A CRACK IN

C000241447

Kathy Shuker was born in nor
working as a physiotherapist, she studied along
freelance artist in oils and watercolours. Writing became her
passion several years ago and *A Crack in the Varnish* is her fifth
novel, the first of the Dechansay Bright Mysteries.
She lives with her husband in Devon.

To find out more about Kathy and her other novels, please visit:
www.kathyshuker.co.uk

Also by Kathy Shuker

Deep Water, Thin Ice

Silent Faces, Painted Ghosts

That Still and Whispering Place

The Silence before Thunder

A CRACK IN THE VARNISH

Kathy Shuker

A Dechansay Bright Mystery

La Vieille Abbaie, Provence, June 1988

The acrid smell of smoke hung in the air, choking and oppressive. Bits of ash rose and eddied for a few seconds before drifting down to settle somewhere else. The sun hadn't cleared the horizon yet but dawn was slowly illuminating the eastern sky and suffusing the gardens with clear, soft light. Already the lamps that Guillaume had brought looked ineffectual by comparison.

Esther surveyed the charred remains of the building then turned away, trying to clear her head. She needed to *think*. The alcohol of the night before, the lack of sleep and now this pervasive smoke were all conspiring to dull her senses. After all the desperate and feverish activity, the confusion of people coming and going, suddenly it felt very empty. There was nothing else to be done here. The men were clearing the hosepipes away; the women had gone back to the house.

She heard a cough and quickly looked round, peering through the fog of smoke. Guillaume had returned and was standing the other side of the smoking, sodden mess. Was he looking at the devastation or at her? It was hard to tell. He picked his way round to join her.

'The police have gone, Miss Langley,' he said. Tiredness had made his French accent more noticeable than usual.

'Will it be all right, do you think?' she asked anxiously. 'They accepted my story?'

'Yes, I think so. No, I'm sure they did.'

'Good, good. Still, there might be... I don't want gossip

1

about this Guillaume. You know what the press are like. If they find out we had a party and then this…' She glanced reluctantly back at the ruin. 'But you've got contacts, haven't you? You're a local. You know these people.' Her smile pleaded with him. 'Please keep it quiet for me. Whatever it takes.'

'I'll do my best, Miss Langley.'

'Thank you Guillaume. What would I do without you?' On an impulse she leaned forwards and planted a soft kiss on his cheek, then suddenly remembered his hands and looked down. They both had dressings on them. 'How are your hands?'

'They will be fine, thank you. Claudine looked at them for me. Which reminds me: I managed to get that painting out that was downstairs. It's over by the edge of the lawn over there.' He turned and gestured with one padded hand. 'It is damaged though.'

'Thank you. But you shouldn't have risked yourself.'

He shrugged and shook his head. He looked exhausted and she let him go.

Esther walked past the swimming pool which now reflected the opalescent dawn, and onto the lawn. She found the painting; it was in a terrible state. She stared at it for a moment, frowning, then made her way slowly back up to the house.

Chapter 1

Nathan picked up the bottle of varnish and poured a generous finger's depth into a small bowl, watching the new woman out of the corner of his eye. This was her fifth day with them and he was already convinced that she had attitude. Timothy had taken her on to replace Gary. Nathan had liked Gary. He'd been easy-going, co-operative, a real team worker, more likely to crack a joke than to argue. Whereas this woman – Hannah something French, he couldn't remember what – was not going to be easy to work with at all, he could tell.

Nathan focused back on the job in hand, dipped his brush in the varnish and started methodically coating the painting on the table in front of him, working from top to bottom.

It was Friday morning and they were in the Oxford workshops of Blandish Fine Art Conservation, a business Timothy Blandish had started twenty years previously. He had gradually expanded the studios and now employed five restorers plus Daphne, the receptionist. Timothy himself rarely picked up a scalpel or brush in anger any more. His role, as he saw it, was to bring the work in and organise others to do it. He specialised in offering a bespoke service to the wealthy and insecure. For those clients who were reluctant to send their precious paintings away, or for those who simply could not for some practical reason, Timothy sent the restorer to them. Most of

3

their clients had the space and the means to have someone living and working on site for as long as it took.

Presumably Hannah would be on probation for a while, thought Nathan, working in the workshops. That would be good. Timothy insisted on keeping two restorers back at base for what he called their 'tick over work' and Steve Chorley never went away. That would mean Nathan could be released to travel again. He was ready for that.

He forced himself to concentrate on smoothly overlapping the brushstrokes of varnish all the way to the bottom of the picture. It was a portrait by Reynolds which he'd recently finished cleaning. He soaked up the excess in the last bead of varnish with his brush then straightened up and surveyed his work. As always, the varnish lifted the colours and added depth and vibrancy and he felt the familiar glow of satisfaction. Another coat or two and it would be good to go.

'Hi.'

He looked round quickly. Hannah had loomed up and was staring at his work table and the equipment laid out there.

'You are neat, aren't you?' She flicked him a quick, piercing look. 'Which varnish are you using by the way?'

He showed her and she nodded but said nothing. He sensed criticism.

'Finding your way around?' he said. 'I imagine Timothy'll have you started on a project next week.'

'I hope so. I much prefer to be working. But I understand we do a lot of work away from here – in situ?'

'Yes. Quite often. Is that a problem for you?'

'Not at all. I'd welcome it.' She produced a rare smile and gave a little shrug. 'I'm happy to work alone.'

I'll bet you are, thought Nathan.

The intercom on the wall near the door crackled and Daphne's voice chirped at them.

4

'Hannah. Could you come downstairs please? Mr Blandish would like to see you in his office.'

Hannah walked away to the stairs and Nathan watched her go: dark, urchin cut hair; drainpipe jeans; an oversized check shirt and huge trainers with thick rubber soles which made her legs look even skinnier than they already were. She walked purposefully, head held high. Definitely an attitude. Then his eyes narrowed. Why had she been summoned like that?

A moment later, he abandoned the Reynolds – it needed to dry anyway – and went downstairs too. When he reached reception, Daphne pointed one warning finger towards the office at the rear of the room then put it to her lips. The door stood slightly ajar and they could hear the drone of Timothy talking.

'What's it about?' he mouthed, jerking his head in the direction of the office.

Daphne knew everything that went on at the studios. And a surprising number of other things too.

'He's dividing up the next round of jobs,' she said.

'And she's being told first?'

Nathan frowned and half turned, cocking his head to listen. For a man, Timothy's voice had a shrill tone; it carried.

'All things considered, I've decided to send you to Miss Langley's. She's got four paintings that need attention and she's happy to offer accommodation.'

'Esther Langley, the actress,' Daphne mouthed at Nathan. 'Lives in Provence. You must have heard of her.'

Nathan nodded, his frown deepening. Timothy was still speaking.

'...can't stress enough what an important client she is. We're very honoured to have her business. And she's a charming lady; I spoke to her on the phone. Quite charming.'

Nathan rolled his eyes. Timothy became irritatingly

5

sycophantic around pretty women, especially if they were famous and wealthy. He liked to think he had a way with women; his two ex-wives probably disagreed.

'And, of course,' Timothy went on, 'we want her to recommend us to her friends. I gave her an estimate from the photographs she sent me but, as you know, it's difficult to judge a painting's condition from a photo. So do a thorough assessment of the work, what needs doing, how long it'll take, the usual drill, put it in writing and send it to me. Then I'll give her a more accurate estimate of the cost. She said to go ahead anyway which is good. Miss Langley's not at home at the moment. She's off shooting a movie in the States, I gather.'

Hannah was talking now but her voice was softer and more mellow. It was impossible to make out the words.

'Good, good,' said Timothy. 'That's what I thought. Anyway, Miss Langley seemed to think she'll be back before you finish.' There was a brief pause. 'Now look Hannah, your last employer said you were *very thorough. Great attention to detail*, she said. Now I like that, I do, I told you that at your interview. It's good.'

He paused. Nathan could hear the inevitable 'but' in his voice. He imagined the oleaginous smile that always preceded it.

'But don't forget that we always have a waiting list,' said Timothy. 'Do what's necessary, no more, make sure the client's happy, then move on. Don't get carried away and linger. Time is money after all.'

Daphne and Nathan exchanged a look. Hannah replied again inaudibly.

'Of course, of course,' Timothy said dismissively. 'I know you'll use good judgement but don't forget to ring me with a regular progress report. This is the address and contact details. Let them know when you'll be arriving. Get your trunk ready.

Alan explained all about the trunks I assume, showed you where we keep our materials and equipment? It's your responsibility to make sure it's stocked with everything you think you'll need. Daphne'll organise the collection of it and your travel arrangements.' A hesitation. 'And remember, it may be Provence but it's not a holiday.'

'Of course not.' Hannah's voice, raised, firm and indignant, was clear that time.

'Fine.' Another, slightly longer, pause from Timothy. 'Do dress tidily, won't you? It's probably quite a smart place and we do have a reputation to maintain. Still, I'm sure you'll be a credit to us. Oh, here are the photographs Miss Langley sent me.'

'Good advice about the clothes,' Nathan muttered to Daphne. 'Have you seen the things she wears?' He pulled a wry grin.

Daphne glared a warning as Hannah appeared beside him. With those damn rubber soles he hadn't heard her coming but she'd probably heard him. She stared at him for a long moment then turned to Daphne.

'I need to get to a place called Tourbelle la Vierge in Provence as early next week as possible. I understand you can sort that out for me?'

'Yes. I've looked up where it is. You need a flight to Marseille and you'll need a rental car. Miss Langley lives up in the hills. And I should be able to get your trunk collected this afternoon.'

'Great. Thanks.'

'Special food requirements for the plane?'

'No. Anything edible.'

Daphne smiled and picked up the phone. 'I can't promise that.' She referred to a list in a notebook and dialled a number. 'Just think,' she murmured, 'when they finish building the channel tunnel, you'll be able to get a train straight through to Paris. And then…' She shrugged, eyebrows raised. '…well, wherever you want to go.' Someone spoke in her ear and she looked away. 'Hello, yes. I'm looking for flights to Marseille, Monday or Tuesday next week.'

'So–o,' Nathan said to Hannah, trying to sound conversational, 'Provence. Nice call.'

'You were listening.'

'Not exactly. Timothy's voice carries. Still… spring in Provence. That's a good gig when you've only just arrived. I guess you must have quite a résumé. I mean, Timothy usually has new people kicking their heels for months in the workshops, breaking them in. You're not related to him or anything, are you?'

He had meant it as a joke – well, sort of – but it hadn't come out that way.

Her eyes narrowed. 'No, I'm not even *anything*. And I don't believe I need *breaking in*. I guess maybe I have got quite a résumé at that. How long have you been here, Nathan?'

He straightened, pulling back his shoulders. 'Six and a half years.'

'Really? That's amazing. And aren't you allowed out yet? That must be so frustrating.'

He opened his mouth to reply but Daphne cut in, demanding Hannah's attention and the moment had gone.

'The earliest flight I can get is on Wednesday,' said Daphne, her hand over the mouthpiece.

'OK then, that's fine. Let's take that.'

A few minutes later, all the travel arrangement made, Hannah turned back to him.

'I'd better go and sort out my trunk. If you'll excuse me, that is?'

She walked away, head held high, and made for the stairs

to the basement. Nathan watched her go then looked back at Daphne.

'What is it with her?'

'Come on, Nathan, you asked for that. Your jealousy's showing.'

'I'm not jealous.'

'No?'

'Well, maybe.' He sighed, glancing back at Timothy's office door to check it was closed. 'Spring and summer in Provence? And at some fancy villa probably. I could have done with that right now. But it's not just that: it's a matter of principle. I'm the senior restorer here. Why should she get the best job going? She talked him into it, didn't she? A flash of those big eyes and he's putty in her hands.'

'Really Nathan, she doesn't strike me as the type. In fact, I rather like her. It's about time we had another woman working here.' Daphne studied his face. 'You seem a bit tense this morning and you were late arriving. Is everything OK?'

'I had a phone call just as I was about to leave.'

'Your mother fretting again?'

He felt the familiar tension in his jaw. 'Yes. Same old same old. It doesn't matter what I say.' He sighed. 'It's coming up to the anniversary again.'

Daphne nodded sympathetically but didn't comment.

'You know this Provence job might not be so great,' she remarked instead. 'It's not a villa; it's an old abbey, all stone and cloisters. I saw some photos in a magazine. And they say Esther Langley can be a bit… odd. Unpredictable.'

Nathan managed a smile. Daphne was a sweetheart. 'You're just trying to make me feel better.' He pushed his glasses up his nose and leaned against the desk. 'What do you know about Hannah then? You must have seen her file.'

'Yes. She's thirty-eight, same as you more or less, and has

9

moved around a bit. She's worked at a couple of big galleries, one in London, one in Paris plus two private restoration studios.' Daphne shrugged. 'She's had a lot of experience with Renaissance paintings. Oh and she's half French – no surprise there given the surname – and speaks French fluently. So there you are.'

'There I am, what?'

'That's why he's sending her to France. He always sends Michael to Germany 'cause he's half Swiss and speaks German.'

Nathan grunted. He pulled himself away from the desk. 'I'd better get…'

Timothy's office door opened and he appeared in the doorway.

'Thought I heard you, Nathan. Where are you at with that Reynolds?'

'I've just started revarnishing it. Alan's already done the frame. I'm waiting to put the second coat on.'

'Good, good.' Timothy looked at his wrist watch. 'I've got someone coming in shortly. Pop down at twelve, will you? I've got a job for you up in Scotland next: a quick clean ready for an exhibition. I'll tell you all about it then.'

He retreated back into his office and Nathan looked back at Daphne.

'Scotland,' he muttered. 'Great.'

'Scotland's beautiful,' she said, and smiled. 'You wanted to get away.'

*

It was one-thirty on a dull, rainy afternoon on the last Wednesday in March when Hannah arrived at Marseille airport. She picked up the hire car, glanced at the address and map one last time, and hit the road. She had visited France

10

many times, partly for work and partly for pleasure but she didn't know this area at all and drove carefully, windscreen wipers swishing back and forth. It was easy to go miles out of your way on these French autoroutes if you missed your turning. She was heading north and east, the smudgy blue line of the distant Luberon mountain range leading her on.

Esther Langley was British but had lived for several years in the States and usually worked there. Though she still had an apartment in Los Angeles, she now lived in France, a couple of miles outside the town of Tourbelle la Vierge, buried somewhere in that far off range of mountains. Daphne had been the source of this information. Hannah had heard of the actress, knew that she had made some big box office films, had even seen her a couple of years previously playing a brilliant and chilling Mrs Danvers in a new retelling of du Maurier's *Rebecca*. But Hannah wasn't a movie buff while Daphne apparently devoured both celebrity and house magazines, delighting in the details of other people's lives and their homes. Hannah liked Daphne. She was in her fifties, intelligent, easy-going and approachable.

'Esther's forty-four now and lives with an actor called David Flaxman,' she'd told Hannah. 'He's a Brit who's lived and worked in the States for years. A real hunk. She's pretty gorgeous too. But then they pay a fortune to look like that, don't they?'

'What about the paintings? asked Hannah. 'Is she an art collector?'

'I'm not sure. I'll see if I can find an article about her. I've got a stack of magazines at home.'

But Daphne had forgotten about the magazines. Her elderly mother, who lived with her, hadn't been well over the weekend. Hannah wasn't bothered. It had only been idle curiosity.

11

She'd spent more of her time on the journey thinking about her new job. After all that had happened in these last months, she'd needed the move, the fresh start, and good jobs in art restoration weren't easy to come by. The Blandish studios had a decent reputation and, despite the technical limitations of restoring paintings in situ, she welcomed the prospect of working alone, trusting to her own initiative. Timothy, she had been warned by friends in the art world, was fair but miserly. He was old-fashioned too and suspicious of new gadgets, including computers. Or maybe it was their cost. She had already gleaned that he was a control freak which could prove challenging. Alan was all right and Steve was a pleasant guy; he usually worked at base apparently because his wife needed care. Nathan was a different matter. Serious eyes behind serious glasses and a condescending manner. He couldn't be much older than her. That snide remark about her being related to Timothy still rankled. And what was wrong with the way she dressed? Yes, she liked to keep it casual and fun but there was no point dressing up to work on old paintings. Nathan's clothes were positively bland; he probably had a personality to go with them.

Hannah focused back on the road. She took the Boulevard du Sud, looping west, then north round the medieval walls of Tourbelle la Vierge, and glanced up at it as she passed, a small town pressed tight against the hillside. It looked bleak in the mid-afternoon gloom. Further on, she passed fields of twisted dark olive trees and bare, stunted vines. Some fields lay ploughed but barren. In the grey, moist light of a wet spring day the landscape bore disappointingly little resemblance to the hot canvases of Cézanne and Van Gogh.

One last turning, a lane winding through trees, and she came to a halt in front of tall gates. The rain had stopped but it was still grey and damp. A sign on one of the gateposts read:

La Vieille Abbaye. Either side of the gates a high stone wall, with what looked like electric fencing on the top, stretched away into the trees and out of sight. She got out of the car and walked up to the intercom on the nearest gatepost. A security camera was angled down to examine her. *Press and speak*, was written in both English and French next to one of the buttons on the intercom.

'*Bonjour,* hello. I'm Hannah Dechansay. I'm the conservator who's come to work on Miss Langley's paintings.'

She released the button and waited. There was silence. She was about to speak again when the speaker crackled and a man's voice spoke slowly and clearly.

'Good day, Miss Dechansay. I shall open the gates. After going through, please stop by the building on your right.' The perfect English was spoken with a French accent.

The gates swung slowly back. She drove through and stopped. The building to her right was low and squat, built in the style of a lodge, set back a few feet from the driveway. The gates swung to behind her and a man walked round the front of the car to the driver's side. He was solid and broad-shouldered but not the classic security man she had envisaged. His grizzled hair was medium length and immaculate, his beard closely cropped. He wore dark blue trousers with a finely striped dark blue and cream shirt and a cream linen jacket thrown casually over the top. He was muscular but his movements were easy and fluid. He could have stepped right out of the pages of a men's clothing catalogue.

Hannah brought the window down as he bent over and smiled politely.

'Hannah Dechansay?' he said. 'Can I see your passport please?'

'Of course.' She handed it to him and he studied it, then her face, then the passport again before returning it to her. She noticed his hands were badly scarred.

'Thank you. I am Guillaume Bordier, the security officer here. How long are you going to be staying? Miss Langley didn't specify.'

'I'm not sure until I see the paintings. A little while, I think.'

He nodded slowly. 'I see. Then I shall speak to you again to explain how our security works. Now you must follow the driveway round to the left there.' He lifted one arm and pointed. 'You will see room to park on your left near the house. There will be other cars. From there it is a short walk to the front door. They will be expecting you.'

He was polite enough but something in his manner suggested she wouldn't want to get on the wrong side of him. He straightened up again, looking earnest and forbidding, and backed away to let her drive on. Maybe she was lucky he hadn't made her get out to frisk her.

The house, at first sight, appeared to be a long two-storied building – not perhaps as big as she had expected – built of pale grey stone, its windows hung with soft lavender shutters. She pulled into the parking area and turned off the engine. There were three other cars parked there, one of them a beautiful red Morgan. Nice. She could see a run of three garages over to the left, linked to the corner of the house by an archway of matching stone. Just for a moment, a young girl stood beneath the arch, her long dark hair falling behind her shoulders. She wore a white frock and was slight, ethereal even. The next minute she'd gone and Hannah wondered if she'd imagined her. Or maybe it was a ghost; abbeys had ghosts sometimes, didn't they? Stupid girl, she thought. It had been a long day.

She got out, pulled her case and bags out of the car boot and hefted them towards the front door which, flanked on each

14

side by a large potted box bush, stood way over to the left of the building. High on the wall, another security camera was focused on her. She wondered if Guillaume was, even now, still watching her.

She pressed the doorbell and heard it peal inside. Three or four minutes later the door opened and a man stared at her with an expression of frank surprise. He was a similar age to herself, hair longish and tousled, a day's growth of beard on his face. He wore trainers, knee length shorts and a large shirt hanging loose over a tee shirt. He wasn't what she'd expected.

His expression became curious. 'Yes?'

'I'm Hannah Dechansay. I was told you were expecting me. Blandish Fine Art Conservation?'

He frowned. 'We are? In that case I suppose you'd better come in.' His accent was unmistakeably British.

She dragged her case and bags into the hallway. He didn't offer to help.

'Guillaume usually rings through to say someone's here,' he said, rubbing the back of his hand against the stubble on his face. 'Clearly Sara didn't hear it. But she must be around somewhere.'

He left her standing there, glanced in through a door off a corridor to her right, then walked off down the passageway ahead and out of sight. Hannah looked round curiously. It was a square entrance hall with a flight of stairs leading up and round to her left. Wandering forward a couple of steps, Hannah started to see the true extent of the house and its abbey origins began to make sense. The room the man had looked into was the first in a line of rooms along a corridor to her right. Straight ahead the long passage also had rooms off to the left. Glancing out of a nearby window off the passage showed that the house was built round three sides of a quadrangle and it still had cloisters, framing the garden within.

15

A thin woman now walked towards her along the passage, taking brisk, agitated steps.

'Hannah,' she said, drawing near. A smell of nicotine came with her. 'I'm sorry I didn't hear the bell. Raff told me you were here. I'm Sara, Sara Plascott, Esther's PA.' She held out a bony hand. 'How are you? Good journey, I hope?'

'Fine, thank you. No problems.'

'Then I'll show you to your room. Esther's away at the moment but I believe you have your instructions. My office is just there at the top of the west wing...' She pointed towards the room the man had looked in. '...if you need anything. The paintings are all in the theatre, waiting for you. That's where you'll be working. God knows, it's not used for much else these days.' She surveyed Hannah's luggage. 'Any of this need to go there?'

'No. My working kit is coming in a trunk, by carrier. A big thing.' Hannah used her hands to show the size. 'It should have been here by now. Isn't it?'

'No. Unless Guillaume's put it in the theatre already and not bothered to tell me.' Sara grabbed the suitcase and headed for the stairs, looking distracted. 'He does that sometimes; drives me mad,' she muttered.

It wasn't clear if she was telling Hannah or talking to herself. Hannah followed.

*

They turned left at the top of the stairs and kept walking. The long landing appeared to echo the passage below. Glancing out of windows as they went, Hannah could clearly see the two arms of the building embracing the large courtyard below.

'This is you.' Sara stopped abruptly by a door on her left.

Inside, Sara put the suitcase down and waved a hand vaguely towards a courtesy tray on the chest of drawers.

'Help yourself to a drink. Claudine's our housekeeper and cook and sorts us out with the help of a couple of part-time assistants, Liane and Dominique. Most of our meals are left out in the dining room, buffet style. You help yourself. Claudine's busy and doesn't like being disturbed in the kitchen so bear that in mind. Breakfast's between seven and ten. Lunch between twelve-thirty and two. Dinner seven-thirty to nine-thirty. Claudine doesn't work Sundays. She's a keen church-goer, very devout, but an assistant usually fills in. Any special dietary needs, you'd better see her. She's – what shall I say? – a woman of few words. Have you had lunch?'

'I had something on the plane.'

Sara grunted and fixed Hannah with a look. 'I wasn't told how long you're going to be here.'

'I'm not sure yet either. It depends how long the work takes.'

'I see. You've met Guillaume of course. He manages our security. Do pay attention to his instructions. He's very diligent about enforcing them. Above all, we have a rule here: no-one discusses the abbey or its occupants outside these walls. Esther's very strict about it. No gossip. If she finds out you've betrayed her, you'll be gone so quick …' Sara snapped her fingers. 'Well, just so you know. You get to the theatre through a door down a passage next to the kitchen but I'll come back and show you round later when you've had a chance to unpack.'

She retreated to the doorway, putting her hand to the handle of the door.

'Sara?' said Hannah. 'Who's Raff?'

'Oh, Raff's just… Raff's an artist. He's got a studio out on the estate. I'm sure he'll show you it sometime if you're interested. He likes people to be interested.'

And with that enigmatic response, she'd gone, shutting the

door behind her.

There was a key in the lock and Hannah fingered it a moment, then quietly turned it. It was a bright but subtly furnished room with an en suite bathroom and a small television on the chest of drawers. The room's single window faced east over the grounds and to the woods beyond. Looking out and down, Hannah could see a small annexe with its own neatly tended garden set back a little from the main house. For Claudine perhaps. She wondered how many people lived here.

She peeled off her new linen jacket and threw it on the bed. That was a relief. *Do dress tidily won't you,* Timothy had said so she'd made an effort. She ran a hand through her hair, loosening it and easing the journey out of her system. She'd just had it cut again and it stuck up now in little spikes. She made herself a cup of tea and drank it while she unpacked. Esther's staff seemed preoccupied with how long she was going to stay. From what she'd seen of the place so far, she wondered why it mattered. Would they even notice her?

If she finds out you've betrayed her. Sara's words stuck in her head. Betrayal? Such emotive language. What was there to betray?

Chapter 2

Sara never did come back.

Hannah had a shower and changed and, not one to hang about with nothing to do, eventually went to explore by herself. She found her way back down to the lower hallway but Sara wasn't in her office. There was no-one around. Presumably no-one would mind then if she nosed about by herself.

On the wall in the entrance hallway Hannah found an aerial photograph of the house which helped to make sense of the place. It faced south. The southern range of buildings which would once have closed the quadrangle and completed the cloister walk had long gone. Only part of the abbey's skeleton remained, a shadow of its former self. It stood on a small plateau of ground on the lower slopes of a valley. At the bottom of the valley ran a narrow river – no doubt the reason for the choice of the site for the abbey. At one time water would have been diverted to create fish ponds and washing facilities. Now the river was just part of a valley cultivated with vines, olives and fruit trees. There was a kidney shaped swimming pool in the grounds at a lower level, between the house and the river. Hannah looked closer. The roofs of outbuildings could be seen among the shrubs and trees of the gardens. Guillaume's place at the entrance was visible but there were at least three others. One of them must be the theatre where she would be working.

She started to wander. Beyond Sara's office on the west

wing corridor were two more rooms: a long one fitted out as a leisure room with a large television and a pull-down screen for showing slides or movies, and a bright sitting room with a shuttered window looking out over the valley. Off the hallway in the body of the house was a large formal drawing room, a dining room and a simple morning room. On the corner, to judge from the smells of cooking, was the kitchen. Hannah put her head round the door, planning to introduce herself. It was a huge space, fully fitted, with a couple of doors leading off it but there was nobody there either. She moved on, past the narrow passage Sara had mentioned which gave access to the outside, and down the eastern arm of the building.

She passed a store room but the next room was far more interesting: a chunky wooden arched door fitted neatly into an old stone arch and, on either side, another smaller arch each framed a thin panel of stained glass. This had to be part of the original abbey. Hannah was intrigued. She tried the door but it was locked.

'No can go,' said a man's voice. 'That's Esther's library. She has to invite you to go in there. You have to be *favoured*.'

Hannah turned quickly. Raff was standing further along the corridor. His hair was wet and plastered to his head and he had a towel draped round his shoulders over a loosely tied cotton waffle wrap. His legs were damp and bare and he was wearing flip flops.

'I'm sorry,' said Hannah. 'I was just curious.'

'Oh you don't have to apologise to me.' He grinned.

She gestured towards the door with her hand. 'This looks like part of the original abbey.'

'It is. That's why she's adopted it for herself. Esther's into stuff like that. Very spiritual when the mood takes her. To me, it's just a bit of old stone but hey...' He shrugged then thrust out a hand. 'I'm Raff by the way. Sorry I didn't, you know,

20

introduce myself earlier. You caught me off guard.'

She shook his hand. It was damp too. 'Hannah.'

'I've just been for a swim. A bit chilly yet but bracing. I can recommend the pool. The water's warm at least. There are towels in the pool house. Did you bring your costume?' The grin became teasing with a challenging glint in his eye. 'Not that it's essential, not when Esther isn't here anyway. We don't mind.'

'Is that so? But I did actually – bring my costume that is.'

'Ah. How disappointing.' He regarded her curiously. 'So you're from some fine art conservation company, right? I did hear that Esther had been buying more paintings. I must take a look. Her taste is, shall we say, variable? Not sure she knows what she's buying to be honest but she sometimes has a lucky find. I'm an artist myself, you know.'

'Sara did mention it.'

He raised his eyebrows. 'Did she? Well good. My studio's in the grounds, the old bake house for the monks once upon a time. Not that you'd know now. Anyway, do come and see it. You might be interested in my work.'

'I will. Thanks.'

'Oh you're welcome.' He hesitated. 'By the way, the next room's out of bounds too: it's what Esther calls her private lounge. She likes to escape us all, you see, and be alone.'

'There don't seem to be many people here to escape.'

He looked amused. 'No, I suppose not.'

'Miss Langley's away, I understand. Who else is here at the moment?'

'Who else indeed? Well, David's not here. No doubt you're going to hear it from someone so it might as well be me. David and Esther had a little falling out. He left. He may or may not return. I suspect not. But what do I know?' Raff shrugged. 'Then, apart from Sara and me and Guillaume,

21

there's Claudine and her husband Pietro who does the gardening and odd jobs. And their granddaughter of course. Strange little thing. But other people do descend on the place, trust me. Favoured people, of course. At least, they used to. And in no time you wish they'd all go away again and leave you in peace. If you're here long enough, you'll see. How long *are* you here for?'

'I don't know yet.'

'Ah well, see you.' He smiled thinly and walked past her and into the heart of the house.

Hannah stared after him then turned back to look at the entrance to Esther's private library. But Raff and his insinuating remarks had left her uneasy and suddenly tired of the house. She decided to go in search of the theatre.

*

Raff found Sara in her office, her restless fingers typing a letter on her new computer. She had told Esther that a computer would make her work easier so Esther had bought her one. Raff couldn't understand the appeal himself but Sara seemed pleased with it. He supposed it smacked of efficiency. It was also impersonal and she'd like that. She was always typing something or scribbling notes or on the phone to someone. He wondered if it was all necessary, if she didn't just create work. Sara liked to look busy. The implication was always that no-one worked as hard as she did. But really, she just co-ordinated things and fielded phone calls and enquiries. Though keeping Esther's affairs running smoothly and the actress herself calm and serene was a challenge, he'd give her that.

'So tell me about this Hannah woman,' he said as he came to stand by her desk.

'I'm working,' she said.

She dragged her gaze from the screen, took in the cotton

22

waffle wrap, the damp towel and the flip flops and sighed.

'When do you ever work, Raff?'

'I work. I work when the muse inspires me.'

'Which isn't often, it seems.'

'That's not true and you know it. Don't be crabby, Sara. You have to go with the flow of creative energy when it hits. I've told you before: you can't timetable it.'

'Hell, Raff, you could at least channel it.'

He tutted. 'Now, now, don't swear within the holy walls. You know Esther wouldn't like it.'

'Why don't you go and meet with your muse and leave me alone.'

Sara turned her face back to the screen, her fingers poised over the keys.

'But you haven't answered my question. About Hannah.'

She kept her eyes resolutely on the small screen. 'She's here to do some restoration work on Esther's new paintings. You know that already. They're very old, some of them.'

'Really? Valuable or junk?'

'They're valuable to Esther I imagine.'

He sniffed and pulled a face. 'But what do you know about Hannah, the woman?'

She sighed and raised a resigned gaze to his face. 'Nothing much. It's a well-regarded company of long standing and she's one of their staff. Esther presumably checked them out. She didn't ask me. I think someone she knew had already used them. That's it. That's all I know.' Her eyes narrowed. 'Why are you so interested anyway?'

'Why shouldn't I be? She's a bit tasty, don't you think? Big eyes. Dark blue, I think. Rather an arresting face – not beautiful but very paintable.' He laughed. 'And that spiky hair fits with her personality, I'm guessing. She's a bit feisty, isn't she? I've just bumped into her. I found her wandering.'

'Damn, yes. I forgot to show her round.'

'Well she's showing herself around. Independent you see. I like that.'

Sara produced a wry smile and shook her head. 'You do dream, don't you? You're wasting your time. She's a smart, intelligent professional with a job to do, not one of your modelling bimbos. Have you looked in the mirror lately? She's out of your league.'

'Thanks Sara. Thanks a lot. But what does that make your sister?'

Sara's mouth tightened into a hard line. She fixed her eyes back on the computer screen. 'She was out of your league too. She was just a fool about you. Now go and let me do some work.'

Raff was starting to feel cold anyway and went upstairs to his room. Maybe Sara was right, maybe not. A lot of women liked his bohemian lifestyle: they found it mysterious and sexy. Anyway he thought Hannah might. She played with pictures for a living after all, tinkered at the edge of other people's dreams. She might be tempted to tag onto the edge of his.

*

The theatre, when Hannah found it, was locked too. She hadn't thought of that. Thanks to the aerial photograph, she had found it down a gritty path which wound between beds of oregano and sweet violets interspersed with euonymus and holly bushes. A small wooden canopy arced over the entrance and overlapping carved masks of tragedy and comedy, lightly gilded, hung on the door. There was an old-fashioned metal latch above a large keyhole but no key. No doubt there'd be one in the house but what were the chances of her tracking anyone down? Presumably Guillaume had one too. She went back up the path and turned left. If she circled round the house, it stood to reason that sooner or later she would find the entrance driveway and his lodge.

She didn't get that far. She passed another path to her left – to Raff's studio perhaps – then reached the end of the eastern wing of the abbey. The ground fell away soon after and there was a series of winding stone steps to a lower level and the swimming pool. She paused, trying to recall the photograph and orientate herself. Of course the driveway had climbed a little but she hadn't really noticed it in the car.

'Are you lost?'

Guillaume had appeared behind her. Had he been watching her?

'I was coming to look for you,' she said, disconcerted.

'Good. Is there a problem?'

'I want to get into the theatre. Have you got a key?'

He pulled a key ring out of his trouser pocket. An assortment of keys hung from it.

'Yes. Shall we go there?'

'Yes,' she answered cautiously and fell into step with him. 'Why is it good that I was coming to see you?' she asked.

'Because I was coming to see you too.'

She didn't ask why and he didn't expand. At the theatre he fitted the key in the lock and let her in, stepping back as she surveyed the space.

It was an oblong room with a wooden stage at one end and sumptuous brocade curtains pulled back against the wings. A short run of steps on each side led up to the apron of the stage and a door beyond presumably gave access backstage. The wooden seats for the audience had been stacked up to the sides leaving the floor clear and a large table had been placed there instead. There was even a small studio easel, empty and ready for her to use: a thoughtful touch, though there was a folding one in her trunk. Each side wall was punctuated with three tall

25

windows, set high, all of them hung with thick curtains which had been pulled back. Natural light streamed in. It was perfect for her work.

And there were the paintings, propped up against the front of the stage. Curious, Hannah automatically walked towards them, scanning them. First impressions confirmed what she'd seen from Timothy's notes and the photographs: they were quality pictures but three of them were badly darkened, displaying their age in places, and the fourth was a modern piece. She glanced round. There was no sign of her trunk. Damn.

'So my work trunk hasn't been delivered?' She looked at Guillaume hopefully.

'Nothing has been delivered for you, *Mademoiselle*.'

'I'll have to chase it up. And I'm going to need a key to the theatre. Can you supply me with one?'

'You should ask Sara. I do not keep spares.' He looked round. 'This is a good place for you to work?'

'Yes, very good, thank you.' She smiled. 'Why did you want to see me?'

He produced a piece of paper from an inner pocket of his jacket. 'I need to tell you about our security measures. You have seen our front gates.' He handed her the paper. 'There are two codes on there. The first is for the security pad at the front gates. The gates have a sensor on them so, as soon as you are clear of them, the gates will close again. You don't need to do anything to close them.'

'And the second code?'

'That is for the gate to the woodland path to town. That one has to be manually opened after you put the code in. Close it after you and re-enter the code from the other side, otherwise the gate will not lock.' He paused, fixing her with a look. 'I'm going to try to get something better fitted but, until then, if you decide to use that gate, I cannot stress how important it is that you always lock it afterwards. There is CCTV on it but I cannot watch it all the time. Miss Langley has a lot of admirers. Unfortunately, not all of them respect her privacy or her property. There are many – how do you say? – cranks out there. Her safety is my priority.'

Hannah nodded.

'Any questions?' he demanded.

'No. Yes. How long does it take to walk into town?'

He looked surprised. 'About half an hour, maybe less. It depends how fast you walk.'

'Of course.' She waited. 'Was there anything else?'

Again, he studied her face. 'Yes. It is a rule with all the staff who work here, permanent or temporary, that we do not talk about Miss Langley in the town – or about any of her business. Most of the locals are protective of her but, as I said, there are always the cranks. And there's always gossip. Talking about her only encourages them and Miss Langley expects loyalty. We don't take photographs of anything or anyone here either. If you do that and I find out you have, say, sold them to a newspaper, we will not hesitate to prosecute. There are strict privacy laws in France. Naturally you will also be asked to leave, immediately, and your employer informed.'

'I see. Well that's pretty clear, isn't it?' Hannah said crisply. She met his gaze with a frank stare. 'I don't know whether I shall meet Miss Langley while I'm here but, in any case, I'm here to do a job. That's all I'm interested in.'

'Good. There's no problem then.'

'Not of my making certainly.'

He frowned, as if unsure of her meaning, then wished her a cool '*bonjour*' and walked out, leaving the door open.

She stood for a moment and let out a long, heavy breath. The man irritated her but it would be unwise to get on the

27

wrong side of him. So many rules; so many warnings. Perhaps it wasn't surprising that so few people lived here. She glanced round again. There was no phone in the building that she could see. She left the theatre, closing the door behind her, and made her way back to the house. She needed to locate her trunk and she needed a key.

Sara was in her office this time. Hannah apologised for disturbing her.

'No problem.' Sara looked up and smiled distantly. 'I'm sorry I forgot to show you round. Raff tells me you've been exploring.'

'Just a little. I found the theatre. It was locked and Guillaume opened it for me. Do you have a key I can keep while I'm here?'

'A key?' Sara looked surprised. 'Of course, a key. Yes, I'll see if I can find one for you.'

'And my trunk hasn't arrived. I need to make a phone call to find out what's happened to it. Can I use your phone?'

A moment's hesitation. 'Yes, there's one in the morning room. You know, next to the kitchen?'

'Yes, I know. Thank you.'

Hannah made her way back along the hallway. The morning room held a small pine table and chairs and a couple of wingback armchairs either side of a fireplace. The phone sat on a narrow oak desk under the window at the far end of the room. She sat down and dialled through to the studios in Oxford.

Daphne answered promptly.

'Blandish Fine Art Conservation. How can I help you?'

'Hello Daphne. It's Hannah.'

'Oh good. I was planning to try and get hold of you. Are you all right?'

'Yes, but my trunk hasn't arrived.'

28

'No, I'm afraid it went to the Brussels depot by mistake. It's now sitting just outside Paris.'

'Paris?'

'I know. The carrier company seemed quite proud of itself for having tracked it down so quickly.' Daphne sounded aggrieved. 'As if losing it in the first place was to be expected. But they've promised it'll be with you by the end of the day tomorrow.'

'I hope so. I can't do much until it arrives. Does Timothy know?'

'Oh yes,' Daphne said drily. 'Timothy knows. He insisted on speaking to them himself.'

'Good. He won't blame me then.'

'What's it like there?'

Hannah turned and glanced first towards the closed hatch in the wall between the morning room and the dining room, then towards the door. The real threat of eavesdropping however probably came from someone listening in on a phone somewhere else in the house.

'Very nice,' she said carefully. 'It was raining when I arrived but it's brightening up now. I'm speaking from the house. I've got a separate place to work in but it doesn't have a phone.'

There was a pause. Hopefully Daphne was picking up the subtext. 'Ah. Good. Well, you take care dear and I'll ring if I hear anything different about your trunk.'

Hannah thanked her but before she put the receiver down, she heard another click. In future she would find a public phone somewhere to ring from, maybe in town. There weren't many people here but definitely too many ears.

Chapter 3

On the Thursday morning, Hannah woke up to sunshine. The window of her bedroom faced east and the morning sun flooded in. It took her a couple of minutes to remember where she was but she was used to that; she had stayed in several different places over the last few months, often from necessity, sometimes from choice. *Ants in your pants*, her mother used to say when she was little and wouldn't stay in one place. *Why can't you settle?*

The night before, Hannah had turned up in the dining room just after seven-thirty. The food had been laid out on a long side table: four covered metal dishes on hot plates, a baguette cut into slices in a basket, a bowl of green salad and a cheese board with a few grapes, loosely covered with a cloth. At the end of the table a small fridge contained three individual dishes of a creamy dessert, each with a slice of kiwi fruit on top. Nearby was a plate of sweet nutty biscuits half-coated in dark chocolate. A large jug of water with a profusion of ice cubes stood on the main table. She helped herself to a couple of spoonfuls of a beef stroganoff, some rice and a portion of baby carrots and wondered when the others would arrive. In the end she ate alone. Tiredness had driven her to bed early and into a fitful sleep.

Now she glanced at her watch. Ten past seven. Would the trunk arrive today, as promised? It was anyone's guess. Either

30

way, she had time to kill but she couldn't just laze in bed. Breakfast would already have been put out. She got up.

There was no-one in the dining room again. Hannah helped herself to orange juice, cereal and some crusty bread and jam and sat in silence. She heard odd sounds from the kitchen. Maybe she'd bring her Walkman down next time and at least she could listen to some music. A jug of filter coffee was keeping warm on a hot plate but there was water in a kettle too and she made herself a cup of tea using one of the tea bags provided. She'd finished and had stood up to go when a woman appeared in the doorway and quickly surveyed the serving table. She was broad-shouldered and above average height with the olive complexion of a Provençal native. Her hair, once very dark, was now peppered with grey.

She saw Hannah and reluctantly nodded, her dark eyes guarded. 'Good morning, *Madame.*' She spoke in heavily accented English.

'Good morning. It's *Mademoiselle* actually. Are you Claudine? My name's Hannah Dechansay.'

'Yes, I know who you are.'

Hannah smiled and switched to French. 'Thank you for the meal last night. It was delicious.'

Claudine looked at her suspiciously. '*Je vous en prie.*' A moment later she had gone.

Well I tried, thought Hannah.

Half an hour later, she was in the theatre. Sara had given her a key the previous afternoon, exhorting her, in her anxious way, not to lose it. Hannah couldn't do much until her trunk arrived but she could at least see what issues she would be dealing with.

She put the first painting on the easel and stood back to look at it. About a metre high by seventy centimetres wide, it was an image of the Madonna with the infant Jesus, painted in

31

oil on panel. She picked up the sheet Timothy had given her listing the details of each picture. Esther had provided these: the attributions and provenance of each painting as told to her by the galleries or auction houses where she had bought them.

'This must be the Bellini,' she murmured.

What a find. A painting by Giovanni Bellini, the fifteenth century Venetian master. It was a typically tender image, finely executed, as far as Hannah could judge through the darkened, dirty varnish. Somewhere buried under here would undoubtedly be the rich colours for which Bellini was known. She thought she could detect signs of previous restoration but her equipment would show that up better when it arrived. And there was some flaking paint down the central section. She turned it round to look at the back. The wooden panel had been made from two planks, dowelled together probably, and there had been some shrinkage. That would need attention.

That seemed straightforward. She propped the painting back up against the stage.

She straightened up and stretched her neck, letting her gaze roam over the stage. The place had a forlorn, abandoned air now but it must have been used in the past. What performances had been put on here? Had all sorts of famous actors trod these boards? Hannah loved the immediacy and energy of the theatre, had even briefly toyed with going into set design but her mother hadn't liked the idea. *There's some very loose living in the theatre business,* she'd said. *Very dubious.* Hannah gave a rueful shake of the head. Her mother had lived in a very shuttered world. *Why don't you consider teaching?* she'd said. *Elizabeth loves it.* Elizabeth might. But Hannah and her older sister were very different people.

Hannah wandered across and through the door at the side of the stage. Backstage were three dressing rooms, a cloak-room, a locked door to the outside and a small kitchen. At least she had somewhere to wash things out and clean up. An electric kettle, a mug, a jar of instant coffee and some tea bags had been left out on the side, along with a carton of long-life milk.

Hannah made herself a mug of tea and returned to the auditorium. She put in her earphones, switched on the Walkman attached to her belt and checked through the remaining paintings. Two were listed as School of Rembrandt: *Saint Peter Denying Christ* and *Christ Receiving the Holy Spirit*. Both were dirty and had other issues which Timothy hadn't noticed from the photographs and which might take time to resolve.

The last painting was different in every way. The listing said it had been fire-damaged and that much was obvious. It was covered in a heavy film of smoke and soot but she could still just make out a beach scene: a man and woman running into the sea hand in hand, both naked and viewed from the rear. The surface of the painting had bubbled and peeled in places and the frame was badly scorched. It was signed Amanda Jay: a slightly known impressionist British artist of the early twentieth century.

Hannah walked around, her head swaying side to side, her feet moving in time to the beat of *I'm Still Standing* by Elton John. Music usually helped her think. So… fire-damaged. Interesting. In fact it was interesting that Esther Langley had this picture at all; it didn't fit with the religious themes of the others. Just as a person's bookshelves told you something about their owner, Hannah always thought that the choice of paintings on the walls did the same.

So what did these pictures say about her absent hostess? The three religious pictures would not have been cheap, despite their condition. The attributions and provenance made them serious investments and there was the cost of restoration on top. Esther must have really wanted them.

Hannah stopped jigging and paused in front of the more modern work. This was quite different: a captured moment of abandon. The couple looked like carefree lovers, laughing and splashing, naked, into the water. Hannah sucked the inside of her lower lip thoughtfully.

Her skin prickled and she spun round suddenly to face the door. The girl with the long dark hair was standing just inside the doorway, watching her.

Hannah's heart slowed down again. She smiled.

'*Bonjour*,' she said, tugging the earphones out. '*Ça va?*'

The girl said nothing. Eyes wide, she stared at Hannah for another moment then ran out of the door. Claudine and Pietro's granddaughter presumably. What a nervous little soul. There again, it was hardly surprising: this was a strange place for a child to live.

*

'All right?' Sara enquired at lunchtime, leaving the dining room just as Hannah entered. She was wearing a crisp blouse beneath a three-quarter sleeved jacket and kept fidgeting the collars of the blouse down in what looked like a nervous tic. 'Settling in? Finding your way around?'

'Yes, thanks. I thought I might explore the grounds this afternoon, if that's OK?'

Sara produced a distant smile. 'Of course.'

'My trunk should arrive today.'

'Good. I'll get Guillaume to bring it to the theatre.'

She left and Hannah heard her steps clicking briskly down the passage.

Hannah turned her attention to the side table. There was one long baguette and half of a second. Sliced ham and smoked sausage lay under one plastic cover; butter, cheese and a selection of yoghurts were arranged under another. A few large ripe tomatoes nestled in a bowl nearby. Hannah made herself a ham and tomato sandwich and, rather than sit in the dark dining room, took it out into the courtyard.

The old abbey garth was sheltered and warm in the midday sun. A couple of climbing roses had been trained up the columns and iron and wicker seating, loosely arranged around an ornamental iron table, made the most of the south-facing position. Two small bay trees in terracotta pots demarcated the end of the patio and the entrance to the herb garden. Lavender and thyme, oregano and hyssop, chives and fennel grew in triangular beds, all separated by paths radiating from the centre where a sun dial stood on a pillar of stone. It was delightful.

Hannah sat on one of the wicker seats to eat, then wandered out into the grounds, trying to remember their layout from the map in the entrance hall. There were steps down to the lower gardens but she stayed on the higher level, meandering along pathways between shrubs and trees. Coming round to the rear of the house, the land rose again and there, on ground given over to fruit bushes and a kitchen garden, a man stood hoeing the soil between neatly drilled lines of seedlings. He looked up as she approached and smiled broadly. He was short and solid with a lined, tanned face and grizzled hair poking from beneath a flat cap.

She introduced herself in French and reached out a hand. He looked surprised, then laid down the hoe, glanced at his hand to check it was clean and shook hers.

'Pietro, *Mam'selle. Enchanté.*' He hesitated. 'Your French is very good. Not many visitors here speak much French.' His own French had a pronounced Italian accent.

'My father's French, *monsieur.*'

'Ah.'

She pointed at the seedlings. 'Rocket?'

'Yes *Mam'selle*. For Claudine to use in the kitchen. Claudine's my wife.'

'Yes, we've met. In fact I think I saw your granddaughter this morning too. Long dark hair? She came to the theatre.'

'Yes, that would be Marielle. I'm sorry if she disturbed you. She has been off school with a stomach upset but I think she must be better. She does wander, I'm afraid.'

'It's not a problem. She was there one minute and gone the next. I was told she lives with you.'

Pietro frowned. 'Yes. Was someone complaining about her?'

'No. I just asked who lived here.'

'I see. Well, yes. Sadly, my daughter passed away when Marielle was four and her father, well...' Pietro shrugged expressively. '...he'd already deserted them. Not that anyone missed him. He was an evil man: used to knock my daughter about. Anyway, Miss Langley was kind enough to let Marielle come to live with us.'

'That's good.' The first really positive comment anyone had made about Esther. 'How old is Marielle now?'

'Eight. She's very timid though. Good, *Mam'selle*, but well, a bit troubled sometimes. And you know, we had a...'

He stopped speaking suddenly.

'It's of no matter,' he added quickly. 'Do say if she gets in your way, won't you?' He smiled more tentatively and hastily picked up the hoe again. 'I think I'd better get on *Mam'selle*.' He touched a hand to his forehead and resumed his hoeing.

Hannah left him to it. She glanced at her watch and headed back to the house. Pietro seemed like a nice guy. Why did he suddenly clam up like that?

*

Raff was in the dining room when Hannah arrived that evening, loitering along the side table, examining what was on offer. He turned as she entered and smiled with relief. A chance for some different conversation for once. Sara could be so boring.

'Hannah. How delightful. I was just wondering whether to stay here or take my meal over to the studio.'

'You don't have to stay on my account.'

'You want to get rid of me.'

'No. I don't want you to neglect your work if you've got something on the go.' She eyed him up shrewdly. 'Grasp the muse while you can.'

'You're mocking me. Or could it be that you truly understand the artist's life? I'll assume the latter.' He bowed and turned back towards the food on offer. 'We have some sort of stew and roast potatoes tonight.' He sniffed. 'With garlic, I believe. And the usual side shows of course.' He waved a hand towards the basket of bread, the salad and the cheese board. 'Why do we have to have salad all the time? Who eats all this salad?'

Hannah came alongside and peered at the stew he was regarding with such distaste.

'That's a *navarin d'agneau*,' she said. 'Lamb with carrot, turnip, potatoes, sometimes peas. Very traditional.'

He stared at her, still holding the cover off the dish. 'My, we're very knowledgeable, aren't we? I just sometimes wish there was a choice.'

'There is,' said Hannah. 'Eat or don't eat.'

'My God, you're telling me I should be grateful. Well, I dare say you're right.'

'My mother said it to me once when I was whingeing. She didn't have time for fussy eaters. To be fair, she didn't have much money.'

37

'Ah yes, mothers. The true source of wisdom. Except mine perhaps, who managed to lurch from one toxic relationship to another.'

He produced a synthetic grin, helped himself to what was on offer and took his plate to the table. He started to eat but watched Hannah work her way along the hot plates. She was an interesting woman, this. Not like any woman he'd met before. She came over and sat down, not quite opposite him.

'Are you settling in then?' he enquired.

'I think I've got my bearings now, thank you.'

They ate for a few minutes in silence. Then Sara walked in and they turned their heads in unison. She looked surprised to see them.

'Perfect timing, Sara,' remarked Raff. 'We can actually have a communal meal together with our guest, like a normal household.' He shot Hannah a look. 'Well, maybe not exactly normal.'

Sara didn't respond but helped herself to food and sat down. She meticulously unfolded the linen napkin by her plate and laid it across her lap.

'I was relieved to hear that your trunk has arrived Hannah,' she said. 'Guillaume's taken it over, I hope?'

'Yes. I've got no excuse not to start work now.'

'I don't know,' said Sara, without inflection. 'Raff can always think of one.'

'Sara, unlike you,' Raff said to Hannah confidentially, 'has no understanding of the artistic life.' He finished eating and laid the cutlery down. 'Speaking of which, I must come and see what you do. I mean, I know in principle, but I've never seen a conservator in action, so to speak.'

'I'm sure Hannah doesn't want an audience,' Sara remarked.

'It depends what I'm doing,' said Hannah, 'on how much

38

concentration is required.'

'I'll be sure to make an appointment then,' Raff said archly.

Hannah picked up the jug of water and offered it round. Sara accepted and Hannah poured some into a glass and passed it over.

'Not for me, thanks,' said Raff. 'Water, I ask you.' He sighed. 'Esther's absolutely made of money and she gives us water.' He rolled his eyes at Hannah. 'When she graces us with her presence we're sometimes allowed a little wine if we've been good. Even then, she keeps a very tight grip on the key to the drinks cabinet. It's ever since she's gone all religious and spiritual.'

'What nonsense,' said Sara. 'We often have drinks.'

'Only when she's in residence. I'm surprised she doesn't put up a flag too, like royalty.'

Sara tutted. 'You drink too much anyway.'

'Pots and kettles, Sara.'

Sara glared at him then concentrated back on her food.

Raff got to his feet. 'Anyway, as Hannah so cleverly guessed when she arrived, I'm in the middle of something that might be very good. Or not. One never knows. Either way, I'll take my bread and cheese over to the studio.'

He left the dining room, clutching a few pieces of baguette and a small round goat's cheese all bundled up in his napkin. He walked towards the little passage beside the kitchen but didn't exit through the door. Instead he turned back and trod softly back and into the morning room, crossing silently to stand by the closed hatch. He could hear nothing from the neighbouring room though. Then as if they had been waiting for him to be out of earshot, the two women both spoke at once.

'Sorry,' said Sara. 'I was just saying that Raff often works late or even all night at the studio.' She laughed awkwardly.

'It's why you don't often see him at breakfast.'

'Artists do tend to work strange hours,' said Hannah.

'What were you going to say?'

'I just wanted to ask about the pictures I'm due to work on. I see that three of them were bought at auction but the fourth wasn't. It's fire-damaged and it's unusual for a gallery to sell a picture in that condition.' There was a brief pause. 'I wondered if you knew where Miss Langley got it from. It has no label on the back.'

Raff leaned slightly closer to the hatch, curious to hear Sara's reply.

'Oh Esther didn't buy it,' said Sara. 'Well she did buy it of course, but not like that.'

'I'm sorry?'

'I mean it wasn't like that when she bought it.'

'So… it got burnt here?'

There was the clatter of a knife and fork being put down roughly on a plate. That was Sara probably, thought Raff. She was getting rattled. When she spoke again, Sara's voice had its familiar anxious, breathy tone.

'Look, I don't know anything about Esther's paintings. If you need to know more about them you must ask her yourself when she returns.'

'All right,' said Hannah slowly. 'Do you know when that might be?'

'She rang today but she's not sure yet.'

'I see.' There was a pause and then the scraping of a chair on the stone floor. 'I'm going to get one of the desserts. Can I get you anything?'

'No, I'm fine,' said Sara. 'I'll go out and have a cigarette in a minute. Esther doesn't like people smoking in the house.'

The fridge door was opened and closed. The chair scraped again.

40

'You know, Hannah, you shouldn't pay too much attention to what Raff says.' There was another silence. Raff was almost holding his breath to hear what was coming next. 'I mean, he's a flirt obviously...'

A short laugh. 'I had noticed.'

'But the way he talks about Esther. You mustn't take any notice of it. It's just talk. He doesn't say these things when she's here.' More softly, in that quirky personal monologue of hers, Sara added, 'Not usually anyway.'

'Sara, what's Esther like?'

There was another brief pause and then Sara's bright public voice. 'Esther's a very private person but she's very kind. She recognises how privileged she is and generously supports a number of...'

Raff decided that this was his opportunity to leave. He had no desire to hear Sara trotting out her glowing press talk. But it was useful occasionally to hear what people said when they thought you weren't around. It could be very revealing. It was certainly news to him that Esther had put that particular painting to be restored. He hadn't even realised she still had it. What had possessed her? Sara had dodged the question about it rather well but he doubted that Hannah would be fobbed off for long. She wasn't the type.

He trod softly out and away to his studio.

Chapter 4

On the Friday morning, Hannah finally got round to unpacking her trunk. It had been cleverly designed – Timothy boasted that he'd had them made to his own specifications – and held an impressive amount of equipment: paints and pigments, varnishes and cleaning solutions, brushes and scalpels, a folding easel, an ultra violet light and a camera. It even had pockets for stationery and for the temporary storage of small paintings. Hannah laid out some of the equipment on the table by the easel and already felt better. She was itching to get started.

She began her formal assessments of the paintings, working through them slowly and thoroughly this time. She did the Bellini first again, taking photographs of it on the easel to record its condition as she found it. Then she checked it with ultraviolet light for any retouching – yes, there was some – and gently felt the integrity of the paint surface. She took it off the easel and put it flat on the table, studying it from different angles, shining a raking light over it to throw up any other surface issues. And she took notes as she went along. All the while, she listened to music as usual. In her youth, she'd been obsessed with rock and beat bands: the Beatles, the Rolling Stones, the Moody Blues, Dave Edmunds and many more. In more recent years, her tastes had softened and broadened and, depending on her mood, she'd listen to ballads and blues, boogie woogie and jazz.

The next painting she put up was the painting of *Saint Peter Denying Christ.* While she studied it, she listened to the husky tones of Louis Armstrong, sometimes shuffling her feet to the beat, occasionally singing along. She was wrapped up in her own world when she turned and started. Marielle had let herself in and was standing motionless near the door, silent, watching. *Troubled*, Pietro had said. Poor kid, Hannah thought. She pulled out the earphones, switched off the Walkman and smiled a welcome.

'*Salut* Marielle. *Viens si tu veux.*' Come in if you want to.

Marielle stared at her but didn't move, though nor did she run away. Hannah made a show of searching for something on the table, not looking at her and a few minutes later Marielle slipped away.

'Well, that was progress, I suppose,' Hannah muttered, and went back to work.

By the end of the afternoon she had written out her findings on all the pictures, including her estimates of timescales. She found an envelope and addressed it to Timothy in Oxford, then hesitated. She had seen a fax machine in Sara's office which would have been much quicker but, after a moment's reflection, she licked the envelope and sealed it. Intuitively it seemed wiser here to keep her head down and not ask for favours. The assessment could go by post.

After a brief search, she found Pietro in the kitchen garden again. He was the person who seemed most approachable.

'Where's the nearest post box?' she asked him.

'There's one at the bottom of the lane to the abbey. On the junction.' He glanced at his watch. 'If you go now, you might catch the last post.'

Hannah let herself out of the main gates and walked briskly down to the box. As the gates swung open on her return, she saw Guillaume appear by the lodge door. He offered a brief, sombre nod of acknowledgement and appeared to turn away. But she was aware of him, still in his doorway, watching her walk the long drive back to the house and out of sight.

*

Hannah began work in earnest on the Saturday morning, determined to make up the lost time.

She started with the picture of Saint Peter. It was an oil painting on canvas, a waist-up portrait of an old man with a white beard and hair, a quarter turn away from the viewer, his expression agonised and tormented. So the auction house had classed it as School of Rembrandt. It certainly had the dramatic use of light and shadow associated with the great master but with paintings that came from the Renaissance workshops, there was often doubt about who had produced the work: the master or one of his apprentices. The vague attribution reduced the price of the painting but also reduced the chance of the work being returned as a fake. So this might be an original Rembrandt, or sections of it might be his. It was the kind of thing that Hannah loved about this job: you never knew what might be passing through your hands. Little gems of art history perhaps.

She ran the ultraviolet light over it. It had been restored before – there were small areas of infill painting, some of which had started to pull away – and she could see some flaking of the original paint too. The frame, an ornate gilt affair, had a few chips in it but was otherwise sound. What Saint Peter needed more than anything else was a good clean.

With the picture face down on the table, she removed the old iron nails holding it in its frame and, with a soft brush, removed the dirt and dust which had accumulated around it. Then, with the naked picture balanced back on the easel on its

44

stretcher bars, she collected a handful of tiny cotton swabs, fine wooden sticks and some weak solvent and set to work to remove the grime and varnish, starting on Saint Peter's beard. The first swab came up virtually black and she wrinkled up her nose. This was going to be a long job.

She took Sunday off. It was the first day of April, sunny and warm, and she explored the grounds again, going down to the lower gardens this time and finding mixed orchards of plum, cherry and fig. The swimming pool glinted invitingly in the sunshine and was achingly deserted. She stood for a moment, glancing around. What was it about this place that felt so odd, so unnerving? It was beautiful but it felt so empty, so uninhabited and yet she couldn't shake off the feeling that she was being watched.

Back at the house, she sat in the little sitting room, reading an old paperback novel she'd found on one of the shelves. For a brief moment, Sara appeared in the doorway, bringing an earthy, pungent smell in with her.

'Ah, you're here,' she said enigmatically and smiled perfunctorily.

'Were you looking for me?' Hannah started to say but Sara had already gone. The smell lingered behind her though and Hannah knew what it was. On a night out with friends as a student, she'd smoked cannabis herself once. Horrible stuff.

With the start of the new week, Hannah settled into a working routine and every afternoon, after school was out, she had a visitor. Marielle would come into the theatre and loiter at a distance, eyeing her up with a nervous, curious gaze. On the Monday, she stayed by the door; on the Tuesday she came closer. On the Wednesday, Hannah returned from a late lunch to find the door to the theatre ajar and the girl standing by the table, staring at the equipment laid out across it. As Hannah watched, she reached out a hand to a pot with brushes sticking

45

out of it and touched the head of one of the larger ones.

'*Bonjour Marielle. Ça va?*'

The girl visibly jumped and spun round, looking cornered.

Hannah smiled. 'I have a fascinating table of art stuff, don't I?' she said in French. 'Would you like me to show you?'

The child said nothing but didn't move either, watching Hannah warily.

Hannah joined her by the table. 'I repair and clean old paintings. Perhaps your *grand-maman* told you that already?'

She reached a hand to the pot with the brushes. 'These are just some of the brushes I use. I've got a lot of really small ones too.' She began pointing at different things on the table, keeping her tone light and conversational. 'I've got different kinds of paints, and pigments too for when I have to mix special ones to match the colours on an old picture. And I've got tools for scraping and cutting. In my case over there I've got solutions and solvents to clean the pictures, and varnishes to protect them too. Cool, huh?'

'What does that do?' Marielle said suddenly, pointing at the ultraviolet lamp.

Hannah picked it up and switched it on. 'It's a special light that shows me when someone has put new layers of paint on an old picture. Here, I'll show you.'

She took it across to the painting of Saint Peter and shone it over the surface.

'See how this looks really dark here. And here. And here. That's where someone in the past has put paint on to try to fill in where old paint has been lost.'

Marielle nodded, apparently fascinated. She looked round and reached out a hand towards the table again.

'*Mais ne touche pas, chérie,*' Hannah said kindly.

The hand withdrew at lightning speed. The child shrank back into herself.

46

'It's all right, Marielle. You haven't done anything wrong. But this equipment doesn't belong to me and it's expensive. I have to look after it very carefully. Also, some of the liquids and the knives here, they're dangerous and I don't want you to get hurt. So no touching, OK? That's a very important rule.'

Marielle was watching her face intently as she spoke.

'You understand?' persisted Hannah.

Marielle nodded.

'Good. Do you like to draw?' No response, just big eyes watching her. 'If you want to do some art of your own, I could give you paper and crayons, pastels they are. You could sit at the end of the table there and draw some pictures. Would you like that?'

Marielle appeared to give the suggestion serious consideration. 'Maybe,' she said. Then she ran to the door, pulled it open wide and ran out.

Hannah returned to work. She felt sorry for Marielle; she seemed like a sweet kid, harmless. She rather liked having her around.

*

Raff lifted the lid on the first dish on the hot plate and peered inside hopefully.

'Bloody brilliant. Cannelloni. My favourite. I thought so. I could smell it. No doubt we have Pietro to thank for this.'

Sara glanced up but said nothing. She was already sitting at the table, a plate of food in front of her, a paperback book lying open to the side of her plate.

Raff served himself a generous helping from the dish and took a couple of chunks of garlic bread as well. It was eight forty on the Wednesday evening and he was feeling good. He'd just finished a painting – at least he hoped it was finished – and he thought it wasn't half bad. Maybe even quite good. He sat

47

down opposite Sara and tucked in, surprised at the depth of his hunger.

'So...' he said after a few minutes, '...where's Hannah?'

Sara didn't look up from her book. 'She's already eaten. She was leaving when I arrived.'

Raff grunted and kept on shovelling food into his mouth.

'I never seem to see much of her,' he said.

'She's working. You have heard of the concept?'

'Yeah, yeah. Very funny. Painting *is* working. It takes a lot of concentration and skill.'

Sara flicked him a sceptical glance and returned her eyes to her book.

'So what have you told Hannah about the fire?' Raff asked.

She looked up sharply. 'Nothing. You?'

'She hasn't asked me.'

'She asked me. She's got that painting to restore and it made her curious.'

'So what did you say?'

'I told her to ask Esther.'

Raff looked at her a long moment. He'd been wondering if she'd said anything else to Hannah since the conversation he'd overheard. Did he believe her? Probably, but you could never be sure with Sara. She only ever told you what she wanted you to know.

'But what will Esther tell her?'

Sara's eyes narrowed. 'I have no idea. You can't tell with Esther these days, can you? You know what she's like. I just try to keep her stress to a minimum. When she comes home at the end of this shoot, she's going to want to be quiet for a while; she won't want to answer questions. I think I should keep Hannah away from her as much as possible.'

'Good luck with that then.'

48

'What do you mean?'

He shrugged and swallowed the last of the cannelloni. He picked up the second chunk of garlic bread.

'I just think Hannah's the sort of person who likes her questions answered. Still, you're right: it's better for all of us if Esther doesn't get too worked up.'

Sara looked at him, a frown puckering the bridge of her nose. She said nothing and returned to her book.

*

'*Qu'est-ce que vous faites là?*'

Hannah barely glanced round. It was Friday afternoon and Marielle was back. Hannah pulled the ear pieces out before answering.

'I'm cleaning the dirt and the old varnish off this picture.'

Hannah could feel the child standing close behind her. Watching.

'It's very dirty,' Marielle murmured.

'It is. But the old varnish thickens and yellows with age too. It hides the picture.'

'So why do they put it on?'

'Because it protects the painting. I'll put some fresh varnish on when I've finished cleaning and repairing it. Modern varnishes don't yellow like the ones they used in the past.'

Marielle said nothing and Hannah continued to work, meticulous and slow. She felt Marielle's restlessness behind her. It was boring just to watch.

'I left some paper and pastels on the table for you,' she said. 'Why don't you draw me a picture?'

There was a pause before Marielle walked over to the end of the table. Certain that the child would turn up again sooner or later, Hannah had left a wooden chair beside it for her and

49

Marielle knelt up on it and fingered the pastels.

'What do you want me to draw?'

'Whatever you want. What do you like most? What interests you, Marielle?'

There was no answer and Hannah glanced round. The child had picked up one of the pastels and was staring hard at the paper in front of her, an intense expression on her face. Hannah wondered if she ever laughed or even smiled. She seemed old before her time.

Hannah worked on and Marielle began to draw, silent and focussed. It was three quarters of an hour later when she stopped and put the pastels down. Hannah, absorbed in her work, didn't notice until, out of the corner of her eye, she saw Marielle wandering round the theatre.

'Have you finished?' said Hannah. 'Can I see?'

Marielle came back to the table and, diffident, picked up the paper and handed it over. Her fingers were smudged with colours.

It was a drawing of a painting. At first, Hannah thought Marielle had drawn one of the paintings propped up against the stage. But, though this was an image of the Madonna with the infant Jesus in her arms, it wasn't like the one by Bellini; it was a very different pose and it was bordered by a profusion of flowers. It was a good drawing though. For her age, the child undoubtedly had a gift and she had chosen her colours well, even blending them in places.

'This is good,' said Hannah. 'Did you do this from your imagination?'

'No.' She sounded indignant. 'That's *The Lily Madonna*.'

Hannah frowned. 'What's *The Lily Madonna*?'

'Don't you know? It's famous. It's a beautiful icon in the church in Tourbelle.'

'Really? Then I must go and see it. You like it do you?'

Marielle looked disdainful. 'It's not something you like or you don't like. It's special. Blessed. *The Lily Madonna* protects us from our enemies and from illness. Of course we have to be very good and pray a lot while we look at Her, otherwise nothing happens.'

Hannah sensed Claudine's devout hand in this and Marielle had clearly learnt her lessons well. At least she'd finally found her voice.

'I see,' said Hannah. 'Then I must definitely go and see it.'

'Marielle, what are you doing in here?'

They turned as one to face the doorway. Sara had come in and now approached Hannah, flicking Marielle a reproachful look.

'You shouldn't be here,' she said to her sternly. 'You know that.'

The little girl immediately ran to the door and went out.

'She wasn't doing any harm,' protested Hannah. 'I wouldn't let her stay if I was doing something tricky. I gave her some paper to draw on.' She held up the drawing then smiled sympathetically. 'She seems a bit lost.'

'You shouldn't encourage her.' Sara was unusually abrupt. 'She's naughty for going places she's not supposed to. Miss Langley's complained about her eavesdropping and her endless watching. She finds it creepy, I think. Miss Langley's an actress, remember. She's very highly strung. The trouble is Pietro's soft on the girl and spoils her and Claudine's too busy to keep an eye on her. She's left to run wild.'

'Well, she hasn't troubled me.'

'That's as may be. But you don't live here, Hannah. You don't...' Sara shook her head and seemed to collect herself. 'Anyway, that isn't why I'm here. I thought you should know that Miss Langley has just returned home. The filming finished

51

more quickly than she expected. And I must warn you: Miss Langley likes to have some quiet time when she returns from a film shoot. She finds it very draining so she mustn't be disturbed. If you have any questions, perhaps you could write them down and give them to me. I'll approach her about them at a later time.'

'No problem. There's nothing particular I need to see her about, not at this time anyway.'

'OK.' Sara's eyes lingered on her a minute then she glanced round without apparent interest. 'Everything all right for you here?'

'Yes, it's fine, thanks.'

She left and Hannah tried to settle back into her work. Poor Marielle. Always in the wrong place.

And now Esther was back. Hannah did have questions, but she would ask them herself.

Chapter 5

Hannah keyed the security code in to the pad on the post next to the garden gate and heard the lock release. She went through, pulled it closed and keyed the code in again on the other side. The lock re-engaged with a clunk. It was Saturday and she was making her first trip to town. Seeing Claudine at breakfast, she had taken the opportunity to ask about *The Lily Madonna* and, for once, the housekeeper was keen to talk.

'Have you not heard of it, *Mam'selle*?' she said proudly, determinedly speaking English. 'It is very famous. Since you work with paintings, you are certain to find it interesting. People call it Tourbelle's *Mona Lisa*, though of course it is – how do you say? – a picture for prayer and devotion, not simply a painting. You must visit the church and see it. Today is a good day. It's market day and there is a lot to see.'

'Is it easy to find?'

Claudine produced a short, amazed laugh. 'The church is at the top of the town, on the square. You cannot miss it. You take the path through the woods. You turn left when you reach the end. Go up to the square and *voilà*.'

Tourbelle's *Mona Lisa*. This I have to see, thought Hannah.

Intrigued but in no particular hurry, she set off, enjoying the walk. There was a biting wind but the sun shone and there was birdsong in the air. The woods were a mix of oak trees, both evergreen and deciduous, and lines of light streamed through the broken canopy. She hadn't walked far when she came across a small shrine with a painted statue of the Virgin Mary in it, the paint peeling in places. A posy of flowers had recently been left at her feet. By the side of it was an old weathered memorial but Hannah couldn't read the inscription cut into it and soon moved on.

The woods thinned out as she reached the outskirts of the town and the ground fell away. She descended a long flight of stone steps and finally emerged between a house and an undertaker's yard onto a narrow sloping street: Le Chemin de L'Abbaye. Hannah turned left and climbed again and a few minutes later she was in the square.

Claudine was right: the church was unmissable. It stood to her left, dominating the square and, with its tall stone tower, the whole town. It was stern and imposing. By contrast, the Place de l'Église, shaded by four huge chestnut trees, was filled with colourful market stalls and with people jostling to do their weekly shop. There were stalls of assorted breads, fruits and vegetables, cheeses, olives and spices, lavender goods, honey and preserves – a treasure trove of local produce. Hannah decided *The Lily Madonna* could wait and explored them. She bought herself a chocolate brioche, a small bag of crimson grapes and some lavender sachets for her clothes. From the edge of the square radiated several narrow streets, winding down the hillside, all lined with stalls but the wind funnelled up from below, throwing dust in her face and making her hug her jacket closer. She abandoned the market and crossed back over the square and up the steps to the church.

It was dark after the brightness outside and she paused to let her eyes adjust. The familiar heaviness settled on her along with the familiar frustration that she hadn't managed to grow out of it. Old churches always oppressed her; they brought back too many memories. Her mother had been like Claudine, very devout, and the church they'd attended, Anglican but high church, had been old and dark like this. The lighting had been inadequate; it had obscure corners where the young Hannah was sure she'd seen things move. When her father left, her mother had struggled to accept the fact and they had attended more frequently. Elizabeth never seemed to mind but, between the intensity of her mother's despair at being abandoned and the dismal atmosphere of the services, Hannah had grown to dread going. She would sometimes have nightmares about it. As a rebellious teenager, she had finally refused to go at all and religion became the thing she and her mother always fell out over.

Hannah regretted all the arguments, now more than ever, and being here just brought it all back. It was a bad idea to come. She took a deep breath and let it out slowly. There was an icon to see. She could do this.

The air smelt of stale incense mingled with guttered candles. The woodwork was dark and heavy, but, now that her eyes had adjusted, it wasn't quite so sombre. A succession of tall windows on each side of the nave filtered sunshine in through thick old glass, illuminating the dust motes hanging in the air. Every corner and alcove had painted statues of saints. There were colourful children's drawings pinned on display boards to her left and a range of prayer cards and postcards on a table nearby. On the far side stood the confessional box though there appeared to be no-one else around. She relaxed a little.

She walked slowly up the centre of the nave.

'*Bonjour Madame. Bienvenue à notre belle église.*'

The voice offering her a welcome came from the side aisle to her left and she turned quickly to see a middle-aged priest cutting smoothly through the pews to join her. He introduced himself in French as *Père* Diluca.

'*Bonjour Père.*' She stuck out her hand. '*Mademoiselle* Dechansay.' She hesitated. 'Hannah,' she added.

''annah.' He smiled. '*Enchanté*. Are you on holiday here?'

'No, I'm working at the old abbey.' He said nothing but looked at her curiously, prompting her to add, 'I'm a painting conservator.'

'That is wonderful work you do then, *Mademoiselle*. Most interesting, I imagine.'

'It is. In fact, I've been told about a painting you have here, an icon called *The Lily Madonna*?'

'Ah yes, our special Lady. Let me show Her to you.'

He led the way back to the side aisle from which he had just come and to an arched alcove with a metal grill fastened across it. Standing on a gilt easel and illuminated from above, was the icon. It was a simple, almost crude, depiction of the Virgin Mary with the baby Jesus in her arms. Mary held the child tightly and the infant Jesus reached one hand up to pull the blue covering draped around his mother's head. The colours were still vivid, the upper part of the background had been gilded, and both mother and child had raised golden haloes. An orderly profusion of flowers formed an informal border. Marielle's drawing had been surprisingly accurate.

The whole painting, enclosed in its raised gilt frame was no more than thirty-six centimetres by fifty. It was an unremarkable, rather banal rural icon, painted as an act of piety and devotion. Hannah wasn't surprised but she was disappointed, having hoped that it might have been something special. Her professional eye took in its physical condition: old and worn, painted in egg tempera on panel. Even seen from a remove and behind a metal grill, it was obvious that the paint surface was cracked and a little flaky in places – a tired and much travelled piece.

'Wonderful,' Hannah said, trying to sound genuine. 'It must be very old, I imagine.'

'She is thought to be fourteenth century, though perhaps you would already know that, being an expert in the field.' The priest looked at the painting affectionately. 'We are told that She was painted by a monk with much prayer and fasting. As a testament to his immense faith, She saved the community from the black death when it raged through the region in the fourteenth century. The local people were warned to shelter at the abbey and, though many thousands died elsewhere, the abbey and its occupants were not touched. Then later, during the wars of religion, meditation on the icon warned of imminent Protestant attack and they were prepared and victorious.' He glanced at Hannah apologetically. 'Of course, the religious wars were terrible times. So little tolerance. Anyway there has been a succession of amazing stories attached to this painting – miracles you might say.' He shrugged his sloping shoulders dismissively. 'An icon is just a channel for prayer of course, a point of mediation, but some people feel She grants them illumination. She is much revered.'

'Yes, I can see that. Well, thank you, Father. It's a wonderful story.'

He dropped his head and fixed her with a beady look, the corners of his mouth lifted. 'And yet you don't believe it.'

She hesitated.

'I'm not Catholic, Father. And I deal with paintings all the time. I find it hard to see them as anything other than works of art.'

'We don't understand everything in this world, *Mademoiselle*. There are some things which have to be taken on faith.' He frowned lightly. 'Forgive me, your French is very good but you have a slight accent. Are you...?'

'My father is French but my mother's English.'

He nodded an acknowledgement as if he thought that explained everything, and they parted.

Walking back to the abbey, the image of the icon lingered in Hannah's mind. Miracles indeed. And such a nondescript painting.

*

Raff hadn't expected to see her yet. Esther had been home little more than twenty-four hours but she was there, sitting in her accustomed seat at the head of the table. It usually took at least a couple of full days before she surfaced after working abroad, taking her meals in her bedroom or in her private lounge. But now Raff arrived to the queen in residence and Sara sitting to her left. It was a quarter to nine and to judge from their plates, they had both recently sat down to eat. Sara looked up and met his gaze as he walked in and he guessed that she too had been taken by surprise. It was strange how, when they were alone in the house but for the servants, they never got on, but when Esther came home they drew closer, became almost united. A defence maybe. Perhaps that's what siblings were like, thought Raff. He'd never had any so he supposed Sara was as close as he'd get to having a sister.

'Hello Raff,' Esther said and smiled.

She had a beautiful smile. It came in different temperatures but this evening it was quite warm. She was a beautiful woman in fact and, no matter how she felt, she always took the trouble to dress well and to do her make-up. Polished was the word that came to mind.

'Hello Esther. Sara.' He went to the side table and began serving himself. Tonight they had a beef stew, Dauphinoise potatoes and green beans on offer.

'I was hoping to see you here,' said Esther. 'I was beginning to think you weren't coming.'

There was a subtle note of criticism and he turned. 'I didn't know you were expecting me, Esther. Honestly, I thought you might still be resting after your journey.' He waited but Esther said nothing. 'My dealer just called. She thinks she's got a buyer for one of my works.'

'I see. You must be very pleased.'

Esther was looking up at him. Her voice was always the same: soft, warm and mellifluous; it oozed compassion. Sometimes her eyes gave her away but she seemed to be in a good mood.

'Of course.' Raff finished loading his plate and came over to join them. 'As you know, it's not easy to sell paintings if you aren't a big name.'

'There are certainly a lot of artists out there,' remarked Sara. 'Too many, really. They can't possibly all make a living.'

It sounded suspiciously like a dig in his direction. It had been wishful thinking to imagine that anything bound them together. When it came to his work, Sara never took his side.

There was silence for several minutes while they all ate.

'How did the filming go?' Raff enquired eventually.

Esther ate one more forkful and stopped eating, dabbing at her mouth with her napkin.

'Quite well, thank you. A few delays and a producer getting stressed. It's tiring trying to keep everybody happy. The usual things. No doubt some of the scenes I shot are already on the cutting room floor.' She managed to make it sound unimportant and paused, glancing between them. 'And you? Has everything been all right here?'

'Yes, of course, absolutely fine.' Sara spoke a little too hastily. She finished eating and picked up the jug of water, pouring some into each of their glasses. 'We've got the woman

59

from the art restoration company here but she's over in the theatre so we don't see much of her.'

Esther looked round, a little theatrically. 'Doesn't she eat though? She's staying here, isn't she?'

'Yes. Oh yes,' said Sara. 'I think you just missed her. She tends to eat early.'

'I see. But there are no problems?'

'No.'

Esther looked at Raff who shrugged and shook his head, finished his last mouthful of food and laid the cutlery down.

A moment later, Claudine appeared wordlessly to clear the dishes. Had she been listening? Esther thanked her and waited till she'd gone.

'I've got some really rather special paintings this time. Quite moving. You know how… well, how much I'm valuing religious paintings at the moment. Anyway, I'm really looking forward to seeing them restored.'

In honour of Esther's return, a freshly made *tarte au citron* had been put out on the side. Raff always thought it ironic that Claudine went to this extra trouble when Esther was at home, despite the fact that her employer ate very few desserts. However a large bowl of fresh fruit had been put out as well.

'Does anyone else want a slice of that tart?' Raff enquired, standing up.

'No thank you,' said Esther. 'You could fetch me one of those peaches though.'

'Just a small slice for me please,' said Sara.

Esther put the offered peach on her side plate and waited. 'I believe I saw her today – the art restorer, that is. Hannah, isn't it? It must have been her. Short dark hair? Slim, wearing leggings? I was looking out of the side window in my bedroom and I saw her returning to the house.'

Raff handed Sara a plate with a slice of tart on it and sat

60

down with his own.

'In fact I believe I saw you talking to her, Raff,' Esther added. 'You looked very earnest.' She smiled. 'What was that about?'

Raff was taken aback. He'd assumed that Esther would have been closeted up in her bedroom.

'Yes, I did bump into Hannah in the garden. She was just coming back from town. She'd been to see *The Lily Madonna*, she said.'

'Really?' Esther immediately became more interested. 'And what did she think? Did she say?'

'I'm not sure what she said about it honestly.' It wasn't true; Raff remembered the conversation well. He'd invited Hannah to visit his studio again. He'd told her she had a wonderful bone structure and asked if she'd ever considered posing for a life drawing. She'd laughed. No she hadn't considered it. And didn't intend to. 'I think we just talked generally,' he said now. 'She'd bought some things from the market.'

'I see.' Esther sounded disappointed. 'Dear me, I am tired. Still it's good to be back. There's something very cleansing about this place.' She wearily pushed a strand of hair away from her forehead and sighed. 'I think I'll go across and see this Hannah myself. I'd like to see the paintings again and find out what she's going to do with them.'

She started cutting into the peach with a knife and Sara and Raff exchanged a look.

*

Saint Peter looked better. Hannah had removed the dirt and the varnish from his face, hair and beard, and he had come alive again, like someone stepping forward into the spotlight on a stage, ready to impose themselves on an audience. She was

61

now sitting in front of him, working slowly to clean the dark background. There was music playing in her ears as usual. This time it was piano music: a selection of pieces by Gershwin. Her mother had been a piano teacher and piano music was the soundtrack to her childhood. There had been lullabies to help her sleep, dance music when Hannah had too much energy and it needed channelling. and dramatic classical music when her mother felt frustrated or angry. When Hannah's father had left, she'd played Beethoven and Rachmaninov for days. Everything went into the piano. It wasn't until her mother became ill that Hannah had started listening to piano music again. She still wasn't sure why.

It was Sunday afternoon and she had decided to work. Living at the abbey, she'd found, was a strange, dislocated existence and paintings were good company. No under-currents; no insinuations.

She was engrossed, twisting round to the table to jettison a dirty swab from the stick and replace it with a fresh one, when a movement at the corner of her eye made her turn. A woman had walked into the theatre dressed in loose, pale blue silk trousers and a silk top a couple of shades darker. Their simplicity and cut suggested expensive. Her short auburn hair was glossy and immaculately cut to swing round her face at chin level. She looked exquisite. Round her neck hung a gold chain with a plain gold cross on it. She looked quite different to that person playing Mrs Danvers but this had to be Esther Langley.

'Hannah, hello. So good to meet you.' Esther smiled warmly. Her accent was transatlantic, neither British nor American.

She came closer and held out a hand. Hannah put down the swab and stood up, pulling the earphones out and switching off the Walkman. She took the proffered hand.

'It's good to meet you too.' She felt unusually tongue-tied. She'd heard too many opinions about this woman and wasn't sure what to expect but the woman certainly had presence.

'What are you listening to?'

'Gershwin.'

The finely drawn eyebrows lifted.

'I suppose it helps keep you entertained.'

Hannah smiled. 'It helps me focus actually.'

'I'm slightly surprised to see you working on a Sunday,' Esther said genially.

'You don't mind? I'm here to do a job.'

'No, of course I don't mind. I'm impressed.' She offered the suggestion of a mischievous smile. 'Just don't tell Claudine. She's very devout and is careful to keep Sunday as a day of rest. I have my beliefs of course but I often end up working on Sundays. I think the way we exercise our faith is more personal than formal religion allows. We all navigate life in our own particular way, don't we, trying to find the right path?' The smile had faded and her gaze became distant, her voice dreamy. Hannah noticed that her eyes were slightly different colours, one grey-blue, the other grey-green. 'It's all about the spirit inside us. The soul, I suppose. That's what we're all working with in our own way, isn't it?'

It wasn't clear if she expected a reply. Hannah nodded, unsure exactly what she was agreeing with. There was an eerie silence for a couple of minutes.

'So tell me about the paintings,' Esther said suddenly, coming out of her apparent reverie and looking at the picture on the easel, alert again, interested. 'Saint Peter looks better already. Aren't you clever? He was an amazing man, you know. He was so scared, so out of his depth for a while there, but such a strong person too. Christ's rock. I think the artist has captured something of that, don't you, that conflict inside?'

'Yes, I think you're right. It's very powerful.'

'Yes, yes, it is. Will he need a lot of work still?'

'There's a bit of degradation to the paint surface which I'll need to address but his main problem was a thick, yellowed varnish and a lot of dirt.' Hannah hesitated. 'Can I ask, Miss Langley, did you acquire all these paintings recently?'

'Oh call me Esther, please. Yes and no. I've bought them over the last twelve months. I always knew they'd need attention. It's a risk when you buy at auction, isn't it? You're never sure quite what state they're in underneath.' She looked amused. 'It wasn't me who made them so dirty, if that's what you're suggesting.'

'Of course not. I just wondered how long you'd had them.'

Esther wandered across to the other paintings and walked slowly past them, pausing by each one, staring intently at them.

'A couple of them will need a lot more work than the others,' ventured Hannah. 'I've found more damage than Mr Blandish could see on the photographs. Has he been in touch with you? I sent him an assessment of them. The thing is, I'm afraid they might take a little longer than he initially quoted for. He said he'd send you a revised quote.'

Esther turned and smiled at her. 'I haven't had anything yet. Though perhaps Sara has. Either way, don't worry about it darling. You do whatever needs to be done.' She stopped by the fire-damaged one and became suddenly serious. 'And this one? Can you do something with it, do you think?' There was a subtle change in her voice, hard to define.

'Yes, definitely. There's considerable bubbling of the paint on one side. It'll need work to stabilise it and probably some infill painting. Of course, it'll need cleaning first. Smoke and soot leave a thick residue.' Hannah hesitated. 'I asked Sara about this painting. I thought perhaps you'd bought it like this. It's unusual for an auction house to sell anything in this condition. She said it wasn't like this when you bought it but she was reluctant to talk about it. She said I should ask you.'

Esther nodded. 'Yes,' she said slowly, 'I imagine she would be reluctant.' She dragged her eyes from the painting and turned back to face Hannah. 'We had a fire, you see and that painting was a casualty. I know I should have done something about it sooner but you know, I was...' She hesitated as if about to say something else, to explain, but didn't.

'You had a fire here? Were you hurt?'

'No, no, I wasn't, but thank you for asking.'

'How long ago was it?'

Again the hesitation. 'Nearly two years now.'

'What happened?'

Esther frowned. A flicker of annoyance passed over her features, quickly gone.

'Well, I suppose it might help you to understand the damage. You see, when I bought this house there was a little chalet thing down by the pool – a bit of nonsense really – called the Garden House. Built of stone but with a lot of wood too. The same people who built that, built this theatre.' She looked up and around. 'It was a couple who worked in musical theatre. I rather like this. Anyway, there was a bad fire at the chalet a couple of years ago and that painting you've got was on the wall. The building wasn't worth saving so I had it knocked down and had the pool house built instead. It's so much more useful.'

Esther's manner changed suddenly and she made a point of looking brightly over Hannah's equipment, waving an expansive and flippant hand.

'Don't you need a lot of equipment to sort out old paintings?' She turned to look at Hannah again, solicitous now. 'I hear little Marielle's been bothering you. You must ask her to leave if she's a problem. I don't want her to disturb your work.'

'No, she doesn't bother me. She seems lonely. I gave her some paper and crayons to draw with and she was quite happy. She was no trouble.'

'That was kind of you, Hannah. Thank you. Yes, I think she's lonely too. Poor child.'

Esther began to drift elegantly towards the door then stopped half way and turned.

'You must join us for dinner one evening – all of us sitting down together. Really, I know we all have our separate lives and the buffet is practical but it's like being back at school, isn't it?' She gave a tinkling laugh. 'We really should make more effort, don't you think? Of course Raff sometimes works all evening and half the night.' She raised her eyebrows and one expressive hand. 'He says he's more productive then. How he's more productive in the dark is a mystery to me. Still, I can't have you eating alone every night; it's not very hospitable so I'll get Sara to organise something. What about Tuesday evening? Suppose we converge on the dining room for eight o'clock? Let's get to know one another.'

She flashed another smile and left, shutting the door behind her. Hannah sat for a moment, frowning at the closed door. Esther was a very gracious and charming woman. Undeniably so. But she was very intense. And there was something about the fire that wasn't being said. The more they all chose not to talk about it, the more curious Hannah became.

She turned back, switched on the music again and picked up the clean swab.

Chapter 6

Hannah had a shower and wrapped herself in a towel then spent more than half an hour examining her limited wardrobe, trying things on, unable to decide what to wear. It was Tuesday evening and she had to join the others for dinner. But nothing she had felt glamorous enough for Esther. Did that matter? Neither Sara nor Raff were glamorous either. *Dress tidily,* Timothy had exhorted her. She sighed and eventually settled on a casual cotton dress with a little cardigan to throw round her shoulders. She'd be glad of that. The dining room enjoyed little direct sunshine and, still early in April, it was cold. She pushed her fingers through her hair and put on a pair of bright red earrings to match the flowers in the dress. Hannah liked colour.

She arrived a couple of minutes early. The hot plates stood cold and empty; no food had been left on the side tonight. The dining table had been attractively laid with four settings at one end complete with folded napkins neatly shaped into crowns and a small vase of freesias. A basket of bread sat on the table, along with the jug of water and four glasses. Hannah's attention drifted to a painting on the wall between the two windows and she crossed to look at it. She had noticed it before and wondered and, yes, it was a Sisley, one of his river scenes. There were the familiar barges, the houses bordering the choppy water on one side, long grasses on the other. It was a pastel on cardboard. Lovely.

'Evening Hannah.' Sara had arrived and Hannah quickly moved away. Suddenly they were all there and Esther immediately took charge, sitting at the head of the table and insisting that Hannah sit on her right, obliging Raff to sit further down.

'Your conversation's more interesting than mine,' he quipped to Hannah in an aside.

'I'm sure it is,' remarked Sara drily.

'What a lovely bright dress, Hannah,' said Esther. 'Pretty. Have you ever thought of wearing blue? To match your eyes? You should.'

'Er no. Well yes, sometimes.'

Liane, one of Claudine's helpers, brought in a tray with the starters on and put it down on the sideboard behind Esther's chair.

'*Bonsoir* Liane,' said Esther. 'How are you?'

'I am good, Miss Langley, thank you.' Liane smiled shyly, transferred four plates of duck pâté with green salad to the table and retreated with her tray.

There was an awkward silence. Hannah wondered if Esther said grace before eating – her mother always had – but Raff was already buttering a piece of French bread and the other two had started eating. Hannah did the same.

Esther ate a morsel of bread and pâté then paused and poured herself a glass of water. She fixed Hannah with her unusual eyes.

'Raff tells me you went to see *The Lily Madonna*.'

'I did. Marielle mentioned it to me so I went to have a look. Father Diluca was there and he told me its history.'

'And what did you think?' asked Esther. It sounded like a loaded question, too important somehow.

Hannah hesitated for the blink of an eye. 'I thought it was

really interesting. What a fascinating story.'

'But not a great work of art,' remarked Raff.

'Really Raff,' objected Esther. 'Show some feeling. It's an icon. Many people think *The Lily Madonna* can work miracles. They hold it in great affection.'

Again there was silence. 'I suppose that's the difference, isn't it?' Hannah turned to Raff. 'The icon was painted as an act of devotion, not as a work of art. You can't judge it in the same way. But it's certainly wonderful that it's survived all these centuries.'

'Very diplomatic,' grinned Raff, putting his knife down. The pâté had gone; the salad remained.

Esther finished eating too and sat back, flicking Raff a baleful look, before fixing back on Hannah. 'I think it's wonderful too.'

'Do you think it's true though?' Sara looked avidly from Hannah to Esther and back. 'Can it work miracles? I've often wondered.'

Glances were cast but no-one replied.

'The priest said it was a channel for prayer,' Hannah offered. 'He said people claimed it offered illumination. Maybe that's what some see as a miracle.'

Sara became thoughtful but said nothing.

'I think it's all about faith,' said Esther vaguely, letting her eyes roll around the room as if seeing something nobody else could. She focused back on Hannah. 'Did the priest tell you about the monk?'

'The monk?' Hannah shook her head. 'No. What monk?'

Liane came in to clear and Esther bestowed a smile of gratitude on her before answering.

'There's a shrine on the path to town and a grave by it.'

'Oh yes, I've seen that. There's an inscription on the memorial but I couldn't read it.'

'It's very worn and it's in Provençal.' Esther lifted her chin, looked ahead of her, and began to recite: 'I, a nameless servant of God, died at the Abbaye Val du Bois in 1790, the last of the Cistercian brothers to live and work here. May God show his mercy.'

Claudine had appeared in the doorway carrying two plates of pan-fried sea bass. She waited until Esther had finished, then put one in front of Esther and one for Hannah. She crossed herself and went out. A moment later Liane brought in the other two plates and Claudine came back with a dish of tiny roast potatoes and a bowl of ratatouille. The side dishes were passed round for them to help themselves.

'I had someone translate it for me,' said Esther, spooning ratatouille onto her plate. 'It's a very moving story. Back at the beginning of the twentieth century, an archaeological dig found a skeleton over there somewhere on the edge of the woods. They were looking for the chapel that used to be there. Cistercian abbeys didn't allow the public access to their own church, you see. They used to erect a chapel at the gates for pilgrims and lay worshippers to use. Anyway, they found a skeleton and it had blade marks in the skull, God rest his soul.' She shuddered and forked a delicate mouthful of fish into her mouth.

'How horrible,' said Hannah. 'And they're sure it was a monk?'

'I think it's like, I don't know, *The Name of the Rose*,' said Raff. 'Wasn't that the film?'

'It's nothing like *The Name of the Rose*,' protested Sara impatiently.

'Well, how should I know? I'm no film buff. I've never seen it.'

'Then why say it?'

Esther glared at them both. 'Have you two quite finished?'

Sara and Raff fell silent and ate. Esther offered Hannah an apologetic smile.

'As you probably know, Hannah, most of the abbeys and churches were looted during the Revolution and some were completely destroyed. Many of the monks fled or were offered pensions to leave. It seems that that is what happened here, except that the last monk at this abbey refused to leave and he was murdered. After the dig, they reburied the skeleton by the shrine and put up the memorial. It's a holy place, you see. A place of sacrifice.'

Hannah nodded, unsure what to say. It was clearly very personal for Esther. They all continued to eat in silence.

Raff finished first, took another piece of bread and tore it in two.

'It's probably why people say the abbey is haunted.' He rammed a chunk in his mouth.

Hannah turned quickly. 'Do they?'

'That's nonsense,' Sara interposed quickly. 'Why do you say these things?'

'Because it's true. Little Marielle says she's seen a ghost. Pietro has too.'

'The monk?' asked Hannah.

'Presumably. I don't think he stayed around long enough to answer questions. Probably just walked through a wall or something.'

The blood had drained from Esther's face. Her make-up seemed to stand proud on her translucent skin. 'It's not a joking matter,' she said. 'Please stop.'

'Sorry Esther, but I'm not joking. Really. I just don't think ghosts are something to worry about.'

'Well, *I've* never seen a ghost here,' said Sara firmly, though she looked pale herself. Her fingers, as she put her cutlery down, shook slightly. 'And Marielle's hardly a reliable

71

witness. She probably sees unicorns in the wood and fairies in the garden as well.'

There was a pained silence.

'This is an amazing building,' Hannah said and looked at Esther. 'There's clearly a lot of the abbey still here. How long have you lived here?'

Esther bestowed a grateful smile on her. 'Just over ten years now.' She abandoned the remaining food on her plate and dabbed her mouth with her napkin. 'It was already a house, of course. The old abbey had been stripped for stone after the revolution and only parts of it remained. Then, years later, someone decided to rebuild parts of it and make it into a home. It's had several owners since then and everyone has changed it to suit themselves. But a lot of the cloisters are original and so is the entrance to the chapter house. That's where my library is now. I'll show you some time, Hannah.'

'I'd like that.'

Hannah noticed Raff look across at Sara but she seemed to be pointedly averting her eyes.

Liane came in to remove their plates. Claudine came close behind with a cheese board and fruit and the offer of dessert. Only Raff accepted and was served a tiramisu. Esther ate a few grapes then made her apologies and left, complaining that she was still tired from her travelling.

No-one spoke for several minutes after she'd gone as they listened to her soft footsteps disappearing into the distance.

'You're honoured,' Raff said suddenly, finishing his dessert, plucking one grape off the bunch and sitting back. 'Most people aren't invited to see Esther's library. The inner sanctum.'

'I wish you wouldn't tease her about ghosts,' complained Sara. 'You know how it spooks her.'

'That's because she believes in them. She's haunted. It

would be better for all of us if we just admitted it.'

'We shouldn't talk about it.' Sara flicked a sideways look at Hannah.

'For God's sake, Sara, Hannah's going to find out sooner or later. She's got that damn painting to restore.' Raff's expression became serious. 'Anyway, not talking about it just makes it worse. For everyone. It's all about the fire, you see, Hannah. Isn't it, Sara?'

Sara didn't respond. 'I could do with some coffee. Anyone else?' She got up and pressed the call button on the wall behind Esther's chair.

Raff got abruptly to his feet. 'I need a drink and since there's none to be had here, I'm going somewhere I can find one.' He paused and looked down at Hannah. 'It seems Esther likes you, Hannah. But beware: she can turn on you if you say the wrong thing. Just like that.' He snapped his fingers. 'Haunted *and* temperamental, you see. Oh, and get Sara to tell you about Jemma.'

Liane came in as he went out. Sara asked her for a pot of coffee and the young woman disappeared wordlessly.

Hannah waited but Sara refused to meet her eye and said nothing, her fingers fidgeting around the remaining cutlery on the table in front of her.

The pot of coffee arrived on a tray, along with two cups and saucers and a small jug of milk. Liane cleared the cheese and fruit off the table and withdrew.

'Esther told me you'd had a fire at the Garden House,' Hannah said.

Sara looked across sharply. 'Did she? What did she say?'

'Just that. And that it had been razed and replaced with the pool house. No coffee for me, thanks. I don't drink it.'

'Oh. Would you like tea?'

'I'm fine, thanks.'

Sara poured herself a coffee and left it black. She took a sip, savouring it in her mouth before swallowing.

'Raff talks too much. He likes the sound of his own voice.' She glanced quickly at Hannah and away again. 'And he's purposely provocative.' She paused. 'Jemma is the only reason he's allowed to stay on here.'

Sara took another sip of coffee and carefully put her cup down.

'Jemma and Esther were friends – best friends if you like. Do you believe in "best friends", Hannah? Don't they always fall out in the end?' She shrugged. 'Well, they'd been friends ever since they were at drama school together. And Jemma went on to be an actress too, just not as successfully as Esther. Some work; no work. You know how it is with actors. Anyway, Jemma was engaged to Raff and Esther let them live here off and on. She let him set up a studio here too. I'm not sure why.'

'You said she *was* engaged? So what happened?'

Sara drank some more coffee. Her fingers still fidgeted as if she they were missing a cigarette to hold. She swallowed.

'Jemma died in the fire.' Suddenly Sara met Hannah's gaze. 'That's why Esther doesn't like talk of ghosts. Raff's right: she's haunted.' A pause and a meaningful lift of the eyebrows. 'And frankly I'm not surprised.'

She picked up her cup, finished the last of her coffee in one gulp and stood up. Nodding to Hannah, she left the room.

*

The painting of Saint Peter was as clean of old varnish and dirt as Hannah could safely make it. She had now started removing the flaking paint to make the surface stable before she could go any further. Late in the afternoon on the Thursday, Marielle popped into the theatre again. School had just broken up for the Easter holidays and she was excited and restless. She asked to listen to Hannah's music – Elton John was playing again – and jigged along to it for a couple of minutes then lost interest and gave the Walkman back.

'They'll move *The Lily Madonna* this weekend,' she told Hannah. 'She'll be taken from the alcove and put up on the high altar for the Easter services. She only ever comes out twice, you see: once on Easter Sunday and once in August when She leads the procession for the town festival.'

'There's a procession?'

'Oh yes. And a market, and music and dancing. It's a very special occasion.'

The little girl nodded gravely. She was definitely too serious for someone so young.

'Will you come to the *fête*?' Marielle asked.

'I'll probably have finished working here by then and I'll be back in England.'

Marielle said nothing. She stood and stared at the painting as Hannah, peering through a huge magnifying glass on a stand, painstakingly picked off tiny scraps of paint with a small pair of tweezers.

'What are you doing?'

'I'm taking off the bits of the old paint which are loose. Then I can touch it up with new paint so it all makes sense as a picture again. Then I'll varnish it to protect it.'

'Protect it from what?'

'Pollution in the air, dirt, accidental scratches.'

Marielle stared at the painting for a moment as if it might transform in front of her eyes, then turned away. A couple of minutes later, she'd gone.

Hannah put her earphones in and settled back to her work. Claudine had made a point of speaking to her at breakfast time, instructing Hannah not to let Marianne disturb her.

'Tell her to leave you alone. I have told her but she doesn't listen to me.'

'She doesn't disturb me, Claudine. But if I do need peace and quiet, I'll lock the door. I promise.'

Mollified, Claudine nodded.

'And if she does come, I would like you to make her speak English. She knows a lot of English and it's good for her.'

'I will.'

Hannah hadn't seen Esther to speak to since the dinner. They'd all resumed their self-service meals, living separate lives, passing like ships in the night. The conversation of that evening circulated in her head though. She had thought, prior to the actress's return that, having met her, she would be able to form her own judgement of the woman. Hannah wasn't one to automatically accept what other people told her. But as yet her impressions were confused. And Sara's remarks lingered in her mind. *She's haunted... And frankly I'm not surprised.* Why wasn't she surprised? Because Esther was so devoted to Jemma? Or, reading the accusatory look in Sara's eyes, because Esther was culpable in some way? *Do you believe in 'best friends', Hannah? Don't they always fall out in the end?* Did they fall out?

On Easter Saturday morning, Hannah walked into town again. Studying a map of the town centre on a stand at the corner of the square, she located the library and walked down Rue Victor Hugo to find it. The library shared a double-fronted building with the town museum. There were shelves of books and magazines through a door to the right and a display of the history of the town and locality in the rooms to the left. What interested Hannah, however, was the local newspaper archive which was held upstairs.

She was hoping to find out more about the fire. It must have been a significant one for it to gut the Garden House and

76

for someone to have died in it. So the local newspaper must have reported the incident. Hannah asked the librarian for the issues for 1988. It was a weekly paper and they were held in two binders, January to June and July to December. She opened the first one and started in April, slowly scanning the pages, looking for the item. Esther Langley was a big name, their local celebrity. It would be a prominent piece surely; there would probably be a photograph.

There was nothing in April, nor May. In the third week of June, she finally found a small headline over a very short column, buried inside the paper.

Fire in poolside chalet.

Last Saturday, a freak fire destroyed a small building in the grounds of the old converted abbey on the outskirts of town. The house belongs to actress, Esther Langley, who was unhurt. The police said the fire appeared to have been started by candles left unattended after a barbecue. The residents were able to extinguish the flames but one of the guests sustained significant burns and died in the inferno. Next of kin have been informed. Miss Langley said she is devastated at this tragic accident.

It wasn't much and told Hannah nothing that she didn't already know. But it was surprising that someone with as big a profile as Esther hadn't merited a more detailed and prominent story. More than surprising. It had clearly been hushed up. Was that the influence of a big name? Or the persuasion of money? On the face of it the fire and the death were innocent tragedies, yet something made Hannah doubt it. The secrecy perhaps, or Esther's odd behaviour. And Sara's veiled remarks… And why was Jemma alone in the Garden House anyway?

She left the library and wandered back up the street towards the square, passing stalls set up down the middle of

77

the road. Nearing the top she saw Raff standing on the pavement pressed in close to one of the shop fronts, talking intently to a young dark-haired woman, gesturing with an emphatic hand. Drawing nearer, Hannah could hear him speaking fairly basic French with a pronounced English accent. She walked past them with the briefest of nods in Raff's direction but a couple of minutes later he caught up with her. He was alone.

'Hannah, I didn't know you were coming in today. Did you walk in?'

'Yes.'

'So what brings you here? The market, I suppose. It's not bad.'

'It's very good. Anyway, I like the atmosphere. What brings you here – apart from chatting up the local talent that is?'

'I wasn't chatting her up. Not exactly. I was trying to persuade her to pose for me. She did it once before and she was quite good.'

'But she's not keen?'

'Her boyfriend isn't.'

'Ah.'

He waved a paper package at her. 'I came to collect some charcoal for drawing. The art shop here gets it in specially for me. It's an American brand. Look, have you finished here? I brought the Morgan in. How do you fancy a spin in her?' He glanced up at the blue sky. Only a few white clouds scudded across it. 'Just the day for the top down and a good run. We could have lunch in Bonnieux. On me. You should accept. I don't often have the money. Have you been there? Stunning views.'

Hannah looked into his face. Behind the studiously unkempt look, he was quite good-looking really. A flirt and irritating at times, he was also articulate and funny. She smiled.

'No, I haven't been there. Sounds good. Why not?'

He looked surprised then grinned. 'Excellent.' He looped his arm through hers. 'The car's parked down here. Come on.'

It was an undeniable pleasure, driving along in the sunshine with the wind in her hair, watching the fields of vines and olives on either side, passing red pantile-roofed farmhouses and signs to small, family run vineyards. It was good to be away from the abbey for a while. And Bonnieux was a charming village, built like Tourbelle on the side of a hill with steep, winding streets, but smaller and more relaxed. Raff took her to a restaurant at the top which boasted a sweeping panoramic view over the plain below and to the distant mountains. They ordered – an omelette and chips for him and a salade niçoise for her – and sat drinking a small glass of beer each.

Raff talked art, mostly about his favourite artists: Édouard Manet, James Whistler and Paul Cèzanne. The bohemian image might be carefully manufactured but he was clearly passionate about art. He asked about her work, about the artists whose paintings she had restored over the years.

'Do you enjoy it? Don't you find it frustrating to work on other people's paintings all the time? You must have some artistic skill. Do you never ache to paint yourself?'

She laughed. 'No. Yes, I can draw. And I used to paint a bit when I was younger.' She shrugged, fingering the condensation on her glass. 'But I was never going to be good. Not really good. I opted for a job that would pay me. I get to see all sorts of wonderful pictures and hopefully do something good for them. Of course I see some dross too but it's still an interesting job. Lots of challenges. I like that.'

Their food arrived and the conversation faltered while they ate.

Raff gobbled his food as usual and finished first. He sat back with the remains of his beer, watching her speculatively.

'I'm sorry if our meal proved a bit... heavy the other night,' he said. 'Esther tends to bring her own particular gloom with her these days and it settles over all of us.' Hannah offered him a token smile while she ate but said nothing. 'And then Sara toadies to her. I may have talked too much in consequence. It gets me like that sometimes.'

Hannah finished and picked up her beer too.

'Sara told me about Jemma in the fire, Raff. And that you were engaged. I'm sorry. I had no idea. How long had you known her?'

A soft sigh. 'About six years. I was staying with a friend in London and we met at the National Gallery, both staring at *Combing the Hair* by Degas. Have you seen it? It could have been painted yesterday. Amazing. Jemma thought so too.' He grinned. 'Corny, huh? Like something from a romcom.'

She smiled. 'I think it's wonderful.' Her expression clouded. 'But what happened to cause the fire, Raff?'

'Candles, they say. *I* don't know. We'd been having a little barbecue, letting our hair down. We'd had a few drinks. Maybe too many.'

'But how did Jemma come to be the only one hurt?'

Now Raff looked angry. 'Because we'd had a row and I'd left her there, OK? You think I'm proud of that?' He fixed her with a warning look. 'Now you know why Esther behaves the way she does and I'd advise you to leave it there. You see, she'd left Jemma there too. We all had, so we don't talk about it. It's history. Asking questions is definitely not a good idea around here.' He drummed on the table with his fingers then forced a smile. 'Dessert? No? Coffee?'

'No thanks.'

'I'll get the bill then.'

He made a sign to the waitress who came a few minutes later and laid the bill on its saucer on the table. He paid and they walked back to the car. Raff was unusually quiet, morose even, and said little on the journey home.

At the gates of the abbey, Hannah got out to key in the code and they sailed through to a cursory wave from Guillaume.

'This should get a few tongues wagging,' said Raff, brightening up. 'You going for a drive with me.' He almost laughed.

He pulled the car to a halt in the parking area and killed the engine. Neither seemed in a hurry to move.

'I'm kind of surprised you stay here,' said Hannah. 'Doesn't it have too many bad memories for you?'

Raff hesitated. When he did reply he talked to the dashboard.

'I don't really remember a lot about it. I'd been drinking, like I said, and I was dead to the world. By the time someone hammered on my door and I surfaced, it was all over. It was too bloody late. Guillaume and Pietro had got hoses out, David too, and they'd managed to stop the fire razing the whole building. But the upstairs was gutted and Jemma was gone. Just like that. I comfort myself that she was so smashed, she didn't know anything about it. They say the smoke would probably have got to her first anyway.' He tapped a finger against the steering wheel. 'I've got board and lodging and a great studio. It's more than most artists can boast. Or maybe I stay just to annoy Esther. Who knows?' He turned and fixed her with a look. 'Jemma was Sara's sister. I guess she didn't mention that, did she? She doesn't usually. And *she's* still here. We're a sad lot really.'

Chapter 7

Timothy was away from the office for a few days. It was a rare event. He constantly complained that he never had a holiday but Nathan had no sympathy; it was his own fault. Timothy was a control freak and thought the whole business would grind to a halt without him. But his daughter from his first marriage was about to get married on the island of Jersey and he had agreed to give her away. For a few weeks at least, he and his first wife – Monica – had been on speaking terms.

Nathan's job in Scotland had been straightforward and brief and now he was back and nominally in charge. Timothy had left a raft of scribbled notes for him on a notepad on his desk. Nathan checked them on the Tuesday morning after the Easter weekend. There was the telephone number of the hotel where Timothy was staying, 'in case of any issues which won't wait till I come back.' There were notes about clients who had made enquiries but not yet formally commissioned work, and one about a possible client – a friend of a previous client – who might ring. All pretty straightforward. It was hard to imagine anything so urgent in a business like this that it wouldn't wait until the following week.

Now it was the Wednesday lunchtime and Nathan, who had been working on a Corot in the workshop, called in to see Daphne in reception on his way out to grab some lunch.

'Timothy rang again,' she said as he came in.

'Of course he did.' Nathan leaned against the desk. 'He's going to ring every day. He can't stop himself.'

'He doesn't seem very happy about his daughter's wedding.'

'He's probably thinking about how much it's costing him. He may not have had much say in how it was done but he'll probably be picking up more than half the bill.'

Daphne grinned. 'You're so cynical. By the way, this arrived this morning.' Daphne held up a large brown envelope. 'It's addressed to Hannah. Do you think I should send it on?'

Nathan took the envelope. It had been franked with the name of an art restoration business in Cheltenham.

'It's from the place she worked at before she came here,' said Daphne. 'I suppose it might be important.'

Nathan felt the envelope. It felt like there was something much smaller inside, in fact – he poked and prodded it some more – maybe a couple of things. He turned it over. The sealing flap was weakly gummed or hadn't been moistened sufficiently; it gaped for most of its length. He tipped the envelope on its end, making the loose objects fall against the flap, then squeezed to make the flap open a little.

'Photographs,' he said, trying to work them to show more out of the end and failing. 'I thought that's what they were. Oh look, the seal's completely broken now. This was a crap envelope, wasn't it?'

'Honestly Nathan, you are the limit. You did that on purpose.' Daphne shook her head. 'If Hannah finds out…'

He slid the contents out: three photographs and a short letter. He read it.

'Apparently Hannah left these behind by mistake in a drawer of her desk. They'd got caught or stuck in the drawer above. Gosh, a desk of her own. Why don't we have desks?'

'Because you don't need them?'

He ignored her, putting the letter down and examining the first photograph. A family group: mother, father and two girls. The second one was of a middle-aged woman with a young woman, unmistakeably Hannah as a late teenager. The third was a more recent one of the mother alone. Nathan examined the one of mother and daughter. Hannah had dyed her hair bright red and wore huge dangling earrings. He produced a wry smile at the image. She was looking belligerently at the camera. The hair was no longer red but he thought the obstinate set of the mouth was recognisable.

He handed them to Daphne to look at.

'These are quite old,' she said. 'Look at the clothes. That's Hannah, isn't it? So that must be her mum.'

'Yep, it's the same woman in both pictures. They're not urgent are they, so I don't see any need to send them on.' He grinned. 'I'm sure Timothy would rather save the postage. Anyway, they might get lost again. Keep them here till she gets back.'

He replaced the letter and photographs in the envelope and smoothed the flap down. The gum had been so weak that the part he'd pulled open hadn't torn at all.

'You'd better tell her it came like that in the post,' he said to Daphne, handing it back. 'It's almost true. It is a crap envelope.'

She rolled her eyes and put it in a drawer.

'Have you heard from her at all?' he asked.

'No. Nothing. Timothy asked that yesterday on the phone. He was complaining he hadn't heard from her since soon after she got there. You know what he's like about having regular updates. But she strikes me as a pretty conscientious worker.'

'That's just you and your female solidarity.'

'No, it's not. Timothy said she was conscientious. Maybe too conscientious, he suggested. Anyway, I always think no

84

news is good news.'

'Not always,' said Nathan cryptically, and left in search of food. Hannah didn't strike him as the kind of person who'd ask for help or advice, even if she needed it.

*

That same Wednesday afternoon Hannah was in the theatre, sanding down the filler she'd pressed into the chipped frame of the picture of Saint Peter. She was working late, feeling pressured to get on and determined to at least put a first coat of primer on the filler that night. The infill painting had taken her longer than she had expected; lots of small losses had made it a more painstaking job. It occurred to her that she should have rung Timothy by now to give him an update but she wanted to finish this painting first and have something concrete to say. He clearly liked progress. He was an odd man to work for. Polite and pleasant enough but obsessed with 'getting the job done.' And moving on to the next. Wherever she'd worked, there had always been commercial pressures – restoration was a slow business and people always wanted to see results – but it had usually come from the client, not the boss. The irony of it here was that Esther didn't mind how long she took.

She was still smiling to herself at the thought when Marielle appeared beside her. Hannah straightened up and stretched the knots out of her back and neck.

'Hello Marielle, how are you? See, I know you can speak English. Your *grand-maman* told me.'

'A little.' Marielle thrust out her hand which was clutching a small envelope.

Hannah took it. 'Thank you. What's this?'

Marielle shook her head and shrugged.

The envelope had Hannah's name on it, written by hand in a looping script. The French inside was equally flowery.

Mademoiselle Dechansay,

I apologise for approaching you in this way but be assured it is because my mission is of the utmost importance and also very confidential. I should be deeply grateful if you would do me the honour of coming to see me tomorrow night. Please come to the rear door of the presbytery at 19.30 H. I have something I must discuss with you.

I beg you not to talk about this to anyone. I shall give this letter to Marielle after the catechism class but I shall not tell her what it contains. If she shows curiosity, please say that I have invited you to join us for worship next Sunday.

Yours most gratefully,

Père *Diluca*

Hannah read it twice then looked up at Marielle who was watching her intently.

'Father Diluca has invited me to attend church on Sunday.' Hannah had slipped back into French without thinking. She smiled ruefully. 'I'm not much of a church-goer, I'm afraid.' She slipped the note back in the envelope. 'But thank you for bringing it to me.'

'Aren't you frightened of not going to church?'

'Frightened? What should I be frightened of, Marielle?'

Marielle's eyes grew big. 'Hell,' she murmured, as if scared even saying it would call it down upon her.

'Ah. Yes, I see.' Hannah hesitated. She was walking on eggshells here: someone else's culture; someone else's religion. 'Well, I think you can be a good person without going to church but you have to learn all about it before you can make that decision. When you're grown up, you can figure it out for yourself.'

Marielle gave this due consideration, frowning, but appeared to accept it. Hannah was relieved. Her own mother inevitably came to mind. She'd once said she thought Hannah would go to hell too.

*

The Place de l'Église was quiet. Rain spat intermittently in a chill mistral and those out and about, going home or heading to restaurants for dinner, kept their heads down, moving purposefully. The *presbytère* stood next to the church, a plain stone building with a dark, imposing carved front door. There was an alley between it and the neighbouring building, an old house now used, according to the plaque by the door, as a lawyer's office. Hannah slipped down the alley, pushed open a wrought iron gate and went into the presbytery's rear courtyard. Father Diluca was watering the potted plants and immediately put the watering can down and came to greet her.

'Thank you for coming, *Mademoiselle*. Come in, come in. My housekeeper's out this evening.' He ushered Hannah into his study, a large book-lined room, the woodwork and furniture all mahogany, the chairs covered in worn dark brown leather. 'Can I get you something to drink?'

'No, I'm fine, thank you. But I am curious to know what this is about Father.'

'Please sit.' He gestured towards one of the leather chairs. He sat down too, then paused, arcing his fingers together, watching her anxiously.

'I'm afraid we have a problem, 'annah, and I dearly need your help. *The Lily Madonna* – you remember our precious painting – has had a small accident at the Easter festivities.' He hesitated and leaned forward solicitously. 'Are you sure I can't get you a drink?'

'No, really, thank you. You said the icon had an accident?'

'Yes. She has... er... sustained some damage. We rather hoped you might be in a position to help us restore her to her beautiful self?'

Hannah stared at him, trying to take in the implications of what he was asking.

'Some damage? What sort of damage? How?' She looked round, thinking she might see it.

'She had been moved to the high altar for the Easter service. Francesca – it wasn't her fault; she is a wonderful servant of the church – was trying to be helpful. She picked it up after the service to put it back in its niche. Unfortunately, she caught her toe as she was carrying it and fell, and the icon fell to the floor too. It has lost a little paint.' One hand strayed down to touch a battered old suitcase by the side of his chair. He smiled apologetically. 'It was my fault, not hers. Normally it is my job to move it. I forgot and had become involved doing something else.'

'I'm sorry, Father, but I don't see how I can help.'

'I assure you I would not ask if there had been any other choice. *The Lily Madonna* is held in such regard here that it is essential for the well-being of the people that She be quickly restored and put back in a prominent position. The people believe that She is there to protect them, that something terrible will happen to the town if She is gone for long.' His eyes pleaded with her. 'At the very least, She must be ready for the great annual festival in August, on the Feast of the Assumption. In the meantime I shall tell people that the picture needs a little cleaning from all the candle smoke. I have sworn Francesca to secrecy about the fall. She only suffered a bruise or two fortunately.'

'I see. But I'm afraid I have my hands full with the work I'm doing at the abbey.' She shook her head regretfully. 'I know of a couple of very good restoration workshops in Nice but you should consult your insurance company for their advice before taking it to anyone.'

He nearly laughed. 'Insurance company? She isn't insured, *Mademoiselle*. We did ask once, years ago but the premium was so high. We are a small church and the young people don't attend the way they used to.' He shrugged. 'There aren't the resources, you see.' He hesitated. 'But we might be able to pay something towards your materials. We wouldn't want you to be out of pocket.'

Hannah said nothing. It was an absurd suggestion. She couldn't do it. But Father Diluca looked so distraught, his soft brown eyes so pathetic, so desperate.

'I suppose if it's just a small problem,' she ventured. She was curious to see it.

Almost before she had finished speaking, the priest had the suitcase flat on his desk and open. Hannah got up to stand beside him. The icon was wrapped in a large soft cloth. He carefully lifted it out, peeled off the swaddling and handed *The Lily Madonna* to her.

Hannah's mouth dropped open. *It has lost a little paint*, he'd said. A little? It was a nightmare. The corner which had born the brunt of the fall was impressed and flattened, the paint cracked back from the point in a succession of parallel fissures like the ripples a falling stone makes in a pond, revealing underlayers of paint down to the gesso and disturbing the continuity of the floral border. And there was more: the paint was flaking over the Christ child and his mother's sleeve and, worse still, chunks of paint were missing from the Virgin's face.

Father Diluca put his hand in the case again and pulled out a long, unsealed envelope. He pulled back the flap and gently pressed it lengthways to make it open, holding it out for her to see inside.

'We picked up all the pieces of paint we could find. We thought that might help.'

Hannah glanced at the intermingled slivers of coloured paint nestling in the bottom of the envelope, then looked back up at Father Diluca's hopeful face.

'Really…' she began.

'Is it reparable?' His voice sounded strangled; his face had gone pale.

Hannah stared back down at the vandalised image, automatically scanning it to assess the damage, trying to gauge what was involved in restoring it. Her first instincts were always to try to make a picture 'better'. It was what she did.

'Yes,' she said distantly. 'I'm sure it could be repaired, but restored…? And it's a big job. Huge.' She shook her head. She didn't have the time and it was such a responsibility. What's more Timothy would probably sack her on the spot. 'I really can't do this, Father.'

She tried to hand it back to him but he wouldn't take it.

'Please think about it, *Mademoiselle*, I beseech you. Your help is needed now. It is not a coincidence, I think, that you are here at this time. I believe God sent you.'

'Really Father.'

'Just because you don't believe, doesn't mean it isn't true, 'annah.' He dipped his head down as if beaten and despairing then looked up at her through his lashes imploringly. 'Suppose you take Her and see what you think you can do? Then you can let me know.' He brightened. 'Here, this is my phone number. Or you can send me a note with Marielle. Please be discreet.'

Hannah studied his face. He looked so innocent but he was a wily man, this priest. He could see that she was torn and he was playing her. If she were smart, she'd hand the picture straight back to him and go. This was a can of worms, whichever way she looked at it. No, she wouldn't do it.

Half an hour later, Hannah approached the rear gate into the abbey grounds carrying a large cardboard carrier bag with the swaddled painting in it, a bag boasting the name of a smart dress shop in the town. Only now did it occur to her in passing to wonder how the priest had such a bag. But it was lucky that the picture wasn't any bigger for the suitcase would have drawn attention. Now it just looked as if she'd been shopping. Did it? She tried not to look up at the security camera over the gate. Guillaume was probably watching her.

Chapter 8

Esther had been home for two weeks when she finally invited Hannah to join her for afternoon tea. On first impressions, Esther liked Hannah. A bit of a kindred spirit, she thought. Hannah appreciated old things and religious artifacts. She seemed a sympathetic sort of person too and quite genuine, and she'd coped well with Sara and Raff's foolish chatter that night at dinner, steering the conversation back onto more comfortable ground. The way those two bickered just set Esther's nerves on edge. Hannah had been a breath of calm, fresh air.

Esther wasn't finding it easy without David. Of course, it was a temporary thing and she was sure he'd return. All couples went through this, didn't they? He'd said he needed space. Goodness, she often liked time to herself too and they were lucky that their work allowed for it: his filming and hers rarely coincided. It was just that this time he'd made a thing about it and time had gone on. Still, she was fine. She was, really. She didn't like the fashionable parties and gossip round Los Angeles. Now less than ever. She cherished her own home here in the country between shoots, with the occasional dinner party or close friends to stay; otherwise she liked quiet.

She didn't usually get up early and Claudine would bring breakfast to her bedroom: a glass of orange juice, a bowl of grapefruit and a little toast. When Claudine brought the tray up on the Friday morning, she asked her to give Hannah a message, inviting her to tea that afternoon at four o'clock.

Hannah arrived promptly and knocked at the door to Esther's lounge. She wore a long baggy white tee shirt and cropped leggings, and her short hair stood up in random spikes. Dragged through a hedge backwards was the phrase that came to mind. She had clearly hurried. There was a smudge of something reddish on her right cheek and something similar near the neck of her tee shirt. Esther decided not to mention it and smiled.

'Come in Hannah. I'm glad you could make it. Have I dragged you away from your work?'

'I'm putting the finishing touches to the frame for the painting of Saint Peter.' Hannah ran a restless hand through her hair. 'It was badly chipped, if you remember? I've been regilding it.'

'Wonderful. Aren't you clever? So it'll be finished soon?'

'I hope so.'

'I'm looking forward to seeing it. Do take a seat. Claudine has just brought the tea.'

There were two sofas at right angles to each other, both half turned towards the view over the valley. Hannah sat gingerly on one. A low glass table stood in the angle between them with a tray of tea things on it. Esther sat on the other sofa.

'Ceylon, Earl Grey, Darjeeling or camomile?' she enquired.

'Ceylon please.'

'My favourite too.' Esther opened two sachets and put a tea bag in each cup then poured hot water from a tall covered pot onto the tea. 'Though I'd have used a teapot if I'd known you liked the same tea. Much more what I was brought up to and, well, more like a proper cup of tea.' She looked at Hannah as she handed her the cup and saucer. 'Showing my British roots, aren't I?' She hesitated. 'Between you and me, my parents always make builder's tea.' She laughed. 'So strong.'

'Thank you.' Hannah put the cup and saucer down on the table, leaving the bag to steep. 'Where are you from originally?'

'Yorkshire. But I went to drama school when I was eighteen and made sure I lost the accent. I was told it would make it easier to get work.' Esther removed the tea bag from her cup and put it in a bowl on the tray. 'What about you?'

'I grew up in Gloucestershire. But I trained in London and worked there for a while.'

Hannah removed her tea bag as Esther proffered a plate with a mixture of French cakes and a couple of buttered scones. 'Can I tempt you? Claudine's been baking.'

Hannah took a scone. Esther hesitated then took the second one. 'But you didn't stay? Not a city girl?'

'I wanted to experience different work. I've moved around a bit.'

'And you've only recently joined Timothy Blandish, I gather. Don't look so surprised: he told me you were new. But very good. He stressed that.' Esther smiled. 'With all this moving around, I'm guessing you're not in a long-term relationship then?'

'No. Not at the moment.'

'No, well, relationships can be… difficult. Still, it gives you more freedom, doesn't it?' Esther took a small bite of her scone. 'Mm, good. I must say Claudine is getting quite good at baking scones. She'd never seen one till I gave her a recipe for them.'

Hannah bit into hers. 'Mm, they're good.' She hesitated. 'Do you miss Yorkshire then, and England? Or are you settled here?'

'There are a few things I miss. My parents still live there

and I don't get to see them as often as I'd like.' Esther abruptly stopped speaking and frowned, looking out of the low window to the view beyond. 'They never seem to want to come here. It's too hot or it's too far. Or it's too French.' She put her plate with the remains of her scone down on the table and picked up her tea. 'Different worlds, I suppose, Hannah. We inhabit different worlds now.' She smiled politely. 'Do you see your parents?'

'I see my father occasionally. He lives in Paris.' She hesitated. 'My mother passed away recently. She had early onset dementia.'

'Oh I *am* sorry.' Esther looked at her with concern. 'And how are you? I mean, how have you coped with losing her?'

Hannah shifted uncomfortably in her seat. 'I'm all right. Of course, I miss her.'

'Naturally. She was taken too soon, wasn't she? I do understand.'

Hannah didn't respond and they drank the rest of their tea in silence.

Esther put her cup down and glanced across at Hannah's. 'Have you finished? Let's go next door and I'll show you my library.'

Esther led the way and unlocked the door, letting Hannah go in first.

Hannah stood and slowly looked round. 'This is a wonderful room.'

'I thought you'd like it.'

Esther stood beside her and surveyed it too, enjoying it anew. There was an entire wall of wooden bookshelves on one side, a richly grained mahogany cabinet against the opposite wall with a small painted statuette of the Virgin Mary on it, and a desk and chair under the window. Two wing back leather chairs stood at ninety degrees to each other with a low table between them. The stained glass in the arched side windows cast a mysterious, unearthly light over the whole space.

'I love this place,' Esther said softly. 'It has soul don't you think? As I think I told you, this was the monks' chapter house, or part of it anyway – the central focus of the monastery where they conducted business and received visitors or had meetings. They read from the scriptures here too.' She looked down. 'I found these floor tiles in a salvage yard. They're very old. I loved all the birds and animals and, well honestly, I'm not sure what they all are. They're probably not even real creatures but they felt right here.'

Hannah nodded, still scanning the room. She moved closer to the bare wall where a single painting hung.

'This looks old.'

'Fifteenth century, the gallery said. *Christ Healing the Blind Man*. They didn't know the artist but it didn't matter to me. It's a miracle told in the Gospels. Well, you probably know that. It's very moving, don't you think?'

'It is.'

'I wanted to show you this too.' Esther pulled open a drawer of the cabinet and took out a tooled leather-bound book with a metal clasp. She handed it to Hannah reverentially. 'This is fifteenth century too.'

Hannah opened it and carefully leafed through the pages. It was an illuminated Book of Hours.

'It's beautiful,' she murmured, gazing on page after page.

'I probably shouldn't use it but it's too precious to me to lock it up under glass. I find it a great help.' She paused. 'Perhaps you should try and find something like that for yourself, Hannah. You might find it helps.'

'Helps?' Hannah glanced up at her in surprise.

'With your loss.'

'I see.' A couple of minutes later Hannah returned the

book and they were about to leave the library when she paused by the cabinet to look at a couple of framed photographs which stood either side of the statuette.

'That's me with David,' said Esther. 'David Flaxman, the actor? He's the man who shares my life.' She stared at it a moment then looked at the other picture. 'And that's Jemma. She was a friend. A very dear friend.'

'Sara's sister.'

'Yes. You know?'

Hannah hesitated. 'She told me that Jemma died in the fire you had here. I am sorry. That must have been awful for you.'

Esther felt winded. They had talked about it behind her back? She took a moment to get her composure back.

'Yes, yes it was. I… hadn't realised you… What else did she say?'

'Nothing. That was it.'

Esther stared at her a moment then picked up the photograph and studied it, stroking a finger along the frame. 'It's a terrible feeling. She was an actress too, you know. Very talented though not everyone saw it.' She paused. 'And now she's gone. Taken too soon, you see. Another one.' She glanced back at Hannah. 'We've all known each other a long time. Well, except Raff…' She offered a woebegone smile. 'Still, we keep her here with us.'

Hannah nodded respectfully, then offered her thanks for the tea and for the tour of the library.

'I'm so glad you like it. The others just don't get it I'm afraid. You must come again. And do make yourself at home while you're here. Use the pool, won't you? There's no point Pietro cleaning it if nobody uses it.'

'I've seen Raff use it.'

'Oh yes, Raff.' Esther smiled distantly. Yes, Raff would, she thought. Raff didn't have a problem with ghosts. 'Well, even so, Hannah, you should too – if you want to, of course.' She smiled graciously.

'Thank you.'

Esther watched Hannah walk away then went back into her library. She stood in front of the painting of *Christ Healing the Blind Man* and gazed on it once more. She had been right about Hannah. She had sensed the woman's loss, had recognised the air of confusion and guilt. Definitely a kindred spirit.

*

The painting of Saint Peter was securely back in its frame. It was finished. After breaking off to go and have tea with Esther, Hannah had worked late the night before to put the last touches to it. Now it was nine o'clock on the Saturday morning and she was back in the theatre. The wind that had plagued them all week seemed to have blown itself out, taking the rain with it. Sun streamed through the high windows. Hannah put the fire-damaged painting by Amanda Jay up on the easel and studied it again. This had to be done next: she needed to try to get the soot off it. It should have been cleaned long since, soon after the fire, to stop the acid doing any more damage.

Looking at it made her think of Esther and the strange 'audience' she'd been granted the previous day. Esther was a gracious hostess, beguiling even, but she was unnerving too. It was hard to get a handle on her. Was she genuine? All that stuff about being taken too soon, and the way she kept focusing on something in the distance, like she was communing with spirits. It gave Hannah the creeps. The woman was certainly haunted by something, but sympathise as she might, Hannah had no intention of being sucked into a conversation about loss and about her mother. That was her business and hers alone.

So what was making Esther so haunted? Maybe I should

have asked Raff more over that lunch in Bonnieux, Hannah thought, but, for all his jokes and bonhomie, Raff wasn't that approachable or forthcoming. He seemed very controlled in his bestowal of information, as if he'd planned it out in advance. And he might describe the household as a sad lot but they almost seemed to enjoy their sadness, their dysfunctionality. They wore it like a badge of honour.

Hannah sighed, still staring at the smudgy, burnt painting and its pitiful frame. The frame would have to be replaced. She'd noticed an art supplies and framing workshop in town; she'd call in one day and get a selection of moulding samples. In the meantime, there was a lot to do. She should forget about the fire and the strange behaviour of the people living here; she had enough on her mind.

She took the Jay down again and put it back against the stage, then automatically glanced towards the door, even though she'd locked it behind her. She put her hand deep into a big cotton shoulder bag she'd brought from the house and carefully pulled out the swaddling bundle that Father Diluca had given her. For two nights the icon had been hidden in Hannah's wardrobe like a guilty secret. She was already tired of it and wished she'd never accepted it. Had anyone seen her bring the bag over? Did it really matter? It was just a painting after all, and not a very good one at that. The secrecy was a burden and felt absurd.

She unwrapped *The Lily Madonna* and put it on the easel, stepping back to consider it again. Maybe it had just been the surprise of the priest's request. Maybe it would look better this morning.

It didn't. Whichever way you looked at it, it was a mess. She surveyed it from different angles then walked up to it and examined it from close range. There was no pretending otherwise, it was a horrible job and she couldn't justify the time it would take. Moreover, she didn't want to get involved. It was not her problem.

But it refused to be put away from her so easily. She kept hearing her mother's voice – odd, silly things, completely unrelated, but still they taunted her: *You lack any purpose in your life, Hannah. Yes, I know you've got your work but it's not healthy, shut up all the time with paintings, picking at tiny details. Where are your relationships? You need to get out and meet people. You might find someone then. I'd love grandchildren. Don't leave it too late, will you?*

And: *I'm sure you rebelled against the church just because of me. It was your protest. But you really should try it again. Why don't you come with me again? Please Hannah, next time you come to stay. To please me if nothing else.*

And: *I saw a programme on the telly last night about Leonardo Da Vinci. It was fascinating. I think perhaps I can see why you like working on those paintings so much. Some of his are amazing. I loved* The Virgin of the Rocks. *You must tell me if you work on anything like that.*

Hannah shook her head, not even sure what she was shaking her head about. So many arguments. The trouble was that Hannah followed too much after her father. She and her mother had come at life from two very different angles. A tear escaped and ran down her cheek. She'd loved her mother, despite their differences, but the thing with the church had just been a running sore. They had rubbed along as only families do, but they'd never got ahead of it. Then the dementia had come and any hope of a meeting of minds had been lost. Her mother's illness had cruelly and rapidly robbed her of the ability to engage in conversation; she constantly forgot what had just been said. Then she became confused about where she was and what day it was. In her last months she didn't even know who Hannah was.

Hannah walked briskly to the kitchen to make herself a mug of coffee. These memories didn't help. Being sentimental wasn't going to resolve what she should do with the icon.

She returned to the theatre and drank the coffee, gazing at it once more. To restore this painting, she would need reference material. She had only seen the undamaged image once and, though such icons had a traditional design, the portraits within them were always individual and unique. This was a cherished and familiar image and would need to be restored keeping faith with the original. That would be impossible. She couldn't do it. She would have to have photographs, good ones, to ensure a close copy of the Madonna's face and other details. Even then, she couldn't do it.

'I'm sorry, mum,' she muttered, and quickly took the icon down from the easel and wrapped it up again, stowing it away in her trunk where she could lock it up before leaving.

She put the beach scene down on the table and began to carefully prise the burnt frame away from the picture.

But by the end of the morning, she had admitted defeat. Hannah let herself out of the garden gate and walked to town. She carried a sealed letter in her bag addressed to *Père Diluca* and marked *personnel*. It had taken her some time to write:

Father Diluca,

In order to restore The Lily Madonna, *I would need your help with reference material: good, clear photographs of the painting to give me exact information about how it looked before.*

I would also need a written authorisation from you requesting me to do the work, on the clear understanding that I will do the best I can, given the considerable damage to the painting, and that I am not responsible if it does not

look as it did before. Please state this explicitly. I will not
start any work without it. I must point out that time is of the
essence.

Yours sincerely,

Hannah.

When she got to the square some of the stalls were already being dismantled and the market was winding down. Hannah walked to the presbytery and paused by the letterbox in the front door, glanced round to check no-one was watching her, then quickly pushed the letter through and walked away. If the priest provided neither photographs nor authorisation, she could hand the icon back and step away from the project with a clear conscience. In the unlikely event that he had some decent photographs, she thought she could just about get it done in the time. The evenings were getting lighter and she had nothing else planned for them; she could work and Timothy need never know.

*

On the Monday afternoon, Hannah found Sara in her office and asked if she could use the house phone to ring Timothy. She was tired and it was warm and she couldn't face another walk into town. In any case, this was going to be a boring call. If anyone wanted to, they were welcome to listen in.

'Of course,' said Sara. 'Is there a problem?'

'No, just a routine call to let him know how it's going.'

'Use the phone in the morning room, then. Esther has a separate line so she won't be affected.'

The morning room was quiet; indeed the abbey was quiet. Esther's presence had changed the atmosphere in some way though it was hard to put a finger on how exactly. The routine hadn't changed. And Hannah hadn't seen much of her hostess since having tea with her, just an occasional wave if she saw Hannah in the grounds. Esther wandered a lot, without any apparent purpose, drifting from one place to another with a faraway look in her eyes.

Hannah rang the number in Oxford. Daphne answered it promptly.

'Hannah,' she exclaimed with apparent pleasure. 'How are you?'

'Fine, thanks. And you?'

'Can't complain dear. If you want Timothy, I'm afraid he's not here. Back tomorrow.'

'Oh. Right. I was only checking in, letting him know my progress.'

'I could put you through to Nathan? He's filling in and it would save you ringing again. He's in Timothy's office now as it happens. Hang on, I'll tell him you're on.'

There was a click and silence before Hannah had had a chance to stop her. Great: Nathan. Just the person she wanted to speak to.

'Hello Hannah. Nathan here. How can I help you?'

Her eyes narrowed. Cocky devil. How can I help you? Really? He clearly enjoyed being in control, playing the boss. Especially with her. Don't give him an inch, she thought.

'Hello Nathan,' she replied coolly. 'Can you pass a message on to Timothy for me? I've finished the painting of Saint Peter and I've now started on the Amanda Jay.'

'OK, good.' Nathan spoke slowly as he scribbled notes. 'Anything else?'

'No.'

'No problems?'

'No.'

'Good. I'm sure Timothy will be relieved to hear it. He

was wondering when you'd get in touch.'

'I've been busy.'

A grunt then a brief pause. 'What's it like there?'

'It's quite beautiful. The weather's getting warm and there's a lovely pool. Oh and the food's amazing. But look, I must go. Thanks. Bye.'

She put the phone down before he had a chance to reply and smiled. Well he did ask. She returned to the theatre and went back to work.

On the Wednesday afternoon she received a reply from Father Diluca. She was cleaning soot and smoke off the beach scene, peering through the magnifier, listening to the *Rumours* album by Fleetwood Mac when she saw a movement out of the corner of her eye and jumped. She pushed the magnifier away, pulled the ear pieces out and straightened up.

'You nearly gave me a fright, Marielle.'

'I have another letter for you,' the child said in meticulous English. It sounded practised.

She thrust out her hand. In it was an envelope with the same looping script on it as before. Hannah opened it.

My dear Mademoiselle *Dechansay,*

Thank you for your letter. I rejoice that I am able to provide you with all that you require. However another visit to the presbytery would be unwise and might create suspicion. I shall bring the photographs to the shrine on the woodland path near the abbey. Please meet me there at 19.30H tomorrow night.

Yours most gratefully,

Father Diluca

'Oh good grief, what cloak and dagger,' muttered Hannah,

without thinking.

'Is he asking you to come to church again?' said Marielle, frowning and slipping back into French.

'Is that what he told you?'

The girl shook her head. 'He didn't tell me anything. He said I was a good girl and that he knew I wouldn't tell anyone about the note.'

Hannah smiled ruefully. That priest was good at manipulating people.

'It's something different, isn't it?' Marielle prompted, eyeing Hannah up shrewdly. 'I'm good at keeping secrets.'

'I can see that you are. But I've been sworn to secrecy too so I can't tell you what it's about. Not right now anyway.'

Marielle thought for a moment. '*D'accord*,' she said. Another moment's hesitation. 'Would you play pétanque with me some time?'

Hannah grinned. 'OK. But I've never played it so you'd have to show me how. Maybe at the weekend?'

Marielle smiled and nodded. It was the first time Hannah had seen her smile. Then she'd gone.

The following evening, Hannah was at the shrine early. A posy of fresh flowers had been laid there again but there was no-one about. She was standing, facing the memorial stone, trying to match the words to Esther's interpretation of it when Father Diluca came hurrying up to join her.

'*Mademoiselle,* I am sorry. Have you been waiting long? The phone rang as I was about to leave.' He glanced round nervously. 'I have what you asked for.'

He thrust an envelope at her, unsealed and chunky. She opened the flap and slipped out the pictures. Photographs, old and glossy. Hannah flicked through them. Three of them had been taken during the festival parade, snapped from below at different angles while the icon was being carried in procession through the streets. People were crowding in, trying to reach out and touch The Lily Madonna, pressing and pushing and obscuring the view. None of them were of any use.

The remaining three photographs were close ups, taken inside with a flash, leaving holes of white where the flash light had reflected off the varnished surface of the picture. They hadn't been taken from the same angles so the flash had registered in a different place on each one. It did at least mean that, between them, she might be able to fill in the gaps.

'They were the best I could find without giving away why I needed them,' said Father Diluca, anxiously. 'Do they help? Oh, and there's this.' He produced a crumpled sheet of folded notepaper out of his pocket and gave it to her.

> *I, Father Diluca, priest of the parish of Tourbelle la Vierge, give* Mademoiselle *Hannah Dechansay full authority to do all that is required to restore the icon known as* The Lily Madonna *which has been damaged. I understand that, when the work is finished, it is possible that the image might not look the same as it did before.*

It was signed and dated. It was what she needed.

Father Diluca reached out with both hands and gripped hers. 'We thank you for doing this. God will bless you. He recognises your good works, 'annah. He can see you are a good person.' He turned and was gone.

Hannah watched him scuttle away and sighed. She pushed the paper and the envelope into one of the pockets of her jacket and headed back to the abbey. For good or bad, she had to do this now.

Chapter 9

Hannah swam a final length and climbed out of the pool. It was only nine-thirty on the Saturday morning but it was warm and still. The weather over the final days of April had settled into a run of dry, sunny days, the temperature nudging up into the twenties. The mistral had blown itself out. She wandered into the pool house and showered the chlorine off then towelled herself down and stretched out on one of the loungers to dry. She had breakfasted early and come down on a whim, hoping it would still be quiet, a chance to relax.

After a few minutes, she lifted her head again and turned it, raising a hand to shield her eyes as she looked up at the pool house. She wondered what the Garden House had been like. After the fire it had been razed. Was that because it was so badly damaged or because Esther wanted to obliterate it and forget? Hannah let her gaze roam around the pool. In the sunshine it was a pleasing, peaceful place. The kidney-shaped pool had a wide edging of stone, and a large paved area near the pool house was inset with a mosaic design of frolicking dolphins. It was sheltered here, buffered from the wind by the terraced bank up to the house and, elsewhere, by small trees and shrubs. To her right was a sea of cotton lavender; to her left, beyond the pool, stretched a neatly tended lawn. She could imagine a casual barbecue being held here on a summer's day, a relaxed gathering. Then it had all ended in tragedy. But where were all the candles that had supposedly caused the fire? Was that believable?

She pushed herself up into a sitting position and stared at the pool house. Though the shower area and a couple of toilet cubicles occupied more than half of the building, there was a small kitchen area to the other side. She supposed that you could still have a party down here though the abbey didn't feel like a party place any more.

'Lovely day, *Mademoiselle*.'

She turned her head quickly to see Guillaume standing not far away.

'Yes, isn't it? The temptation to use the pool was too strong.'

'It's good. It isn't used much these days.'

'Do you never use it?'

'Sometimes. When I'm sure I won't be disturbing anyone else.'

She nodded. 'I felt like that too. That's why I came early.'

He smiled an acknowledgement of their shared deference to the residents' use of the pool. It broke the ice a little. She turned to sit facing him, shrugging a light wrap over her shoulders as she did so. She gestured to the nearby lounger.

'Do sit down for a few minutes. Please.'

He hesitated, then sat, forearms on his knees. Beneath the crisp cotton short-sleeved shirt – no jacket today, she noticed – he looked strong, his muscles well-defined, but her eyes lingered briefly on the scars on his hands.

'Is the work going well?' he enquired.

'Yes, thanks. The theatre is an ideal place to work. But I can't imagine what your job must be like. Aren't you always on duty?'

He shrugged the question away dismissively. 'Yes and no. I try to be available when I'm needed. It's a – how would you

108

say? – a tie. But I have a friend who fills in for me so I can have a holiday.' A brief grin and an expansive wave of the hand. 'But it's a good place to live and work, no?'

'Definitely. It's beautiful.' She paused. He seemed in the mood to chat. 'How long have you been here?'

'Seven years. Before this, I was in the police. I worked all hours then too, believe me, but the conditions here are much better.'

'I can imagine. Your English is very good.'

'Thank you. I learnt it at school and enjoyed it. I kept learning.' He hesitated. 'Have you travelled a lot with your work?'

'Quite a bit. I go where it takes me. There are paintings everywhere.'

'Indeed. I'm a little jealous. I'd like to travel. Perhaps when I retire.'

They were both silent. She toyed with asking him if he had someone to travel with – he seemed to live a lonely existence – but didn't. An orange tip butterfly fluttered over the pool and they both watched it dip and rise, then fly away.

Hannah looked back at him, trying to sound casual. 'Miss Langley was telling me about the fire down here at the Garden House. And about the tragic loss of her friend. I was just trying to imagine it. It must have been terrifying. Of course you were here; you must have seen it.'

Guillaume frowned. 'I'm surprised,' he said guardedly. 'Miss Langley doesn't usually talk about it. But, yes, indeed it was a terrible thing.'

'I'm working on a painting that was damaged in the fire. It's in an awful state. But I'm surprised it was down here at all. I presume the Garden House was something like this?' She pointed towards the pool house.

A hesitation. 'No, it was bigger than this, like a miniature house. The downstairs had doors that folded back. It had a sort of kitchen and a dining area plus a shower room. The first floor was a casual sitting room with a daybed and a balcony. It was intended as a party house, I suppose. A foolish thing.'

He sounded quite bitter as he described it then stopped suddenly, as if he thought he'd said too much.

'The painting was downstairs,' he added, as an after-thought. 'In the dining area.'

'I see.'

Guillaume got to his feet. 'I hope you have a good weekend, *Mademoiselle*.' He paused, looking down at her with an intense, penetrating gaze. 'You do understand, I hope: you must not talk to anyone, and I mean anyone, about the fire?'

She nodded. 'I had no int…'

'I also sincerely advise you not to think too much about it. It is not necessary in order to restore the picture, I think.'

As he walked away, back towards his cottage and the entrance, Marielle approached from round the back of the pool house. Her manner suggested she had been waiting for Guillaume to leave.

She came to stand in front of Hannah's lounger.

'Can we play pétanque now?'

Hannah smiled distantly. 'Sure. But I need to go and change. I'll meet you by the pit in twenty minutes.'

Marielle ran off and Hannah made her way back up to the house, flicking one last look down at the pool house as she went.

*

There was no-one in the surrounding gardens when Hannah let herself into the theatre that afternoon. She'd checked. Even so, she turned the key in the door behind her. She made herself a mug of tea then unlocked the trunk and got *The Lily Madonna* out. She put it up on the easel and stepped back, grabbed the mug of tea and regarded the painting balefully.

It was as yet untouched. The previous afternoon, after finishing her work for the day, she had done the same thing: placed it on the easel and just stared at it, the photographs Father Diluca had given her spread out on the table nearby.

She was trying to get a sense of this painting. It was old but was it in fact medieval? She had her doubts. Who had painted it? There was no way of knowing; icons were rarely signed and they had timeless designs, repeated over the centuries with only minor variations which might give away a particular hand. As a devotional piece, it was intended to be 'read' following set rules. The monk who had painted it would not have considered human pride in his work appropriate.

She picked the icon up and turned it over, wary of disturbing any more of the fragile paint. But there was nothing to be seen. The reverse had been painted in a plain dark ochre, cracking and flaking in places but giving no clues to the picture's origins or its age. She doubted there was a separate frame. The painting's raised gilt border was probably part of the same piece of wood as the picture, with the central section chiselled out to form a painting surface. As she had done the previous day, she shone the ultraviolet lamp over the image but could still only find one previous piece of retouching, an area over the bottom of the Virgin's robes, though it was possible the damage had obscured others.

Other thoughts intruded, less professional ones: why did people think it held any power? They wanted to believe it, presumably. Or had someone genuinely seen something amazing happen because they had the icon with them, something which had made them believe in it? Oh come on, she berated herself. You don't really believe that. But the train of thought persisted in spite of herself. Did being damaged affect its power? Could she in effect restore its power by restoring the image. No, that was complete nonsense. Even so the piece intimidated her a little and she wasn't used to that. It's just another painting, she told herself, and not even a very good one. Treat it like all the others.

But what would her mother have said? Hannah closed her eyes and tipped her head back, letting out a long, slow breath. Was she watching her even now? Did that happen? Maybe. A whole confusion of thoughts about belief and religion churned at the back of her mind but she wanted to think it could be true.

It was more than an hour later when she finally got out a swab and some weak cleaning solution. The picture had to be clean before she could do anything else with it. She dipped the swab in the solution and began a gentle circular motion on a tiny area of the smoke-yellowed surface.

*

Raff and Sara had both just started eating when Hannah arrived in the dining room that night. Raff glanced at his watch. It was eight-forty.

'Hannah,' he said tauntingly. 'You're late this evening. What *have* you been up to?'

She hesitated for the blink of an eye. 'This and that. I lost track of time.'

He watched her help herself to a couple of herb-roasted lamb chops, roast baby potatoes and green beans from the hot plate and sit down next to Sara who smiled a faint greeting at her while she ate.

Then Esther wandered in. She embraced them all with a benevolent smile, murmured 'hello everyone' and drifted along the side table, lifting the lids on the hot dishes but putting them back without taking anything. She went to the head of the table and stood facing them, prompting them all to stop eating

112

and look up.

'Well I don't know,' she said vaguely. She lifted a hand and ran a couple of fingers along her forehead. 'I think perhaps I'll tell Claudine that I'll eat in my room.' Her gaze drifted around the room as if she'd forgotten what it looked like. 'Yes, I think I will.'

'Esther?' said Hannah. 'I've finished the painting of Saint Peter. Would you like me to bring it over to the house?'

'The painting of Saint Peter? Oh yes.' A beautiful, grateful smile. 'Thank you, Hannah. Yes, that would be lovely.'

She wandered out again. There was silence.

'I think she's getting worse,' murmured Sara, looking towards the door.

'I told you that weeks ago,' said Raff. 'You didn't believe me.'

Sara started eating again. 'I didn't want to believe you.'

'You know, I saw her the other day in the garden,' said Raff. 'She stopped and put her head on one side as if she was listening to someone. But there was nobody there. It's getting really creepy.'

'Was that down at the bottom?'

'Of course.'

Sara glanced at Hannah as if only just remembering she was there. 'Don't mind us, Hannah. It's just that Esther does have these moments.' She met a quick look from Raff. 'Actors do rather live on their nerves, don't they?'

Raff snorted, cleared the last of the food on his plate and pushed it away. He got up and went to look at the offered dessert but returned to the table with nothing, looking restless. He sat again, watching the two women who were still eating.

'Don't just sit there watching us,' said Sara. 'Why don't you ring for some coffee?'

He pulled a face and looked away. Hannah finished, put

113

down her cutlery and took a drink of water.

'Why don't you both come over to the studio?' Raff looked from one to the other. 'I've got proper drinks. And you...' He fixed Hannah with a reproachful look. '...still haven't seen my paintings.'

'Aren't you going to work?' Sara wiped her mouth with the napkin. 'I thought this was supposed to be your creative time.'

'I probably will. Later.'

'It's tempting.' Hannah turned to Sara. 'What do you think? Shall we brave it?'

Raff eyed them up warily. He didn't like the sound of that 'we'; he didn't want Hannah siding with Sara.

'Why not?' Sara laid her cutlery down neatly on her plate. 'I could do with a drink.'

The sun had long since set but there was a clear sky and the moon was full, shedding a clear, silver light over the garden as they all traipsed over to Raff's studio. He went to a stone on the side of the building, eased it out and retrieved a key.

'Saves losing it,' he muttered to Hannah as he unlocked the door.

He flicked the light switch and ushered them in.

'Welcome to my studio.' He looked round with both pride and affection. 'This is where the magic happens. Don't scoff, Sara. Some people have got more soul than you've got.'

It was an oblong room, not as big as the theatre but the biggest space he'd ever had to work in. Ahead of them was his working area: a huge wooden studio easel and a cluttered table. Beyond that was a small raised platform with a chaise longue on it, and the far right hand corner of the studio held a large plan chest and a racking system for his canvases. Against the back wall stood a big old pine wardrobe and, to the left, was a clean-up area with a ceramic sink and a wooden draining

114

board. Closer to them a battered three-seater sofa nudged up against a cupboard on which stood a number of bottles. Raff walked up to it and stood, peering into the assortment of odd glasses there, trying to work out which, if any, were clean.

'Who's for what?' He spun round to look at them expectantly. 'I've got red wine and whisky, Ricard and something masquerading as beer – it's not cold though.'

'Red wine please,' said Hannah.

Sara hesitated. 'Yes, I'll have wine too.' She walked closer. 'I need a smoke. Got any cigarettes, Raff?'

'You should have brought your own.'

He opened a drawer at the top of the cupboard and pulled out a packet and a lighter, offering them to her. She took the lighter and put a cigarette in her mouth.

'Outside,' he said. 'You know the drill. No smoke on the paintings. Your wine'll be here when you get back.'

She sighed but went outside and he poured wine into three odd glasses, handed one to Hannah and took one for himself.

'I didn't know you smoked,' said Hannah.

'Just one, now and then, when the muse fails me. Come and look at what I can do when she doesn't.'

She followed him across to his easel where the first lines of an image had been loosely drawn with thin brown paint on a primed canvas, landscape format.

'Landscape?' she said. 'From the way you spoke I thought maybe you only did figures.'

'I like to mix it up. Anyway, you can't get the models. Or they expect too much money.'

'It's not an easy job. Staying still for ages, often in horrible positions.'

'So you have modelled for an artist before?'

'Not me. But my father's an artist. He paints figures sometimes, nudes occasionally.'

'Oh. I didn't realise. Would I know him?'

'I don't know. Eric Dechansay.'

Raff's mouth fell open. 'Of course, I should have connected the name. I mean I don't know him but I certainly know of him. He's based in Paris isn't he?'

'Yes.' She took a sip of wine and wandered towards the racking. 'Show me some of your work then.'

He was a little nonplussed. Eric Dechansay was very successful. Still, Hannah didn't paint. He pulled out a few paintings for her, propping them up against the wall beyond. As always, he looked at his own work with a mixture of pride and disgust. He talked it up but he was never really happy with it. His landscapes were figurative and carefully drafted. He wished he could work more loosely but they never seemed to come out right.

'And then there's my figure studies.' These were usually more successful but harder to sell. He pulled out another canvas and propped it up. 'This is David.'

She frowned. 'David, as in Esther's boyfriend?'

'More likely her ex. He sat for it under sufferance. He's not a patient man. Anyway, Esther commissioned it but now...'

'Esther spoke to me as if he was still very much in her life.'

'Well she would, wouldn't she? She dotes on the man for some godforsaken reason. But whether she'll want the picture...' He shrugged and drank some wine. In the portrait, David was a handsome, broad-shouldered man with an open face and a forthright gaze. 'I made sure he looked every inch a hero.' He snorted a laugh.

'Why? Isn't he?'

'Actors – they're never quite what they seem, are they?'

'And you don't think they'll get back together?'

116

'Not the way Esther's going. He couldn't cope, you see. He walked out. I mean, he's a bit arrogant too but still, you've seen her. She's lost a loop somewhere along the way. The fire was the final straw.'

Raff pushed the painting of David back into the rack and pulled out another. It was a nude. He watched Hannah look at it but he could tell she wasn't particularly interested. She sipped at her wine, then turned to look at him.

'When I asked about the fire, you mentioned candles,' she said. 'But I don't understand how they could have burnt down a whole building.' She was frowning. 'Were there a lot of them?'

Raff flicked her a glance then drained the last of his wine.

'Does it matter?'

'No. I'm just puzzled. I guess I'm also scared of saying the wrong thing to Esther. It would help if I knew what happened.'

Hannah's glass was still three quarters full so Raff walked to the cupboard and poured himself more wine. He drank another mouthful before coming back to join her.

'Since you're going to be here for a while, I guess you'll hear the gory details sooner or later.' He slid the nude back into the rack and pulled out another. 'It was June, sunny and warm. Like I said: we'd had a barbecue and drunk too much as usual.'

'Who's "we"?'

'Esther, David, Sara, Me... and Jemma. And there was a couple too: friends of Esther who used to live the other side of Tourbelle. They'd driven and weren't staying over so didn't drink much. He didn't anyway. He's American, she's French.' He took another mouthful of wine. 'Come to think of it, I haven't seen them in ages. Anyway, they left early. Sara's boyfriend, Pascal, had finished with her a couple of weeks before so she was really down. Perhaps we were all drinking

117

as moral support.' He laughed and drank again.

'So what happened?'

'Like I told you: Jemma and I had a row.' He paused. 'A stupid thing about going back to England for my mother's sixtieth. Jemma didn't want to go. She was all prickly and emotional. I guess it was that time of the month. Anyway, I left them to it and came back here to do some work, then I went to bed. A bit later on everyone else drifted away to bed too. That's what I was told. All except Jemma and Esther. Old friends putting the world to rights, I guess. Jemma was probably complaining about me. It had gone dark anyway and they'd lit a load of candles, even though there was electricity there. How dumb, huh? I mean, the state they were in… Then Esther wants to go to bed and Jemma says she'll stay a bit and finish the booze. She was already smashed. And Esther left her there. Can you believe it? Serves her right if she's racked with guilt. She should be.' He drank again. 'Jemma must have knocked a candle over or something. Comatose, probably, while the bloody building burnt around her.' He shrugged and flicked Hannah a glance. 'Course, I wasn't the only one who'd argued with her. David did too, I think. Don't know what about. And Sara was in a real nag after being dumped.'

As if on cue, Sara chose that moment to come back in. She glanced across at them, taking in the intimacy of their conversation, but said nothing and walked across to the cupboard, dumped the lighter on it and picked up her wine. She drank several swallows in one go then topped up the glass and came over to join them.

'You looked positively guilty then, Raff. Have you been telling stories again?' She didn't take her eyes off his face. 'I swear he could make his way writing fiction, Hannah. Probably a better living than he's making from painting anyway.' She finally dragged her eyes away and drank another mouthful of wine. 'What were you talking about?'

Raff didn't answer and put the nude away, poking among the canvases, looking for something pleasing, something successful to show Hannah.

'Raff was telling me about the barbecue and how the fire started,' said Hannah.

Sara drifted away towards his work table and Raff straightened up and watched her warily. Her fingers flicked agitatedly through the pages of one of his sketch books.

'Strange thing to talk about,' said Sara. She swallowed some more wine and looked back at Raff. 'Even stranger considering he left the barbecue and didn't return.' She paused. 'He said.'

'You said you left early too,' he responded aggressively. 'There's no need to sound so suspicious.'

Sara wandered to the easel and stared at the painting then glanced round the studio. Big eyes, staring, probing.

'I prefer not to talk about it,' said Sara. She turned her restive eyes on Hannah. 'And you shouldn't be asking about it either.'

'I'm restoring the painting that was damaged. It got me wondering how it happened exactly.'

Sara took a drink of wine and looked away. 'Who knows what happened? We weren't there. We know Esther feels guilty.' She rammed her hair back behind her ears with her free hand. 'Of course, their relationship wasn't always sweetness and light. Esther sometimes complained that Jemma only hung around her because she was successful and could do things for her. And it was true. Jemma did do that.' Sara produced an ironic laugh. 'But I guess that's what we all do, isn't it, Raff?' She finished the last of her wine and put the glass down on his table. 'By the way, David's coming home.'

'David?' said Raff. 'When? How do you know?'

119

'He's got a flight Wednesday. He rang and couldn't get through on Esther's phone for some reason.'

'Well, well.' Raff looked at Hannah. 'You see? You never know in this house.'

'I see you've been telling our visitor the dirty laundry on David and Esther as well,' said Sara. 'Does it never occur to you, Raff, that you should follow the rules of the house and keep your mouth shut?' She walked to the door, said, 'Night,' over her shoulder and left.

'God, she's becoming a frustrated old spinster,' said Raff bitterly. 'Always playing mother and moralising.'

'I'd better be going too.' Hannah took a long draught of wine and put her glass down; it was still half full. 'Thanks for the drink and the tour.'

'Oh, OK.' Raff fixed her with a reproachful look then turned abruptly away. 'See you then.'

Chapter 10

'Look, look at this David.' Esther had brought the painting of Saint Peter through to the drawing room and propped it up on the back of the chest of drawers. 'I told you I'd got a restorer in to sort out those paintings I bought. Do you remember this one? She's just finished it. Isn't it wonderful?'

'Yes, very good.' David spoke absently then looked more closely. 'It is actually. What a transformation.'

'Isn't it? We need to decide where to put it. Where do you think?'

He looked at her warily. 'But I thought you weren't doing this any more.'

'Doing what?'

'Oh come on, Esther. Don't play games. We talked about it on the phone. All the obsession with religion and spirits and absolution. I wouldn't have come back if I'd thought nothing had changed. You said you were better.'

'I wasn't ill,' she retaliated coldly.

'No.' He sighed, walked away a few restless steps and turned. 'No, you weren't ill. If you had been ill, we could perhaps have done something about it. But I always felt that you chose to punish yourself. I never could understand it and I don't understand it now. You're still doing it.' He waved a hand towards the painting of Saint Peter.

'It's just a painting, David. A painting I like. I don't see

121

what's wrong with that.'

'And how many others are there, all vehicles for your meditation, no doubt?'

'You've come here with preconceptions. You're not giving me a chance. I've got a couple of other pictures, yes. I've also asked the restorer to work on the painting of the beach, the one that got damaged in the fire.' She paused, glaring at him indignantly. 'You see, I *have* moved on. I couldn't even look at that picture before. Now I'm ready to put it back on the wall when she's finished with it. It has good memories for us both, doesn't it? It was a special painting.'

David looked at her a moment then prowled round the room, saying nothing.

'I am better. I'm... calmer.' She released a slow breath. 'It takes time to get over something that traumatic. I don't think you're being fair to me.'

David stopped walking and faced her, a puzzled frown creasing his brow.

'Why have you got a picture restorer on site? Wouldn't it have been better to send the pictures to them?'

'It was a service they offered. We've got space. Since there were several, it seemed like a good idea. It's more personal.'

'And more expensive, I imagine. Still, it's your money.' He paused. 'So long as she's not in the way.'

'She's not. She's a really nice woman in fact. I must introduce you. Her name's Hannah... Hannah...' She tutted. 'I can't remember what.'

'Odd name.'

'What? Oh.' She smiled. 'Very funny.'

He grinned back. 'That's better. You are so lovely when you just let yourself relax.'

She came across and looped her arms around his waist.

'But it wasn't all me, was it?' she pouted. 'You struggled to get over it too. You just coped in a different way: all silent and moody. Typical man.'

He put his arms round her too, leaned forward and kissed her softly on the lips.

'Possibly.'

'I think we should go out for dinner tonight. I don't want to share you with anyone else. Not tonight.'

He looked into her face, examining it thoughtfully.

'You do look much happier.'

'I told you: I am.'

'And how is everything here?'

'It's fine.'

He looked at her sidelong. 'But? I definitely heard a "but" in there.'

'It's fine, really. Sara and Raff are at each other's throats all the time – you know what they're like, but that's normal. It's a bit draining but, you know… Anyway I don't want to think about them tonight. You've only just got here.'

'I know.' He pulled away and threw his tall frame down on one of the sofas. 'Jeez, planes, rental cars, time zones. I'm exhausted.' He patted the seat next to him. 'Come and sit with me.'

She did, leaning into his side while he put his arm round her shoulders. It felt good, having him there. They sat in silence for several minutes. She allowed herself to relax properly, nestling in, feeling that security.

'I don't know why you let Raff stay on,' said David.

She stiffened. 'Please don't start that again.'

He sighed. 'It makes it difficult for us though, Es. You know how I feel about him.'

'And you know why I can't ask him to leave. I feel responsible, David.'

'For God's sake, Esther. Not again. It wasn't your fault.'

She reached up and put a finger to his lips.

'Please don't let's talk about it tonight. Can't we just enjoy being together again?'

'OK, OK.'

He rested his head back and closed his eyes.

'Where do you want to eat?' murmured Esther. 'What about Dominique's? She'll let us use that top room and give us some privacy. I'd better call her and make a reservation. Even midweek it'll be busy now, I guess.'

There was no answer. She glanced up. David's mouth had dropped open slightly and his breathing had slowed. He'd fallen asleep.

Esther stayed where she was. She wouldn't wake him. Anyway, it was good just being there with him. At that moment, she thought it would all sort out. There were things he didn't know, that he didn't need to know. They were a perfect fit; that was all that mattered.

*

By mid-afternoon on the Friday, Hannah had cleaned the majority of the soot off the beach painting. It had been a tedious job and, having got the worst off, she needed a change of focus for a while. She picked up the second of the Rembrandt school paintings: *Christ Receiving the Holy Spirit* and put it up on the easel. The picture surface was dirty – straightforward grime and old varnish – and there was some flaking paint but her main concern was a fraying hole in the canvas which she'd found on her assessment. It was only the size of a small coin but the edges of it were frayed and it could rapidly grow. She examined it at length through the magnifier and fingered it gently then straightened up and regarded the painting thoughtfully.

Having told Timothy in her assessment that it should be repairable, she wasn't so sure now. The whole canvas looked too fragile. She took the picture off the easel and laid it flat on the table, face down, to carefully unscrew it from the frame. The screws were rusty and it took her a while to free them. Now with the stretched canvas flat on the table she could examine the back of it more safely. Very small holes could sometimes be mended with size and careful abutment of the edging fibres; bigger holes could often be patched. But she doubted that this canvas would tolerate a patch: it was too brittle and weak and the patch might create tension on the fabric and cause more damage. And the canvas was starting to pull away in a couple of places where it folded over the stretcher. The whole picture might benefit from being relined which meant sending it back to the workshops in Oxford.

She replaced the painting back on the easel and stared at it again, wondering what Timothy's response would be. It was an expensive option and some conservators disliked relining; they thought that sticking another canvas to the back of the painting damaged the texture of the surface. But with modern equipment, glues and handling methods that wasn't usually a problem. Timothy had a low pressure vacuum table in the workshop.

Hannah made herself a mug of tea while she decided what to do. She was reluctant to try cleaning it if the canvas was that fragile. Did she need to speak to Esther about it before sending it off? She had seen Esther earlier in the week when she'd taken the painting of Saint Peter across. The actress had been in her lounge and had been effusive when she saw it.

'He's wonderful, absolutely wonderful, Hannah. You are *so* clever.' She'd reached out to take it and stared at it, rapt. 'He just… I mean he glows now, doesn't he, the way I'm sure the artist intended.'

'I'm glad you're happy with it.'

Esther looked up. 'Oh, more than happy.' She put the painting down, propping it up on top of a cabinet against the rear wall of the room. 'Take a seat. What about a drink? I've got some of Claudine's home-made lemonade here. It's delicious.'

'No, I'm fine, thank you. I won't stay. I've got something I need to get back to in the theatre.'

'Working again? Well, I won't keep you then.' Esther hesitated. 'Perhaps I should say...' She reached out a hand to Hannah's arm. 'I'd like to tell you because we've become so close, haven't we? My dear David is coming back this week. Silly of me I know but I'm so excited. It's been a while, you see, since he was able to be here.'

'That's wonderful. Will he be able to stay a while?'

'Yes, I think so.' Esther smiled warmly, then became coy. 'You really must find someone too. It's the most marvellous thing.'

'Well... I...'

'You must pray Hannah. Do you do that? Whenever I need to clear something in my head or make a decision or need something, I pray... or meditate on something soothing. I prayed he would return quickly and see?' Esther draped herself back down onto the sofa. 'I can see Peter perfectly now so that's what I shall do: sit and meditate on this wonderful painting you've restored for me. Thank you.'

Thinking now about that conversation, Hannah had answered her own question. No, speaking to Esther about her decision wouldn't be a good move. The woman was acting strangely; she wouldn't care what Hannah did provided her precious paintings were preserved and improved. The painting would go back to be relined. There was no issue with the timescale. It was only the fourth of May; it could be relined

126

and returned easily for Hannah to finish the necessary work on it before she left. Decision made.

An hour later, Hannah locked up the theatre and walked into town to ring the workshop. She didn't like using the house phone and it was a fine day; she welcomed the activity. When Daphne answered, Hannah asked her to arrange a carrier to collect the painting and take it back to Oxford for relining.

'Is Timothy there?' she asked.

'I'm afraid not. He's out doing an assessment. He won't be back at the office today. I could get Nathan if you like?'

'No, no, it's fine. I'll put a note in with the painting to explain. Tell the couriers that I'll leave the picture with the security guy by the gates. Thanks Daphne.'

Back in the theatre, Hannah locked the door behind her, got *The Lily Madonna* out of the trunk, and put it up on the easel. The smoke deposits had largely gone but she could do little more until she'd stabilised the paint. She picked up a pair of tiny tweezers and began cautiously feeling at the loose fragments of paint, picking off those that clearly couldn't be saved.

*

'Hannah, this is my David. David, this is the lady I was telling you about who's doing such wonderful things with my paintings.'

David held out a hand.

'A pleasure to meet you,' he said with a warm smile.

Hannah smiled back. 'Likewise.'

Raff watched them make small talk. It was the Saturday night and Esther had arranged for them all to have dinner together. Now they were having preprandial cocktails in the drawing room. David fancied himself as a connoisseur of cocktails and always did the honours when he was here.

Hallelujah that David had returned, thought Raff, otherwise they'd still be drinking water and fruit juice. Not that Raff had much time for David. Even so…

Raff wandered off, a Singapore Sling in hand, to look at a painting by Mary Cassatt hanging on the wall to the side, a portrait of an actress sitting in front of a mirror in her dressing room. He'd looked at it countless times before. It was good. It was also something to do. He had a feeling it was going to be a tedious evening. Sara came to stand beside him.

'Wonderful brushwork,' he remarked, glancing sidelong at her.

'Mm.'

She hadn't even looked. Art passed her by. She sipped at her cocktail.

'What's that?' He nodded towards her glass.

'A Gimlet.'

'Hm. Might have one of those next.' He glanced across the room and back at Sara. 'We're just kind of making up the numbers tonight, aren't we?' he murmured to his drink. 'The sideshow for the main event.'

'What do you mean?'

'Esther's showing off her latest toy to David. And she's showing off David to Hannah too, her prize, her doting man.'

'You really are unbearably cynical.'

'Just realistic, Sara. We both know that Esther likes to cultivate people. Like they're her favourite plants, put in a hothouse and coaxed to bloom perpetually.' He nodded to himself with a satisfied smile. 'That was good, don't you think? I haven't thought of that one before. Sums her up though. When they stop blooming for her, she puts them outside in the cold and lets them wither.'

Sara turned her head to fix him with a stony stare.

'But it was David who left *her* last time,' she said. 'He'd

128

had it; he just walked out.'

'I know.' Raff's smile faded. He took a sip of his cocktail. 'I really didn't think he would come back.'

'Neither did I.' Sara looked round at the other three who had sat down across two of the sofas, still talking, though Esther was monopolising the conversation.

Raff wandered across and sat on the third sofa, finished his drink and ostentatiously leaned forward to put the empty glass down on the coffee table. Sara joined him a couple of minutes later though, annoyingly, her glass was still half full.

'So you could be asked to go almost anywhere,' David was saying to Hannah, 'and be given pretty much any kind of painting to restore?'

'In theory,' she replied. 'But we do a lot of work back in the workshops too.'

'It must be fascinating. I'd be curious to see a bit of what you do, if you don't mind showing me sometime while you're here.'

'Of course. I'm sure we could arrange something.'

'Great.'

'How long will you be here?' said Hannah. 'I mean, have you got another film project lined up?'

'Not immediately.'

Esther reached across and squeezed David's hand, smiling up into his face proprietorially.

'We're going to take some quality time together for a few weeks, aren't we darling?' she said. 'Sometimes, with film schedules, we hardly get to see each other. It gets crazy.'

David smiled briefly at Esther then transferred his attention back to Hannah. 'I've got a couple of film scripts to read, see whether they appeal or not. It'll be good to spend some time here to do it.'

'You have a choice of scripts?' remarked Raff. 'Well. And

when do we get to see your last film? Some sort of action caper was it?'

David's eyes narrowed. 'It was a thriller. And it's due out in October, as if you were really interested.'

Raff didn't pursue it. It was tempting to have a go at David – he rose to the bait so easily – but it didn't do to push Esther too far. She hated David being teased. No sense of humour, that woman.

'That's enough talk about work.' Esther got to her feet. 'It's time we went through for dinner. I don't want to keep Claudine waiting.'

David stood up and Esther put her arm through his as they went through to the dining room, Sara following close behind.

Raff made a point of moving alongside Hannah.

'I'm sure Claudine would have let us know by now if she was waiting,' he remarked. 'Haven't you noticed that she has a way of looming into the doorway which is quite unnerving?' He took Hannah's hand and put it through his arm. 'It's going to be a long evening but you seem to be having a good time anyway. David's quite the hunk, I'm told.'

Hannah stopped short and turned to look at him, gaze unflinching. They were still well short of the doorway.

'If you have some personal feud going on Raff, leave me out of it, OK? That's not a game I intend to play.'

She eased out of his arm and walked off ahead of him. Raff, eyebrows raised in amusement, followed. She had spunk that girl.

He was right: the dinner was tedious. But the food was good and at least they had wine, both red and white and Raff drank as much of both as he dared. He spent most of the meal surreptitiously watching what he had described as the main event. David was like a juggler, keeping Esther, Hannah and Sara entertained. He was doing a good job; Esther looked

130

happier than she had for some time and Hannah smiled and laughed and told a couple of entertaining stories. Even Sara lost her perpetually anxious look now and then. He was a charming man, David Flaxman, Raff had to reluctantly admit.

Outside the door of his studio later that night, Raff, mellowed with alcohol and good food and not feeling remotely ready to work, stood to enjoy a cigarette. It was dark with only a glimpse of the waning moon appearing intermittently between the clouds. There were odd sounds from the gardens, birds settling perhaps or other creatures about which he knew nothing.

The evening edged back into his mind. He wondered idly where they were all going and how long they'd be able to keep this up, how long he'd be able to keep it up. He hadn't reckoned on David coming back though he still wasn't convinced the man would stay.

But it was Hannah who lingered in his thoughts. Hannah, the wild card. She was only passing through of course, a few weeks or months at most. But she could cause a lot of trouble in that time. Raff had watched the way David interacted with her; he'd seen the way Hannah responded. He'd also seen Esther watching the two of them. Hannah might have no designs on David – she struck him as irritatingly honest – but Raff knew how jealous Esther could get; he'd seen it before. It wouldn't take much to set her off again.

Chapter 11

The painting of *Christ Receiving the Holy Spirit* was collected on the Monday afternoon. Hannah assumed Daphne had told Timothy about it but she heard nothing from him. He wouldn't want to ring the house to speak to her though, unless there was a significant problem. And why should there be? She carried on working on the beach scene. She had finished cleaning it and was now picking over the bubbled paint, assessing which bits might be salvageable and which would have to be removed.

She was still working through this process on the Thursday afternoon, tweezing occasional fragments off, when a deep voice spoke behind her.

'Hannah?'

She jumped and turned.

'David.' She pulled the ear pieces out. 'I didn't hear you come in. I always listen to music while I'm working.'

He grinned sheepishly. 'Sorry. I did knock but there was no answer so I tried the door. I'd hoped to catch you to ask about coming over but I've hardly seen you.'

'No, well, I've been kind of busy.'

'And I've been thoroughly lazy, I'm afraid: lying in bed till all hours, lounging around the pool and swimming. Very decadent.'

'It is your home. And you're on holiday. I'm not...' She

grinned. '…as my boss is keen to point out.'

'Ah. One of those is he… or she?'

'He.'

David glanced round her work station. 'This all looks very scary to me. I have no idea what you do with all these things.'

'I'll show you.' Hannah glanced at her watch. 'I'm due for a drink. Would you like tea… or coffee?'

'Coffee please. Black. No sugar. Gotta look after the waistline.' He patted his already flat abdomen.

'Have a look around.' She raised a warning finger and wiggled it side to side with a mock frown. 'But don't touch anything.'

'Wouldn't dare.'

In the kitchen, she boiled the kettle, spooned coffee into one mug and dumped a teabag in another. She wasn't sure what she had expected Esther's boyfriend to be like but David wasn't it. He was approachable and easy to be with. Maybe she'd expected someone more full of himself, more wrapped up in the Hollywood bubble and his own publicity. He certainly fitted the image physically: well-toned body, pristine white teeth and a winning smile. Deep set eyes gave him an enigmatic, soul-searching air. His speech was sprinkled with Americanisms but his accent leaned more towards Britain than America.

She returned to the theatre with the coffee. David was staring at the painting on the easel.

He turned, offering her his dazzling smile. 'Great, thanks.' He took the offered mug. 'You're sure I'm not disturbing you? I'd hate for you to get into trouble with your boss.'

'I won't tell him if you don't.'

He mimed zipping his lips together. 'My lips are sealed.'

Hannah put her mug down on the table and began a quick summary of her equipment and what it all did. David listened attentively, occasionally asking a question. Then she showed him what she had done to the Jay and explained why and what she still had to do.

'My God, Hannah, you must have a hell of a lot of patience.'

She shrugged. 'Every job needs patience, doesn't it? I hear actors have to spend hours waiting around on set. I'd hate that. It must get pretty boring.'

'I guess I see what you mean.' He looked back at the painting. 'I'm glad you can do something with this. I thought it was beyond help to be honest. It was the first thing Esther and I bought together, in a little gallery in Bloomsbury. It already looks a hundred times better.'

'Well, there's a way to go yet and it's going to need a new frame.' She hesitated. 'It was a terrible thing, the fire, wasn't it? I heard about Esther's friend. What a tragedy.'

'Yes, it was.' He pulled his gaze from the painting and turned back to Hannah. 'Did Esther tell you?'

'Yes, a little.'

'Good. I'm glad she can talk about it now. She... Well let's say she struggled some after the fire. We all did.' He nodded towards the picture. 'It'll be good to get this back up. Like a fresh start.'

'I'll do my best.'

'I'm sure you will. Anyway, I've taken up enough of your precious time. I'd better let you get on.' He placed a hand on Hannah's shoulder. 'Thank you so much, Hannah. That was really interesting. You're a clever lady, no question.'

He walked to the door, said 'See you around', and left.

Hannah took a little while to get back to work again, restless, her mind in the wrong place. David had unsettled her. He was attractive and charming. He made her feel interesting and unusually good about herself but she rather suspected he did that with every woman he met and she wasn't going to go there. In any case, he was just a little too smooth for her tastes; men like him couldn't be trusted in her experience. Either way, he was attached and that was an end of it. Dangerous territory.

*

As Nathan returned to the studios after visiting the post office, the driver from their regular art carrier was just leaving. In fact, the man held the door open for him. Intrigued, instead of going back up to the workshop, Nathan wandered into reception and examined the wooden crate the man had just delivered. He read the label, frowned, and glanced up at Daphne.

'This has come from Provence. From Hannah. You must have signed for it. Do you know anything about it?'

'Hm?' She looked up and took a moment to focus on him. Her mother had been ill again and had been in hospital since the Sunday night, having tests for shortness of breath and palpitations. 'Sorry, Nathan. Oh yes. Yes, I do. I forgot to tell Timothy about it.'

'Forgot to tell me what? What's that?'

Timothy had just emerged from his office and he approached the crate and read the label too.

'It's from Hannah,' said Daphne superfluously. 'She rang on Friday afternoon and asked to speak to you. It's a painting that needs relining. I forgot to tell you, Timothy. Sorry.'

'You should have put her through to me,' said Nathan.

'I offered.' Daphne looked at him indignantly. 'She refused. Said she'd put a note in explaining about it.'

'She might have tried ringing again,' grunted Timothy, 'tried actually talking the matter through with me before sending it over. She's a bit too self-reliant for comfort and she's only just started with us, for Christ's sake.' He drummed a finger on the side of the crate. 'Anyway, take it upstairs,

Nathan, and see what's what. I'll pop up in a few minutes and have a look.'

He handed Daphne a letter to post and retreated into his office again.

Nathan went over to lean on the reception desk.

'What did Hannah say exactly?'

'I can't remember now, can I? Nothing much.'

Nathan nodded slowly. 'Well, it's not going down well with sir,' he muttered. 'He likes to be in control.'

'He's in a mood today,' said Daphne wearily. 'Anyway, she's several hundred miles away. He's got to trust her.'

'She's got to prove she can be trusted first.'

'Give her a chance.'

'Sure. But it's not up to me, is it?' He sniffed and straightened up. 'Right, I'll go and have a look at this painting and hope, for Hannah's sake, that it does indeed need relining.'

*

Another week had slipped by and here it was, the end of a Friday afternoon again. Hannah had just finished removing all the unusable burnt paint from the beach scene so this was a good place to stop. She pushed the magnifier away and rolled her shoulders, stretching her neck back. She was stiff and she ached; she fantasised about a long, hot soak in a bath but she had no bath so she'd have to make do with a shower. That would be good too. She sighed wearily. Not until she'd done some more work on the icon.

She took the swaddled painting out of the trunk and put it down on the table then wandered off to visit the cloakroom and make herself another drink. When she returned carrying a mug of tea, Marielle was standing there. Hannah realised her mistake immediately and her heart sank: she had forgotten to lock the door.

She came closer. The icon was loosely wrapped still but not in quite the same way and one glance at Marielle's face told her that the girl had peaked inside. She looked both amazed and scandalised.

'You've got *The Lily Madonna*,' she whispered in French.

'Yes.'

Her eyes grew bigger. 'It's broken.'

'Yes. That's why I've got it here. To make it right again.'

Hannah put down the mug and walked over to lock the door, cursing herself for forgetting. Coming back to stand beside Marielle, she hesitated.

'You know, Marielle,' she said gently, 'you shouldn't look inside things that belong to other people, not without asking first. Things are wrapped up for a reason.'

The girl frowned and her head dropped.

'I know,' she said in a small voice. 'I'm sorry.'

Hannah put her hand flat on top of the cloth-wrapped painting.

'You see, this is a secret. It's Father Diluca's secret. I'm going to explain it to you but you have to promise me that you will keep this secret because it's not mine. And it's very important.'

She nodded.

'Promise?'

'*Oui, je promets. Naturellement.*'

Hannah peeled back the cloth to reveal the icon. She heard Marielle's sharp intake of breath when she saw it again.

'*The Lily Madonna* fell and, as you can see, it's badly damaged. Father Diluca asked me to repair it but he doesn't want anyone else to know because they'll be upset. Very upset.'

Marielle's eyes roamed over the icon. Hannah had removed a lot of the loose, flaking pieces of paint but the surface was still far from stable.

'She looks kind of sad at the moment, doesn't she?' said Hannah.

Marielle looked back into Hannah's face. 'Can you put Her back together again?'

Humpty Dumpty flitted into Hannah's mind.

'I hope so.'

Marielle's hand came up suddenly and grabbed Hannah's. 'She will help you,' she said earnestly. 'If you pray and focus on her, *The Lily Madonna* Herself will help you.'

Hannah managed a smile and squeezed Marielle's hand.

'I'm sure she will. Now, I must get on and this needs a lot of concentration so I'm going to have to be alone to do it. OK?'

'*D'accord.*'

'And remember: it's a secret.'

'*Bien sûr*. I'm good at secrets.'

Apparently reassured, Marielle skipped away to the door and let herself out. What an odd little girl, thought Hannah, locking the door after her. She sincerely hoped the child would keep to her word.

She placed the icon on the easel, took stock of what she'd done so far, then began to remove another section of loose paint. If she could just get the whole thing stable, she could start to infill paint and maybe get it something like it was before.

She worked on the background gilding around the Virgin, and on her halo too which had suffered a severe crack in the fall. The traditional red underpainting, which was used to add depth and vibrancy to the gilding, hung by an edge and the bole – the thin clay cushioning layer for the gold – was cracked and loose. It would all have to be removed.

She carefully picked off the redundant paint, then tested the bole again, wondering if it could be saved. But each

138

cracked fragment moved and in the end she decided that it would be better to remove a chunk of it and replace it rather than risk leaving it unstable. With the aid of the magnifying glass, she picked at each piece laboriously with the tweezers, dismayed at how much of it eventually ended up coming away. The job was getting bigger by the minute.

Taking the last loose piece out down to the gesso below, she put down the tweezers and pushed the magnifier away, rubbing her dusty hands round the sockets of her eyes, leaning her head back and stretching her shoulders again.

'Oh Francesca, Francesca, why did you have to drop this painting?' she complained to the empty room.

At least this part of the picture now had a stable surface; the rest of it could wait. Her stomach was rumbling. It was time to pack up and leave for the night. Over the weekend, with fresher eyes, she might try and finish the preparation.

But as she lifted the icon off the stand to wrap it and return it to the trunk, something caught her eye. Was that really a fleck of colour in the gesso? She put it back on the easel and looked more closely. It didn't make sense. Gesso was made from plaster of Paris or lime and covered the whole of the panel to provide a smooth, inabsorbent surface for the paint. It was nearly always white. Indeed the sections she'd revealed so far were all white. But a tiny fleck of the gesso had come off with the bole revealing what looked like the flash of gold beneath. Hannah shook the idea away with a rueful smile. It had been a long day and her eyes were tired. It was so minute as to be almost a trick of the light.

She swung the lens in again and peered through it. She moved closer to the lens, frowning, then moved the lens over to the area near the frame where there had been so much damage. There had been something strange there too, she remembered now, but she'd brushed it off, thinking she'd imagined it. Now she studied it afresh, then moved the lens back to the middle. And then back to the area by the frame. And back to the middle.

She sat back in her chair, mouth open, and pushed her hair back from her face with her dusty hand. There was definitely both gold and colour showing through under the gesso. At some point this icon had been completely repainted.

Chapter 12

David had gone off for the day to play golf. Again. His third time in the last five days. Esther came to a halt on the main path round the eastern side of the house, uncertain what to do next. She wondered why he found hitting a tiny ball into a hole so appealing. And if he wasn't doing that, he was going for a workout in the gym behind the garage. It had been getting worse. And they kept falling out, over silly things. He had been home two and a half weeks now and their reunion wasn't proving as smooth as she had expected.

It was Saturday morning and sunshine bathed the grounds in dazzling light. The days were stretching out and the temperature was inexorably rising. They would have to start closing the shutters through the day soon to keep the house cool. She must remember to speak to Claudine about it. The thought was a welcome distraction from the turmoil in her head.

David had woken early and brought her tea in bed. He tended to wake before her, had always seemed to manage on less sleep than she did and had too much energy, wanting to be up and doing things. The tea had been a nice thought though, except that he hadn't got back into bed but had sat on her side of it while they drank it.

'You know that little avant-garde theatre in Avignon?' he said. 'They're putting an English language play on at the moment. In fact tonight's the last night. I can't remember what it's called but I thought it'd be good to go. I rang up and reserved a couple of tickets for us.'

'When did you do that?'

'Yesterday evening.'

'Really David, why didn't you ask me first? I'm not sure I want to go.'

'That's why I did it. You always say no if I ask you first.'

'So you're trying to bully me into it?'

'No, I'm...' He gritted his teeth. 'Why don't you want to go? We haven't been to the theatre together for ages.'

'Darling, a theatre's a very public place.' She turned to put her cup back on the tray. 'It's tedious when people recognise you all the time. You can't relax.'

'So we go incognito. We've done it before and it's worked. It'd be fun. And we don't have enough fun these days.'

She ran a hand through her hair, pushing it back into place, making it bob prettily. 'I suppose we could. What's the play about?'

'It's about a woman accused of witchcraft. Modern day but in a small rural community. Something to do with the music she writes and performs. Lots of chanting.'

'It sounds weird.'

'It's supposed to be very good. Thought provoking.'

'Darling, I really don't think it's me.' She smiled her sweetest smile then pouted, seductively, she hoped. 'I don't need thought-provoking. I believe I think quite enough as it is. Anyway, I like spending time here with you.'

David sighed and walked to the window. 'You spend too much time here, Esther. It's not healthy.'

'Nonsense. It's a wonderful place to unwind and regroup. You're too restless,' she added crossly. 'Why do you have to be doing something all the time? Why can't you just be?'

'Because doing something is what life is all about. I don't want it to pass me by. I don't want to find myself old one day and full of regrets over all the things I never did. I guess you'll be telling me I should meditate, examine my soul, maybe repent my sins. Well, I'm telling you: I know I've made mistakes but that's part of being human. So have you, so get over it, Esther.'

'Honestly, David, you...'

'What the hell do you spend all this time meditating about? You're so busy meditating and praying, you're not living any more. You know one of these days you won't be able to act either because you'll have forgotten how to live.'

He'd left her then. He'd bathed, dressed and gone off in a temper to hit a stupid ball around the stupid golf course.

Now, with the sun high overhead, Esther was wandering the grounds, restless. She knew she'd handled the situation badly and, though she'd tried to relax after he'd gone, there had been no chance of any more sleep. She couldn't read either, the words not sinking in, so she'd given in and got up. She'd suddenly had the idea to find Hannah, half expecting her to be in the house somewhere. Esther needed to talk to someone and Hannah was the first person she thought of. Hannah would listen and understand.

But Hannah wasn't in the house. Claudine said she'd had breakfast some time ago, said she had no idea where she was. On a sudden impulse, Esther turned and took the path to the theatre but the door was locked which only irritated her more. She knocked but there was no response. She retraced her steps and wandered on, then saw Marielle hanging around her grandfather who was spreading mulch over one of the flower beds.

'Have you seen Hannah?' she asked.

143

'No Miss Langley,' said Pietro.

Marielle pointed towards the trees and the gate to the woodland walk that was out of sight. 'She has gone out,' she said in careful English.

'Thank you, Marielle.'

Esther drifted back inside disconsolately.

*

Over the preceding week, Hannah had examined the icon repeatedly, alternately convinced there was another painting beneath the gesso then equally sure that she was mistaken, that they were just flecks of colour which meant nothing. She was fascinated at the alternatives that presented themselves yet appalled at the possible repercussions if she was right.

So now she was in the little museum in town, walking round its exhibits, hoping they might offer her more information on *The Lily Madonna*. The museum was only open until lunch time on the Saturday. There were several people already there, all tourists to judge from the languages being spoken. There were boards explaining the history of the town from its foundation in the twelfth century to the present day and a similar display about the abbey, all neatly illustrated with a floor plan of what the original building would have been like including a three-dimensional drawing. They told the same story that Esther had related about the ransacking after the revolution and the fate of the last monk. How much evidence there was to substantiate the story was unclear.

And there was a special display reserved for *The Lily Madonna* with a large photograph of the icon and an account of what it had done for the village – all information she already knew. She supposed she should have known better than to expect anything else. She idly browsed, glancing at leaflets and booklets in case there was something more in depth but found

144

nothing and left, emerging onto the sun-washed street, her brain still worrying at it.

Of course, she knew it didn't matter whether the icon was original or not, whether it had been repainted, whether it was a complete fake or whether it had been painted by a five-year-old in a nursery one boring wet afternoon. So long as it held some significance for the people of Tourbelle la Vierge, what was it to her? She didn't have time to bother with it one way or the other. She barely had time to finish restoring it in time for the August festival without any further delays or enquiries. She could have nightmares about what Timothy's response would be if she suggested staying on longer to finish a little sideline restoration project on the very remote chance it was something interesting. And she could hardly expect Esther to give her free board and lodging while she did so.

Earlier in the week, she had taken out the bag of paint fragments which Father Diluca had left her and examined them under the microscope from her trunk, studying each piece meticulously before moving on to the next, trying to gauge how recently the overpainting had been done. Pigments and binders could generally provide a clue but it was slow and painstaking work and it was a field of expertise in which she had only limited experience, and her microscope was small and basic.

She'd been sceptical all along that the painting everyone revered was early medieval. Now she felt vindicated but proving it would be difficult. Her preliminary study of the fragments of white paint was unhelpful. They contained lead white, a pigment which had been superseded by zinc white in the nineteenth century. So the icon wasn't a modern copy but that didn't make it medieval either.

Then she'd studied a succession of blue paint fragments and was almost certain that she'd found Prussian blue. That localised the time scale more tightly. A German had discovered Prussian blue early in the eighteenth century and it was produced soon afterwards in France, its use becoming widespread as the century progressed. So it seemed likely that the present image was painted in the latter half of the eighteenth century. This was progress.

But all this examination and enquiry had meant that her progress on the icon had ground to a halt. She still hadn't finished removing all the loose fragments but she couldn't just carry on picking away at it. The issue puzzled and obsessed her; she needed to know. Or maybe not. Maybe, she told herself for the umpteenth time, she should just repair the thing as well as she could and hand it back.

She weaved through the crowds heading back up towards the square, glancing at the stalls blocking the road as she went. It was the middle of May and tourists now swelled the local shoppers, idling and nosing and hardly moving. It was warm too, high twenties; Hannah was hot by the time she reached the square. She toyed with sitting at one of the café tables which bordered it but they were all taken so she moved on.

Then a man waved at her from a table on the terrace outside Bistrot Michel. She ignored him at first but when he stood up and called her name she looked across. He wore a floppy hat and dark glasses and wasn't immediately recognisable. Then she realised it was David and she walked over to see him.

He gestured towards the free chair opposite. 'Join me, why don't you?'

She hesitated. 'I probably shouldn't. I've got things to do.'

'Nonsense. It's summer. Everyone should take the time to kick back and feel the sun on their skin. Sit down.'

'Well… if you're sure you don't mind? Thanks. I could do with a drink and I'd never have got a table.'

David sat again, managed to attract the attention of a waitress nearby and Hannah ordered a cup of tea. He sat back and let his gaze wander over the hubbub of the square. The table was on a front corner of the terrace and afforded a good view.

'The market brings everyone in, doesn't it?' he said. 'I tend to forget when I've been away.'

'Do you miss it?'

'The crowds? No. The place? Yes, but I like it best out of season. That's when you can truly feel the place and the culture, when people have time to chat.' He grinned. 'And the locals huff and shrug and wave their hands in frustration at me because I can't understand what they say. I like to watch them play pétanque though. Slow, earnest, very competitive, then they go for a pastis together. Perfect.'

The waitress brought Hannah's tea. Hannah thanked her and waited for her to go.

'Do you play?' she asked.

'Not often.' He paused as if he was going to say something else, then didn't.

Hannah dunked the tea bag in the cup and watched the water darken. After a couple of minutes she removed it and took a sip. 'Mm, good.'

David smiled absently then looked out towards the square, apparently lost in his own thoughts. Though he was sitting in the shade he still wore both the hat and the dark glasses making it hard to read his expression, but something about the set of his face suggested contemplation, or even melancholy.

Hannah watched the crowds too, listening to the babble of voices, the market traders shouting, a group nearby laughing.

'Isn't that Sara over there?' she asked, with a nod in her direction. 'Over by the fruit stall.'

David glanced round. 'Yes.' He watched her a minute then

looked away. She didn't appear to have seen them and David clearly had no intention of attracting her attention. Sara moved on and out of sight.

'Are you involved with anyone, Hannah?' he blurted out suddenly.

'No. Why?'

'Very wise. Don't get involved. It's an endless…' He shook his head despairingly. '…quagmire. So many ways to do the wrong thing without intending to. I mean people do dumb things, don't they? Bad things they never intended sometimes. Then spend the rest of their lives regretting it. You should definitely stay solo.' He sighed heavily then smiled. 'Sorry, getting a bit heavy.'

He finished his coffee in one gulp. 'Have you got any plans in town or did you just come for the market?'

'Partly for the market but also to pick up some moulding samples so you can choose a new frame for the Amanda Jay, try them against the painting to see the effect.'

'Ah yes, the painting. Of course. Yes, that would be good.'

He sounded disinterested and lapsed into silence again. Hannah drank her tea.

'David, can I ask you something?'

'Sure.'

'What was Jemma like?'

He looked round sharply.

'What was she *like*?'

'Yes. Esther told me they were good friends and that Jemma had been an actress too. I just wondered.'

'I see.' He seemed surprised by the question and thought for a moment. 'Well, she was pretty. And knew it. Good fun. Liked a party. A fair actress but not good enough to make waves.' He looked directly at Hannah. She wished she could see his eyes properly. 'Does that sound harsh? Maybe it is. But

148

it's a harsh business. Too many actors and not enough work to go round. Some are bound to miss out.'

'I guess you need luck or to be in the right place at the right time? That happens in most professions.'

'Or who you know? Certainly. Esther and I don't make a living out of it because we're the best in the world. We've both had some luck though, make no mistake, Esther is a seriously good actress. She really is one of the best I've known.' He looked down at his hands suddenly then felt in a pocket for his wallet. He glanced at the two bills left under the clip and threw some money on the table. 'I ought to be going.' He stood up.

'I've offended you,' said Hannah. 'I'm sorry. I wasn't suggesting that you and Esther aren't good, only that…'

'No, you haven't offended me. I know what you mean and you're right; there's always an element of being in the right place.' He paused. 'The truth is, I do need to go.' He glanced round, aware that he was attracting attention and sat down again. 'I'm sorry, I'm being rude. You asked about Jemma. I guess it's difficult for you, thrust into a household where you have no idea what's gone on. And things are referred to but never actually said. Sometimes I feel like we're stuck in a time warp and we've never moved on.' A fly landed on his glasses and he brushed it away, then took them off and rubbed them on his shirt. He fixed her with a sharp look. 'Did Esther say anything else about Jemma?'

'No.'

He nodded slowly. 'OK. Well… she could be a delight but she could also be very difficult. She traded on Esther's name when she could. That's the way of our business: you do what you can to be noticed. But she was high-handed with Sara and they often argued. You know they were sisters, right? There again, Jemma and Esther argued too. Even Jemma's relationship with Raff was stormy. The truth is, Hannah,

Jemma was self-centred and hard-nosed. She got away with it because she was fun and she could talk. She had the gift. She could persuade you to part with a thousand bucks, and somehow convince you that it had been your idea all along. The shame was that, for some reason, it never worked on casting directors. Or maybe her reputation went before her, I don't know. She just never made it.' He smiled sadly. 'I don't like to speak ill of the dead but maybe now you'll understand the atmosphere. She's causing almost as much trouble now, dead, as she did when she was alive.'

He put the dark glasses back on and stood up.

'Thank you for the tea,' said Hannah. 'And for telling me.'

'The pleasure was mine. See you later.'

She watched him walk away. Her tea had been drunk but she still sat, his words going through her head. Then she saw Sara again, standing on the pavement at the side of the square. And Sara was watching her, expressionless, then pointedly turned her head to look in the direction in which David had gone. A moment later, she walked away. There was no doubt in Hannah's mind: Sara had been watching her with David. And Sara wanted her to know it. It seemed that Hannah had broken one of Esther's rules. She was rocking the boat.

*

Esther was in her private lounge, sitting on the sofa reading a magazine, when David walked in.

'I'm sorry,' David said, almost as soon as he came through the door. He stood full square facing her. 'I said some things this morning that I shouldn't have said. I lost my temper. I was... disappointed, I suppose.'

Esther frowned. 'Disappointed? Because I wouldn't go to the theatre with you?'

'Partly.'

Esther nodded, just once. 'Then I'm sorry too. I… I'm not trying to be a burden, David. I'm just working my way through the best I can. These have been difficult times.'

'I know, I know.' He moved to stand in front of the patio doors, looking out over the valley.

She waited, thinking he would say something else but nothing came.

'Your golf didn't last as long as usual today,' she remarked.

'I didn't play today. I decided I wasn't in the mood. I walked into Tourbelle instead, saw the market.'

'Ah. Busy?'

'Yes. Very.'

'See anyone you knew?'

'The place was heaving, Esther. You could hardly see anything.'

'Just got back?'

He turned away from the doors to look at her. 'Not exactly. I got my clubs out of the car and put them back in the gym. Then I had a shower. I was sticky after the walk.' His eyes narrowed. 'Why the twenty questions?'

'Sara called in just now. She'd been into Tourbelle too. She said she saw you there.'

'Oh right, here we go. OK, OK, yes, I did see Sara but not to speak to.' He watched Esther's face. 'She told you I had coffee with Hannah, didn't she?'

'I'm just wondering why you didn't.'

'Not again.' He sighed heavily. 'Because I knew you'd make something out of it when it wasn't anything.'

'You make it seem like something when you hide the fact.'

He shook his head. 'I was at a table at Bistrot Michel. Hannah came along looking for a seat but there weren't any. I saw her and offered she could sit with me. We drank coffee, or

151

rather tea in her case, and made polite conversation. All innocent. Period.'

'Good.'

He studied her face. 'Good? Really? Is that the end of the inquisition then?'

'Of course.' She produced a smile. 'Why not? If that's all there was to it.'

'Because you usually go all jealous as soon as I speak to another woman.'

'Jealousy shows how much I care.'

'Men and women can just talk, Esther. They can be friends.'

'Of course they can.' She paused. 'I've changed my mind about the play. I think we should go. If you still want to?'

'Sure.' He watched her face warily. 'That's good.'

Esther offered him a sweet, apologetic smile. 'I'm sorry for this morning, David. I am really.'

Chapter 13

'Daphne? Hi. It's Hannah.'

'Hannah. Good to hear from you again. How's it going?

'Fine thanks. Are you free to talk for a minute?'

'Of course. Timothy's out on a consultation again. What is it? Is there a problem?'

'No, no. I want to ask a favour.'

'Oh OK. If I can help...'

'There's a book I've got at home which I'd like to have with me here if possible. I wondered if you could get it for me and send it on? My next door neighbour has a key. The thing is, it's quite a chunky book.'

'Ye–es, I suppose I could.'

'I could do with a couple of things from my wardrobe too. I also thought you could wrap the book in them and that'll protect it.'

'All right. This book: is it urgent?'

'No, not really, but well, soon would be good if you can, given that it'll take a few days to get here.'

'I see. Then I'll go and get it today.'

'Thanks.' Hannah gave her the details of the book and where to find it. She also described a dress, a shirt and some cropped trousers she wanted. She waited while Daphne wrote them down.

'Hannah wants a book from home.' Daphne's voice was

muffled now; she'd clearly covered the mouthpiece.

'Who are you speaking to?' said Hannah quickly.

'Nathan's just here. He was wondering what was going on. Oh here, he wants to speak to you.'

'Hannah. Hi.' Nathan's hearty voice assaulted her ear. Her heart sank. Did he ever do any work?

'Hi.'

'Everything OK?'

'Yes. Why not?'

'You said something about needing a book? What's that for?'

'For my personal edification,' she said tartly.

There was a brief pause. 'It was a fair question,' he said crisply.

'It's my own book. I don't understand the need to ask.'

'Fine. If that's the way you want it. I was trying to be helpful.'

There was silence the other end and then Daphne was back.

'Hannah?' Her voice was kind but insistent in her ear. There was a hesitation. Perhaps she was waiting for Nathan to go upstairs. 'Are you sure there's no problem? Are you all right?'

'Yes, fine. Why?'

'You sound strained. I just wondered.'

'No everything's fine. Thank you for getting those things for me. I'll warn them here that I'll be getting a parcel.'

'Right. I'll get on it later.'

'Thanks Daphne. I owe you.' She hesitated. 'Is Nathan still there?'

'No.'

'Tell me, is he always this interfering in what other people do or have I been singled out?'

'Look I know he can be a bit high-handed but he's OK, Hannah. Give him a chance. Everyone has their own problems, you know.'

Closing the call and heading back through the woods towards the abbey, Hannah reflected on the conversation. *Give him a chance.* Daphne was right of course. Hannah and Nathan had got off on the wrong foot and she hadn't been able to let it go. Defensive, that's what she was. Always the same. Now she wished she hadn't reacted like that although Nathan didn't make it easy. But then there had been that cryptic reference to problems. So what problems did the neat and efficient Nathan have?

Hannah's thoughts moved on to the book. It had probably been a foolish idea. The book was old and out of print but had been a go-to classic for late medieval up to Renaissance painting in its day. She had often found it helpful, sometimes just throwing a light on an artist's work, putting it in context. Whether it would help her with *The Lily Madonna* was moot. And now Nathan knew that she'd asked for it. He'd probably tell Timothy and she'd get the third degree from him too next time they spoke.

She reached the shrine and paused a moment to look at it. It was Tuesday morning and still relatively early. She ought to get back to work but a few minutes wouldn't harm. Her brain was tired; she felt muddled and fraught. The icon had occupied her thoughts all weekend and, remembering the book, she'd grasped at the idea, hoping it might show her some illumination. Illumination. She gave a brief laugh. Isn't that what the icon was supposed to give you itself? Of course, she'd have to pray and meditate on it to achieve that and, given the state it was in, that idea was even more preposterous than usual.

Standing, contemplating the shrine did compose her a

little though. It was peaceful here. See mum, she thought, maybe I'm not completely lost after all. And maybe that's what her obsession with the icon was all about: it was something to show her mother.

*

Hannah had removed the loose bubbled paint on the Amanda Jay and now carefully eased adhesive behind the sections she could save in order to bed them back down again. It was late on the Thursday morning when she finished doing it and the canvas needed to dry thoroughly before she could do anything else. She left the painting balanced on the easel, picked up the bag with the moulding samples she'd chosen at the weekend and left the theatre.

There was no reply from Esther at her lounge door and no sign of her around the house but Sara was standing in the courtyard, smoking a cigarette. She drew on it firmly and watched as Hannah approached her, then exhaled ostentatiously and fixed her with an enquiring look.

'Hi Sara,' said Hannah. 'Is Esther about?' She lifted the bag. 'I've got some moulding samples for her to look at to choose a new frame for the Amanda Jay painting.'

Sara sucked on the cigarette again as if it were life-saving. She held the smoke a second before letting it go.

'Esther's gone out for the day.' She paused. 'With David,' she added with emphasis. She stuck out a hand. 'If you leave them with me I'll see she gets them.'

Hannah hesitated then passed over the bag. 'I intended to invite her over to the theatre to see them against the painting. It's not finished but it would give her a better idea of what the final effect will be. I mentioned it to David the other day. He seemed quite keen.'

'Was that while you were drinking coffee with him?'

156

Hannah frowned. 'Tea actually. But yes.'

Sara shook her head despairingly. 'What were you thinking?'

'I don't know what you mean. I wasn't thinking anything.'

'Evidently.'

'Look, I met him by chance and he offered me a seat when there were no others available. It wasn't a big deal.'

'It will have been for Esther. I did warn you not to upset her. David is off limits.'

'I have no designs on David. Besides, it can only upset her if she knows about it. Did you tell her?'

'Yes. Do you think we should lie to her and hide things?' Sara scoffed. 'In my experience, Esther always knows what's going on, sooner or later. It's a small place. The only smart thing to do is not mess up.'

'Look, it was completely innocent.'

'Good. But what you intend or don't intend isn't the point. It's what it looks like that matters. I suggest next time he offers you a drink...' She paused for effect. '...or anything else, that you refuse. It would be in your own interests. And in all ours. We have to live here, remember.'

She raised her eyebrows meaningfully and drew again on the cigarette then tossed the stub on the ground and trod on it.

'*Do* you have to live here, Sara?' said Hannah curiously.

'What do you mean by that?'

'I'd have thought, given what happened, that you'd prefer to move on.'

'You think jobs like this are easy to come by?' Sara shrugged. 'Maybe I'm just too much of a coward to go somewhere new. This is kind of home now.'

Hannah didn't pursue it. 'By the way, I've got a parcel coming from the UK. Just a few extra clothes and a book. I thought I should warn you.'

'Fine,' Sara replied coolly, and bent over to pick up the stub. 'I'll let you know when it arrives.'

'Thanks. I'll tell Guillaume.'

'It's OK. I'll tell him.'

Sara walked away to the cloisters and then back into the house.

Hannah returned to the theatre and resumed her work, putting a thin layer of a synthetic varnish on the areas where she needed to touch in with new paint. The varnish would make it easy for future restorers to remove her infill painting, if they needed to, without disturbing the original.

As she worked, the conversation ran through Hannah's head. Presumably Sara told Esther about the meeting with David in order to curry favour, to show how faithful and dependable she was. Sneaky was the word that came into Hannah's mind. She toyed with seeking Esther out later to explain but immediately rejected the idea. Sara was probably exaggerating anyway. She was altogether too much in thrall to Esther. They all were.

When the varnish was dry, she began mixing colours to touch in the lost paint. It was late in the afternoon when she became aware of someone behind her. She lifted her brush from the canvas and turned in her seat, pulling out the ear pieces.

'Marielle, you're going to give me a heart attack one day,' she protested in French. 'Or make me ruin a painting.'

'Sorry.'

Hannah smiled. 'It's all right. You're just super quiet and I listen to too much music. Anyway, I should have locked the door. My fault.' She noticed the way the girl was standing. 'Have you got something behind your back?'

Marielle brought a hand forward. She thrust a small posy of flowers at Hannah.

'For me? Thank you, Marielle. They *are* pretty.' She put her brush down and stood up. 'Let's see if we can find a jar to put them in. Here. What about this? Why don't you go and put some water in it while I make some tea? Do you want a drink? I've got some orange juice in the kitchen.'

Marielle shook her head but went with Hannah to the kitchen and filled the jar with water. Hannah encouraged her to arrange the flowers nicely then gave her some paper and pastels.

'Why don't you draw the flowers?' she said. 'They're such lovely colours.'

Marielle wrinkled up her nose and shook her head.

'Fine,' said Hannah. 'Draw something else. What about a butterfly?'

'Can I draw a horse?'

'Of course.'

They both worked silently. Hannah stopped to drink her tea before it went cold and glanced over. Marielle seemed completely absorbed in her task.

'Do you draw much at school?' Hannah asked, speaking slowly in English.

Marielle looked up. 'Sometimes.' She concentrated back on her drawing.

Hannah worked on, pausing now and then to lean back and appraise what she'd done. There was still a way to go but this poor burnt painting was going to be all right.

'I have finished,' Marielle sang out.

'Can I see?'

Marielle slid off the chair and brought it over. She had drawn a picture of a rearing horse and it was remarkably good for her age. Horses were difficult enough to draw at any age.

'That's very good, Marielle. Are you pleased with it?'

A pause; a pursing of the lips. 'Ye–es.'

'Then you should sign it.'

'Where?'

'Wherever you like: it's your picture. But most people sign at the bottom, either on the right or the left hand corner.'

The child stuck her tongue out of the side of her mouth as she leaned on the table and crayoned in her name.

'Have you seen many horses?' said Hannah, curious.

'No. This is a...' She frowned. '...a necklace.'

'A necklace?'

'Yes. *Le pendantif.*'

'I see. The pendant on a necklace. Is it yours?'

Marielle shook her head. Something Claudine owned perhaps.

'Do you want to take the picture to show your grand-parents?'

The girl shook her head again and stood up, fidgeting. 'Can't I stay here?'

'I'm sorry. I'm doing something quite tricky now so I need to be alone.'

Marielle pouted a little and didn't immediately go.

'Do you like David?' she asked suddenly.

'I'm sorry?'

Had the girl seen or heard something about the stupid drink in Tourbelle? Did everyone know about it?

'David. Do you like him? Everybody likes him, I think. *Bien que...*'

'English Marielle. Even though what?'

She hesitated. 'Everybody argues when he is here.'

'I see. Don't you like him?'

Marielle just shrugged.

'Has he done something to make you not like him?' said Hannah gently, concerned.

Again, the child shook her head, but there was clearly

160

something behind her remarks. Hannah waited. It didn't work to push Marielle too much.

'I've seen him angry.' The girl had switched to French again. 'He gets angry very quickly.' Her eyes became big then she looked away. 'And I saw him hit Raff one day. And Raff fell over and his nose was bleeding.'

'That must have been scary. Do you know why he did it?'

Another shrug. She looked at Hannah curiously. 'But you like him?'

'I don't know him very well,' Hannah said carefully. 'But he seems very pleasant.'

Marielle said nothing and a moment later she was gone. Hannah locked the door and went back to work, wondering what had sparked that particular conversation, if anything. Marielle had a way of coming out with odd questions. But she was soon absorbed in her task again and it slipped out of her mind.

*

Esther had had the frame moulding samples in her possession for several days before she went over to see Hannah in the theatre. The delay had been intentional; she wasn't going to dance to Hannah's tune and she wanted Hannah to be forced to wait. It was the end of the afternoon on the following Wednesday when she tried the door. Finding it locked, she rapped on it but there was no reply. She glanced at her watch with a heavy sigh – four-forty – and rapped a second time. There was a pause and she heard the lock turn and the door was pulled open. Hannah smiled, a little uncertainly Esther thought, and stood back to let her in.

'Hello Hannah.' Esther showed the bag with the moulding samples. 'I've come to choose the frame. I know you invited David to share in the decision but he had to be somewhere else.' She produced a plastic smile. 'I was sure you'd understand.'

Esther hadn't been back to the theatre since that visit early in April and she looked around, unsure what exactly she expected to have changed. It all looked much the same. She regarded Hannah. The woman's hair was tousled and had flecks of colour in it as if she'd pushed paint smeared fingers through it. She wore an oversized paint-stained shirt. fastened with two buttons, over a tee shirt and knee length cotton trousers. It was warm in the theatre and her cheeks were flushed; she wore no make-up. She looked a mess but appeared careless of her looks and completely wrapped up in her work. Her apparent vulnerability belied the assured and highly professional woman Esther knew her to be, but it was irritatingly engaging. It could appeal to a man. And she did have big eyes. Despite it all, she was an attractive woman. Esther was surprised at herself for not having noticed before, taken up as she was with having found someone she thought she could talk to.

'I'm still working on the picture,' Hannah was saying now, 'infilling some paint loss but it's nearly done. The paint I'm using dries quite quickly but we can avoid touching the risky areas anyway. Come and have a look.'

The beach scene was up on the easel. Esther stood in front of it while Hannah offered up each of the samples in turn to the edge of it. Each piece of moulding was about fifteen centimetres long which ought to have given her an impression of what the result might be but Esther found it hard to imagine. She stared at each one carefully. She also cast frequent glances at Hannah between times. The argument she'd had with David about that shared coffee in Tourbelle lingered in her mind. She had been naïve before. She hadn't expected Hannah to be a problem.

Refusing to consult Hannah's opinion, she finally settled on a moulding.

'Fine,' said Hannah. 'I'll get the new frame made up in town.'

'When will it be finished?'

'I've got maybe another week's work on it. And the framer was running on a two week turnaround when I called in. So maybe three weeks. Not long.'

Esther nodded. She was aware of Hannah watching her face.

'I was able to save some of the bubbled paint,' said Hannah, 'and the soot hasn't caused as much damage as I'd feared.'

'It looks amazing,' Esther said, stunned into honesty. 'Amazing. I never thought…'

She didn't finish the thought, turning away suddenly as images from that awful night began to crowd in on her. For distraction, she walked towards the stage to look at the paintings still awaiting Hannah's attention.

'Can I make you a cup of tea. Or coffee?' offered Hannah.

'No… thank you.'

Esther continued to survey the paintings, collecting her thoughts. Walking over from the house, she had almost decided to ask Hannah to leave; she could finish this one picture and then go. The decision had been fermenting inside her for days. She couldn't bear to let David be taken away from her and she certainly wasn't going to share him. But Hannah was clearly very good at her job and Esther dearly wanted her paintings restored. She could warn the woman off, of course, but that could backfire on her. She'd known women who became more determined to get the man, just for spite. No, Hannah would have to stay and Esther would just have to keep a close eye on both of them.

She turned and flashed Hannah a brief smile.

'David and I were thinking of having a few friends over on Saturday for drinks and a casual dinner. You will come won't you?'

Chapter 14

It was the closest thing they'd had to a party since the awful night of the fire. Drinks and canapes in the garth before going back inside for dinner in the dining room. Raff was intrigued. This had to be David's doing but how had he managed it? It was pleasingly casual; there was idle conversation and some laughter. The usual suspects were there: Esther and David, Sara and Raff, Hannah, and Raff's agent, Jaz Tissington, who'd turned up on one of her biannual visits. Plus there were two couples, both of them people who worked in the 'business': Susie and Bill, both actors, and Frieda and Morgan, an actor and a director respectively. And then there was a single man, an up-and-coming male actor called Chris Maunby. David was doing the honours mixing cocktails again. He was irritatingly good at it. And irritatingly aware of how good he was.

'This is a bold step, isn't it?' Raff remarked to Sara. They were standing together at a slight remove, sipping at their cocktails. It was strange how often that happened, like the ugly sisters at a ball, he thought, and just as appealing. The analogy amused him.

'What *are* you talking about?' said Sara, frowning.

'Having all these people here. Actors too. David has clearly been working on our Esther. I suppose they're all staying over.'

'She used to have parties like this all the time.'

'My point exactly. But not since that night.'

'It's Hannah.'

Raff turned his head, frowning. 'Hannah? What do you mean?'

'Hannah is making Esther nervous. You notice there's a spare man?'

Sara transferred her forensic gaze to a small group standing together talking: Esther with her arm looped possessively through David's, Hannah, and Chris.

'Esther's making a point to Hannah,' murmured Sara. 'She's got David and she's introduced Hannah to the spare man. Though she probably wouldn't care if one of the other men fancied Hannah. It's all the same to her.'

Raff looked at her curiously. 'It's about time we found you another man, Sara. You're getting way too cynical.'

'That's precious coming from you.' She looked him straight in the eyes. 'Anyway you? Find a man for me? That's a laugh.' She looked back at Chris Maunby. 'That actor's pretty dishy mind you.' She pursed up her lips suggestively. 'I could fancy him.'

'You'd better elbow Hannah out of the way then.'

'She'll be gone soon.'

'Unless Esther buys more paintings. Oh look, now Hannah's been dragged away and persecuted by Jaz, probably trying to sell her one of my paintings. She has no shame, I'm glad to say. Still, I'd better go and rescue her.' He didn't move however. 'Not sure about your theory, Sara. Looks to me like Esther's monopolising that young man too. Maybe she's trying to make David jealous.'

'Maybe. I need a cigarette.'

'Have a good one,' he said with a grin to her retreating back.

166

Raff ambled across the courtyard to join the two women.

'I hope you're telling her how brilliant I am,' he said to Jaz.

'Yes. And how modest.'

'It's my artistic nature: one day I think I've painted a masterpiece; the next I want to take a knife to it. It's what makes me so good.'

Jaz rolled her eyes at Hannah. 'Excuse me, I'm going to mingle.' She drifted away to speak to Susie nearby.

'So–o, how are you enjoying our little get together?' said Raff softly. 'Finding the atmosphere with Esther a bit cool?' He tutted. 'You really shouldn't have had coffee with David, you know.'

'Tea. I don't drink coffee. I presume Sara told you.'

'Of course.' He smiled blandly. 'You can't do anything around here without someone noticing. And then they tell everyone else. It's only polite. Incidentally, I haven't seen you much since. What have you been up to?' His flicked a glance across to Esther again and dropped his voice further. 'She's determined to keep that man. Look at this: she hasn't had a party since the fire. Obviously making an effort to please him, scared you'll steal him away.'

'I have no intention…'

'It's about time she realised she has to do more than pout. You've done us a favour.'

He raised his glass to her.

'Sara doesn't think so. She's thinks I've made Esther more difficult.'

'Nah. Sara's a glass half empty kind of person. Not me.' He grinned. 'Glass half full every time, or better still full. Speaking of which I'm going to get a refill. You?'

'I'm fine thanks.'

The party moved inside to eat but the evening dragged for

Raff. He was glad of the visitors. They were a useful buffer, stopping it all becoming choked and inbred. Bill fortunately was a bit of a raconteur and appeared to have a limitless number of stories to tell. God knew, a party like this needed some outside blood to keep it alive. It also made them all behave and stopped them bickering for the duration.

He watched Esther drink a little wine, saw David take her glass and refill it. Esther looked at him gratefully then reached over and stroked his cheek. Very sweet. Did David have an agenda, he wondered, coming back like this or was it love? The genuine kind of love that won't die just because someone drives you mad with the way they behave? Or was it because David's career was never quite as spangled as Esther's and he needed the reflected light from her carefully cultivated varnished image. David was quite a good actor apparently though Raff had no idea himself; movies didn't interest him that much. But he didn't have Esther's charisma, that was clear, just classic good looks. Raff was sceptical about the man but then he usually was; he assumed most people had an agenda.

Like Jaz who didn't need to come and see him like this but made a point of doing it regularly, hoping to meet potential new clients. Anyone who hung around Esther Langley's place was likely to have money and buy paintings was her reasoning. And it was fine by him. Jaz had been a good agent for several years now. She looked after him as well as she could, given how prejudiced the art market was against unknowns, how much a slave to fashion and gimmickry.

She sat to his right at the table.

'I gather you've shown Hannah some of your work,' she said over the oyster hors d'oeuvres. 'Could be a useful contact.'

'In what way?'

168

'Come on Raff, wake up,' she murmured. 'She works in the art business. Wealthy clients who are interested in easel paintings. I gave her a wad of your cards. I'm surprised you didn't.'

He smiled winningly. 'That's why I employ you darling. I just paint the pictures. You're the one with the head for business.'

Raff glanced across at Hannah who was sitting further up on the other side of the table. She was exchanging conversation with Morgan on her left. As he spoke, Hannah was attentive, nodding occasionally, eyes alert and occasionally straying to take in what was happening elsewhere in the room. She looked arty and head-in-the-clouds but she was no-one's fool. He rather doubted she would be a useful contact for him. Hannah had an agenda too, he suspected; he just wasn't sure what it was.

Claudine suddenly appeared in the drawing room and walked briskly to the head of the table, followed by Guillaume. They both stood talking to Esther and David. Raff was intrigued: Claudine looked unusually flustered. He saw Esther turn her head and speak to Hannah saying something about someone having come to see her.

Then a man appeared in the doorway. He was tallish and casually dressed with short light brown hair and dark-rimmed glasses gave him a studious air. After a moment's hesitation, he joined Claudine and Guillaume but turned to face Esther.

'I'm so sorry to disturb your dinner,' he said. 'My flight was really late arriving. I checked into my accommodation and then got lost on the way over here.'

'I told you to wait,' said Claudine crossly.

'I know. I'm sorry.' The man offered her an apologetic smile. 'I thought, since I was the one causing the trouble, I should at least come myself, and explain. I didn't want you to

169

be blamed.'

Claudine looked grudgingly mollified. Raff admired the man's style.

'It's all right, Claudine,' said David, standing up. 'We'll sort this out now.'

She nodded and withdrew, glancing accusingly at the stranger one last time. Guillaume went with her.

'And you are…?' prompted Esther, getting to her feet too.

The man stuck out his hand and smiled again. 'Nathan Bright. So sorry to barge in like this. I work with Hannah.'

*

'What are you *doing* here?'

Hannah's voice spat at him, made more venomous by her effort to keep the volume down. Her eyes smouldered with anger.

'I brought your parcel.' Nathan gestured towards a brown paper-wrapped parcel standing on the console table against the wall in the entrance hall. 'Daphne said you needed it. I've also brought your relined canvas. We did the relining then put it back on the stretchers.' There was a box under the table.

They were standing near the front door. Hannah had insisted on taking Nathan away from the dining room and back down the hall. Claudine had returned to the kitchen and Guillaume had gone. They were alone.

'And I really don't think you need to keep your voice down,' he said. 'They're all still down the other end there, probably talking about us. They're not likely to hear anything we say.'

'Yes, and thank you for that. That's just what I wanted: to become the topic of conversation and ridicule for not knowing my colleague from Oxford was going to turn up in the middle of dinner. You've made me look a fool.'

'Look, I'm sorry. It was a timing thing. By the time I realised how late it was I thought I ought to come on anyway. In any case, I didn't expect you to be sitting down to a fancy meal with your hosts. You certainly seem to be having a good time here.'

'Really? Now you're suggesting I'm coasting it here? You've got a nerve. I don't have to justify myself to you.' Hannah paced around. 'Why on earth are you here anyway? That parcel could have been put in the post.' She stopped suddenly and glared at him. 'The painting could have been sent too. What is this?'

'Timothy had a commission from a couple with a mural that needs attention. It's not too far from here: just outside Lacoste. Since I was coming to the area it seemed only sensible to bring your things along. Cost-effective you might say. Timothy likes that.' He paused. 'I thought you'd be grateful.'

Her eyes narrowed. 'Timothy sent you to a job in Lacoste? When did that come in? Seems like a remarkable coincidence.'

'I guess so.'

'You're not telling me something.' Her eyes fixed on him. It was the first time he'd seen her dressed up and with make-up on. She looked so different. The challenging gaze hadn't changed though. 'Why are you really here, Nathan?'

He paused. 'OK, look: Timothy saw Daphne wrapping up your parcel to post. It made him curious. You know what he's like. He started asking questions. Why did you want the book? What problem had caused you to ask for it? You know he's obsessive about knowing what's going on, constantly thinking that we could be more efficient or that some major problem is going to throw a spanner in the works. And since I'd just finished a project, he had the bright idea to bump the mural commission up the list so I would be nearby, just in case you needed help.'

'Well I do not need help, thank you very much. If I did, I would ask for it.'

Nathan raised his eyebrows. 'Would you? Really? I doubt it. You strike me as far too independent for that. I think you'd look on it as a matter of pride to sort it out yourself.'

Hannah raised her chin. 'Tell me, how would you feel in a comparable situation if I turned up suggesting you needed my help? Without being asked?'

'I'd be bloody annoyed, you're right. Yep, bloody annoyed. And I did say that to Timothy. But it's your fault. You don't communicate with him enough. You were warned. He hates not knowing what's going on. And Daphne thought you sounded anxious.'

'I was not anxious.'

'Well, she thought you were. She was worried about you.' He hesitated. 'Why did you want the book anyway?'

Hannah went over and picked up the parcel.

'It's just a book. I've had it for years. It's not a big deal. In any case, it's none of your business.'

'Hey, get down off the high horse. Don't blame the messenger. If you've got a problem, take it up with Timothy. I'm just doing my job.'

She fixed him with a long, penetrating look. 'Yeah. Sure.' She glanced towards the front door. 'I assume you can find your own way out.'

'Yes.'

She picked up the box containing the canvas and started for the stairs.

'Hannah?'

She stopped and turned.

'This is the number of the house I'm at if you need to get in touch with me.'

He took a step forward and pushed it inside the brown

172

paper wrapping on the parcel. She met his gaze, saying nothing, then walked upstairs and out of sight leaving him alone in the hallway. He stood for a moment, then crossed to study the aerial photograph on the wall. Before leaving he glanced back out through one of the windows into the garth. This was a strange and interesting place. Still, he'd see it again. Whatever Hannah might think or want, he had his instructions.

*

Hannah worked on the Sunday, glad to be back in the theatre and in her own private world. It had been a painful return to the dining room on the Saturday night, trying to shrug off Nathan's unexpected arrival. She had been obliged to explain that Nathan had arrived to work nearby, that, no, she didn't know he was coming. He'd brought some clothes that she'd asked to be posted. Raff had teased; Esther had changed the subject, fussing over her guests. Then Hannah had spent a restless night, the conversations of the evening playing through her head on a repeating loop.

Now she spent the morning mixing paint and touching in the lost sequences in the beach scene while she slowly unwound. The anger she had felt the night before had dissipated. As usual, she regretted the way she had spoken to Nathan. She might not like the man but she knew he must have had Timothy's backing to be sent here. It was possible that Nathan had put the idea in Timothy's head of course – very possible – but she also recognised that she hadn't contacted Timothy as often as he'd asked. Maybe she had brought this on herself. She had been accused of being too independent before. *Always acknowledge when you're in the wrong*, her mother used to say. *Otherwise you're being small-minded*. OK, OK, so she would acknowledge it. But the next time she saw him would be soon enough.

The days moved remorselessly on. It was now the last week of May. Hannah finished retouching the Jay and began putting layers of varnish on it to protect it again. *The Lily Madonna* remained a dilemma. In the privacy of her bedroom, Hannah had pored over the book that Nathan had brought. It was good to be reunited with it, an old companion, but it hadn't told her anything new, though it had confirmed a few things and set her thinking. It didn't resolve, however, what she should do with the icon. Each evening, after work, she took it out of the trunk and examined it anew, picking at the remaining loose fragments, wondering what exactly lay beneath. An X-ray would be a godsend but she didn't have access to that equipment and she certainly couldn't send it back to Oxford to get it done.

On the other hand, she did have a friend nearby... Why hadn't she thought of that before?

On the Thursday afternoon, Hannah walked into town with the carefully wrapped Amanda Jay under her arm and delivered it to the framers. Afterwards, she went to the call box in the square and made a call, listening to it peal five times before it was answered.

'*Oui, allô?*'

'Sylvie? *Salut*. Good, it's you. It's Hannah. How are you? How's Nice?'

'Nice is frantic and I'm fine, thanks. It's good to hear from you. Haven't seen you in ages. I heard about your mum. I am sorry. Are you OK?'

'Yes, I'm fine, thanks Sylvie. It's been... well, you know. Look, you won't believe this but I'm working in Provence at the moment.'

'What? Why didn't you tell me?'

'It's been busy, kind of complicated. The thing is, I wondered if we could meet. I was hoping to pick your brains.

174

Can we talk? I mean, are you alone?'

'Yes.'

'You've done a lot of work on icons haven't you?'

'Some. Why?'

'Why would one be repainted?'

'Repainted?'

'Yes. Completely overcoated with gesso and painted from scratch?'

Hannah could hear Sylvie blowing air out between pursed lips.

'Icons often suffer a lot of wear, you know. They are handled a lot and moved around. If one was damaged or worn beyond easy restoration, it might be completely repainted. I've heard of it being done but I've never come across one like that. Why? Is that what you're working on?'

'Yes and no. It's a long story.'

'How intriguing. Go on then. Tell me about this icon. You think it's been overpainted?'

'I'm sure of it.'

'So? The original must have been a ruin. Why worry about it?'

'I don't know. I suppose you're right. It's just… if I came over to Nice, would you x-ray it for me? It'll take me maybe a couple of hours to get there.'

'Yes, I guess we could do that. I don't think Henri would be too impressed with you making use of his studio, especially when you turned his job down that time. But if we plan it for when he's not around…'

'What about Saturday?'

'This Saturday? Is it urgent? Though that would work. Henri's away at the moment and I've got something that I doubt I'll finish tomorrow and it is overdue. I'm bound to be here.'

175

'Great. Thanks Sylvie.'

'But you're not coming to see me, are you?' Sylvie said drily. 'You're coming to take advantage of the equipment.'

'Only partly. Of course I want to see you too.'

'Yes, yes. I'll see you on Saturday then. Say eleven o'clock?'

'That'll be perfect. It needs to be kept our secret though. And Sylvie?'

'What?'

'You're a true friend.'

Sylvie said something rude, prompting Hannah to smile as she put the phone down.

Chapter 15

Hannah was in the theatre at seven on the Saturday morning, getting *The Lily Madonna* out of the trunk, putting it carefully in a large canvas shopping bag and taking it as nonchalantly as she could out to her car and stowing it in the boot. She'd eaten her breakfast alone and was on the road before nine. She didn't see Guillaume as she left but didn't doubt that he'd seen her leave.

He'd turned up at the theatre on the Friday morning, knocked on the door and walked straight in with Nathan trailing behind him.

'Excuse me, *Mademoiselle. Monsieur* Bright wishes to see you…' A brief hesitation. '…again.'

'Thank you Guillaume.'

Hannah turned from the easel where she was studying the newly relined School of Rembrandt painting. Nathan was standing near the door, surveying the room. They both waited until Guillaume had gone and had closed the door behind him.

'This is an amazing space to work in,' remarked Nathan. He came closer, still looking around. 'Great light. And privacy too. Impressive.'

'Yes, isn't it?' She regarded him warily. 'What can I do for you, Nathan?'

'Nothing.' He produced an envelope from one of the pockets of his linen jacket. 'I'm afraid, what with everything that happened on Saturday, I forgot to give you this.' He handed the envelope to her. 'It came to the office. Daphne asked me to apologise for the state of it. It hadn't been gummed properly and the pictures fell out. Since they were photos she thought you might want it. And since I was coming anyway...'

He left the sentence hanging. Hannah frowned and pulled the photographs out of the envelope. She glanced through them then raised her eyes to his face again.

'I take it you've looked at these.'

'Yes. I see you've got a sister.'

'Yes.' She pushed the photographs back in the envelope. 'I'm afraid I overreacted on Saturday,' she said. 'I'm sorry if I was rude.'

He regarded her a moment.

'Don't think about it. I imagine it was quite a shock seeing me turn up like that. I hope it didn't spoil your evening.'

'No, not at all.'

He glanced at the Rembrandt then ran his gaze over the Bellini propped up against the stage. He didn't comment; she was surprised.

'Perhaps you'd be interested to come over to see the mural I'm working on sometime,' he remarked instead. 'I know Rick and Mandy won't mind.'

'Thank you, though I really need to press on here. Time is money after all,' she said. 'Isn't that what Timothy always says?' Nathan produced a wry smile. 'Anyway, thank you for bringing the photos.'

She turned back to face the easel.

'You must take some time off though, right? Weekends, that's usual. Even Timothy understands you need some down time.'

She glanced back. 'Your point is?'

He shrugged. 'I thought maybe we could meet up

tomorrow. I don't know this area at all. Perhaps you could show me round a little?'

'I'm sorry, Nathan. I'm seeing a friend tomorrow. I'll be out all day.'

He raised his eyebrows but didn't comment. 'Sunday?'

'I usually work Sundays. You know: get the job done.'

'Look, Hannah, I'm making an effort here. We're both working for the same boss and we've been thrown together. I just think we should try to make it – I don't know – less confrontational. Just make the best of it.'

She frowned and met his gaze. Maybe he wasn't so bad after all.

'You're right, of course,' she said eventually. 'We should. But this weekend I'm really busy. I am truly. Sorry.'

'OK. Another time.'

Now, out on the road, heading east, Hannah wondered what he would end up doing though he must be used to amusing himself when he was away. He slipped out of her thoughts as the icon pushed back in, excitement and nervousness about what she was doing jostling for dominance.

As Sylvie had said, Nice was frantic, the bustling city swelled by thousands of summer tourists. Hannah, who had been there several times before, still found herself caught up in the unfamiliar road system and was relieved to finally park her car and get to Sylvie's workshop.

Sylvie was small, curvaceous and stylish with shoulder length straight dark hair and immaculate make-up. She was as extravert as Hannah was introspective. They'd met years before, soon after Hannah had broken up with a long-time boyfriend, when they'd both taken a job at the Louvre in Paris. They were chalk and cheese but Hannah trusted her implicitly.

'I imagine you still only drink tea?' said Sylvie over her shoulder, heading to the kitchen.

179

'Of course,' Hannah called after her and grinned. 'I'm nothing if not consistent.'

'Is that what it is?' she shouted back.

Sylvie brought back a tea and a coffee and immediately got down to business.

'Come on then girl,' she said. 'Show me the picture. I want to see what this is all about.'

Hannah unwrapped it from its swaddling and the French woman held it up between both hands, running her eyes over it thoroughly before looking at Hannah with a frown.

'It's not much is it? Where did it come from?'

'A little parish church in Tourbelle La Vierge near where I'm working. It's supposed to be early medieval, originating from the abbey nearby. It had an accident at Easter and I was asked to restore it.' Hannah paused, watching Sylvie's face as she ran her eyes over the decimated image once more then brought it closer to examine the damage. 'As you can see, it's suffered badly.'

'To say the least.' Sylvie snorted.

'The locals believe it has miraculous powers.'

Sylvie glanced at her, eyebrows raised, but didn't respond.

'Look closely at the bottom right hand corner, then in the middle where Mary's halo would be.'

Sylvie did as she was told then slowly looked up at Hannah, eyes widening.

'There's something underneath.'

'Exactly. That's what I told you on the phone. I thought all along there was something wrong about it – just a feeling. See the tulips in the border? I checked and found that they weren't introduced to Europe till the sixteenth century. And I think the paint's eighteenth century.'

Sylvie looked back at the painting and chewed one glossy lip.

'But what do you think is under there?' She studied Hannah's face. 'You must have some idea or you wouldn't have come all this way to have it checked out.'

'I'm not sure.' Hannah ran a hand along the back of her neck which felt hot and sticky. 'I've spent a bit of time in the local library, looking at local history books. All I've come up with is a theory. Nothing definite. The thing is, Sylvie, it's all being done on the quiet. The parish priest doesn't want his parishioners to know that it's damaged. It's considered too important. And he wants it back before the annual festival in August.'

'So why don't you just restore it like the man wants?'

'But suppose there's something better under there? Is that what you'd do: just paint over it again? Suppose it's something amazing?'

'Suppose it's not. Why should it be? Anyway, it's not your decision is it? Suppose you get into all sorts of trouble for stripping it back. You can't do that just on a whim. People get very worked up about icons; they're emotive things. And what about your employer here? Won't he mind?'

'It's a woman. An actress called Esther Langley. And there's no reason for her to know. But I need to know. That's why I want you to x-ray it.'

'An x-ray won't necessarily prove anything. They don't always show everything; you know that. If there's lead in the overpainting…'

'Even so. Please?'

Sylvie sighed and picked up the icon.

'We'll give it a try. See what we can see.'

She went into another room and left Hannah idling in her studio, killing time looking over Sylvie's current project. Twenty minutes later, Sylvie was back. She put the x-ray film onto a backlit viewing box and stepped back.

'You were right.' Sylvie peered at the film, eyes narrowed. 'There's definitely another painting underneath.'

'I knew it.' Hannah moved in close and stared at it, barely breathing. The film was shadowy and far from clear but there was undoubtedly the outline of another image. There was a large central figure with the hazy suggestion of others around it but the overpainting confused what could be seen, rendering it blank in places.

'It's a Madonna and saints, I'd guess,' said Sylvie.

'Early medieval?'

'Could be, stylistically, but you know how difficult that is to tell with icons.'

'It doesn't look too badly damaged does it?'

Sylvie peered at it again.

'I don't know.'

'Doesn't that look like a flower?' Hannah pointed to a feathery shape crossing the central figure.

'Maybe. Or the serious damage which made someone paint over it in the first place. There had to be a reason. There are several places where it's not clear there's paint underneath.'

'*The Lily Madonna*,' muttered Hannah to herself, feeling the bubble of excitement growing in the pit of her stomach.

'What?'

'Nothing.'

Sylvie pulled the film down and slid it into a card envelope. 'Does it fit with your theory? What is your theory anyway?'

'I'd need to do more research before I could say.'

Sylvie shook her head impatiently.

'Of course you would. You haven't changed. I bet you're so secretive you don't even tell yourself when you're going out. So what are you going to do about it?'

'I don't know yet. I'll have to think about it. At least I have the information now.' She gave Sylvie a hug. 'Thank you so much. I'll ring you soon and let you know how it turns out.'

'Yes, you do that.' Sylvie waved an admonishing finger at her. 'Don't taunt me with hidden paintings and then not let me in on the outcome. But Hannah?'

Hannah turned in the doorway.

'What?'

'Be careful.'

*

David persuaded Esther to join him at the poolside that afternoon. It was the second of June and a beautiful sunny day with the temperature already high in the twenties. They sat on neighbouring recliners though Esther, desperate not to age her skin, kept carefully in the shade of a large parasol. David had swum a few indolent lengths and was now drying out in the sunshine, the beads of moisture on his skin disappearing rapidly in the heat. He was lying on his belly and Esther looked across at him. He was still in great shape, working out regularly in the gym, occasionally going for a run in the cool of the early morning. She watched him roll onto his back, saw his abdominal muscles ripple as he then sat up.

'I'm going for a cold drink. Would you like one?'

'A Perrier would be good, thanks.'

He stood up and walked away to the pool house. He looked relaxed, at ease. She watched him irresistibly and felt the familiar pang of envy. He didn't seem to have any problem with the pool or the building which now stood where the Garden House had been. She had often wondered what he thought about it but he refused to be drawn.

'It's a building,' he'd say. 'Just a building. It's not a bad place but it's not a good place either. It's just a place. There are no spirits here, Esther, just stone and mortar.'

'But, don't you *feel* anything?' she had said to him once.

He'd shrugged. He never saw spirits, not David.

He had never talked about the fire, right from the first day when the truth of what had happened to Jemma became clear. He'd answered the few routine questions from the local police and then he'd gone silent. And yet there'd been something at the back of his eyes, she wasn't sure what. Upset? Anger? Or was it fear? Did he know what had happened? She was convinced that, though he professed to being frank and open, there was a lot that went unsaid.

David returned with a can of lager and a bottle of Perrier and a glass for Esther. She put her book down – she had hardly read any of it anyway – and took them from him. The bottle was ice cold and pleasing to the touch. He'd already removed the cap and she poured half of the contents into the glass and quickly drank a mouthful, enjoying the slight fizz of the bubbles in her mouth and the chill of the water as it went down.

'Is something the matter darling?'

David was still on his feet, looking over towards the entrance.

'No, I just heard the gates go and Guillaume speaking to someone.'

'Oh? Well I'm sure he has it under control.'

David grunted and sat down.

'Hannah was going out in the car this morning when I was coming back from my run,' he said. 'It's probably her.'

'Was she alone?'

'Yes, I think so. Why?'

Esther affected nonchalance and drank another mouthful of water.

'I just wondered. That colleague of hers called again yesterday.'

'Here? What did he want?'

'I've no idea. Guillaume told me.' She drank some more water then put the glass down. 'Did anything strike you as odd about them? About the way he arrived like that, I mean?'

'It was a bit strange. Hannah looked cross, I thought. Why?'

'I don't know.' She batted a fly away from her face. 'When you take someone into your household, it's an act of trust, isn't it? And we don't know anything about Hannah really. Or this Nathan chap.'

David pulled a face. 'I can't imagine there's any great intrigue going on. Hannah seems pretty straightforward to me.'

You would say that, thought Esther, but decided not to articulate it. They'd have another row and she wasn't going to risk him leaving again.

David set up another parasol to give himself some shade and sat down, took a long draught of lager then settled back on the recliner.

'Perhaps we should ask them both to join us for dinner?' he said. 'Then we can study them at close quarters and see whether there's anything odd going on. Or maybe we could have a barbecue?'

'No. No barbecue.' Esther's response was immediate and sharp.

She glanced across again. David's eyes appeared to be closed but she wasn't sure.

'Dinner then,' he said smoothly.

She toyed with a few different responses but in the end said none of them. In any case, she thought he might have fallen asleep. Maybe he'd forget he'd even said it.

Esther looked back towards the pool house but she didn't really see it. She was focussing on the figure standing in front of it: a young woman with long blonde hair, insubstantial as mist but clearly looking at her accusingly. She threw her feet over the side of the lounger and stood up hastily, grabbed her wrap to tie round her waist and the few personal things she'd brought out with her. The woman had gone now, melted away, but Esther walked purposefully towards the steps and climbed back to the house. Let David stay with the ghost.

*

The weekend rolled into the following week and the days stretched out, hot and sunny. The cicadas sang their insistent, rhythmic call loudly, rising to a crescendo late each afternoon. Hannah was barely aware of it. Having finished the Jay, she had turned her attention to the Bellini, removing it from its frame and attending to the shrunken panels, working on fixing them back together; at the end of each day, she would lock the theatre door and get out *The Lily Madonna*, studying it, peering at the x-ray, uncertain what to do next. Was her theory plausible? Did she just want it to be true?

By the Thursday evening, she had come to no conclusion.

'What do you think, mum?' she murmured. 'What should I do?'

She got out the photographs Nathan had given her and looked first at the one of her mother standing alone. It was the most recent picture she had of her mother, taken when the dementia had only just started. Her mother wasn't quite gazing at the viewer and had a distracted air, but there was nothing unusual about that; she had never liked having her photograph taken. Her smile, if she managed it at all for the camera, always looked forced.

Hannah shuffled the photos to look at the one of the four of them. Her family. It seemed a very long time ago. A different world. She flicked her gaze from one face to the next. Her father had left about two years after this picture was taken.

186

She shuffled the pictures again and studied the photograph of herself with her mother. She had been seventeen then and her sister Elizabeth was already at university. The absurd colour of Hannah's hair was a sign of her ongoing adolescent rebellion against her mother.

Hannah felt yet another pang of regret. All those years when she'd fought against her mother seemed so petty now. And what wouldn't she give to have her there to talk to at this moment, to give her some advice.

There was a short knock on the theatre door and Hannah looked up sharply. She dropped the photographs on the table, quickly took the icon off the easel and pushed it back into the trunk, swinging the door closed.

A second knock and Esther called her name.

Hannah walked quickly over and unlocked the door.

'Esther, come in.'

She stepped back as the actress glided in.

'You're working late,' Esther remarked, sounding taut. 'Have I disturbed something important?'

'No, no, I was just finishing up for the day.' She gestured towards the Bellini, prostrate on the table. 'I've been putting adhesive between the panels to fix them. They'd shrunk and moved. You can't do much until they're solid again.'

Esther walked across to the table and looked down at the panels. She frowned.

'Is that common?'

'Not uncommon in paintings of this age. Changes in humidity and temperature will cause it. Modern central heating can be very drying.'

'I see.' Esther glanced towards the stage. 'That's the other possible Rembrandt, isn't it? *Christ Receiving the Holy Spirit.*'

'That's right. There was a hole in it and the canvas was fraying. It was rather brittle so I sent it back to Oxford to have it relined. Nathan brought it over with my other things the other day. I'll be able to get on with it now when I've done the Bellini.'

'Oh you didn't mention it. I don't think the relining was on the original estimate, was it? Did we discuss it?'

'Er no.' Hannah hesitated. This was a new, exacting Esther. The warmth and charm of their earlier meetings was gone. 'I understood you wanted me to exercise my judgement as to what would be best for each painting.'

Esther smiled but her voice held a warning note. 'Of course. Though it's always nice to know what's going on. I will be paying the bill for this, remember.' She turned her head, caught sight of the photographs on the table and picked them up. 'This must be you with your poor mother?' She smirked and flicked Hannah a look. 'Amazing hair, Hannah.'

'It was a stage I was going through.'

Hannah watched Esther replace the photographs on the table as if suddenly bored with them and cast a glance across the rest of the table. Hannah noticed that she'd left the x-ray envelope on view.

'Is there something I can do for you, Esther?' she asked quickly.

'No... no,' Esther said vaguely, then turned, her eyes suddenly sharp and enquiring. 'So there's nothing surprising about Nathan turning up here? I see he called again.'

'Yes. He'd forgotten to give me these photographs. They were sent on from where I worked before. I'd left them behind by mistake.'

'How sweet of him.'

'Yes.' A crazy idea came into Hannah's head, a chance to get this new Jekyll and Hyde Esther and the whole David scenario off her back. 'In fact, well...' Hannah laughed awkwardly. '...there's a little more to it than that. Nathan and

I have just started dating. I mean, it's early days so…' She gave an embarrassed shrug. 'I don't like to make too big a thing of it.'

'Really?' Esther's face split into a wide smile. 'That's good to hear. I love a bit of romance. Well, this makes my task here quite appropriate. We're having a little dinner again on Saturday night and I'd like to invite you and Nathan to join us.' An arch smile. 'I must say, he does seem very charming. You are a secretive girl.'

Hannah uttered a few non-committal sounds. 'You know what it's like in the early days, Esther: you don't like to jinx it.'

Esther raised her neatly plucked eyebrows. 'Of course. I understand. And perhaps your boss wouldn't approve of an in-house romance either? There's no need to worry on that score, your secret's safe with me.'

'Thank you.'

Esther drifted back towards the door and Hannah followed her.

'Tell me, when do you expect to finish? Only David and I were discussing using the theatre again later this summer. We used to have a lot of fun here and we think it's about time we did again.' She cast a quick agonised glance back towards the stage then caught Hannah's eye and smiled, putting a hand to her arm and squeezing it. 'And we wouldn't want to cast you out into the garden, now would we?'

'I'm sorry, I'm not quite sure how long I'll be yet.'

'No darling, of course. But bear it in mind, won't you?' She opened the door. 'Seven-thirty for cocktails on Saturday. I can leave you to invite Nathan, I'm sure.'

Esther smiled knowingly and was gone.

Hannah hesitated a moment, then locked the door and leant her back against it. She felt drained. She already regretted her clever idea. Proving to Esther that she had no designs on David was one thing but acting out a fake romance with Nathan of all people was quite another. What had she been thinking?

Chapter 16

It was just after seven on the Saturday evening when Guillaume opened the gates for Nathan and allowed him to drive through. Nathan stopped the car and lowered the window as Guillaume came over to speak.

'*Bonsoir Monsieur.*' Guillaume paused, looking both apologetic and suspicious. 'You are quite early for dinner, sir.'

'Yes. Hannah Dechansay asked me to come early to see her first.'

'I see. Do you know where you're going then, sir?'

'I'm meeting her in the theatre. I remember the way.'

Nathan parked his hire car next to the red Morgan, cast an envious glance over it, and followed the same route Guillaume had shown him previously: around to the south of the house, along the flat ridge looking down towards the lower grounds and out to the distant valley beyond. He paused briefly half way along and looked left instead, into the garth and the U shape of buildings encircling it. He'd always been fascinated by historic buildings though how much of this was original was doubtful.

He moved on, turning left beyond the house and weaving along the paths which took him to the theatre. He was about to knock on the door when a movement flickered at the corner of his eye and he turned sharply. A small figure had just ducked behind a holly bush, then a head appeared, craning round to

191

look at him: a small long-haired girl, furtive, watchful. The next minute she'd ducked out of sight again and he heard her running away. He shrugged and turned back to rap on the door. Without waiting he lifted the latch and walked in. Hannah was sitting near her work station with a paperback in her hand. She looked up as he entered.

'I've just been spied on by a little girl,' he remarked as he crossed to join her. 'Very nervous and rather strange. She ran away.'

'Well I imagine you could be quite frightening to a little girl.' Hannah got to her feet and put the book down. 'Thank you for coming early.'

She was wearing a dress, a soft satin affair which flared out from the thigh to fall just below her knees and swing prettily as she moved. Her hair had grown since she'd been in France too and, what with the make-up, she looked altogether softer, less threatening. Pretty even. He hadn't really noticed the other night: she'd been so cross.

Now she was looking at him oddly.

'Is there something the matter?' she said.

'No, no. Nothing. You said we needed to talk.'

'Yes.' She glanced at her watch. 'The cocktails are in the drawing room tonight because of the wind. But we've got time for a tea or a coffee first if you'd like one?'

'Why not? Coffee, thanks.'

She walked away to a door at the end of the room and he followed her into a little backstage kitchen.

'I was kind of surprised to get your call,' he said. 'And the invitation to dinner.'

'I'm kind of surprised myself.'

He watched her switch the kettle on, spoon coffee into one mug and drop a teabag in the other. There was an awkward silence while they waited for the kettle to boil.

'Esther called here on Thursday with the invitation.' She poured the boiling water into both mugs and stirred the coffee round. 'Milk? It's long life.'

'A little, thanks.'

She handed his mug over, removed the teabag from her own and picked it up. She didn't move however and glanced warily towards the kitchen door before speaking.

'I think she was going to invite you anyway, I'm not sure. The thing is...' She hesitated, looking down into her mug of tea. She looked up and straight into his face. 'The thing is, I told her we'd just started dating.'

'What?' He laughed. 'You're joking.'

'Trust me, it's not something I'd joke about.' Hannah took a sip of tea and paused. 'Hear me out, will you? You see, Esther lives with an actor called David Flaxman. They've been together years. A couple of years ago there was a tragic fire here and a friend of theirs died in it. Since then, Esther's been haunted by it, introspective, and David left her for a while. Raff said he couldn't cope with the way she was behaving.'

'Who's Raff?'

'I'll explain later. Anyway, David came back here a few weeks ago and Esther has been very... possessive of him ever since. I made the mistake of having a casual drink with him in town. She's not happy about it.'

'Hell's bells, Hannah. That's not smart.'

'It was completely innocent, for God's sake. It was just a mid-morning drink, not a secret assignation. It was market day and frantic; he had a table and I happened to walk past. He offered.' She shrugged. 'I had no idea I was walking on broken glass. Anyway, the point is, if Esther thinks we've started a... a thing, you and I, she'll be less defensive and just let me get on with the job. She was dropping hints about me finishing and I've still got a way to go.'

Nathan regarded her without speaking.

'Well?' she prompted. 'Is it OK? The thing is, her manner changed from the moment I said it. I think it'll make a huge difference.' She paused. 'I'm asking for your help, Nathan. I need to be able to just get on with my work without her giving me grief. I know we haven't got off to a great start but, well, we could do this, couldn't we? All we need to do is give each other a look now and then as if we're sharing a secret. She'll be happy then. And naturally I'll stay well clear of David.'

Nathan drank some coffee, eyebrows raised with amusement.

'It's not funny, Nathan.'

'It is from where I'm standing. Is this why you sounded so anxious on the phone that time to Oxford?'

'No. Anyway, I told you I wasn't anxious.'

'That's right, you did. Still… you have got yourself into a mess, haven't you?'

'You don't have to rub it in.'

'Faking a romance seems like a pretty dumb thing to have to do.'

'You think I'm happy about it?'

He said nothing.

'So you won't do it?'

'I suppose we might be able to carry it off.' He regarded her thoughtfully, then drank a little more coffee and glanced at his watch. 'We'll be expected over there soon. OK, look, we're going to need to know more about each other or it won't be convincing.'

'We can say we only had one date before I came out here.'

'One date?' He blew out his cheeks. 'All right, yes, that could work. What do people talk about on first dates? I haven't been on one in a while.'

'Me neither.' She hesitated. 'OK, I'll go first. I had a long-

194

term relationship which didn't work out; that was a while ago. Nothing serious since.'

Nathan nodded. 'I was in a relationship for a few years too. It ended six months ago.' He paused. 'Family?'

'My parents divorced when I was eleven. My father's French. He lives in Paris. I've got a sister – well, you saw the photographs so you know. She's married and lives in Cheshire.' She hesitated. 'My mother passed away a few months ago.'

'I'm sorry.'

'Thanks. You?'

'My father died in a car accident when I was twelve. My mother lives in Cirencester.'

'I'm sorry about your dad too.' A pause. 'I hate celery and candied fruit, and I don't like coffee. Or apricots.'

'Sprouts. I hate sprouts. And I don't like apricots either.'

Hannah started to grin and Nathan found himself grinning back.

'So tell me about this Raff,' he said. 'He lives here, yes? Who else is there? Give me an idea of what I'm in for here.'

*

It wasn't the evening Hannah had expected or hoped for. There had been no other outsiders invited. It was as if Esther had decided to put Hannah and Nathan on show, arranging for them to sit side by side, occasionally embracing them both with a knowing and indulgent smile, even teasing them once or twice. Presumably she was doing it for David's benefit. She let him sit at the head of the table while she sat on one side of him and Sara on the other. Hannah was carefully placed at a distance.

'Boy, girl, boy, girl,' she'd trilled, organising them as soon as they'd all walked through to the dining room.

A couple of times, Hannah would have sworn that Esther

195

was even flirting with Nathan: a coy smile, a pointed compliment. David seemed uncaring. While they ate, he asked about the work Hannah and Nathan did, about the most interesting or unusual jobs they'd been asked to do. Nathan proceeded to regale them with several anecdotes, starting with a couple of naturists who'd employed him to work at their house and who never wore clothes.

'Whatever the weather,' he added with a grin. 'And they were no oil paintings, let me tell you. No pun intended of course.'

The stories became more far-fetched. Hannah seriously doubted that they were all true but they were entertaining, she'd give him that. And to think she'd thought he was so strait-laced. Watching him talk, she found herself smiling. He caught her watching him once and winked. Esther noticed it too. Nathan was doing a good job.

The main course dishes were removed and dessert offered. Cheese and more bread were put out on the table along with a bowl of fruit.

'You must have a host of stories to tell from the films you've worked on too,' said Hannah, helping herself to cheese and grapes. She looked expectantly from Esther to David and back.

'They aren't allowed,' Raff interposed quickly. 'Studio rules. No stories from the set. Or production company rules or whoever. Isn't that right? The publicity department don't like too much getting out, displaying the underbelly of the beast so to speak. Got to keep the image looking good.'

'Don't be ridiculous,' said David coldly. 'It's not like that.'

'Excuse *me*. Just a little quip, David. Really, you take things so seriously.'

David's gaze on Raff was filled with dislike. 'You always

claim a joke when you're called out on something. But you never joke. It's always a barbed remark.'

Esther placed her hand on top of David's in her familiar gesture. 'Darling, let's not spoil the evening by arguing. Raff?' She looked at the other man warningly. 'Anyway, I think I've had enough to eat and I'm a little tired. I don't want coffee. I think I might go for a short walk before bed.'

She stood up and bestowed a warm smile first on Hannah, then on Nathan where it lingered a little.

'Thank you for such an interesting evening.' She looked at David. 'Coming darling?'

'Not yet. I'm going to finish my wine then I think I'll have a coffee.'

'Oh.'

'I might come out,' said Raff. 'I've got something I want to work on. I'll walk with you as far as my studio, how's that?'

'Yes... well, I suppose.' Raff was already on his feet but Esther barely looked at him. She had clearly expected the evening to fragment without her but she couldn't sit down again now. She was still looking at David. 'I'll see you in a bit then darling. Good night everyone.'

Raff linked his arm through hers. 'Come on. Come and see what I'm working on in the studio. I think you'll like it.' Still keeping his hold on her, he looked back at the table.

'Nathan. You must come and see my work. Call in sometime in the week, why don't you?'

'I might just do that,' said Nathan.

Esther looked around distractedly and walked out with him.

A few minutes later the rest of them went through to the drawing room where Liane served coffee and a small pot of tea for Hannah.

'Poor Esther,' said Sara, 'having to look at Raff's art.'

'She doesn't have to if she doesn't want to.' David poured himself a coffee. 'Help yourself everyone.'

He walked over to stand in front of the painting of Saint Peter. Hannah resisted the temptation to join him and ask him what he thought. She took her tea to one of the sofas and sat down.

'What sort of art does Raff produce?' said Nathan, waiting behind Sara by the coffee tray.

'You don't want to know. Are you having one too?' She poured coffee into two cups and took hers away black. 'Really, he's not that good.'

'Representational,' said Hannah. 'Multimedia.'

'Does he sell?' Nathan stirred a cube of sugar into his cup.

'Now and then, amazingly.' Sara sat on the other sofa. 'But not much.'

Nathan sat next to Hannah, offering her a conspiratorial smile as he did so.

'He can't do too badly,' he said. 'That's a fine car he drives. They don't come cheap.'

'A bequest in an uncle's will.' David turned his back on the painting and stood, feet apart. The tiny coffee cup and saucer looked absurd in his large hands. 'That's what he said anyway.'

'You don't believe him?' said Nathan.

'I hardly ever believe anything Raff says. He's a compulsive liar.'

'It's true; he is,' agreed Sara.

There was a strained silence.

Nathan finished his coffee and leaned forward to put the cup down on the coffee table.

'Still, I might go over and take a look at his studio. Just for curiosity.'

'Don't let him talk you into buying anything,' said Sara.

'Or promising to make any contacts for him. He can be very persuasive.'

'There's no fear of that.' Nathan grinned. 'I don't have any money and I don't have any contacts. Though one of my old school friends does run a painting and decorating business. Slaps a lot of emulsion about. Do you think Raff would be interested in him?'

Sara laughed. Her face was as relaxed as Hannah had seen it. She seemed to rather like Nathan.

'No, but I'd love for you to suggest it to him,' she said, still smiling.

'I don't think he'd notice.' David walked back to the coffee tray and replaced his cup and saucer there. 'Everything washes off him,' he added bitterly, coming back to stand near the sofas. He had a restless air.

'You shouldn't let him get to you,' said Sara.

'You don't think I see how cross he makes you? And you have to put up with him all the time. At least I get a break now and then.'

'I don't know.' Hannah glanced round them. 'I got the impression that his art is the only thing Raff does take seriously. Like a lot of artists. It consumes them and leaves room for little else.'

'You think?' David looked at her curiously. 'You sound like you're speaking from personal experience.'

'My father's an artist. And while he often pretends not to care, I know he cares very much. Especially when the critics lay into him.'

'What kind of work does he do?' asked Nathan.

'Figurative. A sort of modern-day Degas.'

'Where does he work?' said David. 'Does he drive your mother mad the way Raff does everyone here?'

'No. They split up years ago. He works in Paris. Very left

bank and bohemian. But he does take his art seriously. It even sells. It wasn't always like that, believe me.'

'Don't tell me there's hope for Raff then,' said Sara.

'Maybe,' grunted David. 'Anyway, thanks for a good evening guys. Stay and have more coffee if you want it. I'll be off now.'

Sara left soon after and Liane came in silently to clear the coffee things away.

Hannah stood up and waited until she'd gone. 'That went OK, I think.' She offered Nathan a wry smile. 'Good stories by the way.'

'Thank you.' Nathan got up and walked across to the painting of Saint Peter. 'This is quite a commanding work.'

'Yes. It came up well.'

'It's one you've just been working on?'

'Yes.'

He nodded, impressed, and studied it more closely, then looked back at her.

'Do you think Esther'll expect me to stay the night?'

'Well, I certainly don't. We've only just started dating, remember.'

He grinned. 'Don't panic. I was only teasing. I'd better be going.'

She walked him out to his car for form's sake. He took hold of her hand, in case they were being watched he said, though they saw no-one on their route. He released her by the car and she thanked him for helping out.

'It was – what shall I say? – an interesting evening,' he replied. 'We'd better plan something else or they won't believe it. We should go out for a meal or something.'

'I suppose so. I'll ring, shall I?'

'Or I'll ring you.'

'It's not easy here, taking calls. It's better if I ring you.'

He let it go and she watched him drive off back towards the main gates.

There was a bright half-moon rising in a cloudless sky, shedding a clear, silver light. Hannah decided to go to her room through the gardens, to stretch her legs and clear her head of the evening's chatter. It was calm and peaceful. There was the odd sound of a bird somewhere up in the trees, the occasional rustle at ground level. She walked past the swimming pool which glittered in the moonlight and took the steps up to the higher grounds.

Passing by the path which led to Raff's studio, she heard voices. Esther was still there, standing just outside the door, leaving perhaps. She sounded upset and cross. On an impulse, Hannah ducked carefully and quietly in amongst the shrubs and eased herself closer.

'You don't mean that,' Raff was saying.

'Yes I do.' A pause and a more resigned voice. 'No, no, I suppose I don't.'

'It's not really that much, Esther. Only sales haven't been great lately.'

'All right, all right, I'll write you a cheque tomorrow, I promise. Just be patient, Raff. Be patient and… and be kind. Be kind. Don't give me away.'

'Darling. Of course not.'

Hannah waited until Esther had passed by and gone and Raff had retreated inside the studio before emerging from the shrubs and walking slowly back to her room. That had been the unmistakeable sound of Esther being blackmailed.

*

The church in Tourbelle La Vierge was cool and dark after the sunshine in the town square outside. It was nearly four o'clock on the Sunday afternoon and, too early for mass, it was empty but for an elderly woman, sitting praying near the front. Hannah walked slowly up the main aisle and turned in to sit on one of the wooden pews, its seat polished to a weary shine by countless shuffling bottoms. She lifted her gaze to sweep round the painted statues and the ornate memorials and wondered yet again why she was doing this. She could just walk away. It wasn't her icon and it wasn't her job to sort it out. She had been manipulated, put under emotional pressure.

She was tired. It had taken her a while to get to sleep after the dinner the night before, the conversations of the evening and that disconcerting encounter between Esther and Raff still running though her head. And then there was issue of *The Lily Madonna*.

She dropped forward, resting her elbows on her knees. Praying didn't come easily to her. Too much baggage.

She heard someone approaching and the discreet clearing of a throat. She hastily straightened up. The priest was standing at the end of the pew and she offered him a strained smile.

'*Mademoiselle* Dechansay, *bonjour,*' he said. 'It's good to see you.'

'*Bonjour Père* Diluca.' She hesitated. 'I was hoping to have a word.'

'Of course, you are very welcome.' His face clouded. 'You look concerned.'

He glanced towards the elderly woman at the front of the church then beckoned Hannah to follow him with an urgent finger. He led the way to a pew in the side aisle and invited her to sit beside him.

'Is there a problem with *The Lily Madonna*?' he whispered.

'Problem? Well...' She hesitated. '...yes and no.'

'I'm sorry, I don't understand.'

'It's complicated, Father,' she murmured. 'Something has

come to light and I need your advice.' She paused. 'Suppose someone had painted over the icon, covering up an existing painting that was actually quite special. The new painting is simple in comparison and now, as time has passed, everyone has forgotten what the previous image looked like. They revere the new one simply because of its reputation.'

'Painted over it? But why would anyone do that?' The priest's eyes narrowed. 'Why paint over something that was special in the first place?'

'I'm not sure. There could have been many reasons. Anyway, that's what I think has happened to *The Lily Madonna*. Now, with the new paint surface damaged, there are small glimpses of the picture beneath. Tiny but...'

The old woman got up from the pew and slowly walked out. Hannah watched and waited until she'd gone.

'I had it x-rayed,' she said. 'There is definitely an image underneath. So the question is this: should I go ahead and restore the simple painting on the top or should I remove it to reveal what's underneath?'

'You're sure there's something underneath?'

'Yes.' She paused. It had become clear to her how much she wanted to strip it down, to see what was underneath but for that she needed his agreement and he had to know the truth first. 'I'm not sure how complete it is though. It too might have been damaged.'

'The one underneath might have had an accident too, you mean?'

'Something like that. I can't be absolutely sure one way or the other from the x-ray. Or...' she added slowly, '...it could be perfect and someone simply wanted to hide it.'

He frowned but didn't immediately respond.

'That's a very difficult decision then,' he said.

'Yes.' She waited. The priest said nothing, staring into the distance beyond her. 'What do you want me to do Father?'

'Me?' He shifted uneasily on the seat. 'It's no good asking me, *Mademoiselle*; I'm not in a position to say. I know nothing about these things.'

'No, but as the guardian of *The Lily Madonna*, it's your call.'

'No, no. I would leave it to the experts.' He nodded for emphasis but wouldn't meet her eye. 'But we'd have to be certain that it was a precious picture underneath to risk doing something like that wouldn't we? I mean, an icon isn't just a picture, it's a channel for prayer, an object for meditation.'

'Exactly, but if it isn't the true image which people have been contemplating, surely it would only be right to remove it? In a way people have been meditating and praying to a forgery.'

He thought for a moment, brow furrowed, then looked at her shrewdly.

'That is a clever argument, but I still think it would be a risky thing to do. I mean if people didn't know that there was another picture underneath, then I could see no reason to risk upsetting them, especially if there were any doubt about it. It's certainly not something that someone in my position would want to get involved in. What would people say?'

'But suppose the painting underneath is valuable.'

His attitude changed immediately. 'Valuable? *Is* it valuable?'

'I don't know. It might be. Unless I take the top painting off, I can't be sure.'

The priest was silent. She could see the internal arguments playing across his face. She could make a guess at some of them: a poor parish with repairs constantly needed to the fabric of the church, and yet the impossibility of selling something the community thought so miraculous; the prestige it would

204

give the parish and perhaps him too, just for having it there, which might bring people in and therefore the much-needed money. But then there would be the insurance…

'You must have some idea what's underneath?' he said eventually.

'I can only guess.'

'But original? Very old?'

'Yes.'

His cocoa-coloured eyes rested briefly on Hannah's then quickly danced away. 'That would be a fascinating thing to see. Perhaps it is indeed a special treasure and much good might come of it. But I think that the decision has to be yours. You are an expert, after all. I will be guided by you. I cannot take responsibility for this.'

'Really, father, it's not for me to decide. Do you want to ask one of your superiors in the church?'

A man came in at the back of the church and the priest quickly got to his feet.

'This man has come for confession. I must go.' He dropped his voice again. 'No, I will not involve anyone else. I don't want news getting out about it. It could cause a lot of trouble. The decision is yours, *Mademoiselle* Dechansay. You brought this problem to me. It's not my dilemma. But please be sure to get it finished in time for the *fête.*'

He nodded to her and walked away before she could reply.

Hannah sat for a moment, open-mouthed, staring after him: he was washing his hands of all responsibility.

She went out into the sunshine and walked slowly back through the woods towards the abbey. A breeze still cut the air, flicking a lock of hair forwards into her face and she absent-mindedly kept pushing it back, not even noticing. Fragments of her conversation with Sylvie paraded across her mind.

Suppose it's something amazing?

Suppose it's not. Suppose you get into all sorts of trouble for stripping it back. You can't do that just on a whim.

But it's not on a whim, Hannah mentally protested. I know there's something underneath that is important. It's criminal to leave it covered up.

Doesn't that look like a flower?

Maybe. Or the serious damage which made someone paint over it in the first place. There had to be a reason.

She should listen to Sylvie; she was a smart woman who knew what she was talking about. If Hannah ignored her, took the overpaint right back and found there wasn't a complete image underneath, what then? Try to restore the original? It'd be too late for that. She'd be in serious trouble. She'd have desecrated their precious icon and there would be hell to pay. She'd probably lose her job too.

And then of course, there was the more practical problem of whether she could finish the job either way before Esther's work was completed and she had to leave. She trudged home, weary and no wiser. And time was running out.

By evening, she was back in the theatre with the door locked and *The Lily Madonna* back on the easel. There was light and to spare. Anyway, she had a lamp if she needed it.

The arguments for and against doing this could go through her head as many times as they liked but they didn't change anything, and seeing the priest hadn't changed anything either. She had to have a little look, just so she knew. She wouldn't take much off but at least then she could decide.

She picked up a tiny bent-head scraper and began picking away at the gesso that the fall had revealed. It was thick, put on heavy-handedly. Slowly, she chipped away at it. Very slowly, very carefully, so as not to risk damaging what lay beneath.

Chapter 17

The property where Nathan was staying lay on a hillside just outside Lacoste. It was a large country house which had once stood in the grounds of its own vineyard. The land, but for some extensive gardens, had long since been sold off but, despite being in need of some refurbishment, the house was impressively grand. Built in the eighteenth century in a handsome, cream-coloured stone, it had turquoise-painted shutters to the windows and doors and boasted a large swimming pool. It had been extended at least twice and offered generous accommodation on a number of floors. Nathan thought he should feel exultant; it was the sort of commission that dreams were made of. Set on a hill looking down over vines, olive groves and fruit orchards, it was an idyllic setting and the new American owners were easy-going and generous.

The mural he had come to work on was somewhat more problematic: it was a large Italian landscape scene, painted onto the rear wall of a huge single-storied garden room, the front of which was mostly glazed and unshuttered. Sun poured in during the summer months and the guttering had failed at some point in the past, allowing water to run down the rear wall. Though dry now, the mural had been badly damaged by months, perhaps years, of damp and mildew.

Nathan had started cleaning the work and had already found a section of it which was peeling badly. It was going to be a testing job but he liked that. Even so, he couldn't quite relax into it. First, there was the instruction from Timothy to keep an eye on Hannah which, frankly, wasn't easy. Increasingly it didn't feel right either. Then there was this ridiculous situation she'd got herself into over Esther's boyfriend. How absurd to have to play-act some kind of romantic entanglement. But perhaps more than anything, it was the atmosphere at the abbey; something about the place made him uneasy.

'So let me get this straight,' he'd said to Hannah before they'd gone over for cocktails the other night. 'You're saying that this Jemma woman died in a fire in a Garden House down by the pool, after a party where they'd all drunk too much. And she was engaged to this Raff bloke. *And* she was the sister of Esther's PA. *And* she was Esther's best friend?'

'Yes.'

'It all sounds horribly incestuous. And she was in that place all alone *and* it was supposed to be an accident?'

'Yes.'

'Doesn't that strike you as suspicious?'

Hannah fiddled with one of her pendulous earrings. 'Well, yes actually. Of course, it had crossed my mind.'

'Was there an investigation? There must have been if there was a death.'

'I looked in the local papers but they didn't say much. It was kind of glossed over.'

'Famous local celebrity being treated with kid gloves?'

'Possibly. I suspect… well, whatever. Look, we need to go.'

She'd bustled away then and over to the house and there hadn't been an opportunity to discuss it again. Indeed, Hannah had looked preoccupied and introspective at times for most of the evening, especially if she wasn't directly involved in the conversation. Later that night, after they'd parted, he wished he'd pressed her more. She suspected what? What was she not telling him? Did it have something to do with the other people who lived in the house? They were an odd lot in his opinion, all watching each other, as if waiting for someone else to make a slip, to put a foot wrong and give themselves away. At times you could have cut the atmosphere with a knife.

But Hannah had been a bit of a revelation. She had been easier to talk to, less prickly, and, God, she'd restored that painting well; that was a surprise. She was smart, he was beginning to realise. He had underrated her. And she brushed up well, no question. Those eyes of hers were striking, especially when she wasn't glaring at you: big and blue, an unusual dark blue. Though there had still been that high-chinned, obstinate line to her face and that frustrating air of self-sufficiency.

He frowned. She'd said it was *not easy here, taking calls.* Why wasn't it easy? They had phones, didn't they? The place was huge; they probably had several dotted about. The remark suggested her own unease, a concern which she seemed reluctant to admit to him. Maybe he should try and find out a bit more about these people she was living with. And about that fire. Daphne would know something about them probably. She would at least know how to find out. He'd give her a ring later.

*

June drifted inexorably on and the temperature continued to rise. Hannah couldn't use the heavily lined curtains to shut out the sunshine in the theatre – she needed the daylight to work by – but the heat was starting to make her skin crawl. It sapped her energy and made it harder to concentrate. She did switch on the air-conditioning units each morning but they were noisy

209

and inefficient, barely keeping the temperature within manageable limits.

More than a week had passed since the dinner party to which Nathan had been invited, though Hannah had been so busy she had given it little thought. She was aware only of time passing and her own personal race to stay ahead of the calendar. She had finished cleaning and preparing the Bellini a couple of days ago and was now mixing paint and slowly touching in the damage. The adhesive she had used to fix the panels appeared to have worked well so the ongoing restoration should prove unproblematic. The Amanda Jay painting had been reframed and Hannah had gone into town the previous afternoon and collected it from the shop. It stood against the stage again, a cheerful, bright image in marked contrast to the sombre, serious pictures which Esther now seemed to favour. While in town, Hannah had taken the opportunity to ring Oxford. If she didn't keep Timothy abreast of her progress, Nathan undoubtedly would. The man would probably turn up again one of these days, unannounced, to check up on her.

Timothy proved unavailable however and Hannah spoke to Daphne instead.

'Hannah, how are you? It's good to hear from you. Is Nathan with you by any chance?'

'Nathan? No. Why? Should he be?'

'Oh… no reason. It's just that he said he'd had dinner with you at the abbey the other night. I just wondered.'

'He rang to tell you?'

'Yes. Well, not just that, of course. Just a quick call, a few days ago now. It doesn't matter.'

'What doesn't matter?'

'That he's not there with you.' A brief, heavy pause. 'Are you having problems there?'

'No. That's what I was ringing to tell Timothy: everything's going fine. Slowly but as expected.'

'Good. I'm relieved to hear it.'

By the time Hannah rang off she was convinced that Daphne was hiding something. She'd been on the point of saying something then changed her mind. What had Nathan been telling her?

At the end of the afternoon on the Wednesday, Hannah finished with the Bellini for the day, cleaned up her brushes, and went outside to get some fresh air and stretch her legs. She had only gone a few steps when Marielle came up and grabbed her hand.

'*Viens jouer à la pétanque avec moi*?' she said enthusiastically.

'I can't play now, Marielle. I'm still kind of busy.'

'But it's late already. You can't still be working.' She hesitated, eyes growing big, then looked around and spoke very softly. 'Are you still working on *The Lily Madonna*?'

Hannah bent down to her and whispered too. 'Yes.'

'Can I see Her?'

'No. Not till I've finished. And She's still a secret, remember?'

Marielle pulled a face and nodded. 'But you've got time for one game? Please?'

Hannah hesitated. Her eyes were tired and her shoulders ached.

'All right. But only one, then I have to get back to work. And you have to speak English, all right?'

'All right.'

They played and Marielle won again. Hannah suspected she always would but didn't care. The child's innocent company was a pleasure either way. Marielle insisted on walking back with her towards the theatre. She saw a butterfly

211

and chased it for a moment, then came back smiling. She turned in a pirouette, pretending to fly, and nearly fell over, then laughed. The girl had opened up a lot since their first encounter.

Their route took them near the top of the steps down to the lower gardens and the swimming pool. Hannah paused for a moment, looking down to where the sun glinted off the surface of the water. There was nobody there.

'Can you swim, Marielle?' said Hannah. 'I've never seen you in the pool.'

Marielle's expression darkened. She shook her head but said nothing.

'You can't swim? You should learn. It's a good thing to be able to do and it's fun.'

'I can swim. But I do not.'

The child looked down. Hannah followed her gaze. Marielle wasn't looking at the pool; she was staring at the pool house.

'Is it because of the fire?' Hannah said gently. She switched to French. 'It must have been very upsetting for you, seeing the building afterwards and hearing what happened.'

'It was horrible.' The girl's brow furrowed but she still stared down. 'Big flames and so hot. It made your skin feel like it was on fire. It was…' She rubbed a hand up each arm as if she could still feel it even now.

'So you saw the fire, Marielle? Were you out here when it happened?'

The child shrugged her skinny shoulders and shook her head again. Then, before Hannah could even register the movement, she'd gone, running off back the way they'd come.

Was it true or was it just the girl's vivid imagination? Did she really see the fire close up like that? It was unlikely that Claudine and Pietro would have let her stay out that late at

212

night. Assuming they knew, of course. Marielle seemed to slip in and out of their house at will, like a phantom.

Hannah frowned and returned to the theatre.

Half an hour later, with the door locked, she was picking away at *The Lily Madonna* again, Ella Fitzgerald singing in her ears.

*

Somehow or other, Raff had missed lunch. Probably, he reflected, because he'd had breakfast late. Very late in fact, stealing into Claudine's kitchen when she wasn't there and taking some croissants and brioches to eat back in the studio. Now he was starving again and it was only just after six. There was an age to wait till the evening buffet was put out. He wandered across to the house again and put his head round the kitchen door. Claudine was there, preparing vegetables at the worktop. He went in anyway.

'Claudine, *chérie*, have you got something satisfying to fill this hole I've got in my stomach?' He put his arm round the back of her broad waist and pushed up against her. 'Tell me you have. I'm absolutely starving and you're the only one who can save me.'

She pushed him off, brandishing the knife.

'Mister Raff, stop doing this. You should eat at meal times. You are always stealing from my kitchen.'

'Stealing is a very strong word, Claudine.' He put on his most appealing expression. 'You wouldn't want me to go hungry, would you? Please tell me I can have a sandwich? Please?'

She relented with a grudging smile; she usually did when he sweet-talked her. She made him a brie sandwich but complained about him all the while.

'You are my saviour,' he assured her, waving the baguette

213

at her with a beaming smile, and he walked back to the studio, eating it.

When he got there, Nathan was knocking on the door.

'There's no-one in there,' Raff said. 'Can't get the staff these days. A few centuries ago I'd have had apprentices there, churning out canvases ready for me to sign. Still, come in.'

He pushed the door back.

'Thanks.' Nathan walked in, then glanced back at him. 'But where would be the fun in that?'

'In what?'

'Having apprentices to paint the canvases.'

Raff laughed. 'Oh that. I dunno. Moral support maybe or people I could boss about. Just think how many paintings you could produce. I might actually earn some real money.'

Nathan looked round.

'Nice studio,' he remarked. 'Good light.'

'Thanks. Yeah. Too much light sometimes at this time of year.'

'I can imagine.' Nathan wandered closer to the easel, studying the painting on it. 'Do you have difficulty earning a living from it then?'

'Who doesn't?' Raff came to stand beside him. He waited. 'That's Pietro, our gardener and handyman. Also the husband of our housekeeper. I'm working from sketches I did of him. Can't get him to pose properly for me.'

'Great subject. He looks like a bit of a character. How long have you been working on it?'

'Days. Maybe a week now.'

Raff stared at the painting. He wasn't really happy with it yet but he wasn't going to admit that to this bloke. He'd come to the conclusion years ago that the artists who were the most successful were the ones who told everyone how bloody brilliant they were. He'd decided never to tell punters about his artistic insecurities ever again.

Raff finished his sandwich and ushered Nathan to the rack in the corner and began pulling out canvases as he had done for Hannah. Nathan made a few polite remarks then eased away.

'So you're not in the market for a painting then.' Raff straightened up and looked at him accusingly. 'I'm wondering why you called.'

'You invited me. And I was curious to see your studio. I like looking at paintings.'

'I see. I guess I should be used to it by now. The curiosity and the total lack of interest in buying any.' Raff pushed the canvases back savagely.

'Hey, I never said I wanted to buy a picture. I don't make that much money. I just work on expensive paintings. I don't have the spare to buy them myself. I drive a Ford Escort.'

Raff's eyes narrowed. 'Is that a dig? Yes, I know I drive a fancy car. A bequest. I decided to treat myself.'

'And why not?'

Raff wandered grumpily back into the centre of the studio.

'Anyway, my paintings aren't that expensive. Not like the stuff Esther buys. The money she must waste. My God, if I had that sort of money, I wouldn't buy the crap she does.'

'What would you buy?'

'I dunno. A Cézanne if I could. Or a Manet. Nah, they'd be in another league again. Maybe a Dechansay. Hannah's father's paintings are expensive but not that expensive. Have you seen any?'

'No, not yet.'

Raff nodded slowly, eyeing him up. 'I must say, Hannah kept her relationship with you pretty quiet.'

'We've only just started dating. I haven't known her long.'

'Think it'll last, do you?'

215

Nathan frowned. 'That's an odd question. How can you tell when you first start dating? More to the point, why do you care?'

'I might be interested in picking up the pieces when you dump her, ever thought of that?'

Nathan laughed. He waved a hand to embrace the studio. 'Does this give you time to have a relationship yourself? I imagine it's pretty full on, following your muse, burning the midnight candle?'

Raff walked across to the cupboard and picked up a half full bottle of red wine.

'Fancy a glass?'

'No thanks. I'm taking Hannah out for a meal.'

Raff poured some wine into a glass and came back. He drank a mouthful and looked at Nathan speculatively.

'I've had relationships. My last one ended in tragedy. I imagine you've heard about the fire?'

'Yes. Hannah mentioned it. That must have been really tough on you. I'm sorry.'

Raff acknowledged the remark with a nod and drank more wine.

'Has Sara worked here a long time too?'

'Yeah. A few years.'

'Were she and Jemma much alike? I knew a couple of sisters once. They weren't twins but, God, they were alike. Irritatingly so.'

Raff grinned. 'You dated one of them did you? Yeah, sisters are tricky, I always think. Jemma and Sara...' He shook his head. 'They didn't have much in common. Didn't stop them ganging up on you though when it suited.'

'Yep, that's what I found too.' Nathan glanced at his watch. 'I suppose I'd better leave you to your work.'

'There's no hurry.' Raff fixed Nathan with a shrewd and

penetrating gaze. 'It's not obvious, you know, you and Hannah.'

'In what way?'

'She doesn't say a lot about herself. Quite guarded, in fact. And she works all hours from what I can see.'

'You're suggesting I don't?'

Raff shrugged. 'I just don't see you as a couple. Do you have much in common?'

'I'm working on finding out.' Nathan raised his eyebrows. 'You'll forgive me if I don't make a point of letting you know first?'

Raff took another drink. 'Lucky you turned up when you did though. Esther was getting pretty hairy there about Hannah and David. Thought she'd go pop before long. You know the old adage about hell having no fury like…'

'A woman scorned.'

'Exactly. Good timing Nathan.'

'Thank you. Wish I could say I'd planned it then. Anyway, thanks for showing me round. I'd better go.'

Raff watched Nathan walk to the door and leave, shutting it behind him. He stayed where he was and slowly finished the wine. It occurred to him that Hannah and Nathan did have one thing in common: they both asked a lot of questions about Jemma and the fire. Why was that?

*

'I told you it'd be better if I rang you.' Hannah looked across at Nathan accusingly.

'Yes, but you didn't. Anyway, Rick and Mandy told me about an open-air concert in town tonight. It's midsummer and that's the way the French celebrate it so it seemed like a perfect night to go out.' He paused and returned the accusing look. 'Maybe you've been working too hard to notice: you know, all

217

the sunshine and the long summer days?'

They had just left the abbey on foot, walking through the woods to Tourbelle, Nathan's arm casually slung round Hannah's shoulders in case they were being watched. The evening sunshine was still warm and the cicadas were in good voice.

Nathan had rung that morning and Sara had come across to the theatre specially to find Hannah who took the call in the morning room, trying to sound affectionate, coy even, just in case anyone was listening in.

'How could you possibly accuse me of working too hard?' she protested. 'Isn't that why Timothy sent you here: to make sure I wasn't skiving?'

'Don't be ridiculous.'

'We're out of sight of the camera now. You can let me go.'

He let his arm drop and they moved apart.

'There's no need to sound so indignant,' he remarked. 'Can I remind you that it was your idea to fake a romance?'

'I know.'

They reached the shrine. Nathan didn't ask what it was and Hannah didn't bother to tell him. They continued walking in silence.

Tourbelle La Vierge was busy. It was nearly seven-thirty when they got there and all the restaurants round the edge of the square looked full. The square itself had been set up with a stage and microphones and rows of temporary seating.

'I guess I should have thought to make a reservation,' said Nathan, glancing at the restaurants.

'The out of the way places won't be so busy. I know somewhere.'

Hannah led them down one of the side streets to a small place called Chez Niccolo. It had two tables out on the pavement – which were both occupied – and a long, narrow interior.

'This is a good place,' said Hannah.

Nathan peered through the window. 'It looks very French.'

'That's because we're in France. Don't be afraid. I speak the language, remember?'

She pushed the door open and he followed her in. They were shown to a table at the rear where double doors stood open onto a tiny courtyard shaded by a plum tree. A lion's head set in the wall spewed water into a stone bowl below, producing a pleasing tinkling sound.

Nathan drank Perrier and Hannah sipped a Kir while they studied the menu. The specials were written on a large chalk board, brought over and left propped up against the door by the waitress. Hannah had to translate some of the menu for Nathan who ended up staying safe and choosing a steak; Hannah went for a fish pie, the speciality of the house, and they ordered a carafe of the house red wine. After some negotiation, they agreed to share a side salad.

She looked round appreciatively. 'I like this place. It's real. Family run. A proper French restaurant.'

Nathan regarded her thoughtfully. 'Do you consider yourself English or French?'

She shrugged. 'English I guess. I was born in England and grew up there. But I can't deny that part of me feels French too. Have you been to France much before?'

'A couple of holidays and a couple of work visits. I've never mastered the language though, as you've already realised. I don't do languages.'

'My father spoke French to me a lot. He wanted me to speak it.'

'Are you close?'

She thought for a moment. 'Not really. Are you close to your mother?'

'Yes.'

Hannah waited but he was pouring wine into each of their glasses and offered nothing more.

'What's she like? Do you follow after her?'

'Maybe. She's the reason I'm an art conservator. She used to take me to galleries and museums. She loves art and talked about it a lot. Her passion got me interested.' He hesitated. 'Were you close to your mother?'

She frowned. 'Yes, sort of.' Was she? It didn't come close to describing their complicated relationship.

'You must miss her.'

'I do. A lot. I didn't realise...' Tears threatened and she took a sip of wine, refusing to look at him, trying to get it under control.

'It's surprising what you learn about people when they aren't there any more,' said Nathan. 'Or maybe what you learn about yourself.' He paused. 'What was she like, your mother?'

'Like?' The question caught her off guard. She thought for a moment. 'She was a brilliant pianist. Could play anything. She loved music. And she was very devout, a keen church-goer.' She paused. There had been so much more to her mum than that but she'd only recently realised that she'd never thought enough about it. 'She was very good at chess but always let me win. In fact she let me win most games: draughts; snap; Monopoly. And she wore a lot of dark colours.'

He nodded slowly. 'Which is why you wear bright ones.'

'I suppose so. That's a dig, isn't it?'

'No, just an observation. It's not hard to see where you get the art thing from.'

'No.'

The food arrived and they lapsed into silence while they

ate. Hannah found herself thinking about her mother, about the days she'd spent sitting with her at the care home, trying to find subjects to talk about that would get a reaction, anything to strike a chord. Sometimes the most surprising things had made her mum smile. Hannah wished she'd known her better.

Nathan finished first and picked up his wine glass. Hannah felt him watching her as she ate.

'I was curious about your housemates after that dinner,' he remarked. 'So I made a few enquiries.'

'Really? Why?' She waved her fork at the bowl of side salad. 'Don't you want any more?'

He shook his head and she forked the last leaves of rocket onto her plate.

'The fire scenario just seems so suspicious,' he said. 'You said so yourself. Inevitably, you wonder if it was started intentionally.'

Hannah finished chewing, put the cutlery down and picked up her wine glass.

'So what did you find out?'

'Not a huge amount, I'm afraid. Jemma and Esther met at drama school. Esther was noticed early on, was given good parts, on stage and in film, and quickly became lauded and well-known. Jemma's career is less documented: a bit of stage work and a few television roles; a couple of indifferent, low budget films. Adverts too. David has been quite successful, mostly in action movies, thrillers, that kind of thing.'

'David told me much the same thing about Jemma.'

'You discussed her with him?'

'Not exactly. I asked him what she was like. A difficult character apparently. Had a kind of charming way with her but fell out with people.' Hannah glanced round to see if anyone was close enough to hear. She dropped her voice. 'She crowded Esther, hoping to use the reflected glory to propel her

221

own career.'

'Interesting. But it doesn't sound as if it did her much good. She was never more than a small part player. According to Daphne anyway. I got her on the case. She loves doing things like that: scouring libraries, checking magazines, that kind of thing.'

'Ah, that explains it then.'

'Explains what?'

'Daphne fretting over if I was all right when I rang earlier in the week.'

'You actually rang Oxford? I'm amazed.'

'I thought I'd better give a progress report. But Timothy wasn't there.'

The waitress came to clear the plates and offered dessert. Nathan opted for an espresso and Hannah refused anything more.

She sat back, cradling her wine glass. 'So you think the fire was deliberate? It does seem strange that it was barely reported in the press.'

'Yes. But also the set up in the abbey feels toxic. Don't you feel it too? I called in at Raff's studio before meeting you. He made a point of saying how fortunate it was that I arrived when I did, that Esther's jealousy was a dangerous thing. You saw that for yourself. Suppose Esther found out that Jemma had been having a fling with David?'

Hannah pulled a face but Nathan's coffee arrived and she waited for the waitress to go before speaking.

'And she killed Jemma in an attack of jealous rage, you mean? According to Raff, they'd all drunk too much and had lit a load of candles. Esther was the last to leave and blames herself for leaving Jemma alone.' She paused and sipped the last of her wine thoughtfully. 'She certainly behaves as if she's haunted by it. Except I don't go for her guilt-trip thing. I get the feeling she turns it on and off. She's acting all the time.'

'That was my impression too.'

He divided the remaining wine between their glasses.

Hannah leaned forward. 'There's something I saw that night of the dinner after seeing you off. I wonder if it's significant.'

'What?'

'I walked through the gardens to get back and passed near Raff's studio. Esther was just leaving. It sounded like they'd had an argument. She was begging him not to give her away and promised him a cheque the next day.'

'Blackmail.'

'It sounded like it. Maybe he knows what she did that night.'

'Which is why she lets him stay on here, because he's got a hold on her. Why the hell otherwise would she put up with him, basically letting him sponge off her?'

'It's possible. But if you're going down that route, perhaps they all had reasons to start that fire. Raff admits to having had a row with Jemma that night. That's why he walked off and left her. He said they argued over a visit to England for his mum's sixtieth. But maybe he knew she'd had an affair with someone and he came back and lit the fire himself. And then there's Sara: she and Jemma didn't get on either apparently.'

'Typical sisters, from what Raff said.'

'Though that's not exactly motive, is it? I don't get on very well with my sister but I wouldn't dream of setting fire to her. And not forgetting here that our version of events has come from the very people who have something to hide. We've no idea how much of it is true.' She paused. 'Except from David. He had no motive.'

'Why should David be innocent?' Nathan gave her a withering look. 'Because he's handsome? If he'd had an affair

223

with Jemma but wanted to end it and she didn't... Or maybe she was threatening to tell Esther? That would give him motive.'

Hannah sat back and picked up her wine glass, shaking her head. 'We've no reason to suppose he had an affair with Jemma.'

'He seems to know a lot about her.'

'She lived here half the time. We're getting carried away and you've read too many thrillers. It's all speculation. They're just a dysfunctional bunch, acting up all the time. They like to make scenes and strike poses. I'm not sure it means anything.'

They sat for several minutes, finishing the last of the wine. Nathan regarded her thoughtfully.

'I don't think you're taking this seriously enough, Hannah.' He drained the glass and leaned forward as he put it down. 'It may not be play-acting. There might be a murderer at the abbey and you should be careful. You don't know what might provoke them to do it again. No, don't scoff. I'm serious.'

Hannah frowned. She became aware of music drifting in through the open doors. The concert had started in the square.

'We should go,' she said. She glanced at the bill that had been left on the table and pulled some money out of her purse, dropping it on top. 'That's my half, including the tip.'

Chapter 18

Sunday had brought one of their spectacular storms: menacing black clouds, heart-stopping thunder and the sky rent by the dazzle of forked lightning. Then the rain, hellbent, pounding, its hammering intent reverberating off every section of roof in the house. To Esther, the storms sometimes felt apocalyptic. She found them unnerving, but David's presence always reassured her. When he was in the house, calm and unflappable, their threat seemed diminished. The upside was that the world outside looked cleansed afterwards, the dust and grime washed away. Everything sparkled. The downside was that, when the sunshine reappeared and the heat rose and everything dried out, the humidity rose also.

Sitting on one of the rattan chairs in the garth late on the Monday afternoon, Esther fanned herself languidly, feeling clammy. David sat nearby. The humidity didn't seem to bother him. He was reading a script he'd been sent.

'Is it any good?' she enquired.

He looked up slowly as if dragging himself back to the present.

'It's got potential.'

There was a jug of iced Pimm's on the low table with a cloth thrown over the top to stop the flies going in. She leaned forward, took a glass from the tray and poured herself a generous measure.

'Do you want one, darling?'

'Uhuh. Thanks.' He barely looked up.

She poured one for him and sipped her own, then took a cocktail stick from the saucer on the table and stabbed at a piece of kiwi fruit floating in her glass. She popped it in her mouth and chewed on it absently.

'Have you had any more thoughts about coming over to L.A. with me?' she said.

David looked up again and let the script lie flat on his lap. He picked up his glass and took a mouthful.

'I don't think there's any point at the moment.'

'But I thought you wanted to see that producer? You said there were a couple of other projects worth exploring too.'

'Sam's gone away; won't be back for three or four weeks apparently. Anyway, my agent said to hold off a bit longer. He's got something else that might interest me. He's going to send me the script.'

'Oh, I see. Still, you could come over with me anyway. Just to keep me company.'

Raff appeared at the far corner of the house and, seeing them sitting in the garth, walked over to join them. Though now dressed, he had clearly been swimming for he was still damp, his loose cotton shirt and shorts both sticking to him, his hair sticking up in spikes after being roughly towelled dry.

'Lovely day,' he remarked. He saw the jug. 'Great, Pimm's. I could do with some of that.'

He leaned over and poured himself a glass.

'Does it ever occur to you that we might prefer not to have your company?' David said.

'No,' said Raff with a genial smile. 'I can't imagine how that could be.' He sat down on one of the vacant rattan chairs.

Esther felt irritated too; she had been psyching herself up to ask David about this trip.

'Shouldn't you be working?' she said peevishly.

'I needed a break, needed to recharge the creative engine.' He took a long draught of the cocktail. 'You know how it is.'

Sara emerged through a door into the cloister and walked briskly across the courtyard to join them.

'Esther, I've just had a phone call from that magazine I told you about? The one that's been chasing. They want an interview about the new film with a view to putting it in the October issue. It comes out in September, three weeks before the première. I promised I'd get back to them today. Copy time is tight.' Sara was hugging the huge desktop diary she still used to track all Esther's engagements. She opened it at the page marker and ran a finger down the sheet. 'You could fit it in next week when you're in L.A. I've pencilled in the Tuesday afternoon. They're offering a longer piece than most of the others so I thought it was worth giving them a separate slot.'

'Fine.' Esther looked up at her with a frown. 'It's the Monday I'm doing most of the publicity interviews isn't it?' These things were so tedious; they all merged into one in her mind.

'Yes. There's a photo shoot with the other principals that afternoon too. Shall I confirm with the magazine then?'

Esther sighed. 'Yes, you better had.'

Raff was pouring another glass of Pimm's. 'Have a drink with us, Sara,' he said, and held it out. 'Sit for a moment. Relax. You look strung out.'

Sara looked at the glass, then glanced at Esther and David. 'No, I…'

David waved a hand towards the remaining chairs. 'Take a seat, Sara. You have as much right to be here as Raff.' He flicked the man a malevolent glance. 'More.'

'Yes Sara, do join us for a few minutes.' Esther smiled. 'I'm sure the phone call can wait. Since you're here, there was something I wanted to mention.'

'All right. Thank you.' Sara took the glass and sat down. She was the only one without sunglasses and she screwed her eyes up against the bright light.

'I've been thinking it would be good to have a little… celebration of my new paintings when they've been restored. A sort of exhibition of them, a bit of a social event.' Esther turned to look at David. 'What do you think darling?'

'I'm not sure. Would that make a good social event? It'd perhaps be the kind of thing to do in the winter. This time of year, people want to be outside, not indoors studying paintings.'

'Yes, I suppose I can see that. I'm not even sure when they're going to be finished anyway. I hardly see Hannah and when I do I can't pin her down.'

'So what do you all think about Hannah and this Nathan guy?' Raff looked round, taking them all in with his gaze, one by one. 'I really don't see them as new lovers.'

David frowned. 'What makes you say that?'

'The way they behave. He turned up at my studio the other day. He'd come to take Hannah out for a meal and came to see me first. I asked him about her. His attitude didn't feel right. Cool. And they're not seeing much of each other, are they? There's no hot, sweaty desperation about them.'

'Really Raff,' said Esther with an amused smile. 'They aren't eighteen. And he was taking her out for a meal so they're obviously dating.'

'Perhaps you shouldn't judge them by your own standards, Raff,' said Sara.

'Look, I happened to be around when they came back from town later that night and I saw her walk with him back to his car.'

'You mean you followed them?' Sara sounded shocked.

'Yes. And you know what: there was no parting kiss. Not even a hug. A total lack of physical contact. What kind of a new relationship is that?'

They were all silent for a couple of minutes, absorbing this information.

'But why would they pretend?' said Sara.

'I don't know.' Raff shrugged with the suggestion of a smile. He put his empty glass down on the table and stood up. 'I just thought you ought to be aware. No-one's ever what they seem, are they? Maybe they're from MI6. They both ask a lot of questions, it seems to me.' He paused for emphasis. 'Anyone got any dark secrets?' The smile became broader and he left, heading back into the house.

'What did your sister ever see in that man, Sara?' remarked David with disgust.

Sara was frowning but didn't reply. She put her glass down, grabbed the diary, and got to her feet too.

'I'd better get on and return that call,' she said. 'By the way, your plane tickets have come through for Friday, Esther. Excuse me.'

Esther waited until Sara was back in the house.

'What do you make of all that?'

'What? The stuff Raff came out with?' David snorted. 'Nothing. He just likes to make a scene and stir us up. Ignore him. I do.'

She steeled herself. 'But what do you think of Hannah darling?'

David flicked her a look she couldn't read with those infuriating sunglasses on.

'I think she's come to do a job for you and she seems to be doing it well. What she does or doesn't do with Nathan is nothing to do with us. I quite liked the guy.'

It wasn't an answer that told her what she needed to know,

but it was all she was going to get. David had picked up his script again.

'I was thinking I might go and see Gerald and Sonia while you're away,' he remarked casually. 'Get some golf in. He's got that great course just down the road if you remember and he keeps inviting me.'

Esther relaxed a little. 'Fine darling. Good idea.' At least he wouldn't be here with Hannah.

'If you want to have some more friends over,' David added. 'Why don't we have a barbecue, make a proper event of it down by the pool the way we used to?'

'No.' Esther stared at him, aghast. 'No, David, I couldn't. Not down there. How could you even suggest such a thing?'

David removed his sunglasses, pushing them up onto the top of his head. He fixed her with his brown eyes.

'Darling, it's time we put it behind us. Having another barbecue there will draw a line under it. It'll be a fresh start.' He reached out and squeezed her hand. 'We both need that; you know we do. We could plan it for July, after we both get back. Don't answer now; think about it.'

He pulled his sunglasses back down and began to read again.

Esther stared at him then stared out into the garden. She was shocked at the suggestion, upset that he didn't understand. She finished her cocktail, hardly tasting it, then stood up and went inside.

She thought of going to see Hannah in the theatre, trying to pin her down as to when she would finish but decided against it, especially after what Raff had said. She didn't want to be questioned and scrutinised. What kind of questions were they asking, those two? She drifted into her library instead and sat for a while with the little statue of the Madonna in front of her. Now and then her gaze strayed to the photograph of herself with Jemma. In the end she got up and put it in a drawer. She should have done it long ago.

Restless, she got up again and headed out to see Guillaume. Did he know about the questions these people were asking and was he keeping track of them? He was usually so good at keeping a tight rein on their visitors. It wasn't as though she could get rid of Hannah now. It was too late to bring someone else in and they might be no better anyway. What about that insolent visitor they'd had last year, a friend of a friend? He'd kept asking impertinent questions too. Guillaume said he'd give the man a warning. That guy had ended up with a broken arm. Esther never asked how. She didn't want to know.

*

Esther and David both went away on the Friday and Hannah was relieved. Almost immediately the atmosphere in the abbey subtly changed too. Claudine retreated back into terse efficiency and, though there were few people there, the passages seemed to echo with every footstep. Nothing much changed for Hannah: she spent most of her time in the theatre, working.

She had finished touching in the damaged paint on the Bellini and spent the Friday afternoon putting protective layers of varnish on it. That just left one painting to work on: the newly relined School of Rembrandt picture, *Christ Receiving the Holy Spirit*. She checked her initial assessment. The varnish on it was very dark – made worse by ingrained dirt – and obscured the details and flattened the picture plane. There was still some attention needed around the hole in the original canvas but it mostly looked like a straightforward clean-up job. How long was that going to take her? Long enough to finish the work needed on *The Lily Madonna*? It seemed unlikely.

The whole thing had got out of control.

Passing the phone box in the town square on the Saturday morning, she rang Sylvie on impulse, keen to talk about it. Sylvie was at her home number and answered quickly.

'Hannah? It's good to hear from you. I was going to ring you but you didn't leave a number where I could reach you – which is typical of you, I might add. And that actress you're working for is clearly ex-directory. Couldn't find the number anywhere. Come on, I've been itching to know. What's happening with that painting? What did you decide to do?'

'I'm trying to see a bit more of it.'

'A bit more of it how?'

'I've been teasing off more of the gesso so I can see if our suspicions were right and there's a medieval painting under there.'

In fact the gesso revealed in the accident had now all gone. With solvent and scalpel, Hannah had started removing some of the surface painting too, desperate to see what lay beneath.

'Ye–es,' said Sylvie in the tone of an indulgent parent, 'but we weren't sure the picture underneath wasn't badly damaged were we?'

'I think it'll be OK,' said Hannah brightly. 'I do really.'

Sylvie grunted. 'So basically you're just winging it, yes? Or did you get permission to do this?'

'Not exactly.'

'*Ciel*, Hannah. OK, so what have you seen so far? Do you think it is medieval? I mean, is it worth it? Are you sure you're doing the right thing?'

'It's too soon to say. I need to do a bit more to be certain.' She didn't want to admit it to Sylvie but the fragments of the work she could glimpse below took her breath away. That's what kept her going. She had a suspicion that a queen had been dressed in sackcloth. Assuming it was complete…

'You're letting that picture take you over,' Sylvie said impatiently.

Hannah closed the call, thinking she probably shouldn't have rung. Her friend was right of course. She had already reached the point when it was going to be difficult, if not impossible, to restore the familiar image.

You're on a quest for redemption, her mother would have said.

And maybe she'd have been right.

On the Saturday afternoon, Nathan rang again. Hannah was occupied with the icon when Sara came knocking impatiently at the locked theatre door to tell her. They walked back to the house together.

'I'm surprised we haven't seen Nathan here more,' Sara remarked.

'Well, we're both very busy, trying to get our work done.' Hannah smiled conspiratorially. 'Our boss likes to keep us on our toes.'

'It doesn't stop you from ringing him though. Nathan, that is. I mean, if you want to ring, you only have to say.'

'Thank you. But when I ring him I usually do it from town. It seems less of an imposition.'

Sara raised her eyebrows. 'And more private?'

'Well, yes.'

'I understand. But, you know, with Esther and David away, and now Raff away for the weekend, there's hardly anyone here to disturb you.'

'Raff's gone away too?'

Sara emitted a satisfied sigh and offered one of her rare smiles. 'Yes, he's gone to stay with friends. Some party or other. He's not back till Sunday. Isn't that wonderful?'

Hannah smiled politely.

She took the call in the morning room as usual.

'Nathan,' she said brightly. 'I thought we'd agreed I'd ring you. It's a shame to bother Sara and make her have to come and find me.'

'But I so wanted to talk to you. I like to know how you are, what you're doing.'

'I know, but it's not easy here. I'm very busy.'

There was a faint sound on the line, hard to identify, but they both heard it and neither spoke for a few seconds, listening. It was silent again.

'How's the mural coming on?' said Hannah.

'Slowly. The damp had really got to it. It was in a state. But I've started infill painting now. If they'd left it much longer, there wouldn't have been much mural to restore. Look, Hannah, when can I see you? It feels like ages.'

'I know what you mean, Nathan. I'd love to see you too.'

'Great. What about tonight?'

A moment's hesitation. 'It's a bit short notice, Nathan. Could we make it tomorrow night instead? I could meet you in town?'

This time there was silence his end. 'All right. If that's what you want.'

They fixed a time and a place and before she closed the call, Hannah heard the familiar click as Sara replaced her receiver.

*

Hannah had never broken into anywhere in her life, though she did sneak into her mother's bedroom a few times when she was a child. In the early days of her parent's separation, her mother received several letters from Eric, but, other than telling the girls that their father sent his love, she never told them what else they contained. Not that Hannah's sister, Elizabeth, seemed to care unduly, but Hannah did. She missed him. She

234

wanted to know when he was coming back. After all, her mother kept insisting that he was coming back.

So Hannah used to wait until her mother was occupied teaching one of her late afternoon piano lessons, then go into her bedroom and look through her mother's bedside cabinet. That's where she always put his letters. Then, after a while, Hannah stopped doing it. The letters were disappointing, just vague apologies and excuses and references to things Hannah didn't understand. There was nothing about him coming back. In the end, the letters stopped too.

Standing by the back door, looking out over the eastern grounds where Raff's studio nestled among the shrubs and trees, it wasn't a promising experience to draw on. But Raff had gone away and this was an opportunity she couldn't resist. Anyway, she wasn't going to break in exactly: she knew where the key was. Since the meal with Nathan, their conversation had played through her mind several times. She might have disdained his theories but the idea that there was more to the fire than a simple accident refused to be dismissed. She kept coming back to Esther and the apparent blackmail. But if Raff was blackmailing her, he needed something concrete to do it with; nobody who knew him would take him at his word. And if Raff did have something on Esther – perhaps a recording of something she'd said in a moment of weakness or some kind of ill-advised letter – it had to be in his studio. It was his territory alone and neither Claudine nor either of her helpers ever went in there to clean.

The grounds looked deserted. It was half past eight and still light. Sara usually ate at this time and should be safely in the dining room. Hannah slipped quickly along the main path then dodged left along the narrow track to his studio. She glanced round again, then found the loose stone, retrieved the key and let herself in.

Locking the door behind her, she pocketed the key, and caught her breath, surveying the room: cluttered, grubby, disordered. Where to start? Raff's work station – his easel and table and the chaise longue for his models – didn't offer much scope for hiding anything important. There was his drinks cupboard, but she'd seen that open and there were only glasses and half open packets of biscuits and nuts in there. But there was the plan chest and she started there, pulling the shallow drawers out one by one.

The top one held sheets of watercolour paper. The next was full of cartridge paper and coloured pastel papers. Carrying on down, she found sketch books and piles of loose drawings in charcoal and pastel, watercolours too on pieces of stretched paper, cut roughly from the painting board and presumably deemed not worth framing. There were thin boards of varying sizes for oil painting, some primed, some covered in canvas, and the lowest drawers held trays of pastel crayons, charcoal sticks and graphite pencils. No written documents. No cassette tapes. Nothing.

Hannah pushed all the drawers home and straightened up. Perhaps she should be looking for somewhere more secure and discreet. There was no desk but the man must keep some sort of paperwork. Receipts? Bills? Bank statements? Or maybe he spurned organisation of every kind. No. Raff's bohemian behaviour was largely an act. He had a lot in common with Esther.

There was the big pine wardrobe against the wall. It wasn't remotely discreet but perhaps she was looking at it the wrong way. If Raff had something on Esther, he'd have to put it somewhere obscure, otherwise it would be all too easy for Guillaume – as Esther's devoted security guard – to search the studio on her behalf and get her out of trouble. If she trusted Guillaume with her secrets, that is.

It was an old-fashioned men's wardrobe with a hanging area on the left where a couple of paint smeared oversized shirts hung as well as a thick, zip fronted jacket. A full-length satin wrap dangled and swayed from a coat hanger, presumably for use by Raff's life models. Bundled at the bottom of the hanging area were a couple of warm blankets, a sheet and a pillow. Hannah pushed her hand down behind them but there was nothing hidden there. Shelves and drawers filled the right-hand side. A jumble of hats had been rammed onto the top shelf along with some scarves. The next shelf down held loosely folded fringed stoles in gaudy, metallic fabrics. There were other odds and ends Raff had collected, intriguing nonsense for his models to wear.

Finally Hannah found his paperwork and let out a strangled 'yes' of exultation: two shallow drawers at the bottom held all the usual bills and accounts. She kneeled down, pulled them out in turn and leafed through them. There were envelopes with letters still in them, scraps of notes and receipts, some clipped together, some rammed in haphazardly. But nothing unusual and certainly nothing incriminating that related to the fire in any way.

'Damn,' she muttered, glaring at the pile of papers from the second drawer, still spread out on the floor. She glanced at her watch. It was nearly half past nine and the light in the studio was fading fast. More to the point Sara would soon be out of the dining room again, if she wasn't already, and she often wandered in the gardens afterwards, smoking.

Hannah collected up the papers and tried to put them back the way they had been before, not that Raff would be likely to notice one way or the other. She got up, rubbing her knees, and looked round once more. Perhaps the whole idea was unfounded; she'd let her imagination run riot. And yet Raff's continued presence at the abbey did seem inexplicable, especially given the way he behaved. Perhaps he had a secure deposit box at a bank somewhere. She shook her head in the gathering gloom. Most unlikely. That cost money and didn't fit with the man.

Her gaze fell on three empty coffee mugs, abandoned on Raff's work table. Typical of him to just leave them there, to wait until he'd run out of clean ones before bothering to do anything about them. There was a chipped plate too with a fly buzzing round it. Hannah's eyes narrowed. She'd been approaching this the wrong way. Raff wouldn't hide something in a formal place; it would be among his art things or his paintings. She glanced over his table but there was nowhere to hide anything there and she'd already checked the plan chest.

There was a sound outside and Hannah froze. Voices, down on the main path, probably by the junction with the studio one. She listened harder but couldn't make out any words. It was Sara's voice though, and a man's. Guillaume's. Double damn. Did the man go round all the buildings at night checking them? Was he coming here next, dangling that ring of keys? She glanced round quickly: there was nowhere to hide. What kind of excuse could she come up with to explain what she was doing? Maybe she could say she'd lost something and thought she might have dropped it here. She put a hand to one ear. She could drop an earring then miraculously find it when Guillaume was with her. It wasn't good but it was the best she could do. She pushed an earring out and bent over to put it silently on the floor under the table.

She heard a laugh, Guillaume's, and a final few words. Now they'd parted. Hannah held her breath but no-one came to the door. She waited a few more minutes, then retrieved her earring. Now was the time to go while she still could.

Then she saw two watercolours hanging on the walls between an array of oil paintings. Something about one of them made her go across and take it down. It was a loose, impressionistic painting of a nude lying indolently on the chaise longue. It was surprisingly good but the frame was quite chunky for a watercolour. Hannah turned it round. The backing board had been fixed in with flexible tabs. Lots of artist did that so they could reuse the frame if the painting didn't sell. Raff hadn't bothered with sealing tape either which was lucky. She put the picture flat on the floor and eased the backing board off.

'Eureka,' she mouthed.

Producing her travel torch from her pocket, she shone it over the back of the picture. There were two envelopes secreted there. The first held two photographs and Hannah gasped as she pulled them out.

'Good God, Esther,' she murmured. 'What the hell were you thinking to let him take these?'

They were incredibly compromising, presumably taken during a night of passion and probably after a lot of alcohol. The second envelope held a handwritten letter, signed by Esther.

> *Raff darling,*
>
> *How can you turn your back on me like that? Haven't we given each other a lot of pleasure these last weeks? Why stop now? I can't bear the thought of these winter nights alone. Jemma will never know, Raff. She's away so much.*
>
> *Please darling, reconsider. For me. For us.*

So Raff did have a hold on Esther but it had nothing to do with the fire. David had been away or maybe they'd split up for a while and she had taken Raff as a lover. Hannah hadn't seen that coming. Maybe Raff had been a novelty back then; he might have been less irritating before he'd got a hold on her.

Hannah carefully replaced everything, trying to remember exactly how the envelopes had lain, then hung the painting back on the wall. She paused after she'd finished and looked round, checking she'd left nothing out of place, then made for the door.

Chapter 19

The following Sunday was the first of July. Driving to Tourbelle to meet up with Hannah, Nathan realised that he'd been in Provence more than a month already. He was surprised. Perhaps it was because his hosts were so easy and hospitable. They were happy for him to use their pool and the weather had made that a pleasing way to clear his head and loosen his muscles after a long day's work. The size of the mural was a challenge, making for awkward working positions but at least it was moving forward and he had started replacing the lost paint.

He parked the car and made for the square. Hannah was already there, standing in front of the church, head turned to her right to watch a busker who was playing guitar and singing a Jacques Brel song. She stood out as usual, this time wearing a blue and white striped blazer over a red top of some kind and white cropped trousers; the trainers had been ditched in favour of espadrilles. He called her name and she turned and smiled. It caught him slightly off guard. It was friendly, welcoming, a reflex smile he supposed. Getting closer he saw the familiar guarded look in her eyes.

'Am I late?' he said, glancing at his watch.

The church clock struck the half hour and Hannah smiled again.

'Apparently not. I was early. It's a fault of mine. Where

241

do you want to go? The restaurants aren't so crowded tonight. They're usually busier at lunchtimes on a Sunday.'

'Let's have a look at these in the square then.'

'The tourist restaurants?' she teased.

'Indulge me.'

They settled on Le Restaurant au Coin, nestled in the corner of the square, the tables on its outside terrace prettily laid with bright Provençal cloths. They found a table on the edge of it, flanked by a long trough of box hedging. The evening was sunny and warm and the busker still sang on the other side of the square. Nathan had no idea what he was singing about but the sound pleased him, perhaps because he couldn't understand it. It added to the relaxed atmosphere, the sense of being in a different world for a while. The menu, however, unlike in Niccolo's, was written in both English and French and that pleased him too.

They ordered food and both drank chilled Perrier while they waited for it to come.

'So you were busy last night?' said Nathan, unable to quell the sarcasm. 'Are you really living such a hectic life at the abbey? Or was it your night to wash your hair?'

Hannah's eyes narrowed. 'I wasn't aware that I was at your beck and call.'

'You were the one who asked me to pretend to date you. Doesn't that mean that we do in fact have to date? I was beginning to wonder if you'd finished and left.'

'Well yes, OK, you're right. Sorry. But you caught me on the hop.' She paused. 'Esther and David have both gone away. Separately apparently. And Raff's away this weekend too. He'll be back tonight I suppose. Anyway, I'd just found that out from Sara so I had a plan.'

'A plan?'

'Yes.' She glanced across at the nearest other diners. No-one was paying them any attention. 'I'd been thinking about our discussion about the fire and about Raff possibly blackmailing Esther. I thought, with Raff out of the way, it was an ideal opportunity to have a poke around his studio.'

'Are you crazy? I told you to be careful.'

'I was. I'm not an idiot.'

'That remains to be seen.'

She was glaring at him as their lasagnes arrived.

'I'd like a glass of the house red wine, please,' Nathan said to the waiter. 'You?'

Hannah nodded. 'Yes. For me too, thanks.'

Nathan waited for the waiter to be out of earshot.

'And was it worth it?' he said. 'Taking a foolish risk like that?'

'Indeed it was, I found out something quite interesting. But I guess you won't care since you don't think I should have been there anyway.'

He gave her a baleful look. 'Oh please. No games. What was so interesting?'

Hannah put a forkful of lasagne in her mouth, making him wait.

'Mm, good.' She leaned forward, dropping her voice. 'Esther *is* being blackmailed, but it's got nothing to do with the fire. She had a fling with Raff some time back and he's got pictures and a letter from her.'

'Good God. What on earth was the woman thinking?'

'I know. So we're back at square one. It doesn't prove Esther didn't start the fire but there's no reason to think she did it any more than anyone else.'

'Maybe not. Though she was cheating on David and on her best friend. And she does get insanely jealous.'

'True.' Hannah shrugged. 'I said they were all dysfunctional.'

They dropped the subject and ate. After a few minutes, Nathan paused and took a sip of wine. He looked across at Hannah. She was wearing teardrop-shaped earrings, long discs of red which swayed and spun as she ate.

'You're never tempted to dye your hair red any more?'

She gave him a withering look, then stopped eating and picked up her glass too.

'I was a teenager. It was a phase I was going through. Did you never have phases, never did anything that seemed a good idea at the time which made you cringe afterwards? Come on, you must have.'

'Maybe.'

'Such as?'

He carried on eating. She gave him an amused look then did the same.

'I did join a hiking club when I was a teenager,' he said. 'They met on a Sunday once a month. I did it because there was a young woman I fancied and I found out she was in it. Very sexy. The trouble was, no-one told me she was engaged to the guy running it. Big guy. Huge muscles. And I was a scrawny youth. To make it worse I fell off a rock on my first outing and twisted my ankle. Couldn't walk without crutches for weeks.'

Hannah laughed. 'Poor you. How embarrassing.'

'Tell me about it.'

They finished their main course and the waiter brought the dessert menus.

'I think I will,' said Hannah, studying hers. 'I'll have one of these ice-cream sundaes please.'

'I'll have a crème brûlée, thanks.'

They drank the last of their wine. The music had stopped; the busker had gone.

'I spoke to Timothy on Friday,' said Nathan. 'He wanted

to know where we were at.' He paused. 'Especially you. He's keen for the job to be finished. He was asking for details. Really Hannah, you should ring him more often.'

'I forget. I remember sometimes when it's not practical to do it and I forget when it is. Why can't he just wait for me to finish? I'm working as hard as I can.'

'He doesn't know you yet and, even if he did, he can't stop himself fussing. It's better just to go with the flow.'

'What did you tell him?'

'I said you were progressing well. Are you? Hell, I have no idea where you're at. If you'd only keep in touch. I don't want to have to lie for you.'

'I don't expect you to. There's nothing to lie about.' She frowned suddenly, so briefly he wondered if he'd imagined it, then it was gone. 'I've got one painting left to do. It might take a little while.'

'You're sure there's no problem? You're not hiding anything?'

'Why should I do that?'

'Your manner?' He shrugged. 'Forget it.'

Their desserts arrived and the subject was dropped. It wasn't till Hannah put down her spoon that she spoke again.

'Maybe the tension between Esther and Raff over their past is what makes the atmosphere at the abbey so fraught. And David hates Raff too, that's obvious. Maybe that's all it is. No sinister murder attempts. Nothing like that.'

'It wasn't an attempt. The woman died.'

'Yes, but it could have been an accident.'

'Is that what you think?'

'I'm not sure, but what do we actually know? Esther left Jemma alone, pretty smashed from the sounds of it, and there were candles lit all over the place. Everyone else had gone. If someone did it deliberately, it either had to be Esther and she's

245

lying, or someone else went back.'

'Exactly. But any of them could have done that. The problem is there's no way of knowing. It was the middle of the night. Everyone else would have been in bed.'

Hannah studied his face curiously. 'Don't tell me: you read murder mysteries and always have to try to guess whodunnit before the great reveal.'

'I do sometimes read murder mysteries,' he said defensively. 'I read a lot of things. It comes of being away from home a lot with time to kill. What do you read? The classics, I suppose? All very highbrow.'

'Not at all.' She grinned. 'In fact, I read anything that comes to hand. Cereal packets if necessary. And I do read the occasional whodunnit too.' The smile disappeared. 'But real life's different. I can't see who could have done this and it's not a book. We're letting our imagination go into overdrive.' She raised her eyebrows. 'Though I did panic last night when I heard Guillaume outside Raff's studio talking to Sara. I thought for a moment that he was going to walk in and visit some terrible retribution on me.'

'Guillaume? Doing his security rounds, I suppose.' Nathan thought about Guillaume, strong and aloof. He thought about those scars on the man's hands. He leaned forward suddenly. 'Look, you're right, it's not a book and it's not something to joke about either. I shouldn't have even brought the subject up. You mustn't go poking about again. We should forget about it; it's none of our business. Just do your work and go.'

'You're worried about me,' she teased.

'I don't want to have to explain to Timothy how you came to have a nasty accident.'

'I can see that might be embarrassing.'

'I'm not joking.'

She nodded slowly but her eyes had taken on a faraway look.

'Hannah?'

'Hm?'

'What is it?'

A brief shake of the head and an innocent look. 'Nothing. Do you want coffee or should we settle up and go?'

*

David returned to the abbey on the Friday of the following week but Esther had been persuaded to stay over a little longer in Los Angeles. The production company had lined up some extra interviews and appearances to promote her latest film.

'I think she's rather enjoying it,' he confided to Sara. 'Once she gets there it's always the same. She thinks she's happy being a recluse but really she loves the buzz of being in the thick of it. Always has. I wish I could persuade her to spend more time over there.'

'He thinks she affects all the reluctance to go,' Sara told Raff at dinner on the Saturday evening, reporting the conversation. 'Apparently her agent's fixed up a couple of meetings about new projects too.'

'And David hasn't flown out to join her?' queried Raff drily.

'I daresay she didn't encourage him,' Sara responded coolly. 'She's never one to share the limelight.'

'I thought maybe he was avoiding her. That would upset her.' He hesitated with a forkful of chicken casserole half way to his mouth. 'So where is our Hollywood hero tonight? Home alone or out and about, living the bachelor life? Or perhaps he's in the gym, working off all the extra carbs he's no doubt been devouring this last week, honing his temple of a body to perfection.' He rammed the chicken in his mouth and chewed with evident satisfaction.

'At least he makes an effort,' remarked Sara acidly. 'You'd do well to do a bit of honing yourself.'

'My body's already perfect.'

'Who told you that? Your latest fawning model?'

Raff speared a roast potato, looking at her pityingly. 'Ah, I detect jealousy. It's understandable. But you only have to say if you want to model for me you know.'

Sara made a noise expressing her disgust at the idea.

'No, you're probably right. It wouldn't work.'

They both ate in silence. Raff finished and sat back.

'I don't suppose you saw Guillaume going into my studio last weekend, did you?' he said.

'No. Why?'

'Just a thought. Ever since I got back, I've had the feeling that someone's been in there. One of the drawers was slightly open and stuff has been moved; I checked.'

She hesitated for the blink of an eye. 'Is something missing?'

'No. Odd, isn't it?

'Not really. What on earth would anyone want?'

'It wasn't you then?'

'Good God, no.' She paused and their eyes met. 'It might have been Hannah.'

'Yes, I thought that too.'

*

On the Sunday David turned up at Raff's studio in the afternoon, walking straight in, not bothering to knock. Raff was roughing out an idea for a painting on a large piece of cartridge paper, referring to some outdoor sketches he'd made. There was a pile of old farm machinery rusting by a ramshackle stone building on a nearby farm and he loved the

248

shapes they made but couldn't get the composition right. Feeling frustrated, he looked up as David strode in.

'Nice of you to call,' said Raff. 'But knocking always works for me.'

'That would suggest that you had some right to be here.'

Raff put down the pencil and turned on his stool to face his visitor. David's face shone with righteous indignation.

'My, you're sounding very belligerent today. Touch of indigestion, is it?'

'I'm so tired of your pseudo clever remarks,' said David. 'I've been thinking about this while I was away and I've come to a decision. I'm doing what I should have done ages ago: I'm telling you to leave. Pack up your stuff and find somewhere else to doss down. I'll give you a couple of weeks to sort it out and then you go.'

Raff raised his eyebrows. 'And this is what Esther wants?'

'Don't bring Esther into this. You abuse your position here and she's too soft-hearted to stand up to you. She feels guilty about Jemma and you use that. It's sickening. I know it's what she wants.'

'She told you that, did she?'

'As good as. And I'm not going to live here with you sponging off her forever.'

Raff nodded. 'Or else? There's always an "or else", isn't there?'

'Or else you'll know about it.'

'Ah. Duelling pistols at dawn. No, that would be for competitive suitors I think.'

'You can play around with words and joke all you want but it won't make any difference. I've made up my mind and you're going, whether you like it or not. I'll make sure of it.'

Raff nodded again. He needed to be careful here. The man was bigger than him and undoubtedly stronger. A good punch

249

and Raff thought he'd probably be having his jaw wired and feeding through a straw for several weeks.

David was watching him. He seemed to have decided that his message had gone home and turned to go.

'David.'

'What?'

'I don't think you should be too hasty. You've got a bit of a dilemma here. You see, I know about you and Jemma.'

David turned back, frowning. 'What? What about me and Jemma?'

'Well I suppose you were never going to come out and admit it.'

David's frown deepened; colour drained from his face. 'There's nothing to admit. Did Jemma say there was?'

'Jemma and I did have our differences, it's true, and we did have some spectacular rows but I thought the world of her and we did talk you know. I was shocked, I can tell you. Upset. Hell man, she was my fiancé. I mean, come on.' Raff sighed. 'Anyway it's all history now, isn't it. For me anyway. But I don't think you'd want what you did to get out, would you? I mean, what would your fans say? What would Esther say?'

David stared at him. 'You're bluffing. You can't prove that.'

'Care to risk that? But of course you probably didn't know that Jemma kept a diary. Just a small one with the odd note scribbled in here and there: special dates, moments of pleasure.' Raff paused. 'Arguments and upsets. All very interesting.'

'She wrote it all down?'

Raff shrugged. 'And what with the fire and people asking questions – still that lingering suspicion that it might have been started deliberately. Anyway, I'd keep your head down if I were you. Don't make waves. Just a thought.'

David clenched and unclenched his fists a couple of times, an expression of disbelief and disgust on his face. A minute later he was gone and Raff returned to his drawing. Presumably his marching orders had just been rescinded. Esther wouldn't have gone along with it anyway. Raff thought there was a pleasing symmetry about playing both sides off against each other. He had long since realised that scruples didn't put food on his plate or help him pay his bills. He smiled to himself. That thing about the diary had been an inspired bit of bluffing.

*

It was a new week and Hannah went back to work on the Rembrandt school painting, still lifting the thick old varnish from it. The days ticked by. She wouldn't rush, she told herself, no matter what pressures Timothy brought to bear. Try to rush a job like this and you ended up stripping the delicate upper paint layers off by mistake, the fine glazes which gave the picture its depth and life. Every painting had to be treated properly; there was professional pride at stake. Of course there was *The Lily Madonna* to consider too. It was going to be a balancing act, trying to get the icon presentable before the work at the abbey finally ran out. Could she dare work on it during daytime hours to get the job done in time? No. Even if there was no chance of Timothy finding out, she couldn't do that. It wouldn't be right. The icon was her problem now and hers alone.

As she worked, the meal with Nathan replayed several times through her head. He wasn't quite the jobsworth she'd thought; he had a heart and a sense of humour apparently. He was even worried about her, which she found both amusing and touching. And then there'd been that insistence suddenly that they should forget about the fire and stop probing. It was a bit precious because he was the one who'd stirred her up

251

about it in the first place. Typical man really, having some bee in his bonnet which everyone else has to fall in with, then changing his mind and expecting everyone to fall in with that instead. This is why I'm single, she thought, thank God.

But there was no doubt that the fire was suspicious. She kept thinking about what Nathan said about the fire being in the middle of the night. *Everyone else would have been in bed.* Everyone except the one who'd lit it, he meant. But there was someone else out of bed, wasn't there? Marielle. Or so she said. And the more Hannah thought about the child's behaviour, the more convinced she became that the girl knew something: her fear and confusion; the way she looked down at where the Garden House had been; the things she'd said. There was that remark in particular about everyone liking David. It sounded so pointed. What was the significance of that? More to the point, what chance did Hannah have of finding out? She hadn't seen much of Marielle these last days, perhaps because she often locked the theatre door now, but in any case the girl was fragile; it wouldn't be easy nor would it be right to push her about it. It wasn't worth pursuing.

By the Friday, Hannah had cleaned off much of the thick, old varnish and realised it had been masking far more problems than she'd thought. Ironically, it was the best thing she could have found. Someone, she thought, was smiling on her from above.

'Did you do this mum?' she murmured, then rolled her eyes and blew out a long breath. 'Oh God, just listen to yourself, Hannah.'

But it was a reprieve, however it had happened. The oil paint the artist had used had become increasingly translucent with the passing years, allowing his first thoughts on the composition to show through. Pentimenti, they were called: ghost limbs or heads which slowly rose up to the light again, refusing to be buried. So far, she had revealed a shadow of Christ's head. The final position was more bowed, humbler, but the original more upright head was clearly visible now and would need 'burying' again. The wing positions of the dove fluttering over his head had changed too. There would be more yet, she suspected. There usually were. She also found a small area of abrasion and paint flaking and the frame needed some attention too.

With the icon still far from finished, it had bought her some precious time.

Chapter 20

Esther flew back to Provence late the following week and David met her at the airport in Marseille. As soon as he saw her he smiled broadly and embraced her, and she hugged him back. So often, in the past, she had been wary of displaying too much emotion in public. Somebody always took a photograph and the next thing you knew it was all over the press with all kinds of cynical interpretations and insinuations attached. Today she didn't care. She was thrilled to see him waiting for her and they could print what they liked; they made half of it up anyway. She was tired from the journey but underneath it she felt invigorated. The trip had done her good; she felt more like her old self. She had been fêted and praised and treated like royalty. And to think that not long ago, she'd thought of giving up her acting career for good.

David took her bags and they walked out to his car.

'So it went well?' he said as they slotted into the queue of cars waiting to exit.

'Very well, darling. The previews of the film seem to have gone down well. The journalists are all saying nice things. It's a welcome change.'

'Nonsense. They always love you.'

'Darling David, you're sweet but you know that's not true. And you know as well as I do: they'll let you make one bad film but if you make two in succession, look out. Suddenly you're history, past your best.' And age isn't on my side now, she thought, but didn't say it, reluctant to remind him. 'How is everything at the house? Nothing terrible happened since my last call?'

'No. Everything's fine.'

She looked across, studying his profile. 'The painting restoration's still going ahead, I gather. Sara tells me that Hannah and Nathan do appear to be dating, whatever Raff says.' She hesitated. 'Is that your impression too? Have you seen much of them?'

He glanced at her but she couldn't interpret his expression. That had been happening more and more lately. 'No, I've no idea what they've been doing. But I don't know why you bother listening to Raff. I've told you before: he'll say anything if he thinks he can get a rise out of people. To him, it's all a game.' He was silent suddenly, staring at the road again, expressionless. 'Do you think he really cared about Jemma?'

'That's an odd question. Yes, I think he did, to start with anyway. It's hard to tell with him, isn't it? So flippant. I guess they had their issues like everyone else. I'm not sure that Jemma was exactly devoted to him anyway. Perhaps she struggled with the engagement thing. Too permanent for her. She didn't like being tied down.'

Another quick glance. 'Did she tell you that?'

'In a way.' Esther was starting to feel uncomfortable about the conversation. She reached out and lightly touched David's hand on the steering wheel. 'Relationships need working on, don't they? It's so easy to take each other for granted.'

'Of course.'

He was frowning. They had reached the filter lane for the motorway and he became preoccupied, looking back, checking the oncoming traffic before seeing an opening and accelerating into it. They drove on in silence for several minutes. She watched the passing landscape, already feeling it wrap around her as it began to change from the flat lands of the coast to the rising bluffs and ridges on their approach to the mountains. It was late afternoon. Not even lunchtime in L.A., thought Esther. She had been catapulted forward in time and felt the usual disorientation. Bedtime would be the problem: tired from the journey but unable to settle, her body clock still on California time.

The next time they spoke, the tone was lighter. They talked about David's discussions with a producer for his next movie and about a couple of scripts Esther was going to look at. It wasn't until they'd turned onto the winding minor roads which would take them up into the Luberon proper that David mentioned the barbecue.

'Have you thought any more about it?' he said. 'I suggested a date in July but it's already half gone and that'd make it a rush to organise, wouldn't it? Why don't we go for August fourth?'

'Really David, I'm not sure I...'

'Esther, you must. It'll be cathartic, trust me. You need this; we both do. If you don't, that fire will hang over both of us forever. It's for me too.'

'I see.' She hadn't heard thought of it that way; perhaps he was more haunted than she'd realised.

He flashed her a quick smile. 'We'll ask some of our best friends and we'll be there together with them. It'll be fine. We'll have fun and then it'll be over and we'll have fresh memories. The rest will all be gone as if it never was. Doesn't that sound good?'

She thought about it for a few minutes, arguing it back and forth in her head. Could it really be that easy to put it behind them? No, not easy, but perhaps he was right. In any case, if she didn't want to lose David, she needed to engage more with his life and make this effort. It was a part she had to play like any other.

She touched his hand again, squeezing it, and offered him her warmest smile.

'Yes. You're right darling. It's time. Let's do it. But let's make it a proper party. Not like last time. Bigger, better, different. Last time it was too...' She paused, groping for the right word.

'Intimate?'

'Yes, I suppose that's what it was.'

It occurred to her that they had still never talked about the fire and now they never would. They circled it like people with a sick relative, unable or unwilling to give the illness concrete form by discussing it. Hopefully, it would soon be history.

*

The atmosphere in the abbey had changed again. Sara's walk had become more urgent, her steps brisker. Claudine was busier too, her expression preoccupied and intense. She could occasionally be heard firing instructions at Liane or Dominique. Even Pietro's languid movements round the garden seemed to have more purpose. Esther was back, Hannah knew – she had seen her drifting gracefully around the abbey precincts – but she had had no interaction with her. Hannah kept working and kept her head down.

Having found the pentimenti, she had gone specially into town at the beginning of the week to ring Timothy to share the news. He wanted updates so she was going to give him one. He sounded both surprised and relieved to hear her voice.

'Ah Hannah, this is a rare pleasure,' he said drily. 'To what do I owe it?'

'There's been a development in the second Rembrandt school painting, the picture of Christ and the dove? I thought you should know.' He groaned as she explained.

'Pentimenti.' He sighed. 'That's unfortunate. Are they serious?'

'I'm afraid so. There are a couple of different head positions before he settled on the final one and the dove changes considerably too. But it is fascinating, don't you think, to see the artist's first thoughts on his composition? They give you such an insight into his thinking processes. When a picture's finished it looks so right somehow that it's hard to imagine it having been painted any other way.'

'Yes, yes, of course,' he said. Perhaps distracted by the passion in her voice, he didn't question her any further. That had been her intention.

'I suppose this'll mean a bit of a delay,' he ventured. 'Do the best you can to get it sorted quickly won't you?'

'I've already started.'

'This is the last one, isn't it?'

'Yes.'

'Good, good. Well, keep me informed.'

She retraced her steps to the abbey and got back to work.

It was some days later when she heard about the barbecue. She had been into the dining room to grab some lunch and was about to leave, clutching two ham and tomato baguette sandwiches wrapped in paper serviettes, when she met Raff in the doorway.

'Leaving already?' he said. 'Squirreling your lunch back to the theatre? We haven't seen much of you lately. Are you trying to avoid us? Or perhaps you're doing something very secret there?'

'Absolutely. I'm really a foreign spy and I decode messages for a hostile government.' She smiled sweetly.

He nodded, looking amused. 'Very witty. I suppose you know Esther's back? And you've heard about the barbecue?'

'No.'

'Really, I thought everyone knew about it. It's a week Saturday and will be quite the event, I'm told.' Raff raised his eyebrows expressively. 'A fancy affair down by the pool. Lots of friends and food and, hopefully, booze. There's even going to be a small band so, who knows, maybe a bit of dancing. A proper party.' He glanced towards the door theatrically and dropped his voice. 'I don't know how David talked her into it.' He fixed a speculative gaze back on Hannah. 'And yet you haven't been invited. How disappointing. I rather assumed you and Nathan would be included. A chance for you to let your hair down for once. And him too, of course. I'm sure you wouldn't want to do that without Nathan. But if you come, do save a dance for me, won't you? By the way, did you find what you were looking for in my studio?'

She frowned. 'I'm sorry, I don't know what you mean.'

He grinned and turned away to get his lunch. She made her escape but his barbed remarks and insinuations lingered. He was hinting that he knew the fling with Nathan was a fiction but he was probably just guessing, testing her, though the dig about her searching his studio had shocked her. He couldn't really know, could he? She comforted herself that she hadn't taken anything. Still, he'd reminded her that she needed to see Esther – among other things she had two completed paintings waiting to be delivered. Given the atmosphere these days, she should probably make an appointment again.

Later that afternoon she went to see Sara. But Esther and David had gone away again, together this time.

'They're visiting friends in Nice,' said Sara. 'Friends who can't come to the barbecue. They're back on Tuesday but Esther has a busy schedule next week as you can imagine. I'll pencil you in for the Wednesday afternoon. Two-thirty but I'll let you know if that's not convenient for her.'

259

Walking back to the theatre, Hannah wondered how Sara felt about having a barbecue down by the pool again. Didn't she mind? No-one seemed to take her feelings into account but then she didn't express many feelings. Mentioning the barbecue, she could as easily have been talking about an appointment with a solicitor. There again, Raff appeared to be uncaring too; he positively welcomed the idea of the party. And Esther might profess guilt but her behaviour didn't suggest any genuine feelings of loss. Two years on from Jemma's death, nobody seemed to miss her.

*

At two twenty-eight on the following Wednesday, Hannah stood outside the library door, a painting under each arm. She put one down and knocked.

'Come in.'

Hannah walked in and found Esther sitting in the armchair facing the door in a regal pose. She smiled politely but made no effort to rise.

'Ah, Hannah. Sara said you wanted to see me.'

'Hello Esther. Did you have a good trip to the States?'

Esther seemed surprised at the question. 'Yes. Yes, thank you. Very good. Tiring of course, all that talking to journalists but I'm afraid it's part of the job.' Her gaze dropped to the pictures Hannah held. She visibly brightened. 'You've brought my paintings over. Does this mean you've finished?'

'No, not yet. These two are finished but there's still one that needs some work.' Hannah put the Bellini down and held up the Amanda Jay. 'The new frame you chose for this works well, I think.'

She continued to hold it while Esther ran her eyes over the image. For an unguarded minute a range of emotions flickered across the woman's face.

'Are you happy with it?' prompted Hannah warily.

'Yes. Yes, it's… it's amazing that it still looks like that. Under all that…' She took a deep breath and collected herself. 'I must admit that I doubted if it could be rescued but you've done a great job.' She transferred her gaze to the other picture, leaning against the cabinet at the side. 'And the Bellini too.' She got up now and came closer, picking it up and studying it. 'Wonderful. We're having some guests staying over this weekend and I'd like to hang them on the wall, you know, share them.' She put the Bellini down. 'What about the one that isn't done yet? Where are you with that?'

'That's the other reason I wanted to see you. It's the painting of Christ and the dove? I'm afraid it's going to be a longer job than we foresaw. The paint the artist used has become translucent with time. Previous paint layers, – different, early ideas the artist tried out for the composition – are showing through.'

'That's very odd, isn't it?'

'It's not uncommon with old oil paintings. I need to cover them again or the painting looks cluttered and confusing.'

Esther looked at her doubtfully.

'I could show you if you like,' offered Hannah.

'No, no.' Esther waved a dismissive hand. 'It wouldn't mean much to me.' She sat down again. 'How long will this take?'

'Perhaps three weeks? It's hard to say. It's delicate work and can't be rushed.'

Esther nodded, looking pensive. She turned her head away. Hannah assumed that the audience was over and walked to the door but before she could turn the handle, Esther spoke again.

'Is Nathan still working near here?'

'Yes.'

'We're having a barbecue on Saturday, Hannah and, since you're both still here, perhaps you'd like to come? There'll be so many people after all, what's two more?' She smiled and spread her hands in an eloquent gesture. 'In fact, several people are staying over. Nathan might like to do that too, then he won't need to worry about drinking and driving.' She raised one coy eyebrow. 'I thought you might like that too.'

'I see. Yes.' Hannah managed a smile. 'Thank you for the invitation.'

'Sara will give you the details. You'll tell Nathan, I assume? I'm sure you'll want him there.'

Esther reached for her book of hours and gingerly opened its pages. Now the audience was at an end.

Returning to the theatre, Hannah saw Pietro hoeing one of the borders and stopped to speak to him. After exchanging a few pleasantries, she asked after Marielle.

'I haven't seen her for a while. Is she all right?'

'Yes, it's the school holidays and she's gone to stay with Claudine's niece in Arles. She has a boy and a girl, a bit older than Marielle.' He looked hunted for a moment. 'Marielle gets bored if she hangs around here all summer. Then she gets under people's feet and we get complaints. She doesn't mean anything by it. She's not a bad girl.'

'I know she's not. She behaves well when she comes to see me.'

'She likes you, *Mam'selle*, I can tell. And she'll be back on Friday because Claudine's niece is going away herself. She always takes her holidays in August. But we'll have to keep Marielle in this weekend, what with all the guests for the barbecue.' He gave a quick indulgent laugh. 'And that won't be easy: she's nosy.'

Hannah smiled but was preoccupied. She hesitated.

'Pietro, did the fire upset her? I suppose it must have.'

He looked surprised at the sudden change of direction. '*Naturellement*. We were all upset and Marielle especially. We don't talk about it much. Such a tragedy about that lady.' He shrugged. 'It wasn't easy to forget either. The fire smouldered for days, you know, and the smell was horrible. It lingered everywhere.'

'Does Marielle ever talk about it?'

'About the fire? No. But she doesn't talk a lot, *Mam'selle*. I know I ought to try to play with her more but she likes to run around outside, either that or she's up in her room. She's got a box of trinkets: little toys and bits of jewellery, and things she's found like coloured stones and feathers and God knows what. Her treasures she calls them and won't let us look inside. But she makes up stories with them and mutters to herself and it seems to keep her happy so we leave her to it.' He looked at her oddly. 'Why do you ask?'

'No reason. I just wondered.'

That night, Hannah dreamt about her mother again in a series of strange, dislocated scenes. Guillaume was in there too, shouting at her to go, go now, then running away, disappearing into billowing smoke. There was smoke everywhere. And yet Nathan was sitting down on a tiny child's chair in the gardens, his legs bent up like a grasshopper's, telling funny stories, apparently oblivious to the choking haze. And Marielle sat on the grass watching him, saying nothing. Esther's face kept looming out of the smoke smiling, like the Cheshire Cat, then disappearing again. And intermittently Hannah's mother would be standing there, holding out a hand as if reaching for her daughter.

'Hannah,' she called out each time. 'Hannah, listen to me. Why do you never listen to me? You must watch out. Be careful.' The last time it happened, she added, 'And keep her close.'

Hannah came to, sweating. She sat up, kicking the sheet off, and for a few moments the dream was still vivid, making her breathe heavily and roughly push her hair away from her sticky face. She was hot and unsettled and a little scared.

Her mother often used to say that to her: *why do you never listen to me?* Hannah wanted to laugh it off but it didn't feel funny. It had felt too real, too pressing and impassioned as if it were a genuine warning. *Watch out. Be careful.*

'But what of?' she muttered. 'Be careful of what?'

And what about the other instruction: *Keep her close.* Keep who close? Marielle perhaps. Going to bed, the conversation with Pietro had still been fresh in Hannah's mind.

She reached over and switched the bedside light on, then got up and went to the bathroom to sluice her face with water. Back in the room she took a drink from a bottle of mineral water. She was cooling down now and the dream was less vivid. She began to relax.

By the time she got back into bed, she'd brushed it all away as nonsense. Stress, tiredness and the recent loss of her mother had made her brain go into overdrive. It was doubtful she would even remember the dream in the morning.

She drifted into a half-sleep but couldn't shake off an uneasy feeling at the back of her mind that, whatever had happened in the past here, it wasn't finished yet.

Chapter 21

'I feel overdressed,' said Nathan.

He looked across at the beautiful people sunning themselves on the loungers, sunshades on, skin glistening with tanning oil. Three women wore bikinis; one had on a one-piece. One of the men wore only a tiny pair of swimming trunks; the second had shrugged a short-sleeved cotton shirt over his shorts, but it hung open to reveal an impressive tanned six-pack. Nathan was wearing linen trousers, a short-sleeved shirt and a linen jacket. He'd been thinking smart casual.

'I did tell you it was a barbecue by the pool,' said Hannah. 'Sara told me you could bring swimming gear if you wanted and I did pass that on, remember?'

'I remember. I guess I thought it was more of a joke than for real. I mean, it's six-thirty and it's a barbecue. It's expected to go on all evening isn't it?'

'I imagine they'll go away and change later. A lot of these people are staying over.'

'Naturally. Forgive me if I seem a little out of my depth. I've never been to a pool party. I don't move in those circles.' He sipped at his daiquiri and grimaced. 'And I don't like rum much.'

Hannah rolled her eyes. 'Then why did you have it?'

'It was offered. I hadn't had one before so I thought I'd try it. I didn't realise there was rum in it. Did you know there was

265

rum in a daiquiri?'

'Yes.'

He blew out a frustrated puff of air. Of course she did. Her father probably mixed them in his studio. He glanced round again disconsolately. He could cope with dinner parties: they had structure and organisation; you could slot into your place and role. And he enjoyed telling stories when it was his turn; maybe it was the secret performer in him. But he'd never been big on this sort of party. It was too casual, too random. There was no procedure to follow. You were expected to wander and mingle, force yourself into other people's clearly private conversations and pretend you were the person they were dying to meet. If there was a protocol – and there probably was – he didn't know the rules of it and that unsettled him.

David and Esther had clearly splashed money about to make this happen. There was a three-piece jazz trio set up by the lawn at the other end of the pool: a man playing a double bass, another on saxophone and a third with an electric keyboard. A woman occasionally stepped up to the microphone and sang. It gave the event a timeless, chic feel.

Their hosts had brought in a catering service too. A man and a woman, both wearing black suit, white shirt and bow tie, were running a smart cocktail bar with a wide array of drinks on offer. The same company had brought an enormous electric barbecue which stood near the pool house with its back to the bed of cotton lavender, attended by two more very earnest, smartly dressed men. A similarly uniformed woman tended a table where an array of salads and side dishes were being arranged and covered. Whether the neatly laid tables and the accompanying chairs which had been spread out across the lawn had been provided by the same company, Nathan wasn't sure. Perhaps Esther kept spare garden furniture stored somewhere, just in case she felt the need to do some serious entertaining.

And there was Esther, near the bar, standing chatting in a group of four people. She laughed at something one of the men said and touched him on the arm.

'I must say your employer's looking radiant this afternoon,' Nathan remarked. 'Is it afternoon or is it evening now?'

Hannah looked at him, eyes narrowed. 'Are you on some sort of medication that's making you hyper or something? Just chill, will you. Nobody's interested in us anyway.'

All the same she followed his gaze. Esther was wearing a low-cut, strappy, silk sheath dress in a shimmering turquoise. It finished just above the knee and displayed her elegant shoulders and immaculate figure to advantage. Rather than sunglasses, she wore a matching turquoise wide-brimmed hat to shade her eyes from the evening sun. Made to order presumably. David, who had just joined her, was more casual: dark blue Bermuda shorts and a short-sleeved linen shirt in pastel blue.

Another couple arrived and made their way through to speak to Esther. Nathan saw Guillaume standing in the archway of the hedge at the end of the lawn, surveying the gathering. A moment later he'd turned and gone. Nathan had seen him escort each new arrival in. Presumably he organised their luggage too, if they had any, and made sure no-one went astray or, more to the point, went where they weren't supposed to.

'This is quite a turnout,' said Nathan. 'Have you any idea how many people are invited?'

'No. They don't tell me things like that. I see Raff's not here yet.'

'Perhaps he won't come. Maybe he hasn't been invited.'

'Oh, he'll be here, invited or not. I see Sara is.' She nodded towards a small group near the barbecue. 'She looks animated. Nice dress. Prettiest I've ever seen her.' She looked back at the pool. 'Do you suppose those people in swimsuits intend to actually get them wet or are they just for show?'

'They probably can't even swim.' He paused. 'By the way, you're looking... striking yourself tonight.'

Hannah's eyebrows hit her hair line. 'Striking? What does that mean exactly? Bit too bright for you am I?'

He pointedly looked her up and down. She wore a sleeveless, V-necked linen dress which buttoned all the way down the front and finished a couple of inches above the knee. The fabric itself was striped – a delicate pink and white – but the buttons and the broad lapels were deep cerise. Her rapidly growing hair had been pinned back on one side with a bright pink clip and she wore large cerise earrings.

'Eye-catching,' he said.

'Thanks. I'm glad you like it.'

Without them noticing, Esther had joined them from the rear.

'Darling people, I know you've only got eyes for each other but I insist on introducing you to some fascinating people. You've got to meet and mingle; it's a rule of our parties. Perhaps we should separate you for a while? Oh and you need more drinks.'

'Thanks but I'm fine,' said Nathan and Hannah, both at the same time, then looked at each other.

Esther produced her tinkling laugh. 'So cute. Now Hannah, you wait here. I won't be long. And *you*, young man...' She put her free arm through Nathan's. '...come with me.' She steered him away.

*

Hannah watched Esther lead Nathan towards a group of people

and effect some introductions. Nathan was right: her hostess looked in good form tonight. She positively glowed, offering a word here, a smile there, and often that mellifluous laugh. She was the leading lady on her own stage and it was a wonderful performance. She was a beguiling woman and Hannah had been dangerously close to falling under her spell too at first, but now she wondered where the acting ended and Esther's real life began.

Hannah toyed with moving away; two familiar faces from a previous dinner, Susie and Bill, were there and she thought she'd join them. But Esther quickly returned, insisting on taking her in a different direction and joining another group of four near the lawn. Hannah made all the right noises and tried to enter into the spirit of the thing. Her new acquaintances were more people from the movie world: an actor and his wife who was a make-up artist, an actress and her stuntman partner. They were intrigued by her profession, as people often were, and asked the usual questions: how did you get into that; which famous artists' work have you restored; don't you need a lot of patience?

The conversation moved on and Hannah glanced round. Nathan was in conversation with a woman in a backless fishtail dress who seemed to be hanging on his every word. Hannah excused herself and went to the bar in search of another drink.

'Something soft, please,' she said to the barman.

They had a choice of several. She chose something fizzy; there was no sign of food being served yet and she needed the sugar. She swayed to the pulse of the music while the barman poured it.

'I like the sexy movement.'

She felt a groping hand on her hip and turned sharply to see Raff at her shoulder, swaying in time with her.

'Hey,' she said, pushing his hand away.

'Really, Hannah, you promised me a dance and Nathan won't mind.' He glanced at her drink. 'Pacing yourself?' He thrust his empty glass at the barman. 'I'll have another Manhattan. Large. You should try one of these, Hannah. Blows your socks off.' He looked down at her feet. She was wearing strappy pink sandals. 'Except that you're not wearing socks of course. So maybe something else. Depends what you're wearing under that interesting dress.' He affected to peer down her cleavage.

She pressed her hand against her chest. 'Nothing that's any business of yours.'

'Shame.' He grinned, took his new drink from the barman and turned, looking round. 'So what do you think of our little party?' He waved an arm to embrace the nearby knots of people. 'So much posing and superficial conversation. There's enough money among this lot to run a small country, you know. And do they buy paintings?' He scoffed. 'Only when they think it makes them look clever or if it's an investment. Never for the joy of the thing.'

Hannah realised that Raff was already more than a little drunk. If he carried on like this, he'd be comatose by the end of the evening, but maybe that was what he wanted. She edged them away from the bar a little.

'It's always been the same.' She shrugged. 'Art has been treated as a status symbol or for political purposes for hundreds of years. Probably longer. Artists have always struggled to make a living from painting simply what they wanted to paint.'

He peered at her with a bemused expression.

'Not making much progress then are we?' he grunted.

She glanced round, wanting to change the subject. 'It is a good party, though.' She looked over towards the jazz trio. They were playing *Rhapsody in Blue* by George Gershwin. 'I like the music.'

'It's all right.'

'Sara seems to be enjoying it.' Esther's PA was standing alone near the band, swaying and throwing her arms out in languid patterns not quite in time to the beat.

Raff watched Sara for a minute or two. 'She's on a high again, I expect. I saw her disappear for a sneaky smoke.' He turned his gaze back on Hannah. It had changed into a flat, accusing stare. 'I think I've been too frank with you. You seem so nice on first acquaintance, so innocent. But what is it you're up to exactly? Sometimes I think you're the real deal; then I think, no you're not. I've been watching you, ever since you arrived. I thought it was a bit of a game. But *you're* the watcher. And you're surreptitious.' He struggled to pronounce the word and had to say it twice. 'You sneak about and lock the door on that place you've claimed as your own. Yet you keep tabs on us and ask too many questions. Are we that fascinating? What is it you're hoping to find out exactly? And why?'

He was earnest, intent, still staring accusingly at her. It was a side of him she hadn't seen before and she automatically shuffled backwards, trying to get some space between them.

'Nothing. I'm just...' She shrugged. 'I'm interested in people.'

He came closer again and carried on as if she hadn't spoken.

'And if you do find something out, what are you going to do with it? You see the watching's not the problem exactly. It's the interfering. I like you but, you know – and I've been thinking about this a lot – you've crossed a line.'

'What line?'

He smiled wryly, slowly shaking a heavy head.

'I suppose you were never going to admit to it. But nobody likes an interfering busybody, however nicely they do it. Our business is our business.'

He stabbed a pugnacious index finger in the air towards her a couple of times, then wandered off.

Hannah frowned, watching him go. A moment later he was talking to the make-up artist, waving a hand expressively as he spoke, then laughing. She was stunned; she hadn't expected the accusation or the simmering resentment. Maybe it was just the drink talking.

She saw Nathan approaching the bar and joined him. He glanced at her glass.

'Is that an alcoholic drink masquerading as pop?' he said.

'No, it's pop. But I think I need something stronger now.'

'Why? I saw you with Raff. I thought there was something up. What's the matter?'

'It was just his manner. It's nothing. He's drunk.'

'Too much booze on an empty stomach. They're about to start serving food, thank God. I'm starving. Come on, let's get the drinks quickly and get in the queue.'

*

It was barbecued meat like nothing Hannah had ever tasted before: expensive quality products, perfectly cooked and delicately flavoured. Both she and Nathan were served with a selection then filled their plates with salads from the nearby table. Nathan, his plate piled precariously high, led the way down to the lawn. All the tables were already occupied but two stray chairs had been abandoned off to one side. Nathan sat on one. It was lower than he had expected and he landed heavily, looking bemused. She was reminded suddenly of her dream and felt her skin crawl. It must have shown on her face.

'What's the matter?' said Nathan. 'I thought we were supposed to look like a couple who wants to be alone.'

'It's nothing. Forget it.'

He grunted and turned his attention to his food, eating as if he hadn't had a meal in days.

Hannah sipped her glass of white wine and glanced round uneasily. It had become a big party, bigger than she had expected, perhaps forty or fifty people though it was hard to tell because some were sitting at the tables on the lawn, others had stayed to sit by the pool to eat. Some hadn't bothered with the food yet and stood around talking, laughing and drinking.

'Apparently, Claudine's put me in the room next to yours,' Nathan said between mouthfuls of barbecued steak. 'Esther told me. She said it as though she found it rather funny. Gosh, this is delicious.' He grinned. 'If I need it, she added pointedly. I swear she almost winked at me. It's come back to bite you, Hannah. She's expecting us to share a passionate bed for the night.'

'They're testing us out,' she said lugubriously. 'They don't believe we're a couple.'

'Are you sure? They? Or Esther?'

'I'm not sure there's any difference. They may bicker and backbite but they gang up on outsiders: their only common threat. Anyway, no-one here's going to be able to focus by bedtime, let alone care what we're doing.'

'You think?' He pulled a piece off a chunk of baguette. 'I've seen Esther look this way a couple of times already.'

Hannah paused with a piece of lamb kebab on her fork and glanced quickly across the lawn. Esther had been circling the tables, exchanging a word here and there but now she had turned and, glass in hand, was walking elegantly back towards the pool or perhaps the barbecue. There was no sign of David.

'It's early yet,' said Hannah dismissively. 'She won't be bothered later.'

Nathan grinned but didn't respond and they ate in silence. Hannah finished first, wiped her fingers on the serviette and

273

put the plate down on the grass.

'I had a dream about the fire the other night.'

Nathan looked up. 'What sort of dream?'

'Odd. I suppose with the party being planned down here it wasn't surprising. Except that my mother was in it.' She immediately wished she hadn't mentioned it. 'It doesn't matter. It was just odd.'

'Upsetting though. I still have dreams about my father.' He finished eating but kept hold of the plate.

She looked at him curiously. 'Really?'

'Yeah. I dream sometimes that I'm there when he crashed and trying to get him out of the car. Which is absurd of course because I wasn't there. I was never there.'

'What did happen, Nathan?'

'He travelled with his work. He was a rep for a pharmaceutical company and was on his way home after a trip up north. He hit black ice and shot off the road and rolled down a bank. He wasn't wearing a seat belt.' He pulled a face. 'They weren't compulsory then, of course. He broke his neck in the fall. Died instantly, we were told, which is something.'

'How awful. It must have been tough for you.'

'It was. But it does get easier with time.' He hesitated. 'What did you dream about your mother?'

'It was foolish. Forget it.'

'No, go on. It helps to talk about it.'

She snorted a laugh, embarrassed. 'She was warning me. Telling me to be careful. Typical mother stuff.' She stood up suddenly. 'Look, I think I'll stretch my legs and go up to the house to use the cloakroom.'

'You might miss dessert, though I think I'd rather have some more of that delicious steak if there's any going.'

'Go and see. I'm fine.'

The house was eerily quiet when Hannah went inside, her

274

footsteps echoing along the passageways and bouncing back at her. Presumably most of the guests were using the facilities in the pool house but she'd wanted the walk. She washed her hands and checked her reflection in the mirror, pushing fingers through her hair, touching away some stray mascara. It was tempting to go up to her room, to leave all the fake glamour and camaraderie behind. But she was supposed to be with Nathan; it was an act she had started and it wouldn't be fair to him if she bailed out now.

Returning to the hallway, she could still hear nothing except her own echoing steps but she had an uneasy feeling that there was someone else around. It was probably just Claudine. All the same, walking back through the gardens, she found herself looking round now and then. The setting sun tinged the trees and shrubs in amber and violet and cast obscure and gloomy shadows, but there was no sign of anyone following her. Why would they? It was that foolish dream; it had spooked her.

Back down by the pool, she looked for Nathan but couldn't see him. In the short time she'd been away, the party had subtly changed. The bar was busy but the barbecue had been closed down and the tables on the lawn had been moved to one side. The band had turned up the amplifier and their music filled the air. Several people had started to dance.

'You owe me a dance,' said Raff in her ear. 'You can't refuse me this time.'

'Actually Raff, I'm looking for…'

'Nathan's dancing over there with someone else. He won't mind.'

The band were playing *Aint Misbehavin'* by Fats Waller. Raff took hold of Hannah's hand and pulled her towards the grass, then put his hand round her waist and into the small of her back, pulling her hard against him. She tried to pull away again but he was too strong for her.

'You're hurting me,' she said.

'Then move with me,' he replied, not shifting his grip. 'Feel my body; feel the pulse. See? Like this. Good isn't it?'

It was intrusive and unpleasant but, as soon as the song ended, he abruptly let her go, saying nothing, and walked away. He'd wanted her to feel diminished, wanted to punish her for looking round his studio and for her interference. She felt soiled and got herself another glass of white wine, drinking it quickly. A few minutes later, she got the barman to serve her another, then wandered back to stand at the edge of the lawn. More people had gravitated there and it was a mass of jigging, swaying bodies. She caught sight of Nathan, dancing with an older woman who appeared to laugh at whatever he said. Sara was nearby too, dancing with David.

'Having a good time, darling?' Esther moved smoothly alongside her. 'Is Nathan neglecting you?'

'Not at all. I'm…'

'Men can be so easily led.' Esther rested her hand on Hannah's arm and stared into her face. 'A word of advice, dear: keep an eye on the woman. They're always the ones to watch.'

Esther left with a knowing look and a soft smile.

The band were good and Hannah automatically swayed and shuffled to the beat. She saw Nathan leave the lawn, still with the same woman, and mentally shrugged. She couldn't very well complain. More people piled onto the grass to dance, some alone, some in twos or threes. Hannah took a long draught of wine, put the glass down on a nearby table and did the same, determined to forget Raff and just enjoy the music. A few minutes later, Susie joined her.

'Bill doesn't dance,' she shouted into Hannah's ear. 'Boring.'

Another change of music, another drink, and Hannah saw

Nathan out of the corner of her eye. Was he looking for her? If he was, he'd changed his mind because now he'd turned and was leaving again. Hannah barely thought about it. She had drunk too much, far more than usual, and the combination of the alcohol and the music made her uncaring. It was a wonderful feeling. There had been too much heartache and worry with her mother this last year. This was a chance to be someone else for the night. When Susie left her to find Bill again, she knocked back the rest of her wine and started dancing again.

The next thing she knew, David was dancing with her, touching distance away.

'Great party,' she shouted.

'I'm glad you're having a good time.'

'Sorry?'

He leaned in closer and raised his voice.

'I'm glad you're having a good time. Where's Nathan?'

'I don't know.'

'He won't mind me dancing with you then.'

She shook her head and kept on dancing. Why should Nathan mind? Why should anyone mind? She ignored the warning voice at the back of her head and began waving her arms around, turning extravagantly, singing along and laughing. David's smile broadened, watching her. Then the music suddenly changed and the band began playing a slow, moody piece. David took hold of her, pulling her close and she let him, moving along with his strong, slow sway. She could smell the gin on his breath. It crossed her mind that maybe he was drunk too and that neither of them should be doing this. But it's only one dance, she protested to herself. It means nothing.

Then the song finished and David lifted her hand to kiss the back of it. She bowed her head in acknowledgement and laughed again. One of the barmen came over to speak to him and David apologised and left. Hannah glanced round. Nathan was back dancing again, this time with a blonde in a mini skirt that revealed legs that went up to her armpits. She was half wrapped around him and they were still swaying. He was staring into her eyes dreamily.

There was a huge splash and everyone turned to see who'd gone into the pool. A woman was swimming to the side, shouting at a man who'd stalked off. A couple of men helped her out. She walked away towards the pool house, still fulminating, her dress clinging to her body, her hair plastered against her head and still dripping.

The band started playing again but Hannah didn't want to dance any more. Suddenly it all felt rather pointless, sleazy even; the bubble had burst. And her mouth felt like she'd been hiking through a desert. She made her slightly unsteady way back to the bar and tagged onto the queue of people waiting to be served.

'*Eau minérale, s'il vous plaît,*' she asked when her turn came. '*Non gaz.*'

Édouard, behind the bar, wordlessly poured the water and put two ice cubes in the glass before passing it over. As Hannah went to turn away, somebody touched her on the arm. She expected it to be Esther but it was a woman she didn't know.

'Excuse me, but are you Hannah?' She spoke with a pronounced American drawl.

'Yes. Why?'

'Someone told me to tell you that there's a little girl asking for you. She's very upset about something and wants to see you.'

'Where?' said Hannah, looking round. 'Who told you?'

'I dunno. Some man who said a woman told him. Why he didn't tell you himself, I have no idea. But he said the girl's up in the theatre? Does that make any sense to you?'

'Yes, sort of. Thank you.'

Hannah quickly drank half the glass of water then abandoned it and made for the steps to the upper gardens. The water and activity began to clear her head. The only girl the man could have been talking about was Marielle. But why would she be at the theatre at this time of night? And who were these people who kept passing on the message? Did they think it was a game of Chinese Whispers?

The air felt fresher when she got to the top of the steps, away from the bodies and the smell of food. Down below her, the noise of the party sounded far distant already, little more than a buzz of voices and a pulsing throb of music. The upper gardens were still and sombre in comparison. With the sun now set, a waning crescent moon cast a barely adequate light.

Nearing the path to the theatre, Hannah called out.

'Marielle? Are you here? Marielle?'

There was no reply. But the child couldn't be in the theatre because it was locked. She turned onto the path and walked towards it, calling out again.

'Marielle?'

There were no lights visible. Hannah reached in her pocket for the key. With *The Lily Madonna* still hidden in the theatre, she always had it on her. But getting closer, she found the door already open and stopped short. That was weird. Had she forgotten to lock it? She leaned forward, cautiously flicked a light switch and walked in.

There was nobody there. She called out again: 'Marielle?'

There was the softest of treads behind her but, before she could turn, something hit her hard on the back of the head and the world went black.

Chapter 22

It had needed both the food and a certain amount of alcohol before Nathan truly began to enjoy the party, before its lack of structure and the casual carelessness of its hosts started to make sense. Normally he liked order; he was the sort of person who looked for patterns in things. Now he could see that parties like this needed no order; there was no pattern. Just excellent food, a lot of alcohol and some good music. It was rather like one of Édouard the barman's cocktails: you mixed the respective components together, with flair naturally – and the end result made you see the world a little differently. Of course, Nathan acknowledged to himself, it could be simply that he was drunk.

He had expected to spend more time with Hannah. After all, that was what this whole scenario was about, wasn't it? A secret office romance, except that it wasn't secret and there wasn't really an office. There was certainly no romance. It didn't matter though. If Hannah wasn't bothered about it, why should he be? After she'd left him, he'd managed to scrounge some more steak and filled up his plate with a few side dishes. Finally, too full to eat any more, he'd got involved talking to some actor or other and, somehow, the time had just gone. A woman – what was her name, Amelia? – had persuaded him to dance with her and, against all his better judgement, he'd agreed. He wasn't a dancer. But she was seriously sexy, a little older and definitely more experienced; she certainly knew how to work it. It had all gone rather well, he thought, until she'd been claimed by someone else. That seemed to be the way it was here. Couples split up, flirted, mingled, made passes even, then reunited. All very liberal and casual. Not quite what he was used to.

Still, he got himself another drink and mingled too. It had definitely got easier. Talking to people he didn't know became a breeze. He even ended up telling some stories to a chap who turned out to be a film director. Every now and then, he would look out for Hannah, but when he did see her, she seemed happy without him. Happier probably, so he left her to it. She did a lot of dancing and he watched her surreptitiously a couple of times. She did move well, no doubt about that. But now she was dancing with David. Why, in heaven's name? Did the woman never learn? Here of all places with Esther looking on.

'What a fascinating job you do,' the tall blonde woman standing next to him was saying. He tried to focus back on her again. Her lips were plastered in glossy red lipstick and she kept sipping at a very green cocktail. Nathan wondered that her lips didn't slip off the side of the glass. 'You must go to all sorts of glamorous places.'

Nathan thought of the wealthy but thrifty landowner who had employed them the previous year to 'sort out' the paintings he'd got stored in his barn. Family heirlooms, he'd called them. When Nathan arrived, he'd found the pictures covered in strands of damp hay and mouse droppings and coated with mildew. Rodents had chewed chunks out of several of the frames and had made holes in some of the canvases too.

'Oh certainly,' Nathan replied now with a weak smile. 'But maybe not all as glamorous as this.'

The woman laughed.

'Yes, this is quite the loveliest place, isn't it?' She slipped a hand through his arm and leaned a little against his shoulder.

He became engulfed in a strong, sickly perfume. 'I travel a lot with my work too.'

'You do? Sorry, what was it you said you did?'

'I'm a model, darling.' She affected disappointment. 'Don't you recognise me? I have done a little acting too. I'm hoping to develop that side of my career: you know, films, television.' She had some sort of regional English accent though he couldn't quite place it and she kept trying to cover it up. It sounded bizarre.

'Wonderful,' he said.

'Oh listen, it's a slow one. Shall we dance? Nathan isn't it? Do come.'

She gave his arm a playful tug and he reluctantly went along. He saw Hannah, still with David, now virtually cheek to cheek, and looked away, cross. He allowed the woman to wrap herself around him. She was very attractive and they danced belly to belly, shuffling side to side. Nathan enjoyed the moment. It wasn't his problem what Hannah did.

The music finished. There was a splash from the pool and Nathan looked across but couldn't make out what was happening. Anyway, the music had started again and this woman wanted another dance then half way through suddenly changed her mind and said she'd had enough.

'Sorry darling. My little old fiancé's looking rather impatient over there. He has to be on a flight first thing tomorrow morning. I think we have to go. Bye darling. Keep doing clever things to those paintings.' She kissed him on the cheek and left.

Nathan extricated himself from the dance floor and looked round for Hannah but she'd gone. David had gone too. His gaze raked the dancers again. Sara was over there near the band. No, she wasn't. The woman had turned and it wasn't her. Either way, there was no Hannah dancing.

He weaved his way through to the bar and asked for a glass of water then glanced round again. There was no Hannah by the bar or anywhere round the pool either. Maybe she'd gone up to the house again. The party had started breaking up into groups, twos and fours splintering off, dancing or talking. Some were stretched out on the loungers by the pool again, indolently sipping at drinks. There was no swimwear on show any more, just shiny, glamorous evening wear. But David wasn't here either and, with Hannah gone too, Nathan was worried, though there was no sign of Esther either. Raff, he hadn't seen in a while. Maybe he'd given up on the party and gone up to his studio, but it didn't seem likely that Esther and David would leave their own party before the end.

He drank the water and wandered off, then sat for a few minutes on the low wall at the bottom of the bank, glancing across now and then to the steps up to the house. There was still no sign of Hannah. He saw Sara over by the pool house and went across to speak to her.

'Have you seen Hannah?' he demanded, rather brusquely.

She raised her eyebrows. 'Hannah? No. Have you lost her?' An arch smile. 'Bit careless of you.'

'She's disappeared.'

She snorted. 'She'll be around somewhere. Powdering her nose probably after all the booze.'

'I suppose.'

David appeared by the bar and Nathan left Sara to home in on him instead.

'Have you seen Hannah?'

'No, not since we danced. Why? She can't have gone far.'

The barwoman approached and David turned away to order, apparently unconcerned.

Édouard, drying a glass on a cloth further along behind the bar, came nearer.

'This 'anna,' he said to Nathan, 'she wears a pink and white dress with pink…' He used a hand to indicate the collars. 'Yes?'

'Yes.'

'I saw a woman tell her that a little girl wants to see her. At the theatre, yes? There is a theatre?'

'Yes, there's a theatre. Who was the woman? Was it someone Hannah knew?'

Édouard shrugged and resumed polishing the glass. 'I don't think so. This 'anna, she looked surprised. Perhaps *inquiète.*'

'Worried?' offered Nathan.

'Yes. *Elle avait l'air perplexe.*' In response to Nathan's blank expression, Édouard offered another word. 'Puzzled, yes?'

A sudden chill ran down Nathan's back. He thanked the barman and pushed and elbowed his way past people in his hurry to get to the steps.

*

As Nathan climbed, the comfortable, drink-induced fogginess of his thinking cleared rapidly. It was cooler up here and it was dark. A breeze had whipped up and clouds scudded across the sky, regularly obscuring what little light the waning moon offered. He remembered the layout of the gardens fairly well but wished he knew them better, stumbling now and then off the path.

A number of thoughts jostled for position in his head. Why would a child want to see Hannah? Presumably it was the strange little French girl he'd seen that time. But at this hour of night? She should be in bed. Then he remembered Hannah's odd dream: her mother giving a warning, telling her to be careful. Careful of what? Nathan wasn't sure what he believed

284

about the afterlife but this didn't feel good. What else had happened in that dream? Hannah hadn't told him the whole story but, there again, she never did and she was so bloody independent. Why was he even chasing after her like this? She'd probably already found out the message was a hoax and had gone back to the house, abandoning the party and leaving him to fend for himself.

He was dragged out of these thoughts by a smell and stopped short, sniffing the air. Smoke. It was definitely smoke. Good God, not another fire? He tried to move faster but took the path leading to Raff's studio by mistake and had to quickly retrace his steps, increasingly anxious. The moon reappeared. He found the right path and wound around the shrubberies towards the theatre. Long before he got there, he became aware of a flickering light coming from the windows.

'Bloody hell. There is a fire. And it's in the theatre.'

He reached the door but it was closed and locked tight.

'Hannah?' he bellowed and banged wildly on the door. 'Hannah, are you in there?'

There was no response.

'Shit,' he shouted and thumped the door with his fist again. He tried to ram the door with his shoulder but it wouldn't budge.

'Can you 'elp 'er?'

It took Nathan a moment to register the small voice behind him. He turned to find the little French girl a couple of metres away, watching him, wide-eyed.

'Marielle? Where is she?' He grabbed her by the shoulders. 'Is she in there?'

Marielle tried to pull away from him but he was holding her too tightly. Her eyes flicked towards the theatre then back at him. She nodded. He released her and tried the theatre door fruitlessly again.

'I need a key,' he shouted helplessly. 'Marielle, do you understand? A key.'

'Yes. In the 'ouse. *Ou chez* Guillaume.'

But no sooner had he said it than he realised it was pointless. There was no time for tracking a key down; the fire would engulf the place before he'd got back. He pushed through the shrubs, looking up at the windows. They were set high, narrow but tall and divided into six panels, three each side of a broad central timber. Single-glazed, it looked as if only the top panels on each side opened. But the light was getting brighter; he could feel heat. Somehow or other, he needed to break in.

Below one of the middle windows grew a large evergreen shrub with a strong, woody trunk and branches which leaned in against the building. He grabbed a hand-sized stone from the ground, rammed it in the pocket of his trousers and eased himself up through its stems, getting scratched and poked as he went but barely noticing. At last he could see inside and he peered through the grubby glass and the smoke. The fire appeared to have started somewhere on or around the stage and the timber of its construction was well alight and burning brightly, flames licking up the scenery. The curtains were starting to catch as well.

Then he saw Hannah. She was face down on the floor, not far from the stage and she wasn't moving. 'My God.'

He pulled the stone out of his pocket and looked down through the branches. Marielle was standing at the bottom of the shrub, looking up anxiously.

'Move back, Marielle.' He flapped a hand at her. 'Move away. It's dangerous.'

She retreated into the shrubs. He pulled his jacket sleeve down to protect his wrist and began smashing at the bottom of one of the panes. It gave quickly but immediately smoke billowed out and caught at his throat. He tied his handkerchief round his face and kept tapping on the glass, breaking it away from the frame as fast as he could. With the two lower panels gone, the upper, opening light still seemed to be holding safely in the frame. He tossed the stone inside in case he needed it again and eased his jacket off, spreading it over the frame and any remaining fragments of glass. It was going to be a drop to the floor inside but he'd have to risk it. He eased himself onto the edge and went over.

The interior floor was higher than the ground outside and he landed safely. Ducking down low to escape the worst of the smoke, he ran to where Hannah lay.

He felt her neck. She still had a pulse and she seemed to be breathing. He had no idea if she had anything broken but she had no obvious injuries and he had to get her out of there one way or another. How, he had no idea. He'd never get her up through the window if she was still unconscious. He carefully turned her over and supported her head.

'Hannah?' He patted her face. 'Hannah? Come on, wake up.'

There was nothing. He slapped her cheek a bit harder. 'Hannah, for God's sake. If you don't wake up I'm going to have to break the door down somehow and carry you out. Wake up, damn you.'

He thought he heard a groan and leaned in closer. The smoke kept making him cough but it was too dangerous to try to get through to the kitchen to wet his handkerchief. There wasn't time anyway. He shook Hannah by the shoulders.

'Hannah.'

This time she definitely groaned and her eyelids started flickering.

'What?' she muttered. Her eyes opened and she stared at him blearily.

'You've got to get up. We need to get out of here. The theatre's on fire, look.'

He nodded towards the stage and her gaze slowly turned. The fire was gaining ground and the heat was becoming fierce.

'What the hell,' she said groggily, trying to move. 'What's happening?'

He tugged her up into a sitting position.

'We're getting out of here, that's what's happening. Can you stand?'

'Of course.' She bent her legs and tried to lever herself up but her body didn't respond. Nathan grabbed her under the arm pits and yanked her to her feet.

'OK?' He held her. She was unsteady and began to cough. 'Come on.'

He looked round. He had no idea how they were going to do this. The state she was in, he'd never get her up and through that broken window.

'If only we had a key to the door,' he said.

'But I have,' said Hannah. She fumbled an uncoordinated hand into the pocket of her dress and pulled it out. 'See.' She coughed again. 'I always have it.'

'I could kiss you. Right, come on.' He began to pull her, one hand still under an armpit.

'No, no, we've got to take the trunk.' She was pulling back on him, eyes determined and stubborn.

'Don't be crazy, that stuff can be replaced. We've got to go.'

'Not without *The Lily Madonna* and she's in the trunk. Why don't we just push it. It's on wheels.'

She was already pulling away from him and had one hand on the trunk.

He decided it was quicker not to argue and got the trunk moving towards the door. The next minute Hannah left the

288

trunk and took a few groggy steps back into the room.

'Where the hell are you going now?' he shouted.

'I'm getting the Rembrandt.' She sounded drunk. Maybe she'd been drunk all along.

She grabbed the painting off the easel and they both made it to the door. Hannah was too clumsy with the key and Nathan had to unlock it but suddenly they were out in the fresh air, coughing heavily, but safe.

*

It's going to be a long night, thought Raff. He had been brought from his studio hours ago by the clamour of noise and people shouting. The theatre was on fire and Guillaume had organised a hosepipe and was marshalling as many men as he could find to help. Then Pietro had set up a second hosepipe and that was when they'd started to win and had managed to put the fire out. The main body of the building had been left intact but the interior timber work had been gutted and there had been significant damage to the roof.

It was maybe an hour ago already since the last flames had been extinguished and now here he was with the other abbey residents in the drawing room, all looking serious and accusing. The rest of the party guests had either gone home or gone to bed. It was amazing how quickly a fire could destroy a party and sober everyone up. Claudine had recently brought in a tray of tea and coffee and the others were sitting or standing holding cups and saucers as if it were an afternoon tea party. It was like a scene from a theatrical farce, he thought, all poses and sidelong glances. Nothing in this place ever happened without it becoming a drama.

Guillaume had made a point of homing in on Raff outside as soon as the furore had subsided.

'What do you know about this?' he'd demanded.

'Know about it?' said Raff. 'Me? Nothing. Why should I? Except that I imagine it was an accident waiting to happen: an old building, a bit neglected and all that wood.'

'An accident? How could it have been an accident when there was no-one there?'

'I don't know.' Raff shrugged. 'The electrics perhaps. Probably needed rewiring.'

'Where were you an hour and a half ago?'

'Me? You suspect me? Really Guillaume, be serious. I'd been in my studio for ages. The party got boring so I was working.' It wasn't true but he thought it sounded good.

Guillaume was still here with them in the drawing room and Raff thought he looked out of place in this setting: too muscular, too solid and regulation. He tended to slip back into policeman mode when things like this happened. Now he was taking charge, or trying to because Esther kept interrupting him.

Esther of course was being Esther, by turns solicitous and theatrical. And there was Hannah, the reluctant star of the scene, sitting on one of the sofas with Nathan alongside, insisting that she was fine. One of the house guests was a doctor and had taken a look at her and had indeed found nothing untoward except a small lump on the back of her head. He had advised Hannah to rest for a couple of days, had told her the signs of a delayed concussion and suggested she seek medical advice if she experienced any of them. It hadn't stopped everyone from fussing over her however, repeatedly asking her if she was all right.

'Well, I think we should all go to bed,' Esther was saying now. She turned and put her coffee cup down on the nearby sideboard. 'We're all tired and there's nothing to be gained by going over it all again. I think we've said all that needs to be said for now.'

'With respect, Miss Langley,' said Guillaume, 'I think it's important that we clear up some issues while it's all still fresh in our minds. That was a serious fire.' He glanced at Raff. 'It might have been an accident but we can't be sure. It'll be easier to assess in the morning. I might need some expert opinion.'

'Oh really, Guillaume,' said Esther. 'Don't start going all officious on me. You're being melodramatic, aren't you? I'm as upset as anyone about the fire and our beautiful little theatre.' She offered Hannah an embracing smile. 'But just so relieved that Hannah came to no harm. We shouldn't make too much of it, though. An accident is by far the most likely cause.' She rolled her eyes. 'I don't think we need "experts" do we?'

The smile faded and she made a point of taking Guillaume's arm, manoeuvring him to one side and speaking softly. Raff watched them carefully. Guillaume appeared to be unhappy with what his employer was saying. Did he venture to actually argue with her? Apparently so. Well that was interesting. Esther turned back to the room with a forced smile.

'Guillaume knows someone who is a bit of an expert in these things. He thinks we need to have it checked out. I mean, your studio was probably wired at about the same time, Raff and we don't want another fire. But Guillaume assures me this chap will be very discreet.' She glanced across at her security man and he met her gaze.

'It would also be useful to know what everyone saw,' said Guillaume, glancing round. 'Was there anyone hanging around the theatre, for example?'

'If it wasn't an accident,' said Raff, 'we shouldn't have let all those people leave, should we? I mean, there were a lot of people here. It could have been anyone.'

'Nathan says he saw Marielle,' Guillaume said as if Raff hadn't spoken. 'I'd like to know if she saw anything or anybody.'

'She's in bed now,' said Esther, easing herself down onto the nearest sofa with a pointed, weary sigh. 'Anyway Claudine said she asked her and Marielle insists she didn't see anything, just the fire.' She paused and shared a slow, meaningful look with the whole room. 'I must say, it makes me wonder if the poor child didn't have something to do with it herself.'

'Yes,' said Sara diffidently. 'That crossed my mind too. I mean, she does behave strangely. And what was she doing there at that time of night?'

There were murmurs of agreement.

'It's certainly odd that Marielle asked to see Hannah at the theatre,' remarked David.

'That's supposing that she did,' said Hannah, making them all turn to look at her. She had been very quiet up to now.

'You don't think she did?' said David.

'I think anyone could have passed on that message, knowing that I would go up to the theatre to check it out.'

'Which means it had to be someone who knew both Marielle and you,' observed Nathan casually.

'Exactly. And the thump on my head certainly wasn't an accident.'

There was an uncomfortable silence.

'Well, I suspect it was a sick practical joke that went wrong,' said David, putting his coffee cup down. 'Whatever, I agree with Esther: we'll all think more clearly after some sleep. We are going to bed.'

Esther rose gracefully to her feet, bestowing a grateful smile on him and taking his offered hand.

Raff noticed Sara watching them thoughtfully as they left the room. She caught his eye and raised her eyebrows, giving him a knowing look. He was sure she suspected Esther of being behind this, yet another 'accident'.

'If you're sure you're all right, Hannah,' she said, 'I think

I'll turn in too. It's been a long day.'

'I'm fine, thanks. I'll go up in a minute. Good night.'

Guillaume and Raff departed too, leaving Nathan and Hannah sitting silently side by side on the sofa.

Chapter 23

It was late on the Sunday morning when Hannah came to. For a moment she felt disorientated, confused about where she was. Then she coughed several times in succession and became aware of the rawness of her throat and it all came back in a rush. She eased a tentative hand along the pillow and under the back of her head and felt the lump there. It was exquisitely tender. She had no headache and yet she felt fragile. Even her limbs felt stiff and sore. She lay still for a while and let the evening's events play across her mind, trying to let it all sink in, hoping to make some sense out of it.

She remembered the party and the dancing, and she remembered the woman at the bar with the message about a little girl asking for her. She had gone up to the theatre; the door had been open and she'd gone in. But after the thump on the head, she remembered nothing until she was outside again, with Claudine insisting she come and sit down in her kitchen and have a drink. Would she like tea? Sit here, nice and quiet. Oh and look, here's a doctor to see you; Miss Langley sent him.

What had happened in the theatre was still a blank. At the back of her mind there was a fleeting image of flames now and then but after all she'd been told, she might just be imagining them. Nathan, it appeared, had saved her life by rescuing her from the burning building. He said she'd spoken to him, had insisted that they get her work trunk out of the theatre with them. She had no recall of that. She had also grabbed the Rembrandt school painting, and, once outside, Nathan had teased her that Timothy would be impressed with her conscientiousness, even in the face of a potentially dangerous conflagration.

'I wasn't going to waste all that work I'd put in,' she had apparently replied.

But she didn't remember that either. Nathan had been very good, she had to admit, supportive in a quiet, understated way for which she was grateful. She hoped she had thanked him; she wasn't sure now. He'd said they'd get some time to themselves to talk today; she definitely remembered him saying that. There were things to discuss, he'd said in a very pointed way, and she wondered what he'd meant by that exactly.

She remembered *The Lily Madonna* and sat up abruptly, then wished she hadn't as the world spun for a moment. What had happened to the icon? Her panic subsided. Of course, it was in the trunk which they'd rescued so it was fine. Calm down, she told herself. It's OK. Still, she needed to check on it to be sure. What had they done with the trunk?

She eased herself out of bed and walked slowly and stiffly into the bathroom to have a shower.

*

Hannah looked pale, Nathan thought, which was hardly surprising in the circumstances. He was probably a bit pale himself. They had both had breakfast. Other than Claudine, the only other person who seemed to be up and about was Sara who, leaving the dining room just as they entered, had immediately enquired after Hannah's health and offered any help needed.

'Esther's not up yet,' she added, 'but she did say something last night about asking her own doctor to come and see you if you wanted it.'

'Thank you but that's not necessary.'

'Just for a second opinion?' she offered. 'Well, let me know if you change your mind.'

'I will, thanks.'

Even with the dining room to themselves, they had said little over breakfast. Nathan was reluctant to talk when someone might walk in on them at any moment and Hannah seemed preoccupied with the whereabouts of her work trunk.

'It's in what Esther calls the Rec Room,' he told her. 'I took it there last night on her suggestion. Do you know it? A big room on the passage beyond Sara's office with a large television and a pull-down screen for watching films.' She nodded. 'Anyway, they don't use it much in the summer, she said, so it's not in anyone's way.'

'I need to go and check it.'

'We'll go together.'

'No, it's fine. I'll do it myself.'

'We'll go together. It's not open for discussion.'

She frowned and their eyes locked. Eventually, she gave an almost imperceptible nod.

Half an hour later they were in the Rec Room and Nathan had shut the door behind them. There was even a key and he turned it: there was no-one in this house he thought he could trust. He watched Hannah unlock the trunk and stiffly pull it open. She glanced inside and looked noticeably relieved. She turned and saw him watching her.

'I've got something to tell you,' she said, glancing towards the locked door.

'It's about *The Lily Madonna*, I imagine,' said Nathan. 'It's in there isn't it?' He nodded towards the trunk.

'You know?'

'You told me last night. But I don't know what it is. With a name like that, I'm guessing it's an icon.'

She was frowning at him again. 'I don't remember telling you.'

'We were trying to escape a burning building at the time.' He paused. 'Am I right?'

'Yes. Yes, it is an icon. But there's a story attached.'

'I knew there would be.'

She went to the trunk again, reached inside and pulled out a rectangular bundle swaddled in cloth.

'Before I show you, I need to explain how I've got this.'

Still holding it, she launched into a long story of how the local priest had come to her secretly with their church's most precious possession, pleading for her help because it had been damaged in a fall.

'It was in an awful condition,' she said. 'I refused. In any case I didn't have time to mess with it when I had all the other paintings to do.'

'But he talked you round.'

'Yes. He wheedled me, saying how important it was to the town. Everyone thinks it has miraculous powers, you see. In the end I decided I could do it in the evenings in my own time and that Timothy need never know.'

'I hope you got something in writing.'

'Of course. I'm not fresh out of college.'

'Good. So come on, show me then.'

'Look at these first.'

She put the bundle down, produced some photographs from the trunk and handed them to him. There were a couple of old pictures of the icon as it was being carried in procession and others that Hannah had taken before she started work on it.

297

Nathan whistled softly. 'I see what you mean about the state of it. God, what a mess.' He looked up. 'So I presume you're now going to show me what an amazing restoration you've performed.'

'Not exactly.' She hesitated. 'As I started removing the flaking paint, I found a lot of the bole cracked and loose. And the underlying gesso was cracked in places too. There were glimpses of gilt and colour through it. I could see them through the magnifier. It became clear there was another painting underneath.'

Nathan's heart sank. He suddenly knew where this was heading.

'And?'

'And I got it x-rayed. By a friend,' she added to his surprised, enquiring expression. 'It showed there was another image underneath, a much more complex one. My only concern was whether the whole thing was intact – you couldn't tell from the x-ray.'

'But you decided you had to see it.'

'Wouldn't you have?'

She waited, eyes fixed on him, demanding a response.

'I might have,' he conceded. 'Maybe I'd have just teased at a tiny section to satisfy myself.'

'Exactly. That's what I did. Then I realised it was too special to be ignored and I kept going.'

He threw his head back in frustration. 'And if it isn't intact underneath, what then?'

'But it is.'

She peeled off the cloth and held up the icon triumphantly.

He wasn't sure what he'd expected but not this, and he was struck dumb, taking it all in. It was a brilliant, highly polished painting of the Assumption of the Virgin Mary: the Madonna, holding a long lily stem, was being transported to heaven by a band of surrounding saints. Unlike some icons he'd seen which had been rigid and formal, this painting glowed. It was vibrant and alive, mesmerising. Astonishing. There was still a small section which Hannah hadn't uncovered in the top left corner but not enough to hide the quality of the piece.

'Well?' she prompted, watching his face.

'That is amazing.'

She nodded. She seemed satisfied and put it down. 'That's why we had to rescue the trunk.'

She looked weary suddenly and sank into one of the easy chairs facing the television. Nathan went over and sat on one adjacent to her.

'But what's the priest going to say about it?' he said.

She shook her head, staring towards the blank television. 'I've no idea. I've never done anything like this before. It just became something I had to do.' She paused. 'I'm probably going to get into all sorts of trouble, even though that's a wonderful painting and probably worth a fortune but everyone'll think I've desecrated their famous icon.' She raised troubled eyes to his face. 'Are you going to tell Timothy?'

'What, you think I'm some sort of telltale?'

'I thought that's why he sent you here, to keep tabs on what I was doing.'

He sighed. 'Well… yes, it was really. But I'm not going to tell him about this. You did it in your own time. It's nothing to do with him. You haven't even used his paint.'

She smiled weakly.

'Does anyone here know about you working on the icon?' he asked.

'No. Why?'

He shrugged. 'I thought if someone believed you were

desecrating it, that might be motive enough to hit you over the head and set fire to the theatre.'

'That doesn't make sense. Why would someone try to burn the place down with the icon in it if it was that important to them?'

'Maybe they didn't realise that you kept it in the trunk and thought it was in your room.'

'No. Nobody knew anyway. I've been really careful.'

'Either way, I think it's time you went home for a bit. Timothy'll understand. I'll be finished with the mural soon and I can finish off the Rembrandt for Esther.'

'No.' Hannah's eyes blazed. 'I'm not going to leave a job unfinished. I'm OK. Just a bit feeble today. Tomorrow I'll be fine.'

'Perhaps you will, but someone tried to kill you, Hannah, or have you already forgotten? It's not safe for you here.'

'We don't know that.'

'You're kidding yourself.' He dropped his voice. 'This is a weird bunch of people, Hannah. I wouldn't put it past any of them to have done it. Guillaume gives me the creeps for one. Look at the way he prowls around, all silent and watchful like he's in a secret army. He could have got those scars on his hand setting the fire which killed Jemma, not trying to save her. Maybe he doesn't like having you here, an outsider, asking questions. Or maybe they're right about that kid. She's odd and she keeps popping up in the wrong place. Maybe she's – I don't know – all muddled in her head and thinks it's a game. No, let me finish. Whatever, you aren't safe here. You should leave. Anyway, the theatre's not usable and I guess you've lost a load of equipment.'

'Not that much. I routinely put the most important stuff away; there are too many keys to the theatre. I've got more than enough in the trunk to work with.' Hannah got to her feet.

'I'm going to finish the job, somewhere, somehow. And I have to finish *The Lily Madonna* in time for the festival of the Assumption on the fifteenth. There's a big *fête*. Just another week and I should be done. What happens after that, I don't know.' She fixed him with a look, daring him to argue. 'I'll be careful.'

He didn't argue. There was no point.

*

'Are you sure you're up to it?' Esther asked anxiously when Hannah enquired where she might work now in order to finish the job. 'I mean, that was a horrible thing you went through. I'll quite understand if you want to stop there and go home.'

'Not at all. I'm fine. There's only another week's work I think. I'd like to finish up. Is there somewhere I could be out of the way to get on?'

'Well, yes,' Esther replied doubtfully. 'I suppose you could stay in the Rec Room and work there. But of course, the easel's gone up in smoke, hasn't it?'

'I've got a folding one in my trunk. It'll be fine.'

'All right, if you're sure. I'll get Pietro to make more space for you in there. But my dear girl, are you really all right? Who could have done such a terrible thing? I think David's right. I think it must have been a practical joke that went horribly wrong. I'm inclined to think that perhaps Marielle did indeed do it.'

'I suppose it might have been a joke,' Hannah conceded politely. 'It's a shame about your lovely theatre though.'

Esther gave a dismissive wave of the hand. 'Not to worry. I'd been thinking that it needed refurbishing anyway.' Her manner changed and she fixed Hannah with an intense, steely look. 'You will understand if I don't get the police involved in this, won't you? We managed to keep that other fire quiet but

301

you can never tell. The press do get a hold of these things somehow and make everything sound so sordid.' She hesitated and softened again. 'And think of the upset and trouble it might cause Marielle.' She squeezed Hannah's hand. 'I knew you'd understand.'

Hannah managed a smile.

That conversation took place on the Sunday afternoon. On the Monday morning, when Hannah went into the Rec Room, Pietro had already been in to sort it out. The easy chairs had been covered in sheets and moved out of the way, and a small folding table and a wooden chair had been placed in the middle.

Hannah unpacked what she needed and settled back to work. For all her bravado to Nathan, the assault and the fire had unnerved her badly, but she'd be damned if she was going to show it. Still, every unexpected noise had her jumping and she carefully set up her easel and work station so that she was facing the door, even though she often locked it. Nor would she play any music for fear of being caught unawares.

Raff rapped on the door on the Monday afternoon, immediately making her stomach clench and her heart thump in her chest. He smiled calmly when she let him in. The brief show of bile he'd expressed on the Saturday night appeared to have gone and he was his usual flippant, cynical self.

'You could have set up in my studio,' he remarked, manoeuvring uncomfortably close to look at the painting on the easel. 'It's a much better space than this. More windows for a start.'

'This is fine. And I concentrate better when I'm alone.'

'Point taken.' He walked around the easel and examined the materials spread out on the table, fingering a brush here, a jar of pigment there. 'Nice to see you're not the kind of girl to let a little bit of concussion and a fire put you off your stride.'

302

He stopped and glanced back at her with the suggestion of admiration. 'Quite impressive really. I rather thought you'd be like most women and give in.'

'Give in to what?'

'To fear, I suppose. Thought you'd run a mile.'

'Maybe that's what the person setting the fire wanted me to do.'

He nodded and smiled again.

'Maybe.'

Was it him, she wondered after he'd gone? Why? For fun, because he assumed that someone would rescue her but he wanted to see her reaction? Or to teach her a lesson, maybe, for having poked about in his studio when he wasn't there. Or perhaps for some other twisted reason in his unfathomable mind.

She tried to forget about him. She was back painting over the pentimenti again, each one in turn, trying to 'bury' them back where they belonged. It was delicate work and needed her full concentration. She was glad of it.

But her suspicions were never far away. In every break they crowded back in on her along with the inevitable questions. Nathan thought any of the household could have initiated the attack and perhaps he was right, though Marielle appeared to be everyone's favourite suspect. Because she was a child perhaps, and couldn't answer back. Or maybe because she got on everyone's nerves. She did behave oddly, certainly, but Hannah didn't believe it. The girl was a bit lost; she was lonely and idiosyncratic, but none of those made her dangerous or vindictive. And she appeared to like spending time with Hannah so why would she try to hurt her? There'd been that look in her eyes too when she remembered the fire at the Garden House. She wouldn't have lit a fire. And how had the child opened the theatre door? Hannah had thought it through over and over and she was sure she had locked it. Marielle could perhaps have used Claudine's key and then returned it, but no, she wouldn't have had the height and strength to hit Hannah. It couldn't have been Marielle. Not that Hannah could pin it on anyone else either. Her thoughts and suspicions just kept going round in circles.

On the Wednesday evening, working on the icon with the door locked, something began teasing at the back of her mind, something Marielle had said, something that felt important except that, irritatingly, it refused to come forward. For the life of her, Hannah couldn't remember what it was; she just knew that she hadn't seen the significance of it at the time. She'd remember when she wasn't trying so hard. Just work, she thought. Keep easing the paint off the icon and let it come to you.

And in the end it did. Staring at *The Lily Madonna* after she'd stopped for the night, she suddenly remembered what it was and felt a tingle of both excitement and apprehension. Everything started to slot into place. Maybe, just maybe, she had finally worked out what was going on. She lifted a hand and lightly touched the icon. Illumination, the priest had said the icon offered. Perhaps that was what she'd just got.

Tomorrow she needed to talk to Marielle.

Chapter 24

Esther was in her bedroom on the Saturday evening, changing for dinner, when David finally put in an appearance. He came in looking weary and disgruntled, having been out playing golf since late morning.

'Not a good day?' she enquired cautiously.

'Terrible. My putting's completely left me. It was embarrassing.' He dropped his car keys onto the little ceramic tray left for that purpose on top of the chest of drawers then swore and banged an angry fist down next to it, making them rattle. He peeled off his clothes and disappeared into the shower, leaving the door open as he often did. It made the bedroom a little steamy but Esther didn't mind. She rather liked watching him shower.

'You've cut it a bit tight,' she called out over the hiss of the water, standing in the doorway in her cocktail dress.

'I won't be long.'

His body was already covered in suds and now he was shampooing his hair. She loved the vigour of his movements, the ripple of his muscles and the complete lack of self-consciousness as he did it. He sluiced himself off again then grabbed the towel from the top of the screen and began rubbing himself down.

'I saw Hannah by the lodge when I drove in,' he said, stepping out of the cubicle. 'She seemed to be talking to

Guillaume very earnestly.'

'Really? What about?'

'How should I know? I didn't stop.' He wrapped the towel around his waist and stood in front of the mirror, combing his hair back into position. 'So Hannah's finally finished restoring your paintings. You have to hand it to her for staying. I didn't think she'd want to after last weekend.'

'No. I don't think any of us did.' She watched his face in the mirror. 'She's not sure which day she'll be leaving yet. Her company in Oxford are going to sort out transport for her and for the trunk. I'm hoping it'll be early next week. Once she's gone, we can get back to normal, relax a little. Whatever, I thought we'd make this the parting dinner, so to speak.'

He caught her eye in the mirror but said nothing and turned away, pulling open drawers and wardrobe doors, sorting out which clothes to wear. Just once, she wished he would say that he'd be glad to see Hannah go and to have the place to themselves again, but he wouldn't, she knew, and if she pressed him he'd get cross and defensive. It would achieve nothing.

'Has Nathan been invited for dinner?' David asked, pulling on a pair of underpants.

'I told her to ask him.' She paused. 'I'm intrigued by what it is she wants to show us.'

'She wants to show us something?'

'Yes. I told you this morning; I knew you weren't listening. She said she'd be finished by tonight and that she had something she wanted to show us. She seemed quite excited by it. I've no idea what it is.' Her eyes lit up. 'Maybe she's found a Rembrandt signature on that last painting, hidden under all the dirt and varnish. Wouldn't that be amazing? She's going to hand that one over tonight, she did say that. That could be it.'

He didn't respond, pulling on a shirt and fastening the

buttons.

Esther gave it up. David didn't share her passion for the old masters. She sat at her dressing table and did her make-up in silence. She couldn't shake off a feeling of unease and her thoughts turned to Hannah again. Hannah talking to Guill-aume.

*

Esther and Sara were in the drawing room when Nathan arrived and David was at the drinks cabinet, mixing cocktails. Nathan opted for a simple gin and tonic. He assumed he'd be driving home later.

There was no sign of Hannah. She had rung him the previous evening from a phone box, explaining that she had nearly finished her work and that her hosts had invited her to share a last dinner with them before she left. 'And you're invited too. You will come, won't you?' Seven-thirty for drinks, she'd said; dinner at eight. She had insisted on meeting him here, rather than beforehand because she said she had things to do but she'd refused to specify what.

He glanced at his watch: it was now seven forty and that bothered him. He had already learned that Hannah, surprisingly perhaps, was punctual to a fault. And she'd sounded strange on the phone, even for her. Preoccupied.

'Try and roll with me tonight, will you?' she said. 'I might say things that sound a bit odd. Just kind of back me up, will you?'

'Back you up? In what way? What do you mean by odd?'

'I've got a plan. I'll explain it all later.'

Then the pips had gone and she'd closed the call, leaving him none the wiser. God, she was irritating.

'How's your work going, Nathan?'

Sara was talking to him and he'd only just realised. She

tipped her glass to her mouth and sipped. Her hand shook a little. Her pupils, he noticed, were dilated.

'Very well, thanks. Just a bit of protection to put on the mural now to seal it. A day's work at most.'

'That's good. You and Hannah'll be able to travel back together then.'

'Yes, we might. You'll all be glad to see the back of us, I'm sure.'

She laughed but shot a nervous, sidelong glance at Esther. 'Not at all.'

'Have you seen Hannah this evening, Sara? I mean, she is all right?'

She looked first surprised then worried by the question. 'I'm sure she is.' A quick look towards the door. 'She's just late, isn't she?'

They all made small talk. Nathan saw Esther catch David's eye a couple of times and glance towards the door too but she had her charming, composed face on this evening.

'Do stay over again tonight, won't you, Nathan,' she said. 'Claudine's got the same room ready for you. If you need it, that is.' One of her enchanting smiles. 'But now I'm getting concerned. It's not like Hannah to be late. Even Raff's here before her,' she added as he strolled in. 'I do hope you haven't offended her in some way. Or maybe it's us? Have we said something horrible to her?'

'Where's the guest of honour?' said Raff, looking round.

'Ah, here she is,' said Esther. 'We've been worrying about you, Hannah.'

'I'm sorry I'm late. I got caught up doing something and the time disappeared. My apologies.'

Esther's smile was stretched a little taut. 'Not to worry. David'll fix you a drink and then we'll go through.'

'I'm fine, thanks. I don't want to hold you up.'

'Very well. Let's go and eat then.'

Nathan was too slow and Raff moved quickly to Hannah's side, looping her arm through his.

'Come on, Hannah. Let me take you in. Tell me, what *have* you been doing?'

'Just last minute things, Raff.'

'Nothing too shocking? I am disappointed.'

They all paraded through to the dining room.

*

Esther waved them all to their places, insisting that, tonight, no-one should sit at the head of the table. She put David opposite Sara with herself to his right. Raff was placed opposite her with Hannah on his left. Esther then chivvied Nathan into the seat opposite Hannah. It meant that Esther was in the middle and at the heart of every conversation while Hannah had carefully been placed at the furthest possible remove from David.

They had a salmon mousse starter and David offered a dry white wine. Nathan decided he would stay over for the night and accepted. He had a feeling he was going to need some alcohol just to get him through the evening.

'Before we start, I think we should drink a toast.' David raised his glass. 'To Hannah, with our sincere thanks for all her hard work.'

Hannah's name echoed round the table. Nathan caught her eye briefly but couldn't read what was going on behind that studiously polite expression.

'I was going to thank her myself,' murmured Esther. She darted a reproachful look at David then smiled back at Hannah. 'I wouldn't want you to think I'm not grateful. And after all we've put you through...' She fluttered a hand in the air as if chasing away unpleasant thoughts.

They started to eat. Esther talked about a movie she was going to Prague to shoot in September while David mentioned that he was going back to the States to work on a television miniseries.

'And I'll be going to my studio,' remarked Raff.

'And doing very little,' said Sara.

He offered her a pained smile, abandoned the remains of his mousse and laid his cutlery down.

'So–o, your last supper with us,' he said to Hannah. 'Sounds like a cue for a painting, doesn't it? But I suppose you've seen them all.'

'Hardly. But you never know what each commission will bring.' Hannah smiled and shared it round the table. 'It's amazing what hidden treasures can still be found in the most surprising places.'

'I've seen that mural,' said Esther, dabbing the corners of her mouth with her napkin. 'Da Vinci's *Last Supper* in Milan. It was wonderful despite all that it's been through. A masterpiece, don't you think so Hannah? Nathan?'

They agreed though they both admitted to only having seen reproductions of it.

'But imagine what it must have been like when it was first painted,' remarked Nathan.

'Of course,' said Esther. 'But it's still worth seeing. You must go.' She turned to look at David. 'You haven't seen it either have you darling. We should go together.'

'Really, Esther, you know I'm a complete moron when it comes to art.' He looked apologetically towards Hannah and Nathan. 'No offence, guys. I'm really impressed by what you do. I'm just not a big gallery buff.'

Liane came in to clear the plates and she and Claudine returned a few minutes later with the main course. David produced a local red wine and poured some into everyone's

310

glass. They helped themselves to salad. The conversation bumped along, dominated at first by Esther talking about galleries she'd visited and paintings she had seen, then moving on to places they had all visited.

'Venice,' said Sara. 'I think that's the most romantic city in the world.'

'But it's sinking,' observed Raff.

'I know.' Sara glared at him defensively.

'Perhaps that makes it more romantic,' said David, 'knowing that it won't last. It makes it all the more precious, doesn't it?'

Sara looked at him gratefully. 'Exactly.'

'Rare, perhaps,' said Raff. 'But I don't see how a city sinking into a smelly lagoon is romantic.'

There was a strained silence.

'But Italy's full of lovely cities, isn't it?' said Nathan. 'Personally, I love Florence. It's a beautiful city and it's got the Uffizi Galleries. I mean, what more do you need?' He shrugged, grinned, and spread out a hand of entreaty.

'A golf course?' suggested David.

They all laughed and the mood slackened. The dinner dragged on. Hannah participated in the conversation now and then but seemed to be almost an onlooker, as if she were waiting for something. The look in her eyes had changed and Nathan's unease thickened. What was she waiting for? What the hell was she planning and when exactly was it going to happen?

Dessert arrived along with the cheese board, fruit and a fresh basket of bread. Claudine paused for the briefest of moments after putting down the basket and Nathan could have sworn she and Hannah exchanged a look. This was getting seriously weird.

Raff and Nathan ate dessert; the rest picked at the cheese

and fruit. When Liane brought in the coffee and tea, it seemed that the time had finally arrived for the plan to unfold. Hannah suggested that, as soon as they'd finished their drinks, they should come with her down to the Rec Room.

'I've got something I want you all to see.'

*

Hannah led the way down the corridor and tried to walk slowly. She wanted to appear nonchalant. It had been difficult to sit through dinner, knowing that she had to wait for the right moment while doubts began to crowd in on her that this scheme of hers was crackpot and would never work. Behind her now in the passage she heard Esther teasing Nathan.

'I suppose you know all about this, don't you: Hannah's little secret?'

'Oh please, Esther,' Hannah heard him reply. 'She's a woman. She doesn't tell me anything.'

Esther gave her melodic laugh. 'Oh Nathan, you are funny.'

In the Rec Room, the painting, *Christ Receiving the Holy Spirit*, was on the easel.

'Here we are,' Hannah declared, standing by it and surveying each of them in turn. 'This is the final painting, cleaned and hopefully brought back to something close to what the artist intended.'

'Is that all we've come to see?' said Raff, sounding bored.

'Not entirely. It's the first thing.'

She mentioned the pentimenti and explained them, passing round photographs of what they'd looked like before she'd covered them up again.

'Fascinating,' said David, peering at one of the photos then back at the painting.

Esther was more interested in the painting than the

312

photographs.

'It looks wonderful,' she said doubtfully. 'You didn't find anything unexpected then, like a signature?'

'No,' said Hannah. 'No, it's still unattributed.'

'Didn't Rembrandt put in the final flourishes on his pupils' work though?' asked Raff.

'Possibly. Some experts think so but it's hard to know how the workshops worked exactly after all this time. It's likely he would have at least overseen all the work produced.'

'This is serious art,' said Sara, staring intently at the painting, then equally intently at the photograph in her hand. Hannah noticed the photograph was shaking.

'Yes. Deadly serious.' Raff cast her a scathing look.

'By the way,' said Hannah, 'I nearly forgot.' She produced a necklace from her pocket: a gold chain with a small gold pendant of a rearing horse dangling from it, a single tiny diamond fixed in its head. 'I found this yesterday when I was out in the gardens. Does anyone recognise it?'

They all turned to look. Esther and Sara immediately abandoned the painting and moved closer to examine it.

'It was down near the pool house,' added Hannah. 'I know this will sound strange – I think it's strange too – but I seem to feel that it belonged to Jemma.'

'What makes you say that?' Sara stared into Hannah's face. 'You never met Jemma. How on earth would you know that?'

'It's obvious,' said Raff. 'She must have seen a photograph of Jemma when she was wearing it.'

'So it *was* Jemma's?' Hannah pressed.

Esther nodded. 'Yes. She bought it not long before…' She swallowed. 'She saw it in a jeweller's window and told me afterwards that she had to have it. She loved horses.' She shook her head, frowning. 'But I don't think there are any photos of

313

her where she's wearing that. Certainly none on show. She hadn't had it that long.' She looked round at the others who all shook their heads or shrugged.

David suddenly grabbed the necklace from Hannah's hand and examined it. After a minute, Sara took it off him and examined it too.

'It looks like Jemma's,' she said and passed it back to Hannah, looking confused. 'But you can't have found it. Why should it show up now?'

Hannah shrugged.

'Where did you say you found it exactly?' David ran a restless hand through his hair. 'This feels like another sick joke.'

'Hannah's not the kind of person to play sick jokes,' said Nathan. 'I suggest we just hear her out.'

Hannah looked at him and gave the suggestion of a nod. She hadn't been sure how he was going to react to all this but it seemed like he was on board for the ride. That was a relief.

'I found it over in the cotton lavender below the pool house,' she said. 'It was odd. It was as if I knew it was there. Anyway,' she added quickly, 'the thing I particularly wanted to show you tonight was another painting. But this painting is very different and *very* special.'

Still with the necklace gathered up in her hand, she took the Rembrandt school picture off the easel and stood it up against the wall, then picked up the cloth-wrapped bundle which lay on the table and carefully unwrapped it. She propped the icon up on the easel and stepped back.

'This…' she announced, '…is *The Lily Madonna*.'

Esther's reaction was immediate and indignant. 'No it's not. I mean it's beautiful…' She peered more closely at it. '…but it's not *The Lily Madonna*. I've seen it hundreds of times.'

314

'She's right,' agreed Sara. 'I've seen it too. That isn't it.'

'No, it's not the image you've seen. But it is *The Lily Madonna*, trust me. This is the true one.'

Hannah went on to explain how she came to have it in her possession and how she realised that there was an older, finer image underneath the damaged one that she had been asked to restore.

'At some point, probably in the eighteenth century, this image was painted over with the one you knew.' She pointed at the picture. 'You can see the lily that the Virgin Mary is holding. That's what gave the icon its name. This is the real thing, the icon that brought about all the miracles long before it was painted over.' She touched the edge of it deferentially. 'This is a very special painting and exquisitely executed. Blessed too, some might say. There are those who believe that this can make things right.'

There was silence while they all absorbed this, staring at the image before them.

Hannah opened her hand to reveal the necklace again and looked down at it. She uttered a groan, prompting them all to turn to her again.

'This feels, my goodness, it feels so warm all of a sudden. Hot, really hot.' She frowned, holding the chain up gingerly as if to allow it to cool off away from her skin. Her voice became flat and distant. 'This was thrown away on the night of the fire. Jemma was wearing it and she took it off and threw it.' Hannah fixed on the icon then back on the necklace. She slowly looked up at Sara with a puzzled expression. 'You were there when she did it, Sara. Why did she do that?'

Sara stared at her aghast. 'I don't know what you mean. Of course I wasn't there.'

'You were arguing. It was all about David, wasn't it?'

'What is this?' demanded David. 'I mean what kind of a

stunt are you trying to pull?'

Hannah stared as if mesmerised at *The Lily Madonna* and didn't respond.

'It's the icon,' said Nathan softly. 'Look at it; look at Hannah. Everyone says it's a channel, that it makes you see things clearly. Hannah's worked with it for so long, she's tuned in to it in some way. She believes in it and it's helping her to see.'

'Can it do that?' Sara went closer to the icon, gazing at it reverently.

Here goes, thought Hannah. The final gamble.

'You were cross with her for having an affair with David, weren't you Sara. You loved David.'

There was a moment's silence. Hannah almost held her breath.

'Yes.' Sara reached out a shaky hand to touch the icon. 'I love David. I've loved him for years.'

'What?' said Esther. 'What is this?'

Everyone ignored her.

'And you argued bitterly,' said Hannah, 'and Jemma was cross with you too, taunting you. So you hit her. Then you started the fire.'

Sara looked round suddenly, eyes blazing, resting a furious, challenging gaze on each person in turn. She started to shout.

'Well, wouldn't you? She always put me down, always, ever since we were children. She'd steal my boyfriends, just because she could. OK, she was pretty but she only made it as an actress because she was happy to walk all over people. She didn't care. It wasn't talent. And then she had to have David too. It was the final straw. You see, I was prepared to wait. I knew he and Esther would break up eventually because Esther didn't appreciate him. They weren't right for each other.'

'What on earth do you mean by that?' demanded Esther. 'David?'

But Sara didn't even hear her. Her gaze was fixed back on David.

'And you like me, I know you do. I knew that if I waited, you'd come to me in the end.' She shook her head, eyes wild and staring. 'But then Jemma thought she'd seduce you. It was just a game to her. And you had to give her that bloody necklace, didn't you? She flaunted it at me. I couldn't stand it.' Sara put a hand to her head and seemed to deflate suddenly. 'I haven't been well.'

'Well, there's a turn-up,' said Raff sardonically, looking at David. 'The squeaky clean image isn't quite so perfect now is it? I'd guessed there was something going on but Jemma denied it. That's what our row was about. It's why I stormed off that night. And to think I blamed you for the fire, Esther. I thought you'd found out about the affair and you were the one who'd started it in a moment of drunken anger.'

Esther was shaking her head. Hannah felt a pang of sympathy for her. This was a lousy way to find out your partner was cheating on you. Not that there was a good way.

'I didn't know,' Esther said, looking pale and shocked. She put a hand down to the little work table to steady herself. 'How could you have done this to me?' she said to David. 'No, don't touch me.'

'Sara,' asked Nathan carefully, 'why did you hit Hannah and set fire to the theatre?'

Sara scoffed as if the answer was obvious. She pointed at Hannah and shouted again. 'Because David liked her too much. I saw them dancing together. I could see it was going to happen all over again. It wasn't that I wanted to hurt you,' she said to Hannah pathetically. 'I didn't have a choice.' She rested her fingers against the frame of the icon. 'Do you think *The*

Lily Madonna has the power to forgive? Can it make everything right?'

Hannah watched Sara warily. As she fingered the painting she became introspective and quiet, occasionally murmuring to herself, but she seemed to be in an alternating cycle of behaviour, one minute apologetic and pleading, the next raging and wild. To Hannah's untrained eye, she looked as though she was heading for a collapse. And Esther was no help; she was too upset and cross to think about anyone but herself. She and David kept on bickering in the background.

Hannah turned to Nathan, speaking softly. 'Guillaume's outside the door. He should have heard most of this. Ask him to call a doctor as well as the police, will you?'

Before Nathan could move, Guillaume appeared in the doorway, nodded, and disappeared.

'I think he heard,' said Nathan.

'He'll sort this out now. I explained to him in advance what I was going to do.'

'And he went along with it?'

'I know. Surprising. But it seems he's still a policeman at heart. Apparently he always had his suspicions about that first fire and the second one made him even more concerned.' She smiled at Nathan. 'Thanks for your help,' she mouthed.

'You should have told me what you were going to do.'

'You'd have tried to stop me.'

'True. But you should have told me anyway.'

She shrugged. 'I'm just glad it's over.'

'But I don't understand: how did you find that necklace?'

Hannah glanced at Sara who was still in a world of her own. Even so, she dropped her voice even lower.

'It's a long story. I'll tell you later.'

Guillaume reappeared and between them they persuaded Sara to go with them to her room to have a rest.

318

'I need a cigarette,' she said as they walked along the passage. 'That icon is special isn't it? I didn't realise before what it could do. It's marvellous. You know, I feel better already. I think it's helped. But I really need a cigarette. I've got some special ones. They usually make me feel better.'

Chapter 25

The Sunday morning dawned bright and sunny. Waking up in his abbey room, it took Nathan a few moments to remember where he was. A strange bed, in a strange room, in a strange house. Then the events of the night before began to trickle back into his head and he was quickly wide awake and glancing at his watch. Nine-thirty. He relaxed back into his pillow; there was plenty of time. In fact, he'd rather hoped it would be later. He hadn't got to bed until the early hours. What an evening.

Guillaume still had contacts in the police apparently and, having informed them of the situation, a police doctor had come out straight away along with uniformed officers and someone more senior. Sara had been sedated and taken away. There seemed to be little chance that she'd be fit to stand trial for some time, if ever. Before the doctor arrived she'd had another rant about Jemma, then she'd started to cry, sobbing about how much she loved David. She kept talking about the icon too and repeating how good it had made her feel. Couldn't she take it with her? She had completely lost it; it was a sorry sight.

Esther and David had been happy to leave Guillaume to take charge, too preoccupied with themselves. They had gone upstairs, still arguing. Had they spent the night together despite the row? He had no idea. Maybe that was the way their relationship worked, if you could honestly say that it worked.

All that cheating on each other. It wasn't Nathan's idea of the way a couple should behave.

Raff, left behind, had become unusually subdued. 'Sara, of all people,' he said several times. 'I can't believe it.' Then he'd disappeared too, muttering something about going to his studio, needing some time to himself. Claudine had still been around, appearing from the kitchen now and then, showing concern and offering help, then muttering about what a wicked thing Sara had done. In the end, she went to bed too, assured that there was nothing more she could do.

And with Sara finally gone, Nathan and Hannah had ended up in the drawing room with a bottle of brandy. It was nearly two in the morning but fortunately David had forgotten to lock up the drinks cabinet. Nathan poured a generous measure into two balloon glasses and offered one to Hannah.

She wrinkled up her nose. 'I don't really like brandy.'

'Drink it anyway. It's soothing. To keep me company if nothing else.'

He held the glass closer to her until she took it.

'Why do you need soothing?' she enquired.

'Because you put me through it this evening.'

She pulled a wry grin and sat down heavily on one of the sofas. Nathan sat on the one adjacent, leaning back, stretching his legs out.

'Put *you* through it,' she said. 'That's a joke. Imagine what I went through. I've been planning this for a couple of days. I'm exhausted.'

'You were impressive. Of course, the plan was appalling. I don't know how you got away with it.'

'Thanks, I'll take that as a compliment.' She sipped at the brandy and pulled a face but sat back hugging the glass all the same.

'Tell me. Tell me how you got the necklace, how you

worked out that it was Sara who was behind it all. Tell me everything.'

Hannah tipped her head back a moment, staring at the ceiling.

'Where do I start?'

'The beginning usually works for me.'

She raised her head and gave him a withering look. 'It was Marielle. Marielle sees everything because, despite the best efforts of her grandparents, the child's restless and lonely, so she wanders and she watches. The trouble is that she sees more than is good for her. She was really wary of me to start with then, slowly, she began to talk. I didn't listen though, not properly. I was happy for her to chatter but I was busy and I suppose I assumed she was just talking to get my attention. It was all bits and pieces, seemingly unrelated. It's only recently I realised that there was some kind of link in what she was saying.'

'In what way?'

'She mentioned the fire, how hot it was. It had obviously scared her so she'd clearly seen it, had actually been there. And she drew a picture of a horse. She said it was a pendant but that it wasn't hers which seemed a bit odd. It felt significant somehow. A few minutes later she asked me if I liked David, very intense and serious, and went on to ask why everyone here liked him. I didn't think anything about it at the time, I was distracted because she seemed scared of David. Then it occurred to me that perhaps when Marielle said *like* she really meant something stronger, that they *loved* him. She said it in English you see and *aimer* can translate either way. I also realised…' Hannah looked across at him as if she was about to pull the rabbit out of the proverbial hat. '…that when you see Sara around David, she looks happy. She never normally looks happy. Ever. It all began to fit together.'

322

'That's a bit tenuous. She looks happy when she's around him is not exactly proof of anything.'

'Of course not. But people's body language tells a huge amount. You really should get out more. Watch instead of judging all the time.'

'What d'you mean? I don't judge.'

'Yes, you do. You judged me.'

'And you didn't judge me too? Come on. Everyone does. We make presumptions.' He hesitated but met her gaze. 'They're not always right.'

'No. I'm sure we can agree on that.'

'Good. Go on then. You had a hunch, so…?'

'I decided to talk to Marielle again, see if I could get her to tell me anything. I thought if I suggested Sara as if I already suspected her and Marielle knew anything, she might open up. And she did. She seemed relieved to be able to talk about it. She told me that she was awake and in the grounds the night of the Garden House fire. She saw someone go back to the building quite late, after everyone else had gone and it was all quiet. A woman. So she went in closer and heard two women having an argument. They were shouting at times.'

'But did she understand them? Her English isn't that good.'

'Good enough. Living here, she hears it all the time and Claudine's encouraged her. So she recognised that one woman said she loved David, for example, and she heard the two women using each other's names. She's a smart kid. She knew who they were and she picked up the tone of the argument, worked bits of it out from odd words. Then Jemma got really cross apparently. According to Marielle, she said something like: "If you want it, you have it then. Go and find it." And she stood on the balcony and threw something away into the cotton lavender.'

'The necklace,' said Nathan. 'Of course. So Marielle retrieved it.'

Hannah sipped at her brandy. 'Not straight away. The row continued and got even more heated, then there was an odd noise and it went suddenly quiet. Marielle got scared, ran back home and went to bed. But she couldn't sleep and, hearing a commotion a bit later, went downstairs. Her grandparents had been roused by Guillaume, saying there was a fire and Pietro went to help. Claudine told the girl to go back to bed and went across to the house. Of course, Marielle snook outside again and went to watch. She didn't find the necklace until much later the next day. Presumably, if Sara bothered to look for it, she couldn't find it.'

'And Marielle's kept it ever since?'

'Shut away in a box in her room so Sara wouldn't have been able to find it after that.' Hannah sat forward, looking earnest and intense. 'The thing was, I had to come up with a plan, don't you see? I didn't want Marielle to be dragged into it. I didn't think she'd cope with having to be a witness. Imagine what it would be like for her.' She shrugged and sat back. 'And who would have believed her? She didn't see Sara light the fire. It was all hearsay and conjecture. No, we needed an admission. So I explained everything to Claudine and Pietro. They were a bit unhappy at first but they finally agreed to what I had in mind.'

'That you would pretend to find the necklace yourself and use the supposed powers of *The Lily Madonna* to tell you what happened? I imagine you had to explain how you came to have the icon. That must have been an interesting conversation.'

'It was. Claudine was shocked, upset even, but she came round.'

'What made you think Sara would crumble and admit it though?'

'Because she'd asked about the icon before. I sensed that she was quite superstitious about it. I get the impression that she lives on a knife's edge, smoking to settle her nerves, using cannabis too when she can. Of course the cannabis is probably part of her problem too: it makes her more anxious or even paranoiac.'

'It was a hell of a gamble you were taking.'

'I know. But you have to sometimes, don't you?'

He grunted. 'Like you did with scraping back *The Lily Madonna* I suppose?'

Hannah produced a pinched smile. 'Yeah, well, how that's going to play out is still anyone's call.' Her eyes lit up suddenly. 'Looking at the style and vibrancy of it, my theory is it's by Simone Martini. I've been reading up on him. He was working in Avignon when he died. It's stunning, isn't it?'

'It is. But it was a crazy thing to do. Have you told Father Diluca yet?'

'No. I'm going to see him tomorrow.' She glanced at her watch. 'I mean today. Claudine and Pietro promised they wouldn't say anything before I saw him.'

Now, still lying in bed, Nathan felt a grudging admiration for Hannah's enthusiasm, if not her cavalier attitude to rules and protocols. There was no way he'd have done what she'd done, but she had got results, no question.

He sat up in bed, pushing away the sheet that covered him, unable to relax any more. Hannah had refused his impulsive offer to accompany her to see Father Diluca and he was glad. It wasn't his affair. Whatever happened with the priest, the news of this newly revealed painting, which was a masterpiece whoever it was by, was sure to get out and into the art press if not the nationals. Which meant Timothy would find out; the art world was a small one.

How their boss would react was anybody's guess and

Nathan didn't want to get caught in the crossfire.

*

It was just before noon when Hannah let herself out of the woodland gate and started the walk towards town. The abbey had been quiet when she left. She'd seen Nathan briefly but there had been no sign of anyone else. She wondered if Guillaume had watched her leave. She had misjudged him; he wasn't quite the threatening gatekeeper she had thought.

Her appointment with Father Diluca at the *presbytère* was for twelve-thirty and she'd left time to spare. *The Lily Madonna* was wrapped up again and back in the carrier bag in which Hannah had originally brought it. It felt like an indignity to carry it like this yet the icon had been treated far worse in its time. She supposed it didn't care. Didn't care? What was she thinking? It was a painting after all, just a painting. It was really time she handed the thing back.

It was tiredness. It had been an emotional night and she felt drained. Long after she'd parted from Nathan, she had stayed awake, unable to get the events of the evening out of her head. She wasn't sure now what had driven her on; she was just relieved it was over and that Sara had confessed. Apparently Guillaume had had the foresight to make a recording of the confession too and her voice had been clearly audible on it.

It was still early when she arrived in town and she wandered around the square. It was only three days until the big annual *fête* and already the town was getting ready for the party. Staging had been set up at one end of the square and metal barriers were stacked up against buildings in the side roads, ready to be put out to control the crowds and allow the procession with *The Lily Madonna* to pass through. All those people, Hannah thought, waiting to see their miraculous icon go by, reaching out to touch it if they could. What would their reaction be?

She walked back to the *presbytêre* and walked through the gate and round to the rear yard. Father Diluca was waiting for her and ushered her in the back door with a broad smile.

'Come in, come in, please. Go through. Can I offer you a coffee? No? Are you sure?'

He waved a hand and she was back in his study again. After all that had happened, it felt surreal, sitting in the same chair, seeing Father Diluca behind his desk with the same hopeful expression on his face. He arced his fingertips together and raised his eyebrows.

'I haven't seen you for some time, 'annah. I trust all is well. You said on the phone that you had finished the icon. I am so grateful, I can't tell you. And to have it back before the festival, well, it's a huge relief.' He waited as if he expected her to say something but she didn't so he continued. 'I've thought many times about our last conversation here in the church. Since I didn't hear from you again, I assumed your idea came to nothing? Which is just as well. On further reflection, I decided that it would be best to leave the image as we knew it. Whatever might be underneath it, we're happy with our familiar lady.' He smiled. 'Perhaps, we could describe her as one of our family.'

Hannah frowned. Her heart thumped uncomfortably in her chest. 'But if you felt that way, Father. I'm surprised you didn't contact me to say so. When I saw you last, you said you didn't feel that it was your decision to make.'

'No, well…' A shrug of a shoulder and a pointed lifting of the chin. 'I changed my mind. Anyway, it doesn't matter now.' He looked expectantly at the bag she had rested against her chair. 'Can I see Her?'

'Of course.'

She bent over and pulled the wrapped picture out of the bag, then stood and peeled away the cloths with the face towards her.

'But first I should warn you...' Hannah spoke slowly, but she had to get this over. '...this is the real *Lily Madonna*.' She turned it round.

His mouth dropped open and he stared. And he stared. The blood drained from his face.

'But...' he muttered. He was on his feet suddenly and waving an indignant hand at her. 'No, that's not...'

'This is what was hiding underneath. It's a masterpiece, Father. I think it's by a famous fourteenth century painter called Simone Martini but, of course, that's for the experts to decide. It's very fine, whoever painted it.'

He came round from behind his desk and stared at the painting, wringing his hands together.

'It is. But... but... I mean, look. We didn't agree on this, did we? What are people going to say? *The Lily Madonna* belongs to our congregation and now... this. It's so different.' He looked back at her with an anguished expression. 'What have you done? What am I going to tell them?'

Hannah waited for him to calm down, then spoke carefully.

'This is a stunning painting though, Father, don't you think? It's a wonderful icon. It's the true one, painted with faith and devotion.'

He frowned at her then switched his gaze back to the picture and began to study it properly, his expression changing as a succession of emotions ran through him. He gave an almost imperceptible nod.

'Ye–es. Yes, I can see that this is indeed a very fine painting.' He turned to look at Hannah. 'Painted with faith you say?'

'Undoubtedly. You could tell your congregation that. You could also tell them that it was painted over to protect it from looting when the revolution prompted the ransacking of the abbeys. It was only ever intended as a temporary measure.' She paused. 'And I suppose you *could* say that it's possible that the same monk who wouldn't leave the abbey here and who was murdered, the one whose shrine is so revered, that he might have been the one who did it. It might have been his final act of devotion and sacrifice.'

'Yes.' Another nod of the head. He reached out tentatively and touched the frame. 'Yes, that would be a wonderful story to tell. If this icon could talk, what a tale it might tell.'

'Indeed it might.' She waited, allowing him to digest all this new information. 'You gave me this, Father, if you remember?'

She handed him a photocopy of the authorisation he had given her back in April. He unfolded it and read.

I, Father Diluca, priest of the parish of Tourbelle la Vierge, give Mademoiselle *Hannah Dechansay full authority to do all that is required to restore the icon known as* The Lily Madonna *which has been damaged. I understand that, when the work is finished, it is possible that the image might not look the same as it did before.*

He looked up and met her gaze.

'I have restored it, Father.'

He looked at her for a long moment, then nodded with the suggestion of a knowing smile. 'Yes, *Mademoiselle.* I can see that you have. And it is indeed a beautiful icon.' He hesitated, then handed back the paper. 'Thank you.'

Hannah walked back through the woods, the authorisation back in her pocket. The original was back at the abbey. Her insurance. It seemed terrible to distrust a priest but she had to watch her own back. Whatever Nathan might think, she was no fool.

She walked slowly. There was no need to rush; there was nothing waiting for her to do. Though she must remember to give Sylvie a ring and tell her what she'd found. She felt odd, empty even, to have finally parted with *The Lily Madonna* after all those weeks together. It had got under her skin in a way no painting had ever done before. The dream she'd had – that odd, discombobulating dream when her mother had exhorted her to *keep her with you* – drifted into her mind. She must have meant *keep* Her *with you*: the icon, not Marielle. To protect her in some way? Maybe. Maybe the icon had helped Nathan to find her. Hannah smiled, shaking her head. She wasn't sure she believed it, but she wanted to believe it and that was enough.

'See mum,' she murmured, 'we did this together. You and me.'

*

Raff found Hannah in the Rec Room, pulling bottles and tubes and brushes out of her trunk and spewing them across the table.

'Aren't you supposed to be packing it up, not emptying it?' he queried.

It was ten-thirty on the Monday morning. Raff hadn't long been up. If he'd had his way, he'd still have been in bed but the revelations of the Saturday night had upset his body clock and sleep was proving elusive. He was all over the place and couldn't settle.

'I need to empty it to pack it properly,' she replied. 'In order for it to be manhandled by the carrier, everything has to be securely in place. I'd just pushed things in wherever I found a gap before. But it's being collected this afternoon. Nathan's too.'

'He's finished then?'

'He will have by the time they get there. That's what he said yesterday anyway. He only had a couple of coats of varnish to put on to seal the work. The synthetic ones dry very quickly these days, as I'm sure you know.'

He nodded, pursing up his lips. 'It's going to be… odd not having you around.'

'It feels odd to me now, without Sara here.' Hannah hesitated and stopped extracting tubs of powdered pigment from the trunk. She looked into his face. 'How are you Raff?'

'Absolutely marvellous. How do you think?'

'I mean seriously?'

He shrugged and looked away. 'Oh, I'm fine. I can't say it hasn't been difficult. I told you that I didn't think Jemma and I would have made it in the end, and I knew she was having an affair with someone. Even so…' Another shrug. '…to think of Sara deliberately setting that fire and leaving her there to... It makes my blood run cold.' He shook his head. 'You know, I believed Jemma when she said she'd bought that necklace. Amazing, isn't it? How easy it is to want to be deceived. It's all kind of obvious now.'

He glanced round the materials on the table and idly picked up a tube of cerulean blue paint. He glanced up at Hannah and grinned.

'It's not all doom and gloom though,' he said brightly. 'David's at Marseille airport as we speak. He's got a flight to L.A. later this morning.'

'To leave permanently?'

'Who knows? He may be back. Esther's daft over him.'

'And you,' said Hannah, 'will you stay here?'

'I don't know. Esther's talking about selling up and moving on, but she's done that before. It probably won't come to anything.'

'Do you not think,' said Hannah, choosing her words

carefully, 'that it might be good for you to make a fresh start somewhere else?'

He tilted his head down, looking up at her through his eyelashes. 'Are you really showing some concern for me? That's too sweet of you. But really you mustn't worry about me. I'll survive.'

'I'm sure you will.'

'And what about you?'

'I've got a flight to London tomorrow.'

'Not staying for the annual town party then? They'll be parading your icon through the streets.'

'It's not my icon,' Hannah said quickly. 'I just worked on it. I was put on the spot and I had to do it.'

'I don't doubt it. And then you couldn't stop yourself peeking underneath.' He brushed away her protestations. 'No, you've done them a favour: that's a seriously good work of art you've revealed. But there'll be a few shocked faces when they see it.' Raff grinned again. 'Are you perhaps leaving before they can lynch you?'

'My boss wants me back. I was on the phone to my office this morning. And since Nathan's finished too... Anyway, I'm ready to go home.'

'And what does Nathan make of it all?'

'All what?'

'*The Lily Madonna*? Murderous PAs? Having to rush home just when we're getting into summer party mode?'

'I don't really know.' She hesitated, narrowing her eyes to look at him. 'Nathan and I aren't a couple, Raff. We never were.'

'No, really? I'm shocked.'

'You knew.'

'Of course I knew.' He looked at her sidelong. 'And I suppose you're going to tell me you don't get on?'

'That's right. Singing from different hymn sheets all the way.'

Raff put the tube of paint back down with a curl of the lip.

'Of course you are.'

Chapter 26

Hannah had a window seat on the flight back to London. She looked out as they took off from Marseille airport on the Tuesday morning, and kept watching as everything became smaller and smaller until they were too high for her to make anything out. She turned to look at Nathan on her left. He was reading a British newspaper he'd picked up at the airport and appeared to be completely absorbed by it.

'I feel like I've been away for years,' said Hannah. 'Anything I should know about?'

Nathan dragged his eyes away and turned to look at her. 'Probably. Don't you keep up with the news when you're away?'

'Some. But it's not easy, is it? The English newspapers, assuming you can get them, are always at least two days out of date. I read the French newspapers sometimes but it's all depressing. Iraq's invaded Kuwait and a British Airways plane has been seized; there've been awful terrorist attacks and we've got this new Community Charge and people are protesting.'

'That's right, the Poll Tax. A lot of people are refusing to pay it.'

She grunted. She didn't want to think about all the bad news and the pressures of home life. Not yet. She glanced out of the window again but they had entered a bank of fluffy white cloud and she could see nothing.

'It's always bittersweet to be going home,' she remarked, barely aware that she'd vocalised the thought.

Again Nathan lifted his nose from the newspaper and she became aware of him looking at her. He folded up the paper and rammed it in the pocket of the seat in front.

'You can't have enjoyed much about that stay though,' he said.

'No. And yet you step into a different world when you're away like that, don't you? Then, when you get back, there are all the responsibilities of normal life.'

She remembered suddenly anew, as she sometimes still did, that her mother had gone. A huge responsibility had gone with her, a constant worry and fear, but the thought didn't offer any solace.

'I suppose,' said Nathan.

Hannah remembered Daphne's oblique reference to Nathan's 'problems'.

'Do you have any issues about going home?' she asked. 'I still think about my mum, you know what it's like. Anyway, Daphne mentioned…' She paused.

'Mentioned what?'

'That you might have, well, issues too.'

'Why would she do that?'

'Oh, because you'd been all interfering on the phone. Why did I want my own book? What was it for? I asked her if you were always like that.'

He snorted. 'That's rich. They were simple enough questions. You just hate to give a straight answer. Talk about secretive.'

'OK, I get it. You don't want to talk about it. I'm sorry, I shouldn't have asked. It's none of my business.'

'No, it's not.'

335

Hannah looked out of the window again. Beside her Nathan was still and silent.

'My brother disappeared,' he said quietly. 'He was twenty-four. He'd got a job and everything seemed to be all right. He just disappeared. No sign of him anywhere. It's been eleven years now but my mother keeps expecting him to turn up at the door. She thinks she sees him in the street.' He sighed. 'It's not easy.'

'I'm sorry. I had no idea.'

The flight attendants came alongside with the drinks trolley. Nathan asked for a beer and Hannah chose a mineral water.

'Did you see Esther before you left?' asked Nathan.

'Yes. She was very gracious, very gushing. It was like a replay of when I first met her, as if nothing had happened in the meantime. It was weird.'

'You never said what happened exactly at your meeting with the priest. It was OK, you said. What does that mean?'

'What I said: it was OK. He was a bit surprised, of course.'

'But he was happy with his new, improved icon?'

'Yes.' She was aware of him watching her face but refused to meet his eye.

'Good. Lucky.'

'Luck had nothing to do with it. I did a great job. He's got a serious work of art there, really valuable. It was a travesty that it was covered up like that.'

'I wonder what his congregation will say.'

'They'll be shocked to start with, but I'm sure they'll love it when they get a chance to see it properly and hear its story.'

'Its story?'

'Of course. It's been through a lot that picture. Imagine: commissioned for a wealthy abbey and revered for centuries, then covered in gesso and daubed with more paint days before

336

the abbey is razed and the monks scatter or are killed. Then buried in a corner of a little parish church, incognito.'

'A word of advice?' said Nathan.

Her eyes narrowed. 'Which is?'

'Don't get too lyrical with Timothy when you tell him about it. You are going to tell him about it, aren't you? Because he's bound to find out.'

'Of course I'm going to tell him. And yes, a new, previously undocumented Simone Martini is…'

'If that's what it is.'

'You're just jealous you didn't find it.'

'No, I'm not.' He shook his head and looked away. 'Fine, tell him however you want. I really want nothing to do with it.'

'Good. I think I'll manage, thanks.'

The trolley bearing their lunch arrived and they said little else for the remainder of the flight.

*

'A Simone Martini?'

Timothy looked at Hannah with a mixture of wonder and suspicion. It was Wednesday morning and he had asked to see both Hannah and Nathan in his office as soon as they'd come in.

'That's my theory,' said Hannah, 'according to my research and from the style and technique. Obviously I'm no expert. It's up to the church there to have it verified if they want to. Anyway, I thought you should know. I only worked on it in my own time, in my evenings and weekends, so I didn't hold up Miss Langley's commission at all.'

'No, well good, good. Indeed, from what you say, it seems to have been a very eventful trip.' He hesitated. 'I'm glad you've come to no real harm after the fire and, er, everything. I received a phone call from Miss Langley yesterday afternoon actually. She's very pleased with your work. She was also at pains to apologise for what happened to you. It was a good thing that Nathan was around.'

Nathan was standing to Hannah's right and she flicked him a thin smile.

'Anyway, I'm glad you're both back. We've got work queueing up. In fact, there are a couple of paintings upstairs that you can get straight on with, do an assessment first, all the usual. Came from a rather damp house in Shropshire. The owner's thinking of selling but thinks he'll get more for them if they're given some attention first. Here, I wrote some notes about them.' He held out a sheet of paper which Nathan took. 'Decide between you which one you're each going to do.'

The phone went and he picked it up, waving a final, dismissive hand and they walked back out into reception, shutting the door behind them.

'So, you're both all right?' said Daphne. She gave Hannah an accusing look. 'I heard about your adventures. Fortunately Nathan's quite good at keeping us informed.'

'Yes, I know, Daphne. And I'm not.'

'I suppose you have been kept pretty busy by the sound of it.'

'And I did have easier access to a phone,' said Nathan.

Hannah and Daphne both looked at him with surprise.

'It's true,' said Hannah. 'I was sure calls from the house were being listened to.'

'Really?' Daphne leaned forward and dropped her voice. 'I was shocked to hear of the things that went on at Esther Langley's place. We don't know the half of what these movie people get up to, do we?' She straightened up and smiled. 'Anyway, Timothy's quite impressed at the way you two dovetailed together. His words, Nathan, not mine. Don't look at me like that. He said he thought he might send the two of

338

you on a project together again. He's got one lined up in fact. Thinks your skills complement each other.'

Hannah and Nathan rolled their eyes at each other.

'Is that a problem?' said Daphne.

Silent Faces, Painted Ghosts

Kathy Shuker

Terri is a talented art curator, stagnating in a dead end job in London. Her ex-boyfriend, Oliver, is stalking her. A post curating the retrospective of a famous but reclusive artist seems the perfect escape.

Portrait painter, Peter Stedding lives in the mountains of Provence, in a house he shares with his wife, daughter, and his eccentric sister, Celia. The setting is idyllic; the atmosphere is not: Peter is rude and obstructive, his household strained and silent. The place holds secrets, stories no-one is allowed to tell. What is Peter hiding? And why should Terri care? Her past has its own dark ghosts. Anyway, she's got an exhibition to organise.

Searching through Peter's old paintings, Terri finds a tantalising clue. Soon she is caught up in a cat and mouse game in search of the truth. But is it ever wise to start digging up the past?

Lightning Source UK Ltd.
Milton Keynes UK
UKHW010454100521
383387UK00001B/11